Cream of the Crime

The 15th Mystery Writers
of America Anthology

Cream OF THE Crime

With a Foreword by Hugh Pentecost

Holt, Rinehart and Winston

New York / Chicago / San Francisco

R01 0028 6371

INDEXED IN  SSI 59-63

Foreword

If you have lived long enough to reach what is politely called the Age of Discretion, because there is nothing else very pleasing to call it, you will have witnessed the passing of many art forms. The silent movie is dead—they say. Vaudeville is dead—they say. Yet if you advertise an old Chaplin movie at one of the Art Theaters, you'll be lucky to get a seat during the first six weeks of the run. If you bring a show to Broadway packed with all the old vaudeville routines, clichés, and pratt falls, you'll be lucky to get to see it the first season. The silent movie is not dead because its brilliant techniques are lost; vaudeville is not dead because there are no longer any funny men. They are dead because we live in an age when all the energies and talents of salesmanship and promotion are devoted strictly to selling "the new model."

Detective fiction began its long and vigorous career with the short story. Ask any afficionado about its beginnings and he will mention, in one breath, Poe and Conan Doyle, masters of the short story technique. And yet I suspect if you ask anyone writing in the mystery field today, he will tell you that the mystery short story is dead, or at any rate dying. Except for the talented and heroic efforts of

5

Ellery Queen and his *Mystery Magazine,* the short story fan cannot hope to turn confidently in any specific direction to find this vanishing commodity. The mystery short story is not what today's editors and salesmen regard as a "new model." In the book length mystery we are told that the old-fashioned whodunit is no longer palatable. The modern mystery must be more a novel than a puzzle. The public wants the new model, not the old. The salesmen don't bother to explain why Agatha Christie and Erle Stanley Gardner, strictly producers of the old model, are the best-selling writers in the field today.

The mystery short story, the old and classic model, is in my opinion far from dead, as this volume will certainly prove. Let's face it. You can't become a burlesque comedian simply by putting on a pair of baggy pants, and you can't become a short story writer simply by limiting yourself to X-number of words. The short story is an art which requires highly developed techniques. In this book you will find some of the real masters of this very special art form.

You will still come out of a Chaplin movie laughing and weeping; you will still come away from a good slapstick performance with your sides aching; and I predict you will come away from reading this book richly rewarded and asking yourself where you can find more of the same. Where can you find more Stanley Ellin, more Q. Patrick, more Ellery Queen, more of all of these other gifted performers? These are not dead men and women. They are live, vigorous, gifted people operating in a medium that will never die, in spite of all the sardonic headshakings of all the supposedly knowing salesmen of "the new model."

This is, indeed, the Cream of the Crime. When you've finished reading this book I think you'll join me in thanking its expert authors, and also its publisher who knows a very live corpse when he sees one.

Hugh Pentecost

Contents

8 *Contents*

Cream of the Crime

John Dickson Carr is undoubtedly one of the great masters of the mystery-suspense genre. His name has become synonymous with the classic locked-room puzzle which no one, past or present, does so well as he. He is only slightly less well-known for his brilliant period mysteries, which are so magnificently researched that the reader experiences the sights, sounds, and smells, and even the political emotions of a time gone by. "The Black Cabinet" is one of these.

1

The Black Cabinet

By John Dickson Carr

As the Emperor's closed carriage swung toward the private entrance at the Opera, with the gentlemen's carriages ahead and the white horses of the Imperial Guard clattering behind, three bombs were thrown from the direction of the Opera steps.

And, only a minute before, a small nine-year-old girl in the crowd had been almost mutinous.

She was too grownup, Nina thought, to be lifted up in *maman's* arms as though she were four years old or even six. True, the fusty-smelling coats and tall hats of the men, even the bonnets and crinolines of the women, made so high a black hedge that Nina could see little except the gas jets illuminating the façade of the Opera and the bright lamps of the Parisian street. But it was warm down here: warm, at least for a night in mid-January of 1858.

Then up Nina went, on the arm of *maman*. Already they could hear in the distance the measured applause—the slow, steady clap-clap of hands, as at a play—and a ragged cheer as the procession approached.

But Nina did not even know what it was, or why they were here. "Mother, I . . ." she began in French.

Maman's bonnet, lined with ruffles, was so long-sided that Nina could not see her mother's face until it was turned around. Then *maman's* dark Italian eyes, always so kindly, took on a glassy bulging glare of hatred and triumph as she pressed her lips against Nina's long curls; bright brown curls, like the hair of Nina's American father.

"Look well!" whispered the handsome Signora Maddalena Bennett, in the Italian language. "At last you will see the death of the devil."

And Nina understood. She too hated, as she had been taught to hate, without knowing why. She had been schooled not to sob or tremble. Yet tears welled up in her eyes, because Nina was sick with fear. In one of those carriages must be Napoleon the Third, Emperor of the French.

Clop-clop, clop-clop moved the horses; slowly, but ever nearer the carpet of white sand spread in front and at the side of the Opera. Then, suddenly, Signora Bennett's whole expression changed. She had never dreamed that the murderers—Orsini and his conspirators —would hold their hands so long, or might throw bombs from the very side or steps of the Opera itself.

"No!" she shrieked aloud.

Holding the child closely, Signora Bennett flung the side of her fur pelisse over Nina's head and dropped down into the half-frozen mud among the spectators. Just as she fell, a black object flew over the heads of the crowd, high-sailing against gas lamps.

Through a crack between the fur pelisse and *maman's* fashion-able deep-bosomed gown with the steel buttons, Nina saw the edge of a white flash. Though they were protected, the first explosion seemed to crush rather than crash, driving steel needles through her eardrums. There were two more explosions, at seconds' intervals. But the street went dark at the first crash, blinding the gas lamps, setting the air a'-sing with flying glass from lamps or windows. Nina's scream was lost amid other screams.

Afterward the small girl felt little or nothing.

A curtain of nightmare, now called shock, wrapped soothingly round Nina's mind and nerves. She looked without surprise, or with very little surprise, at anything she saw. Though her mother, also unhurt, still crouched and breathed heavily, Nina stood up on shaky legs.

Most of the black hedge of tall shiny hats had fallen away. It lay motionless, or tried to crawl across bloodied white sand. And, as Nina turned sideways, she saw the Emperor's state coach near the foot of the steps.

"Sire! Sire!" she heard military voices shouting, amid other shouts. And, above it, the bellow of a military policeman: "Sire!"

The great closed carriage was at a standstill. Stabbed with blast and steel splinters and needles of glass, it had toppled partly toward Nina but remained intact except for its windows. Also, by some miracle, one great gold-bound carriage lantern was still burning on this side.

Before the officers of the Emperor's bodyguard could reach the handle of the coach door, the door opened. There emerged a stately-looking man, plump rather than stout, who jumped to the coach step and thence to the ground.

The carriage lamp gleamed on gold epaulets against a blue coat, and white trousers. His (apparently) steady hand was just putting back on his head the overdecorated cocked hat he wore fore-and-aft. Nina knew, if only from pictures, that he was the Emperor. Though he might be sallow-faced and growing puffy under the eyes, yet between his heavy black moustaches and fox-brush of imperial beard there appeared the edge of a cool smile.

"He is not hurt, the Emperor! Louis Napoleon is unhurt!"

"Long live the Emperor!"

Gravely the sallow-faced man handed down from the carriage a pretty, bad-tempered lady, her countenance as white as her long pearl earrings; she must be the Empress Eugénie. Officers, their uniform coats torn and their faces slashed, whipped out sabers in salute.

"Long live the Empress!"

"And the Emperor! And the Emperor!"

A thick, low rattle of drums ran urgently along the line. Foot-soldiers, dark silhouettes, flowed across and stood up at present-arms, so that the Emperor might not see fallen men with half faces or women carrying bomb splinters where they might have carried children. Around that wrecked carriage, with its two dead horses, lay one hundred and fifty persons, dead or wounded.

The Emperor smiled broadly, concealing agitation.

For the first time genuine hatred, a hatred of what she saw for herself, entered into Nina Bennett and never left her. It made her small body squirm, choking back her voice. It may have been due partly to the teaching of her mother's friends of Young Italy, of the *Carbonari*, who derisively called Napoleon the Third "the sick parrot" when they did not call him devil. But now it was Nina's own hatred.

She could not have explained what had happened, even now. Though she had heard something of bombs, she did not even think of bombs—or of the men who had thrown them. Nina felt only that a white lightning bolt had struck down beside her, hurting, *hurting* these people and perhaps even making them die as her own father had died a year ago in Naples.

Yet the yellow-faced Emperor, with his black moustaches and imperial, had taken no scathe. He stood there and (to Nina) smiled hatefully. He had caused this. It was his fault. His!

Instinctively, amid the reek and the drum-beating, Nina cried out in English, the language her father had taught her, and which she spoke far better than French or even Italian.

"Sick parrot!" the small lungs screeched, the words lost. "Devil! Usurper!"

And then her mother enfolded her, feeling over her for wounds and whispering furiously.

"Be silent, my child! Not another word, I tell thee!"

Gathering up Nina under her fur pelisse, and adding indignity to hysteria, *maman* fought and butted her way out of the crowd with such fury that suspicious eyes turned. Up in front of them loomed a military policeman, his immense cocked hat worn sideways.

"The child!" cried Signora Bennett, clutching Nina with true stage effect, and tragically raised dark eyes to a dark muffled sky. "The child," she lied, "is injured!"

"Pass, madame," gruffly. "Regret."

Though the distance was not great, it took them almost an hour in the crowds to reach their fine furnished lodgings in the rue de Rivoli. There waited Aunt Maria, also Italian and *maman's* maid-companion, fiercely twisting the point of a knife into a rosewood table as she awaited news. Afterward Nina could remember little except a bumping of portmanteaux and a horrible seasickness.

For Signora Bennett, Nina, and Aunt Maria left Paris next day. They had long been safe in England when two of the bomb-assassins—Orsini and Pieri—dropped on the plank and looked out through the everlasting window of the guillotine.

And that had been just over ten years ago.

So reflected Miss Nina Bennett, at the very mature age of nineteen, on the warm evening early in July which was the third evening after her return to Paris. Nobody could have denied that she was beautiful. But all those years in England had made her even more reserved than the English, with a horror of elaborate gestures like those of her late mother.

Though the sky was still bright over the Place de la Concorde, Nina Bennett had told Aunt Maria to close the heavy striped curtains on the windows. Aunt Maria was very fat now. She had a faint moustache of vertical hairs, like a tiny portcullis between nose and mouth. As she waddled over to scrape shut the curtains and waddled back to her chair, wrath exuded from her like a bad perfume.

Nina sat at the dressing-table before a mirror edged in gold leaf. Two gas jets, one in the wall on either side of the mirror, set up yellow flames in flattish glass dishes. They shone on Nina's pink-and-white complexion, her dark blue eyes, her bright brown hair parted in the middle and drawn across the ears to a soft, heavy pad along the nape of the neck. The evening gown of that year was cut just an inch and a half below each shoulder, curving down in lace across the breast; and Nina's gown was so dark a red that it seemed black except when the gaslight rippled or flashed.

Yet her intense composure gave Nina's beauty a chilly quality like marble. She sat motionless, unsmiling, her arms stretched out and hands lightly crossed on the dressing-table.

"No," she thought, "I am not unattractive." The thought, or so she imagined, gave her neither pleasure nor displeasure.

At her left on the dressing-table stood a great bouquet of yellow roses in a glass vase of water. Nina Bennett had bought them herself, as a part of her plan of death. In the dressing-table drawer lay the weapon of death.

"I have no heroics," she thought, looking at the reflection of her blue eyes. "I do not think of myself as Joan of Arc or Charlotte

Corday. Though I may be insane, I do not believe so. But I will kill this puff-ball Emperor, who still mysteriously reigns over the French. I will kill him. I will kill him. I will kill him."

Her intensity was so great that she breathed faster, and faint color tinged her pink-and-white face. Suddenly, out of the darkling background in the mirror, she saw fat Aunt Maria, with gray-streaked hair and fishbone moustache, writhing and flapping with anger.

Aunt Maria's hoarse, harsh voice spoke in Italian.

"Now I wonder," sneered Aunt Maria, "why you must close the curtains, and dare not look on the beauty of Paris."

Nina hesitated before she replied, moistening her lips. Despite her flawless English speech and her tolerable French, she had half-forgotten her mother's Italian and must grope for it.

"You are at liberty," she said, "to wonder what you like."

Again Aunt Maria slapped the chair-arms and writhed, almost in tears. Never in her life could Nina believe that these gesticulations were real, as they were, and not mere theatricalism. Intensely she disliked them.

"Out there," panted Aunt Maria, "is the city of light, the city of pleasure. And who made it so? It was your loathed Louis Napoleon and Baron Haussmann, planning their wide boulevards and their lamps and greenery. If we now have the Wood of Boulogne, it is because Louis Napoleon loves trees."

Nina raised her brown eyebrows so slightly that they hardly seemed to move.

"Do you tell *me*," she asked, "the history of the sick parrot?"

The gas jets whistled thinly, in a shadowy room with black satin wall panels figured in gold. Gracefully, with a studied grace, Nina Bennett rose from the dressing-table, and turned around. The monstrous crinolines of the past decade had dwindled into smaller, more manageable hoopskirts which rustled with petticoats at each step. Glints of crimson darted along Nina's dark, close-fitting gown.

"Have you forgotten, Maria?" she asked, in a passionately repressed voice. "In these rooms, these very rooms, where we lived ten years ago? How you took a great knife, and stabbed a dozen times into the top of a rosewood table, when you heard Orsini had failed? Can you deny it?"

"Ah, blood of the Madonna!"

"Can you deny it?"

"I was younger; I was foolish!" The harsh voice rose in pleading

"See, now! This Emperor, in his youth, worshipped the memory of his uncle, the warlord, the first Napoleon. The first Napoleon they exiled . . ."

"Yes," agreed Nina, "and kings crept out again to feel the sun."

Aunt Maria was galvanized. "That is a noble line; that is a heart-shaking line!"

"It is the late Mrs. Browning's. A trifle. No matter."

"Well! This young man (yes, yes, it is the way of all young men) was also a republican; a lover of liberty; a member of the *Carbonari* itself. Once he promised us a united Italy. But he wavered, and more than a few of us tried to kill him. He wavers always; I say it! But has he not done much in these past few years to redeem his promise? Body of Bacchus! Has he not?"

Though Nina was not tall, she stood high above Maria in the chair and looked down at her indifferently. Nina's white shoulders rose very slightly in the dark red gown.

"Ah, God, your mother has taught you well!" cried Aunt Maria. "Too well!" She hesitated. "And yet, when she died six months ago, it did not seem to me that you were much affected."

"I did not weep or tear my hair, if that is what you mean."

"Unnatural! Pah, I spit! What do you care for Italy?"

"A little, perhaps. But I am an American, as was my father before me."

"So I have heard you say."

"And so I mean!" Nina drew a deep breath; the gown seemed to be constricting her heart as well as her flesh. "My father was of what they call New England, in the State of Massachusetts. His money, though my mother sneered, has kept us above poverty all these years." Her tone changed. "Poor Maria; do the closed curtains stifle you?"

Whereupon Nina, with the same grace in managing her hoop-skirt, went to the left-hand window and threw back the curtains. The fustiness of the room, the fustiness of the curtains, for some reason reminded her of men's greatcoats; Nina shivered without knowing why. Then she opened the curtains of the other window.

Outside, to the little wrought-iron balcony above the rue de Rivoli, was fastened a flagstaff at an oblique angle. From it floated the beloved flag, the flag of the Union, the stars and stripes little more than three years triumphant in bitter war.

"Now what patriotism," jeered Aunt Maria, "for a country you have never seen!"

"It is more than that," said Nina, wanting to laugh. "In a sense it protects us. Have you not heard . . . ?"

"Speak!"

"This is our Day of Independence, the Fourth of July."

"Mad! Mad! Mad!"

"I think not. His Majesty Napoleon the Third made a futile stupid attempt to establish an Empire in Mexico. That did not please the States of America." Nina lifted her exquisite hands and dropped them. "But the traditional friendship of France and America has been renewed. This evening, less than an hour from now, your hypocritical Emperor drives in state to the Opera, for a French-American ball, with ceremonies. As his carriage crosses the Place de la Concorde into the rue Royale . . ."

Aunt Maria heaved her laundry-bag shape up out of the chair.

"Blood of the Madonna!" she screamed. "You do not mean this madwoman's gamble for tonight?"

"Oh, but I do." And for the first time Nina Bennett smiled.

There was a silence, while Nina stood with her back to the window, with the soft and magical sky glow competing with these harsh-singing gaslights. And Nina was uneasy.

She had expected Aunt Maria to stamp, to howl, even possibly to shout from the window for help. But the aging woman only fell back into the chair, not speaking. Tears flowed out of her eyes, tears running down grotesquely past her nose and the hair-spikes of her moustache. Nina Bennett spoke sharply.

"Come, Aunt Maria. This is ridiculous! Why should you weep?"

"Because you are beautiful," Aunt Maria said simply.

There was a silence.

"Well! I—I thank you, Maria. Still . . . !"

"Oh, your plan is good." Aunt Maria turned her streaming eyes toward the great bouquet of yellow roses on the dressing-table, and the drawer which held the weapon. "No doubt you will kill him, my dear. Then you will go to the guillotine, in bare feet and with a black veil over your head, because to kill the Emperor is an act of parricide. You will have had no life, none! No laughter. No affection. No love of men."

Nina's face had gone white. For some reason she retorted cruelly.

"And your own vast experience of love, dear Maria . . . ?"

"That too is ridiculous, eh? Oho, that is comic; yes? This to you!" Aunt Maria made the gesture. "For I have known love more than you think! And the good strong passion, and the heartache too. But *you* will not know it. You are poisoned; your veins are poisoned. If an honest lover bit your arm until the blood flowed, he would die. Ah, behold! You shrink in disgust like a cold Englishwoman!"

"No, good Maria. And Englishwomen are not cold, save perhaps in public. It is as stupid a legend as the legend that they are all fair-haired."

"Listen!" blurted Maria, dabbing at her eyes. "Do you know who poisoned you?"

"If you please, Maria . . . !"

"It was your own mother. Yes! Do you think she knew no man except your father? Body of Venus, she had enough lovers to fill a prison! I startled you? But, because she must dedicate you to her 'cause' of murder, she would turn you against men. How long she spoke to you, when you were thirteen or fourteen, in the accursed great cold house in London! Have I not seen you rush out of the drawing-room, crimson-faced, and your sainted mother laughing secretly?"

"I—I have thought of love," she said calmly. "I would love well, perhaps, if I did not hate. And now, Maria, it is time to fetch my jewel box; and set out my hat and cloak."

Aunt Maria paid no attention.

There was a wild shining of inspiration in her eyes, as though at last she had seen some way to turn this inflexible girl from a mad course. But the time was going, the time was going!

"Come, a test!" panted Aunt Maria. "Are you in truth as poisoned as I said?"

"Did you hear my command, Maria?"

"No! Listen! You remember three nights ago, the evening of the first day we came to Paris? How we returned from our walk, and the young man you met in the courtyard? Well, I saw your eyes kindle!" Aunt Maria cackled with mirth. "You an American? You are a Latin of the Latins! And this young man: was he French —or Italian?"

Nina Bennett grew rigid.

"You have strange fancies," she said. "I cannot remember this at all."

But she did remember it. As Nina turned around briefly to look out of the long window, where a faint breeze rippled the vivid colors of the stars and stripes, that whole brief scene was recreated in every detail.

As the courtesy-aunt said, it had been at about this time on the evening of July second. Aunt Maria had marched beside Nina as they returned from their walk. Even in this modern age, the most emancipated American or English girl would not have gone through such tree-bewitched streets, full of summer's breath and mirrors a-wink in cafés without a formidable chaperone.

The house in which they had taken furnished lodgings was unlike most of those in the same street. It was of an older day, patterned after a nobleman's *hôtel*. Through a smaller door in high-arched wooden doors, you passed through a cool tunnel smelling of old stone, with the *concierge's* lodge on the right. Then you emerged into a green courtyard; it had galleries built around on three sides, and stone balustrades carved with faces. An outside staircase led up to each gallery. In the middle of the green, scented turf was a dead fountain.

As Aunt Maria creaked up the staircase, Nina followed her. Vaguely Nina had noticed a young man standing a little distance away, smoking a cigar and leaning on a gold-headed stick. But she paid little attention. In both hands, if only for practice's sake, she carried a large bouquet of red roses in which was hidden a small but heavy object, and two fingers of her right hand held the chains of her reticule. Though strung-up and alert, Nina was very tired.

Perhaps that was why the accident happened. When she had gone six steps up behind Aunt Maria, Nina's reticule—a heavy, flower-painted handbag—slipped through her fingers, bounced down the steps, and landed on the lowermost one.

"Ah, so-and-so!" exclaimed Aunt Maria, and wheeled around her moustache.

There was a flick in the air as the dark-complexioned young man flung away his cigar. He had suffered some injury to his left leg. But, so deft was his use of the stick, that he scarcely seemed to limp when he made haste. In an instant he was at the foot of the staircase.

The cane was laid down. With his left hand he swept off his high, glossy hat, and his right hand scooped up the reticule. His eyes strayed to Nina's ringless left hand.

"If you will permit me, mademoiselle . . . ?" he said.

The man, whether French or Italian, had a fine resonant voice, fashioning each French syllable clearly. His dark hair, parted on one side, was so thick that it rose up on the other side of the parting. A heavy moustache followed the line of his delicate upper lip. His somber dark clothes, though carelessly worn, were of fine quality.

Nina Bennett, who had turned around, looked down the stairs straight into his eyes. Nina, in a dress of dark purple taffeta and a boat-shaped hat with a flat plume, would have denied coldly that she was a romantic.

"But he is undeniably handsome," she was thinking, "and without oiliness or exaggeration. He has endured great suffering, by the whiteness of his face and the little gray in his hair. And yet his mockery of eye, as though he knew too much of women . . . !"

Abruptly Nina straightened up.

"I thank . . ." she began coldly; and then the worst happened.

Nina, still holding the bouquet of red roses, either by accident or nervousness jerked her left wrist against the stair-balustrade. The roses seemed to spill apart. Out of their stems leaped a derringer, short of barrel but large of bore. It banged on the step, and clattered down to the lowermost one. Though it was loaded with wad, powder, and heavy ball, it did not explode; there was no percussion-cap on the firing-nipple.

Nina stood rigid with horror, like Aunt Maria. For a moment, in that shadowy green courtyard under the light of a pink sunset, it was as silent as though they stood in the Forest of Marly.

The young man looked strangely at the pistol, and suddenly jumped back as though he feared it might still go off. Then he smiled. After a swift glance at the lodge of the *concierge*, he dropped the reticule on top of the derringer, concealing it. He picked up both, advanced up the stairs, and gravely handed the fallen objects to Nina.

"Permit me, mademoiselle, to return your reticule and your— your protection against footpads. If I might suggest . . ."

"I thank you, monsieur. But it is not necessary to suggest . . ."

"Alas, I have already done so," he said, and again looked her in the eyes. His French voice both pointed the double meaning, yet smilingly robbed the words of offense. Pressing the brim of his hat against the black broadcloth over his heart, he bowed slightly. "Until a re-meeting, mademoiselle!"

"Until a re- . . ." said Nina, and stopped. She had not meant to speak at all.

Whirling around her skirts, the roses and pistol and reticule like a mortifying weight in her arms, Nina marched up the stairs after Aunt Maria.

And this was the brief scene which returned in every detail to Nina Bennett, in the dark old room with the gas jets, during the moment when she looked out of the long window over the rue de Rivoli. She had only to concentrate, and it was gone forever. But she felt the pressure of Aunt Maria's eyes, wet and crafty, boring into her back; and anger rose again.

Turning around, Nina took four steps and stood over Aunt Maria in the chair.

"Why do you remind me of this?" Nina asked.

"Oh, then we *were* smitten!"

"Hardly." The voice was dry. But when Nina opened her blue eyes wide, Maria shrank back because they were maniacal and terrifying. "Do you imagine that some sordid affair of love would keep me back from the only cause I have for living?"

"This 'cause'!" sneered Aunt Maria. "I tell you, it is a cold warming-pan for a long night, instead of a husband. Away with it! With your looks and your money; body of Bacchus, you might wed any man you chose." Abruptly, amid her tears, the fat woman began to cackle again with laughter. "But not the young Italian of the courtyard, poor Nina! No, no! Not that one!"

"And why not?" demanded Nina.

"Listen, my child. Pay heed to an old conspirator like me! For I have seen them all. I know the ingratiating air, the cringing approach, the mark of the almost-gentleman . . ."

"How dare you!" Nina amazed herself by crying out. Then she controlled her voice. "You will allow me, please, to pass my own judgment on a gentleman."

"Oh, then we were not smitten! Oh, no!" cackled Aunt Maria. Then her laughter died. "Shall I tell you what this young man really is?"

"Well?"

"He is what the French call a *mouchard*. A police spy."

"You lie!" A pause. "In any event," Nina added casually, "it is of no importance. Since you disobey my order to fetch my hat and cloak and jewel box . . ."

"No, no, I will find them!" said Aunt Maria, and surged up out of the chair.

On creaking slippers she wheezed across to an immense dark

wardrobe, beside the door and opposite the windows. Opening one door of the wardrobe, she plucked out a waist-length cape of rich material in stripes of silver and wine-red.

"Well!" snorted Aunt Maria, examining the cape and giving no sign of furious thought. "You will go to kill the Emperor. I have promised not to interfere; good, I keep my promise! But it will be sad for you, hot-blood, when they arrest you—as they will, mark it!—before you have fired the shot."

Nina's gaze had gone to the grandfather clock, near the alcove which housed the big curtained bed. The time—the time was running out. True, she still had many minutes. But there would be a crowd. She must be in place, the exact spot she had chosen, long before the Imperial procession went past.

Now the meaning of Maria's words stabbed into her brain for the first time.

"What did you say, fuss-budget?"

"Enough," muttered the fat woman darkly. "I said enough!"

"Come, good Maria. Is this another of your childish tricks to divert me?"

"Childish!" cried Aunt Maria, now in a real temper. "Was I your mother's companion for twenty years, or was I not? Do I know every dog's-tail of plotting, or do I not?"

"Of old and clumsy plotting, yes. But my device . . ."

"Faugh!" snorted Aunt Maria, past patience. "How do you think Louis Napoleon keeps so quiet his bright city, his toy? Ask the Prefect of Police, M. Pietri—yes, I said Pietri, not Pieri—but above all ask M. Lagrange, the chief of the political police! They buy more spies than the sand-grains at Dieppe! By my immortal soul, Lagrange will stir up a riot for the very joy of showing how quickly he can suppress it!"

Aunt Maria shook the cape. With her own version of a haughty shrug, she reached again into the wardrobe and drew out a very wide-brimmed velvet hat of the same dark red as Nina's gown.

"You don't believe an old woman, eh?" she taunted. "Good! For I have finished with you. But this I swear on the Cross: you have been betrayed."

"Lies and lies and lies! Betrayed by whom?"

"Why, by your young man down in the courtyard."

She was going dangerously far, to judge by Nina's eyes and breathing.

"Little stupid!" she continued to taunt. "Did you not observe how he started and jumped, when the pistol fell at his feet? He thought there might be a bullet for *him*. Did you not see how he looked with quickness towards the lodge of the *concierge*, who was watching? The *concierge*, who feeds the police with a spoon! You a plotter, when you gave your true name of Bennett? Pah! the name of your mother is a very passport to the Prefecture!"

Now Aunt Maria did not actually believe one word of what she had said about the young man. In fact, three nights ago she had scarcely noticed him except as a possible moustache-twisting sinner of the boulevards. But these ideas foamed into her brain; she could not stop; she must speak faster and faster.

For it seemed to her that there was a hesitation in Nina's eyes . . .

Nina moved slowly to the side of the dressing-table, still looking steadily at the other woman. Gaslight burnished the wings of Nina's soft brown hair. With her left hand she pulled open the drawer of the dressing-table, in which the derringer pistol lay fully loaded, and with a percussion-cap resting under the light pressure of its hammer.

"What do you do?" Aunt Maria screamed out. Then, abruptly glancing at the door and holding up cape and hat as though to call for silence, she added: "Listen!"

Outside the door, the only door in the room, was a drawing room with a polished hardwood floor unmuffled by any carpet. There was a sound. Both women heard the soft thump of the cane as the visitor slid forward a lame leg: then silence; then again the bump of the cane. Someone was slowly but steadily approaching the bedroom door. Both women knew who it was.

"My God!" thought the staggered Aunt Maria. "He really *is* a *mouchard* after all!"

A fist, not loudly, but firmly and with authority, knocked at the bedroom door.

Aunt Maria, terrified, backed away towards the bed alcove and held up cape and hat as though they might shield her.

If there had ever been any uncertainty in Nina's face, it was gone now. Her cold movements were swift but unhurried. From the vase she whipped the bouquet of yellow roses, squeezing the water from the stems and wrapping them in heavy tissue paper from the drawer. Gripping the stems in her left hand, she plucked out the pistol. There was a soft click as she drew back the hammer. She made an opening in the roses, hiding the derringer so that nothing should catch in the hammer when she snatched it out. There would still be time to reload if she must dispose of an intruder first.

"Enter!" Nina calmly called in French. It was the language they spoke afterwards.

Their visitor, the man of the courtyard, came in and closed the door behind him. He was in full evening dress, partly covered by his ankle-length black cloak, which yet showed his white frilled shirtfront and a carelessly tied stock. In one white-gloved hand he held his hat, in the other his gold-headed stick.

Again Nina noted the delicacy of his white, handsome face, in contrast to the heavy dark hair and moustache. Even his figure was somewhat slight, though well-made.

"For this intrusion," he said in his fine voice, "I deeply apologize to mademoiselle; and, understood," bowing towards Aunt Maria, "to madame."

Nina's pink lips went back over fine teeth.

"Your best apology lies behind you." She nodded towards the door.

"Unfortunately, no." The stranger, at leisure, put down his hat and stick on a table at the left of the door. His dark eyes, with that odd life-in-death quality, grew strong with a fierce sincerity; and so did his voice. "For I presume to have an interest in you, mademoiselle."

"Who are you? What do you want?"

The stranger leaned his back against the door, seeming to lounge rather than lean, in a devil-may-care swagger which to Nina seemed vaguely familiar.

"Let us say that I am the detective Lecoq, in the admirable police-romances of M. Gaboriau. Lecoq is a real person, remember, as was the character D'Artagnan. Well! I am Lecoq."

Nina breathed a little faster. Her finger tightened round the trigger of the pistol.

"How did you enter by a locked front door?"

"Believe me, I have passed through more difficult doors than that. Stop!" His white-gloved hand went up to forestall her, and he smiled. "Let us suppose (I say merely let us suppose!) that Mademoiselle Nina Bennett had intent to kill the Emperor of the French. I who speak to you, I also live in this house. I can put questions to a *concierge*."

"Did I not tell you?" screamed Aunt Maria, hiding her face behind cape and hat.

Neither of them looked at her.

"To any reader of the French journals, the name of your mother is well-known. The nationality of your father," and he nodded toward the flag outside the window, his nostrils thin and bitter, "you too obviously display. However! If it be your intent to kill the Emperor, where would you go? Assuredly not far from here, or you would have been gone now."

("If you must kill this sly one here," Aunt Maria thought wildly, "kill him now! Shoot!")

"I think," continued the stranger, "you have chosen the corner of the rue Royale and the rue de Rivoli. Every journal in Paris will have told you, with exactness, the route and time of the procession. It is summer; there will be an open carriage, low-built. The Emperor, a fact well-known, sits always on the right-hand side facing forward, the Empress on the left.

"How lovely . . ." His strong voice shook; he checked himself. "How innocent you will look, in your finery and jewels, chattering English and deliberately bad French, on the curbstone! The military, even the military police, will only smile when you walk out slowly toward the slow-moving carriage, and speak English as you offer (is it not so?) the bouquet of roses to the Empress Eugénie of Montijo."

("I was mad, I was mad!" mentally moaned Aunt Maria. "Let him take the damned pistol from her now!")

"Holding the bouquet in your left hand," he went on quietly, "you must lean partly across His Majesty. With your right hand you will take out an old-style single-shot pistol, and fire it at the Emperor's head so closely that you cannot miss. Have I, M. Lecoq, correctly deduced your plan?"

Nina Bennett cast a swift glance at the clock.

Time, time, time! A while ago, when she had looked out of the window, far up to the right there had been a red sky over Neuilly beyond the top of the Champs Élysées. Now the whole sky was tinged with pink amid white and pale blue. It brightened the gaslights in that black-silk-paneled room, which might have been a symbol of espionage since the days of Savary and Napoleon the First.

"Are you the only one," Nina asked levelly, "who knows of this —this plan?"

"The only one, mademoiselle."

With a steady hand Nina took the derringer from among the roses, moving aside the yellow bouquet. It is a sober fact that the young man did not even notice it.

"And now," he said in that hypnotic voice, "I must tell you of my interest in you. It is very easy." He straightened up, his face whiter, and clenched his gloved fists. "You are Venus in the body of Diana; you are Galatea not yet kissed to true life. You are—I will not say the most beautiful woman I have ever met—but the most maddening and stimulating." Cynicism showed in his eyes. "And I have known so many women."

"How modest you are!" Nina cried furiously.

"I state a fact. But I tell you one of the reasons, my love, why I will not permit you to go from this room for at least half an hour."

Again Nina started, almost dropping the pistol.

From the street below, and from the open spaces beyond, there were cries and shouts. She heard the confused running of feet, seemingly from every direction at once, which can conjure up a Paris crowd in one finger-snap. Very faintly, in the distance, she also heard the slow clop-clop of many horses in procession.

According to every newspaper, the procession to the Opera would be headed by the Imperial Band. The instruments of the band were clear rather than brassy; already they had begun with the swinging tune, *"Partant pour la Syrie,"* which was the official song of Napoleon the Third.

> Setting out for Syria
> Young and brave Dunois . . .

There was still time. Nina Bennett's hand was as steady as a statue's.

"You call yourself a detective, M. Lecoq. But you are only a police spy. Now stand away from that door!"

"No, my dear," smiled the other, and folded his arms lazily.

"I will count to three . . ."

"Count to five thousand; I would hear your voice. What matter if you kill me? Most people," and his dark eyes seemed to wander out to the boulevards, "think me already dead. Put your hand in mine; let fools flourish pistols or knives."

"One!" said Nina, and thought she meant it.

The clop-clop of the procession, though still not loud, was drawing nearer. What sent a shiver through Nina's body was the tune into which the band changed, in honor of the French-American ball at the Opera. There were no words. There were only dreams and memories. Slow, somber, the great battle-hymn rolled out.

Mine eyes have seen the glory of the coming of the Lord,
He is trampling out the vintage where the grapes of wrath are
stored. . . .

"In a moment," continued the visitor, unhearing, "I will come and take that pistol from you. It does not become you. But first hear what I have to say." His tone changed, fiercely. "This political assassination is more than wrong. It changes nothing. It is the act of an idiot. If I could make you understand. . . ."

Abruptly he paused.

He, too, had heard the music, clear in the hush of evening. His face darkened. Had Aunt Maria been watching, she would have seen in his eyes the same maniacal glitter as in those of Nina Bennett. And he spoke the only words which could have ended his life.

"By God!" he snarled. "You might have been a human being, without your mother and your damned Yankee father!"

Nina pulled the trigger, firing straight for his heart at less than ten feet's distance. The percussion-cap flared into the bang of the explosion, amid heavy smoke. The stranger, flung back against the door, still stood upright and emerged through smoke.

She had missed the heart. But the pistol-ball, smashing ribs on the right of his chest, had torn open his right lung. And Nina knew that never, never in her life, could she have fired at the Emperor unless he had first uttered some maddening insult.

"I thank you, my dear," gravely said the stranger, pressing his reddening fingers to his chest, and white-faced at his own choked breathing. "Now be quick! Put that derringer into my hand; and I shall have time to say I did it myself."

Then another realization struck Nina.

"You've been speaking in English!" she cried in that language. "Ever since you said 'damned Yankee.' Are you English?"

"I am an American, my dear," he answered, drawing himself up and swallowing blood. "And at least no one can call me a police spy. My name," he added casually, "is John Wilkes Booth."

Margery Allingham is the creator of Mr. Campion, a new-style detective. He is a deceptively simple, believable human being without arcane knowledge and characteristic eccentricities on the one hand, or superhuman endurance and jeJuan sexual proclivities on the other. Neither boringly violent nor frighteningly erudite, he merely understands what most other people only see. "One Morning They'll Hang Him" is a solid story based on logic and character with no frills and no gimmicks.

2

One Morning

They'll Hang Him

By Margery Allingham

It was typical of Detective Inspector Kenny, at that time D.D.I. of the L. Division, that, having forced himself to ask a favor, he should set about it with the worst grace possible. When at last he took the plunge, he heaved his two hundred pounds off Mr. Campion's fireside couch and set down his empty glass with a clatter.

"I don't know if I needed that at three in the afternoon," he said ungratefully, his small blue eyes baleful, "but I've been up since two this morning dealing with women, tears, minor miracles and this perishing rain." He rubbed his broad face, and presented it scarlet and exasperated at Mr. Campion's back. "If there's one thing that makes me savage it's futility!" he added.

Mr. Albert Campion, who had been staring idly out of the window watching the rain on the roofs, did not glance around. He was still the lean, somewhat ineffectual-looking man to whom the Special Branch had turned so often in the last twenty years. His very fair hair had bleached into whiteness and a few lines had appeared round the pale eyes which were still, as always, covered by large horn-rimmed spectacles, but otherwise he looked much as Kenny first remembered him—"Friendly and a little simple—the old snake!"

"So there's futility in Barraclough Road too, is there?" Campion's light voice sounded polite rather than curious.

Kenny drew a sharp breath of annoyance.

"The Commissioner has 'phoned you? He suggested I should look you up. It's not a great matter—just one of those stupid little snags which has some perfectly obvious explanation. Once it's settled, the whole case is open-and-shut. As it is, we can't keep the man at the station indefinitely."

Mr. Campion picked up the early edition of the evening paper from his desk.

"This is all I know," he said holding it out, "Mr. Oates didn't 'phone. There you are, in the Stop Press, *Rich Widow shot in Barraclough Road West. Nephew at police station helping investigation.* What's the difficulty? His help is not altogether wholehearted, perhaps?"

To his surprise an expression remarkably like regret flickered round Kenny's narrow lips.

"Ruddy young fool," he said, and sat down abruptly. "I tell you, Mr. Campion, this thing is in the bag. It's just one of those ordinary, rather depressing little stories which most murder cases are. There's practically no mystery, no chase—nothing but a wretched little tragedy. As soon as you've spotted what I've missed, I shall charge this chap and he'll go before the magistrates and be committed for trial. His counsel will plead insanity and the jury won't have it. The Judge will sentence him, he'll appeal, their Lordships will dismiss it. The Home Secretary will sign the warrant and one morning they'll take him out and they'll hang him." He sighed. "All for nothing," he said. "All for nothing at all. It'll probably be raining just like it is now," he added inconsequentially.

Mr. Campion's eyes grew puzzled. He knew Kenny for a conscientious officer, and, some said, a hard man. This philosophic strain was unlike him.

"Taken a fancy to him?" he inquired.

"Who? I certainly haven't." The Inspector was grim. "I've got no sympathy for youngsters who shoot up their relatives however selfish the old bottoms may be. No, he's killed her and he must take what's coming to him, but it's hard on—well, on some people. Me, for one." He took out a large old-fashioned notebook and folded it carefully in half. "I stick to one of these," he remarked virtuously. "None of your backs of envelopes for me. My record is kept as neatly as when I was first on the beat, and it can be handed across the court whenever a know-all counsel asks to see it." He paused. "I sound like an advertisement, don't I? Well, Mr. Campion, since I'm here, just give your mind to this, if you will. I don't suppose it'll present any difficulty to you."

"One never knows," murmured Mr. Campion idiotically. "Start with the victim."

Kenny returned to his notebook.

"Mrs. Mary Alice Cibber, aged about seventy or maybe a bit less. She had heart trouble which made her look frail, and, of course, I didn't see her until she was dead. She had a nice house in Barraclough Road, a good deal too big for her, left her by her husband who died ten years ago. Since then she's been alone except for a maid who cleared off in the war and now for another old party who calls herself a companion. *She* looks older still, poor old girl, but you can see she's been kept well under—" he put his thumb down expressively—"by Mrs. C. who appears to have been a dictator in her small way. She was the sort of woman who lived for two chairs and a salad bowl."

"I beg your pardon?"

"Antiques." He was mildly contemptuous. "The house is crammed with them, all three floors and the attic, everything kept as if it was brand-new. The old companion says she loved it more than anything on earth. Of course she hadn't much else *to* love, not a relation in the world except the nephew—"

"Whose future you see so clearly?"

"The man who shot her," the Inspector agreed. "He's a big nervy lad, name of Woodruff, the son of the old lady's brother. His mother, father, and two young sisters all got theirs in the blitz on Portsmouth. Whole family wiped out."

"I see." Campion began to catch some of Kenny's depression.

"Where was he when that happened?"

"In the Western Desert." The D.D.I.'s protuberant eyes were dark with irritation. "I told you this was just an ordinary miserable slice of life. It goes on the same way. This boy, Richard Woodruff —he's only twenty-eight now—did very well in the war. He was in the landings in Sicily and went through the fighting in Italy where he got the M.C. and was promoted to major. Then he copped in for the breakthrough in France and just before the finish he became a casualty. A bridge blew up with him on it—or something of the sort, my informant didn't know exactly—and he seems to have become what the boys call 'bomb happy.' It used to be 'shell shock' in my day. As far as I can gather, he always had been quick-tempered, but this sent him over the edge. He sounds to me as if he wasn't sane for a while. That may help him in his defense, of course."

"Yes." Campion sounded depressed. "Where's he been since then?"

"On a farm mostly. He was training to be an architect before the war but the motherly old army knew what was best for him and when he came out of the hospital they bunged him down to Dorset. He's just got away. Some wartime buddy got him a job in an architect's office under the old pals' act and he was all set to take it up." He paused and his narrow mouth, which was not entirely insensitive, twisted bitterly. "Ought to have started Monday," he said.

"Oh dear," murmured Mr. Campion inadequately. "Why did he shoot his aunt? Pure bad temper?"

Kenny shook his head.

"He had a reason. I mean one can see why he was angry. He hadn't anywhere to live, you see. As you know London is crowded, and rents are fantastic. He and his wife paying through the nose for a cupboard of a bed-sitting room off the Edgware Road."

"His wife?" The lean man in the horn rims was interested. "Where did she come from? You're keeping her very quiet."

To Campion's surprise the Inspector did not speak at once. Instead he grunted, and there was regret, and surprise at it, in his little smile. "I believe I would if I could," he said sincerely. "He found her on the farm. They've been married six weeks. I don't know if you've ever seen love, Mr. Campion? It's very rare—the kind I mean." He put out his hands deprecatingly. "It seems to crop up—when it does—among the most unexpected people, and when you do see it, well, it's very impressive." He succeeded in looking thoroughly ashamed of himself. "I shouldn't call myself a sentimental man," he said.

"No." Campion was reassuring. "You got his war history from her, I suppose?"

"I had to but we're confirming it. He's as shut as a watch—or a hand grenade. 'Yes' and 'No' and 'I did not shoot her'—that's about all his contribution amounted to, and he's had a few hours of expert treatment. The girl is quite different. She's down there too. Won't leave. We put her in the waiting room finally. She's not difficult—just sits there."

"Does she know anything about it?"

"No." Kenny was quite definite. "She's nothing to look at," he went on presently, as if he felt the point should be made. "She's just an ordinary nice little country girl, a bit too thin and a bit too brown, natural hair and inexpert make-up, and yet with this— this blazing radiant steadfastness about her!" He checked himself. "Well, she's fond of him," he amended.

"Believes he's God," Campion suggested.

Kenny shook his head. "She doesn't care if he isn't," he said sadly. "Well, Mr. Campion, some weeks ago these two approached Mrs. Cibber about letting them have a room or two at the top of the house. That must have been the girl's idea; she's just the type to have old-fashioned notions about blood being thicker than water. She made the boy write. The old lady ignored the question but asked them both to an evening meal last night. The invitation was sent a fortnight ago, so you can see there was no eager bless-you-my-children about it."

"Any reason for the delay?"

"Only that she had to have notice if she were giving a party. The old companion explained that to me. There was the silver to get out and clean, and the best china to be washed, and so on. Oh, there was nothing simple and homely about that household!" He sounded personally affronted. "When they got there, of course there was a blazing row."

"Hard words or flying crockery?"

Kenny hesitated. "In a way, both," he said slowly. "It seems to have been a funny sort of flare-up. I had two accounts of it—one from the girl and one from the companion. I think they are both trying to be truthful but they both seem to have been completely foxed by it. They both agree that Mrs. Cibber began it. She waited until there were three oranges and a hundredweight of priceless early Worcester dessert service on the table, and then let fly. Her theme seems to have been the impudence of Youth in casting its eyes on its inheritance before Age was in its grave, and so on and so on. She then made it quite clear that they hadn't a solitary hope of getting what they wanted, and conveyed that she did not care if they slept in the street so long as her precious furniture was safely housed. There's no doubt about it that she was very aggravating and unfair."

"Unfair?"

"Ungenerous. After all she knew the man quite well. He used to go and stay with her by himself when he was a little boy." Kenny returned to his notes. "Woodruff then lost his temper in his own way which, if the exhibition he gave in the early hours of this morning is typical, is impressive. He goes white instead of red, says practically nothing, but looks as if he's about to 'incandesce'—if I make myself plain."

"Entirely." Mr. Campion was deeply interested. This new and human Kenny was an experience. "I take it he then fished out a gun and shot her?"

"Lord, no! If he had, he'd have a chance at least of Broadmoor. No. He just got up and asked her if she had any of his things, because if so he'd take them and not inconvenience her with them any longer. It appears that when he was in the hospital some of his gear had been sent to her, as his next of kin. She said yes, she had, and it was waiting for him in the boot cupboard. The old companion, Miss Smith, was sent trotting out to fetch it and came staggering in with an old officer's hold-all, bursted at the sides and filthy. Mrs. Cibber told her nephew to open it and see if she'd robbed him, and he did as he was told. Of course, one of the first things he saw among the ragged bush shirts and old photographs was a revolver and a clip of ammunition." He paused and shook his head. "Don't ask me how it got there. You know what hospitals were like in the war. Mrs. Cibber went on taunting the man in her own peculiar way, and he stood there examining the gun and presently loading it, almost absently. You can see the scene?"

Campion could. The pleasant, perhaps slightly overcrowded room was vivid in his mind, and he saw the gentle light on the china and the proud, bitter face of the woman.

"After that," said Kenny, "the tale gets more peculiar, although both accounts agree. It was Mrs. C. who laughed and said, 'I suppose you think I ought to be shot?' Woodruff did not answer but he dropped the gun in his side pocket. Then he packed up the hold-all and said, 'Good-bye.' " He hesitated. "Both statements say that he then said something about *the sun having gone down*. I don't know what that meant, or if both women mistook him. Anyway, there's nothing to it. He had no explanation to offer. Says he doesn't remember saying it. However, after that he suddenly picked up one of his aunt's beloved china fruit bowls and simply dropped it on the floor. It fell on a rug, as it happened, and did not break, but old Mrs. Cibber nearly passed out, the companion screamed, and the girl hurried him off home."

"With the gun?"

"With the gun." Kenny shrugged his heavy shoulders. "As soon as the girl heard that Mrs. Cibber had been shot, she jumped up with a tale that he had *not* taken it. She said she'd sneaked it out of his pocket and put it on the window sill. The lamest story you ever heard! She's game and she's ready to say absolutely anything, but she won't save him, poor kid. He was seen in the district at midnight."

Mr. Campion put a hand through his sleek hair. "Ah. That rather tears it."

"Oh, it does. There's no question that he did it. It hardly arises. What happened was this. The young folk got back to their bed-sitting room about ten to nine. Neither of them will admit it, but it's obvious that Woodruff was in one of those boiling but sulky rages which made him unfit for human society. The girl left him alone—I should say she has a gift for handling him—and she says she went to bed while he sat up writing letters. Quite late, she can't or won't say when, he went out to the post. He won't say anything. We may or may not break him down, he's a queer chap. However, we have a witness who saw him somewhere about midnight at the Kilburn end of Barraclough Road. Woodruff stopped him and asked if the last eastbound'bus had gone. Neither of them had a watch, but the witness is prepared to swear it was just after midnight—which is important because the shot was fired at two minutes before twelve. We've got that time fixed."

Mr. Campion, who had been taking notes, looked up in mild astonishment.

"You got that witness very promptly," he remarked. "Why did

he come forward?"

"He was a plain-clothes man off duty," said Kenny calmly. "One of the local men who had been out to a reunion dinner. He wasn't tight but he had decided to walk home before his wife saw him. I don't know why he hadn't a watch"—Kenny frowned at this defect —"anyway, he hadn't, or it wasn't going. But he was alert enough to notice Woodruff. He's a distinctive chap you know. Very tall and dark, and his manner was so nervy and excitable that the dick thought it worth reporting."

Campion's teeth appeared in a brief smile.

"In fact, he recognized him at once as a man who looked as though he'd done a murder?"

"No." The Inspector remained unruffled. "No, he said he looked like a chap who had just got something off his mind and was pleased with himself."

"I see. And meanwhile the shot was fired at two minutes to twelve."

"That's certain." Kenny brightened and became businesslike. "The man next door heard it and looked at his watch. We've got his statement and the old lady's companion. Everyone else in the street is being questioned. But nothing has come in yet. It was a cold wet night and most people had their windows shut; besides, the room where the murder took place was heavily curtained. So far, these two are the only people who seem to have heard anything at all. The man next door woke up and nudged his wife who had slept through it. But then he may have dozed again, for the next thing he remembers is hearing screams for help. By the time he got to the window, the companion was out in the street in her dressing gown, wedged in between the lamp post and the mail box, screeching her little gray head off. The rain was coming down in sheets."

"When exactly was this?"

"Almost immediately after the shot, according to the companion. She had been in bed for some hours and had slept. Her room is on the second floor, at the back. Mrs. Cibber had not come up with her but had settled down at her bureau in the drawing-room, as she often did in the evening. Mrs. C. was still very upset by the scene at the meal, and did not want to talk. Miss Smith says she woke up and thought she heard the front door open. She won't swear to this, and at any rate she thought nothing of it, for Mrs. Cibber often slipped out to the mail box with letters before coming to bed. Exactly how long it was after she woke that she heard the shot she does not know, but it brought her scrambling out of bed. She agrees she might have been a minute or two finding her slippers and a wrapper, but she certainly came down right away. She says she found the street door open, letting in the rain, and the drawing-room door, which is next to it, wide open as well, and the lights in there full on." He referred to his notes and began to read out loud. " 'I smelled burning' "—she means cordite—" 'and I glanced across the room to see poor Mrs. Cibber on the floor with a dreadful hole in her forehead. I was too frightened to go near her, so I ran out of the house shouting "Murder! Thieves!" ' "

"That's nice and old-fashioned. Did she see anybody?"

"She says not, and I believe her. She was directly under the only lamp post for fifty yards and it certainly was raining hard."

Mr. Campion appeared satisfied but unhappy. When he spoke his voice was very gentle.

"Do I understand that your case is that Woodruff came back, tapped on the front door, and was admitted by his aunt? After some conversation, which must have taken place in lowered tones since the companion upstairs did not hear it, he shot her and ran away, leaving all the doors open?"

"Substantially, yes. Although he may have shot her as soon as he saw her."

"In that case she'd have been found dead in the hall."

Kenny blinked. "Yes, I suppose she would. Still, they couldn't have talked much."

"Why?"

The Inspector made a gesture of distaste. "This is the bit which gets under my skin," he said. "They could hardly have spoken long—*because she'd forgiven him.* She had written to her solicitor —the finished letter was on her writing pad ready for the post. She'd written to say she was thinking of making the upper part of her house into a home for her nephew, and asked if there was a clause in her lease to prevent it. She also said she wanted the work done quickly, as she had taken a fancy to her new niece and hoped in time there might be children. It's pathetic, isn't it?" His eyes were wretched. "That's what I meant by futility. She'd forgiven him, see? She wasn't a mean old harridan, she was just quick-tempered. I told you this isn't a mystery tale, this is ordinary sordid life."

Mr. Campion looked away.

"Tragic," he said. "Yes. A horrid thing. What do you want me to do?"

Kenny sighed. "Find the gun," he murmured.

The lean man whistled.

"You'll certainly need that if you're to be sure of a conviction. How did you lose it?"

"He's ditched it somewhere. He didn't get rid of it in Barra-clough Road because the houses come right down to the street, and our chaps were searching for it within half an hour. At the end of the road he caught the last 'bus, which ought to come along at midnight but was a bit late last night, I'm morally certain. These drivers make up time on the straight stretch by the park; it's more than their jobs are worth, so you never get them to admit it. Anyhow, he didn't leave the gun on the 'bus, and it's not in the house where his room is. It's not in the old lady's house at 81 Barraclough Road because I've been over the house myself." He peered at the taller man hopefully. "Where would you hide a gun in this city at night, if you were all that way from the river? It's not so easy, is it? If it had been anywhere obvious it would have turned up by now."

"He may have given it to someone."

"And risked blackmail?" Kenny laughed. "He's not as dumb as that. You'll have to see him. He says he never had it—but that's only natural. Yet where did he put it, Mr. Campion? It's only a little point but, as you say, it's got to be solved."

Campion grimaced.

"Anywhere, Kenny. Absolutely anywhere. In a drain—"

"They're narrow gratings in Barraclough Road."

"In a sandbin or a static water tank—"

"There aren't any in that district."

"He threw it down in the street and someone, who felt he'd rather like to have a gun, picked it up. Your area isn't peopled solely with the law-abiding, you know."

Kenny became more serious. "That's the real likelihood," he admitted gloomily. "But all the same, I don't believe he's the type to throw away a gun casually. He's too intelligent, too cautious. Do you know how this war has made some men cautious even when they're being the most reckless? He's one of those. He's hidden it. Where? Mr. Oates said you'd know if anyone did."

Campion ignored this blatant flattery. He stood staring absently out of the window for so long that the Inspector was tempted to nudge him, and when at last he spoke, his question did not sound promising.

"How often did he stay with his aunt when he was a child?"

"Quite a bit, I think, but there's no kid's hiding-place there that only he could have known, if that's what you're after." Kenny could hardly conceal his disappointment. "It's not that kind of house. Besides, he hadn't the time. He got back about twenty past twelve: a woman in the house confirms it—she met him on the stairs. He was certainly sparked out when we got there at a quarter after four this morning. They were both sleeping like kids when I first saw them. She had one skinny brown arm around his neck. He just woke up in a rage, and she was more astounded than frightened. I swear—"

Mr. Campion had ceased to listen.

"Without the gun the only real evidence you've got is the plain-clothes man's story of meeting him," he said. "And even you admit that gallant officer was walking for his health after a party. Imagine a good defense lawyer enlarging on that point."

"I have," the Inspector agreed, dryly. "That's why I'm here. You must find the gun for us, sir. Can I fetch you a raincoat? Or," he added, a faintly smug expression flickering over his broad face, "will you just sit in your armchair and do it from there?"

To his annoyance his elegant host appeared to consider the question.

"No, perhaps I'd better come with you," he said at last. "We'll go to Barraclough Road first, if you don't mind. And if I might make a suggestion, I should send Woodruff and his wife back to their lodgings—suitably escorted, of course. If the young man was going to crack, I think he would have done so by now, and the gun, wherever it is, can hardly be at the police station."

Kenny considered. "He may give himself away and lead us to it." He agreed although without enthusiasm. "I'll telephone. Then we'll go anywhere you say, but as I told you I've been over the Barraclough Road house myself and if there's anything there it's high time I retired."

Mr. Campion merely looked foolish, and the Inspector sighed and let him have his way.

He came back from the telephone smiling wryly.

"That's settled," he announced. "He's been behaving like a good soldier interrogated by the enemy, silly young fool—after all, we're only trying to hang him! The girl has been asking for him to be fed, and reporters are crawling up the walls. Our boys won't be sorry to get rid of them for a bit. They'll be looked after. We shan't lose 'em. Now, if you've set your heart on the scene of the crime, Mr. Campion, we'll go."

In the taxi he advanced a little idea.

"I was thinking of that remark he is alleged to have made," he said, not without shame. "You don't think that it could have been 'Your sun has gone down,' and that we could construe it as a threat within meaning of the act?"

Campion regarded him owlishly.

"We could, but I don't think we will. That's the most enlightening part of the whole story, don't you think?"

If Inspector Kenny agreed, he did not say so, and they drove to the top of Barraclough Road in silence. There Campion insisted on stopping at the first house next to the main thoroughfare. The building had traded on its proximity to the shopping center and had been converted into a dispensing chemist's. Campion was inside for several minutes, leaving Kenny in the cab. When he came out he offered no explanation other than to observe fatuously that they had a "nice time" and settled back without troubling to look out at the early Victorian stucco three-story houses which lined the broad road.

A man on duty outside, and a handful of idlers gaping apathetically at the drawn blinds, distinguished 81 Barraclough Road. Kenny rang the bell and the door was opened after a pause by a flurried old lady with a duster in her hand.

"Oh, it's you, Inspector," she said hastily. "I'm afraid you've found me in a muddle. I've been trying to tidy up a little. *She* couldn't have borne the place left dirty after everyone had been trampling over it. Yet I don't mean to say that you weren't all very careful."

She led them into a spotless dining room which glowed with old mahogany and limpid silver, and the wan afternoon light showed them her reddened eyes and worn navy-blue housedress. She was a timid-looking person, not quite so old as Kenny had suggested, with very neat gray hair and a skin which had never known cosmetics. Her expression was closed and secret with long submission, and her shoulder blades stuck out a little under the cloth of her dress. Her hands still trembled slightly from the shock of the evening before.

Kenny introduced Campion. "We shan't be long, Miss Smith," he said cheerfully. "Just going to have another little look around. We shan't make a mess."

Campion smiled at her reassuringly. "It's difficult to get help these days?" he suggested pleasantly.

"Oh, it is," she said earnestly. "And Mrs. Cibber wouldn't trust just anyone with her treasures. They are so very good." Her eyes filled with tears. "She was so fond of them."

"I daresay she was. That's a beautiful piece, for instance." Campion glanced with expert interest at the serpentine sideboard with its genuine handles and toilet cupboard.

"Beautiful," echoed Miss Smith dutifully. "And the chairs, you see?"

"I do." He eyed the Trafalgar set with the cherry-leather seats. "Is this where the quarrel took place?"

She nodded and trembled afresh. "Yes. I—I shall never forget it, never."

"Was Mrs. Cibber often bad-tempered?"

The woman hesitated, and her firm small mouth moved without words.

"Was she?"

She shot a swift unhappy glance at him.

"She was quick," she said. "Yes I think I ought to say she was quick. Now, would you like to see the rest of the house or—?"

Campion glanced at his watch and compared it with the Tompion bracket clock on the mantelshelf.

"I think we've just time," he said, idiotically. "Upstairs first, Inspector."

The next thirty-five minutes reduced Kenny to a state of jitters rare to him. After watching Campion with breathless interest for the first five, it slowly dawned on him that the expert had forgotten the crime in his delight at discovering a treasure-trove. Even Miss Smith, who betrayed a certain proprietorial pride, flagged before Campion's insatiable interest. Once or twice she hinted that perhaps they ought to go down, but he would not hear of it. By the time they had exhausted the third floor and were on the steps to the attic, she became almost firm. There was really nothing there but some early Georgian children's toys, she said.

"But I must just see the toys. I've got a 'thing' on toys, Kenny."
Campion sounded ecstatic. "Just a minute—"

A vigorous tattoo on the front door interrupted him and Miss
Smith, whose nerves were suffering, emitted a little squeak.

"Oh, dear. Somebody at the door. I must go down."

"No, no." Campion was uncharacteristically effusive. "I'll see
who it is and come back. I shan't be a moment."

He flung himself downstairs with boyish enthusiasm, Miss Smith
behind him, and Kenny, seeing escape at last, following as quickly
as the narrow stairs would permit.

They reached the hall just in time to see him closing the door.
"Only the post," he said, holding out a package. "Your library
book, Miss Smith."

"Oh, yes," she came forward, hand outstretched. "I was expecting that."

"I rather thought you were." His voice was very soft and suddenly menacing. He held the cardboard book box high over his
head with one hand, and with the other released the flap which
closed it. The soft gleam of metal appeared in the light from the
transom, and a service revolver crashed heavily to the parquet
floor.

For a long minute there was utter silence. Even Kenny was too
thunderstruck to swear.

Miss Smith appeared frozen in mid-air, her hands clawing at the
box.

Then, most dreadfully, she began to scream. . . .

A little over an hour later Kenny sat on a Trafalgar chair in a
room which seemed to quiver and shudder with terrible sound. He
was pale and tired-looking. His shirt was torn and there were three
livid nail scratches down his face.

"God," he said, breathing hard. "God, can you beat that?"

Mr. Campion sat on the priceless table and scratched his ear.

"It was a bit more than I bargained for," he murmured. "It
didn't occur to me that she'd become violent. I'm afraid they may
be having trouble in the van. Sorry, I ought to have thought of it."

The C.I.D. man grunted. "Seems to me you thought of plenty,"
he muttered. "It came as a shock to me—I don't mind admitting
it since I can't very well help it. When did it come to you? From

the start?"

"Oh, Lord, no." Campion sounded apologetic. "It was that remark of Woodruff's you quoted about the sun going down. That's
what set me on the train of thought. Weren't you ever warned as
a kid, Kenny, and by an aunt perhaps, never to let the sun go
down on your wrath?"

"I've heard it, of course. What do you mean? It was a sort of
saying between them?"

"I wondered if it was. They knew each other well when he was a
child, and they were both quick-tempered people. It seemed to me
that he was reminding her that the sun *had* gone down, and he
showed her he could have smashed her precious bowl if he had
liked. It would have broken, you know, if he hadn't taken care
it shouldn't. I wondered if, like many quick-tempered people, they
got sorry just as quickly. Didn't you think it odd, Kenny, that
directly after the row they should *both* have settled down to write
letters?"

The detective stared at him.

"She wrote to her solicitor," he began slowly. "And he—? Good
Lord! You think he wrote to her to say he was sorry?"

"Almost certainly, but we shall never find his letter. That's in
the kitchen stove by now. He came back to deliver it, pushed it
through the door, and hurried off looking just as your plain-clothes
man said, as if he'd got something off his chest. Then he could
sleep. The sun had not gone down on his wrath." He slid off the
table and stood up. "The vital point is, of course, that *Mrs. Cibber
knew he would*. She sat up waiting for it."

Kenny sucked in his breath.

"And Miss Smith knew?"

"Of course, she knew. Mrs. Cibber hadn't the kind of temperament one can keep a secret. Miss Smith knew from the moment
that Mrs. Cibber received the initial letter that the nephew would
get his way in the end—*unless she could stop it somehow!* She
was the one with the bee in her bonnet about the furniture. I
realized that as soon as you said the whole house was kept like a
bandbox. No woman with a weak heart can keep a three-story
house like a palace, or compel another to do it—unless the other
wants to. Miss Smith was the one with the mania. Who was to
get the house if the nephew died in the war? Mrs. Cibber must
have made some provision."

Kenny rubbed his head with both hands. "I knew!" he exploded. "The lawyer's clerk told me this morning when I rang up to find out if Woodruff was the heir. I was so keen to confirm that point that I discounted the rest. If he died the companion was to have it for her lifetime."

Campion looked relieved.

"I thought so. There you are, you see. She had to get rid of them both—Woodruff and his new wife. With a young and vigorous woman in the house there was a danger of the companion becoming—well redundant. Don't you think?"

Kenny was fingering his notebook.

"You think she'd planned it for a fortnight?"

"She'd thought of it for a fortnight. She didn't see how to do it until the row occurred last night. When she found the gun on the window sill, where young Mrs. Woodruff left it, and Mrs. Cibber told her that the boy would come back, the plan was obvious." He shivered. "Do you realize that she must have been waiting, probably on the stairs, with the gun in her hand and the book box addressed to herself in the other, listening for Woodruff's letter to slide under the door? As soon as she heard it, she had to fly down and get it and open the door. Then she had to walk into the drawing room, shoot the old lady as she turned to see who it was, and put the gun in the book box. The instant she was certain Mrs. Cibber was dead, she then had to run out screaming to her place between the lamp post and the mail box and—*post the package!*"

Kenny put down his pencil and looked up.

"Now there," he said with honest admiration, "there I hand it to you. How in the world did you get on to that?"

"You suggested it."

"*I* did?" Kenny was pleased in spite of himself. "When?"

"When you kept asking me where one could hide a gun in a London street with no wide gratings and no sandbins. There was only the mail box. I guessed she'd posted it to herself—no one else would have been safe. Even the dead letter office eventually gives up its dead. That's why I was so keen to get her to the top of the house—as far away from the front door as possible." He sighed. "The book box was misguided genius. The gun was an old Luger, did you notice? Loot. That's why he never had to turn it in. It just fitted in the box. She must have had a thrill when she discovered that."

Kenny shook his head wonderingly. "Well, blow me down!" he said inelegantly, "Funny that *I* put you onto it!"

Mr. Campion was in bed that night when the telephone rang. It was Kenny again.

"I say, Mr. Campion?"

"Yes?"

"Sorry to bother you at this time of night but there's something worrying me. You don't mind, do you?"

"Think nothing of it."

"Well. Everything is all right. Smith had been certified by three medicos. The little girl is very happy comforting her boy, who seems to be upset about his aunt's death. The Commissioner is very pleased. But I can't get off to sleep. Mr. Campion, *how did you know what time the afternoon post is delivered in Barraclough Road?*"

The lean man stifled a yawn.

"Because I went into the chemist's shop on the corner and asked," he said. "Elementary, my dear Kenny."

Perhaps because David Alexander is an habitué of and
an authority on horse racing, he has a Runyonesque
way with the characters and the crack-pots who inhabit
those neighboring half-worlds, Belmont and the Bowery,
Bellevue and Broadway. It is a pleasure to watch a real
professional enjoying himself at his trade; certainly Mr.
Alexander enjoys writing about the outrageous Tommy
Twotoes and his equally outrageous coterie. The fun is
infectious and the murder is real—a fine two-horse par-
lay.

3

Coffee and—

By David Alexander

Tommy Twotoes, the three-hundred-pound millionaire penguin-
fancier, entered the office of Terry Bob Rooke, Private Investigator,
on the loglike arm of old Killer Carney, the punch-drunk, rum-dum
former heavyweight who was now a Bowery bum. Maybe I should
explain right off that I'm Rooke, better known to my friends as
"Soldier," and that my agency was subsidized by the slightly fantastic Mr. Twotoes when he began to fancy himself as a crimi-
nologist in the twilight of his hectic life, and figured he needed
a front for his latest hobby.

To describe Mr. Twotoes as eccentric is to lapse into euphemism.
Mr. Twotoes had been everything from a skid-row vagrant to a
multimillionaire during the seventy-odd years of his intensely alcoholic existence. Among other things, he had promoted the fights
of some of the greatest boxers of his time, which is one of the

reasons he was acquainted with such characters as Killer Carney. The private detective agency for which I held the license was just one of his numerous conceits. He had a herd, or maybe I should say a covey, of penguins housed in an especially refrigerated miniature Antarctic on his estate in Tarrytown. Mr. Twotoes maintained you could learn a great deal about human beings from the study of penguins, since he claimed these flightless birds from the polar regions were the most completely amoral and unchristian of all living creatures.

The Killer, who supported the enormous, crippled Mr. Twotoes on his sturdy arm, was something of a character in his own right. As a result of old batterings and raw booze, he'd been on the Bowery for years. When he wasn't panhandling coffee money, he was engaged in baby-sitting for tenement mothers who couldn't afford the union wage scale of the Baby-sitters Local. Sometimes the Killer was paid a few nickels for his time, and sometimes he was rewarded with homemade wine or a dish of spaghetti; but more often he pursued his odd profession through sheer love of the work.

As he entered the office, Tommy was smoking his queerly wrought pipe, the bowl of which was fashioned in the shape of a nude woman. He took the pipe from his mouth, exuded billowing smoke, and boomed in his foghorn voice:

"Soldier! Have you made arrangements for Lieutenant Romano to receive us?"

Lieutenant Romano was an old buddy of Tommy's who was now attached to the Homicide Squad. That morning Tommy had called me to say that Killer Carney had burst into his home in Tarrytown, panic-stricken, and that the broken-down old pug had important information in connection with the town's latest murder, in which a middle-aged college professor named Stephen Dean was being held for the poison slaying of his beautiful young wife.

I said: "The Lieutenant is awaiting us, and you could have saved yourself a trip up in the elevator. If you've got the Rolls outside, we can drive right downtown. But how did a character like the Killer get mixed up with a college professor and a murder in Mulberry Mews?"

"You will hear in good time," said Tommy, "when the Killer tells his unusual story to Lieutenant Romano. In the meantime, we will pause for refreshment."

Tommy produced a blue crock of French brandy from a cavernous pocket of his coat; I produced glasses, and we all had a drink. After that I helped Killer Carney to the elevator and out into the street with the old man, who was so crippled from alcoholic neuritis that putting one foot in front of the other posed a problem for him. Ebony Black, the gigantic Negro who had lost an eye when he was a heavyweight in Tommy's stable, now acted as bodyguard and chauffeur for Mr. Twotoes. Ebony, clad in plum-colored livery, sat at the wheel of the Rolls Royce, which was parked directly in front of a fireplug. The antediluvian vehicle was so familiar on New York's streets, and its owner was so well known to the police, that Ebony Black was contemptuous of such small matters as traffic regulations.

Mr. Twotoes was always nervous when he was riding, and would permit his chauffeur to proceed at a speed of no more than thirty miles an hour, even on deserted country roads. During our ride down to Manhattan-West headquarters of Homicide on Twentieth Street, my penguin-fancying patron nearly suffered a nervous collapse as the car swerved suddenly.

"Sorry, boss," apologized Ebony, "but a ol' dog almost run under the wheels—ain't nothing makes me feel so poorly as hurting a dumb animal."

Mr. Twotoes, whose doughy moon of a face was even paler than usual, did not answer, but revived himself with a long pull at the blue crock. This time he did not pass it to me or the Killer, however.

"Professor Dean, he was a animal-lover, too," said the Killer. "His house was full of animals, it was."

"Killer," I said, "do you mean to tell me you visited the renovated stable in that sublimated alley in Greenwich Village where Professor Dean has his residence? You're moving in swanky circles these days."

"It ain't no stable," declared the Killer. "It's just a little brick house with kind of a concrete garden out in back. And it ain't in no alley, either. It's in what you call a mews, maybe because they got a lot of cats in it. A mews," explained the Killer, "is a kind of little court which has a lot of trees growing out of boxes in it."

We reached the Manhattan-West station and found Romano, the cop with the classic profile, sitting at a battered desk with a green-shaded light on it, and looking sour, like a man who always expects the worst and is seldom disappointed. He nodded at us.

"Yeah," he said, when Tommy started to introduce the Dean murder witness. "I know the Killer. He was one of the characters around and about your place when I was investigating the Denise Darlan Killing last year."

"He has important information for you, Lieutenant," said Tommy, as we lowered his bulk into the stoutest-looking chair in the office.

"Please don't be doing me favors," said Romano. "I got a clean-cut case of poisoning that is all wrapped up in tissue paper and pretty ribbons and ready to deliver to the D.A. for his birthday. This fellow Dean's young wife dies right after she and he have drunk a cup of coffee. Seems her cup was loaded with a little cyanide. Coffee and—, you might say. Seems the Professor's wife, who's about twenty years younger than he is, has been playing around with a pretty-boy artist named Porter, so we got motive. Seems the only alibi the Professor has is a witness who he claims drank coffee with 'em. We found another cup with fingerprints we couldn't identify, but that could easily have been a plant. The Professor claims this witness is a vag he's picked up and asked in for coffee at his nice little house—a very likely story indeed.

"The Professor claims this vag can testify his wife made the coffee, poured it out into three cups in the house, and brought the cups out to them in the garden. The Professor also says this vag can testify he told his wife he suspected her of trying to poison him so that she could inherit his insurance and marry Pretty Boy Porter, and that he challenged her to drink the coffee she'd prepared for him in an extra-big cup he always used. He says they had a heated argument over this, and that finally his wife grabs the big cup and drinks it down before he can stop her, and drops dead. He says the missing vag can testify to the truth of all this. Only trouble is, the vag lams the minute his wife comes down with a hard case of the death throes."

The Lieutenant scratched his classic Roman nose. "So I've got a perfect case until you come along and do me favors by producing the only witness who can knock the whole case to hell and gone."

He stared at the Killer with his brooding, liquid Italian eyes, and the Killer looked uncomfortable.

"How you ever happen to tell the Professor your name is Vanderlip?" he asked the Killer.

The Killer said: "Cecil Vanderlip was a pug which went nine rounds with me oncet when I was good. The name just come into my mind like that. Vanderlip seemed like a name which would please the Professor. The Professor had class."

The Killer looked guilty. He was sweating. "I don't never give nobody my right name if I can help it," he explained.

Tommy said to Romano: "Before the Killer tells his story, you are due an explanation as to why he did not come forward at once, as to why he left the scene of the crime, in which he was in no way involved, somewhat precipitately. The Killer is a derelict. To him, and to all his kind, the police are natural enemies. It has been half a century or more since I feared the police, but I can understand the Killer's attitude. I trod skid row of the San Francisco that existed before the fire, and I avoided the company of cops, just as the Killer and his cohorts do today. The Killer had no intention of withholding evidence, but he did not wish to involve himself with the police, since his standing in the community is somewhat ambiguous. He fled to me for advice. Being a law-abiding citizen, I have brought him to you."

I had to chuckle at Mr. Twotoes' description of himself as a law-abiding citizen. A good part of his fortune stemmed from Prohibition days, when he was reputed to have been the mastermind behind one of the largest and most profitable of the rumrunning syndicates. But Mr. Twotoes held that Prohibition was an onerous and unnatural law, and he deemed himself a public benefactor in assisting his fellow citizens to flout the Eighteenth Amendment.

Romano sighed patiently, like a man who has conditioned himself to the acceptance of the slings and arrows of outrageous fortune. He called a stenographer and said to Killer Carney: "Tell your story, please."

The Killer said:

"Well, it's thisaway. Yesterday morning I ain't even got jingling in my jeans and I got to make a brace, and the Bowery ain't so popular as it used to be with tourists, so touches ain't easy there. So I'm a little off my beat. I'm on Bleecker, which is usually all right for bracing stale rolls off bakeries, but ain't much good for a flop-stake or a booze-stake. Anyway, I'm figuring I'll work my way up to Washington Square, because at this time of day there is usually a lot of ladies with babies there, and sometimes if you goo-

goo at the babies, you get a dime from them. The ladies, I mean, not the babies. Also there is usually some young punks hanging around which is working steady and killing their lunch hours, and some of them are marks which will maybe spring two-bits.

"But I am still on Bleecker when I see this mark, which is dressed too good for the place where he is walking. This well-dressed guy stops and pets a little cur dog which is lying outside a grocery store; then he reaches in his pocket and takes out a piece of dog biscuit and gives it to the pup, and so I figure he must be a soft touch which is anyway good for coffee money and maybe even a flop-stake, and I brace him.

"I give him the old routine about excuse me, Mister, but couldja maybe spare a few pennies for a cuppa coffee. And he straightens up from feeding the dog the biscuit and says: 'Why, you look to me like you could use a little brandy in your coffee. A café royale,' he says, 'is very stimulating, don't you think?'

"I tell him that the joints I patronize do not put brandy in your coffee, in fact you are lucky if they put canned cow and sugar with flyspecks in it. He laughs, and says to come along with him, and he will see I have some coffee which is laced with brandy.

"Well, I figure I have picked myself a screwball, like one of them guys which are always walking around the Bowery with petitions in their pockets for you to sign, so I say: 'Where do we get this coffee with the slug in it, Mister?'

"And he tells me: 'Well, I had thought it might be pleasant for us to go to my house over in Mulberry Mews, which is not far from here, and have our coffee and brandy in the garden, as it is a pleasant day, but I would like to walk around a bit first, and I would like to talk to you. However,' he says, 'I can see your need for refreshment is urgent, so let us drop into this place on the corner.'

"This place on the corner is called the San Remo, and it is a bar which has a big machine for making Italian coffee at one end which is as big as a diesel engine. This machine explodes and sputters a few times and the bartender gets some coffee out of it; then he gets some brandy out of a bottle and pours it into the coffee, and it is very refreshing, although I would personally have just as lief settle for a boilermaker at Grogan's Elite Palace Café and Bar on the Bowery. Well, we have two of these fancy drinks, and he introduces himself to me very politely as Professor Dean, and I tell him I am Cecil Vanderlip because that is the first name which pops into me head, and besides it seems appropriate under the circumstances. The Professor asks me if he might have the pleasure of my company for a stroll around the streets, and says that afterwards we can go to his house for more of the same we have been having, only better, because he owns some rare old Napoleon brandy. I do not figure how I have anything to lose, as he has not asked me to sign any petitions or even gone into the old routine about how did I become what I am, so I do not tell him anything at all about myself, not even that I am once a heavyweight who was good enough to get his fights promoted by the famous Tommy Twotoes.

"We walk up MacDougal Street but do not get very far very fast, because Professor Dean is a great animal-lover, and MacDougal Street is almost as full of animals as it is of people, and it is very full of people. The Professor stops to stroke the cats and regrets that he has no milk for them to drink. He feeds dog biscuits to half a dozen mutts in every block. He even stops and pats the nose of a bony old horse which he addresses as 'Percy' and which is hitched to a vegetable wagon. He puts his hand in his pocket, but I guess he is out of fodder and horses do not eat dog biscuits, because he says: 'Poor Percy, I have nothing for you today but we will meet again tomorrow and I will bring you something nice.' Only I guess he can't keep his date with the horse account of he is in the can today.

"Finally we get to Washington Square park, and he takes a bag of corn out of his pocket and feeds it to the pigeons. The pigeons seem to know the Professor personal, because they roost all over him until he looks like a fan dancer, and they eat corn right out of his hand. After a while we sit down on a park bench, and a minute later I nearly fall off the park bench because he says to me: 'Vanderlip,' he says, 'what would you do if your wife was trying to poison you?'

"Well, I tell him that my wife has been dead a long time but that she was a good cook and never tried to slip no rat poison into the corned beef and cabbage, and if she had of, I would of clouted her a left hook to the button which would of been a lesson to her.

"He then tells me that his wife is so young and pretty that he could not think of clouting her and risking marking her up with a busted nose or maybe a cauliflower ear. He says that his wife is in love with a young character who paints pictures and that they are planning to slip him a fast mickey and live happily ever after on the fifty gees insurance which he carries. I tell him maybe he is just imagining things, like guys on the Bowery which get the stuff in the wrong bottle and go into the rams and see lavender leopards. But he tells me this is not the case. He says he has overheard his wife and this picture-painter planning to slip a jolt of bug-killer into his coffee and brandy, and he says he is in the habit of drinking coffee and brandy at all hours of the day and night, so there is plenty of opportunity for his wife to sweeten it up for him.

"Then he says that he would like very much to have coffee and brandy in the garden of his house, which is just across the park, but he would not dare to drink his wife's coffee unless a third person is present, and he asks if I will go with him. I tell him I guess there is no harm in me going if he's sure his wife won't dunk the DDT in the wrong cup. He laughs and says there's no danger of that, because he has bought a antique coffee cup for himself up on Cape Cod some years ago which is four times as big as most cups and has old sailing ships painted on it. He says he is the only one at his house which ever drinks out of this big cup. Then he slips me a stake for listening to his troubles, and it is a double saw, twenty bucks! It is the biggest brace I ever made in my entire career on skid row, and the shape I'm in, I would of gladly drunk rat poison to get it.

"Well, this Mulberry Mews where he lives is a kind of little blind alley which runs off MacDougal Street, only it ain't a alley, because it has boxes filled with trees in it instead of cans filled with garbage. There are about half a dozen little houses, all old-looking and pretty much alike, on each side and the Professor lives in the next to the last house on the right-hand side. The house has a white door with a brass knocker and a brass bell on it and the Professor rings the bell to let his wife know he is coming, I guess, before he unlocks the door. His wife is a pretty piece who is young enough to be his daughter and it is not hard to see why she might wish to dose the Professor's coffee and brandy if she has a young picture-painter just around the corner. She does not appear to welcome me too heartily, maybe because I am not dressed up like most of her guests, although I am wearing a coat and pants I got practically new from the Salvation Army, I just washed all over three days ago in a public bath and I have recently had a close shave and haircut at the barber's college.

"The professor's house is not like any which I am used to going into. It has wallpaper and pictures in gold frames and shiny furniture and long red curtains at the windows. And it is full of animals. There is two dogs and more cats than I can count and there are bright-colored fish in little glass tanks and there is a cage with two of those little green birds in it that sit smooching each other all day. The Professor introduces me to his pets, but I'm afraid I do not remember the names of all the little bright-colored fishes which he has in his glass tanks.

"We go out into the garden, although it is not much of a garden. It is a place which is paved with what they call flagstones and there is a umbrella and a table and some chairs and there are plants and little trees growing out of pots. The Professor tells his wife to make some coffee and we will all have coffee and brandy in the garden. The Professor and I and one of them big woolly dogs which are supposed to carry a shot of brandy hitched to their collars and one of them little dogs which look like a wienie sit out in the garden talking of this and that while Mrs. Dean is making coffee. Pretty soon she comes out with a tray. On the tray is three cups of coffee, two regular-sized cups and the big cup for the Professor, and a bottle of brandy which looks like it has been laying around somebody's cellar a long time, and a little silver thing with sugar lumps in it."

Romano asked: "Did she bring out the coffeepot or a cream pitcher?"

The Killer shook his head. "No sir," he said. "She must of poured the coffee into the cups inside the house. And we put brandy instead of cream into the coffee."

"Did all of you take sugar?" Romano asked.

"Yes sir," replied Killer Carney. "Everybody took sugar. The Missus and I took two lumps apiece, but the Professor took three or four because he had such a big cup."

"Who poured the brandy into your coffee?"

"The Professor. He poured a big slug in all our cups. His wife said he was pouring too much."

"And he poured from the same bottle into all your cups?" asked the Lieutenant.

"Sure. There wasn't but one bottle. A real old-looking kind of bottle it was."

"And did each of you drink the coffee with the brandy?"

"Well, Mrs. Dean and I start to drink ours, but the Professor says to his wife: 'My dear,' he says, ' do you really think it's safe for me to drink this?'

" 'What in the world do you mean, Stephen?' she asks him.

" 'Are you quite sure you haven't put something special in this big cup of mine?' he asks her. 'Something that might disagree with me?'

" 'Stephen!' she says. 'How absurd can you get?' she asks him.

" 'It's quite all right, my dear,' he tells her. 'I've told Mr. Vander-lip here that you are planning to poison me.'

"This makes me feel very embarrassed, so I drink my own coffee and brandy down at a gulp. Mrs. Dean is blazing mad. She says to the Professor, 'You fool!' she says, 'I wondered why you brought this man here! You must be completely insane,' she tells him.

"The Professor reaches over and slides the cup which she has been drinking from across the table and pushes the big cup with the ships painted on it, which he hasn't touched, towards his wife. He sips coffee and brandy out of his wife's cup and he says to her, 'If you're sure there's nothing indigestible in the coffee you pre-pared for me, why don't you drink it yourself, my dear?'

" 'You poor, crazy fool,' his wife says. 'You need a psychiatrist,' she tells him. Then she stares him straight in the face like she is kind of defying him and before anybody can stop her, she picks up the Professor's big cup with both hands, and drinks it down, even though the Professor jumps up out of his chair and starts yelling that she shouldn't.

"She puts down the cup and she stares the Professor in the face again, and then all of a sudden she has a funny look and she starts to choke and then she doubles up and falls out of her chair.

"Right there is where I lam. I run out of the house and I don't stop until I am in Grogan's Elite Palace Café and Bar on the Bowery. I tell Suds, the bartender, the funny thing which has hap-pened to me, and he reminds me that Tommy Twotoes is a kind of a detective even if he ain't got a badge, so after I get the twenty that the Professor has give me changed, I have a few boilermakers and I take a train to Tarrytown and see Tommy Twotoes and to-day he brings me here and that's all that I know about anything."

"You know too damned much," said Romano. "You know enough to give Professor Dean a perfect alibi and to knock my case into the left-field bleachers."

The Lieutenant turned to Tommy and sighed. "The case was

almost too perfect," he said. "Dean was a professor of chemistry at Empire State University. He had access to all the poison he could use. You see how smart he was? He decided to kill his wife by poison. So he alibis himself in advance by picking up a panhandler to witness the whole thing. This man can swear that Mrs. Dean prepared the coffee and that she poured it into three separate cups, one of them a very distinctive cup, while nobody was looking. He can swear that the brandy they all drank came out of the same bottle and the sugar they all used came out of the same bowl. He'll testify that although Dean goaded his wife into drinking the cup with the poison in it, she actually drank it of her own volition. He can even say Dean made some kind of effort to stop her—too late. I don't know how Dean got cyanide into the cup. He was smart enough to pour a lot of brandy in, too, so the fumes would disguise the bitter almond odor. Dean's guilty as hell. Otherwise he wouldn't have prepared such an elaborate alibi. But proving it is something else. I doubt the D.A. will even bring the case to trial after hearing Carney's evidence."

"Killer," asked Tommy Twotoes, "what kind of coat was Professor Dean wearing yesterday?"

"A sports coat with a kind of zigzag check," the Killer replied.

"Is that the coat he is now wearing?" Tommy asked Romano.

"Yeah," replied the Lieutenant. "A hound's-tooth tweed."

"Where is Dean now?" asked Tommy.

"Matter of fact, he's right in the building," Romano answered. "We brought him here this morning for what we politely term 'further questioning.' "

"Can you arrange to bring him here and allow me to question him in an ex officio capacity?" Tommy asked. "By staging a bit of mummery, I may be able to break him. You see, this whole matter hinges on a horse."

"A horse!" exclaimed Romano. "Why not the dogs or cats or pigeons or tropical fish or lovebirds? It's irregular, of course, but I'll have him down. I'm like the Killer—I've got nothing to lose."

Romano spoke into a phone.

In a few minutes a detective arrived with Dean. You could tell the Professor was an immaculate, self-contained little man under ordinary circumstances, although his clothes were rumpled now from a night in jail and long hours of questioning by the police.

When the Professor saw Killer Carney, his face lit up. "Thank God you've come forward at last, Vanderlip!" he cried.

"This gentleman wants to ask you a few questions," Romano said to Dean, indicating Tommy with a nod of his head. "He's kind of a special investigator in this case."

The Professor regarded the grossly corpulent old man curiously. Tommy Twotoes said: "Professor Dean, please remove your coat."

"My coat?" asked the bewildered Dean.

"Your coat, sir," replied Tommy. "You will hand it to Dr. Rooke, our police laboratory technician. Take his coat, please, Doctor."

I didn't quite know when I'd been awarded a doctor's degree, but I took the coat.

"Now, Professor Dean," continued Tommy, "you were accustomed to taking midday strolls in the vicinity of Washington Square, I believe?"

"Weather permitting, yes," replied the Professor.

"And you were accustomed to carrying with you tidbits for animals and birds you might encounter during your walks?"

"I was," replied Dean. "I have always been fond of animals."

"You often encountered a horse hitched to a vegetable wagon, a horse you addressed as 'Percy,' during these midday strolls?"

"I did," answered Dean, smiling. "I called him Percy because he had such a long, gaunt face, like the caricatures of typical Englishmen. I always found Percy standing hitched to his wagon at the corner of MacDougal and Minetta Lane, while his owner was crying his wares. Percy is a particular friend of mine."

"And you were accustomed to feeding sugar lumps to this horse, Percy?" Tommy asked.

Dean's eyes narrowed. "Yes," he said at length. "Yes, I was. But why on earth do you ask that, sir?"

"You encountered the horse, Percy, yesterday while you were in the company of Mr. Vanderlip here?"

"Yes," said Dean.

"But you did not feed him his usual tidbit of a sugar lump?"

"No. I had forgotten to bring any sugar with me, I'm afraid."

"Isn't that rather odd, Professor?" Tommy asked. "You carried biscuits for dogs and corn for pigeons. There was a bowl of lump sugar available in your house. Yet you forgot to bring a sugar lump for Percy, whom you describe as your particular friend."

"I simply forgot it, is all," said the Professor.

"No, Professor Dean," said Tommy, his tone very stern. "It won't wash. It won't wash at all. You had a sugar lump in your pocket. But it was not for Percy. Mr. Vanderlip here has testified that when you saw the horse, you reached in your pocket, took out a lump of sugar, but that on second thought you returned it to your pocket."

Of course, the Killer hadn't said anything like that. The old fighter's jaw gaped open, but a frown from Romano silenced him.

"You did not give Percy the sugar because it would have killed him," Tommy Twotoes continued. "And you did not intend to kill a horse. You intended to kill your wife. Cyanide of potassium comes in small white sticks which a chemist such as yourself could easily introduce into a sugar lump. A tenth of a gram is sufficient to bring death almost immediately. You could not risk carrying sugar for Percy yesterday because it might get mixed with the lump of sugar you were carrying about awaiting the opportunity to slip it into the coffee you would trick your wife into drinking. It was simple enough for you to drop the poisoned sugar into the big cup, along with the other lumps you took from the bowl."

"This is fantastic," said Professor Dean.

"I am surprised at you, sir," said Tommy Twotoes. "You are a chemist, and you should know that the modern detective depends more upon the laboratory technician than upon the rubber hose."

Tommy turned to me. "Dr. Rooke," he said. "You will take the coat to the laboratory and make the necessary tests. Pay special attention to any microscopic particles found among the lint in the pocket. There is certain to be crystals of sugar—and of cyanide of potassium. We will expect your report as soon as possible. It will wind up our case against Professor Dean."

The Professor smiled. "I had to kill her," he said. "I could not have let her go to the arms of another man. But it doesn't matter much about your tests. I carried the poisoned sugar lump loose in my pocket, so I could reach it quickly when I needed it. Now she's dead, I have no desire to live."

When Killer Carney and I had settled Tommy in the Rolls Royce, the old man said to Ebony Black:

"Ebony, you will stop at a grocery store and procure a package of lump sugar. Then drive to MacDougal Street and Minetta Lane in the Village. We are going to make a present to a horse named Percy, with the compliments of Lieutenant Romano."

Margaret Millar is a distinguished writer of mystery
fiction who is married to a distinguished writer of mystery fiction, Kenneth Millar (John Ross MacDonald).
She deals in mood and irony rather than in blood and
iron, and her work stays with you long after you have
discovered "who dunnit". "The Couple Next Door"
is a good example: simple, gentle people, a quiet neighborhood—of such things are murders made.

4

The Couple Next Door

By Margaret Millar

It was by accident that they lived next door to each other, but by
design that they became neighbors—Mr. Sands, who had retired
to California after a life of crime investigation, and the Rackhams,
Charles and Alma. Rackham was a big, innocent-looking man in
his fifties. Except for the accumulation of a great deal of money,
nothing much had ever happened to Rackham, and he liked to
listen to Sands talk, while Alma sat with her knitting, plump and
contented, unimpressed by any tale that had no direct bearing on
her own life. She was half Rackham's age, but the fullness of her
figure, and her air of having withdrawn from life quietly and without fuss, gave her the stamp of middle-age.

Two or three times a week Sands crossed the concrete driveway,
skirted the eugenia hedge, and pressed the Rackhams' door chime.
He stayed for tea or for dinner, to play gin or scrabble, or just to
talk. "That reminds me of a case I had in Toronto," Sands would
say, and Rackham would produce martinis and an expression of

intense interest, and Alma would smile tolerantly, as if she didn't really believe a single thing Sands, or anyone else, ever said.

They made good neighbors: the Rackhams, Charles younger than his years, and Alma older than hers, and Sands who could be any age at all . . .

It was the last evening of August and through the open window of Sands' study came the scent of jasmine and the sound of a woman's harsh, wild weeping.

He thought at first that the Rackhams had a guest, a woman on a crying jag, perhaps, after a quarrel with her husband.

He went out into the front yard to listen, and Rackham came around the hedge, dressed in a bathrobe.

He said, sounding very surprised, "Alma's crying."

"I heard."

"I asked her to stop. I begged her. She won't tell me what's the matter."

"Women have cried before."

"Not Alma." Rackham stood on the damp grass, shivering, his forehead streaked with sweat. "What do you think we should do about it?"

The *I* had become *we*, because they were good neighbors, and along with the games and the dinners and the scent of jasmine, they shared the sound of a woman's grief.

"Perhaps you could talk to her," Rackham said.

"I'll try."

"I don't think there is anything physically the matter with her. We both had a check-up at the Tracy clinic last week. George Tracy is a good friend of mine—he'd have told me if there was anything wrong."

"I'm sure he would."

"If anything ever happened to Alma I'd kill myself."

Alma was crouched in a corner of the davenport in the living room, weeping rhythmically, methodically, as if she had accumulated a hoard of tears and must now spend them all in one night. Her fair skin was blotched with patches of red, like strawberry birthmarks, and her eyelids were blistered from the heat of her tears. She looked like a stranger to Sands, who had never seen her display any emotion stronger than ladylike distress over a broken teacup.

Rackham went over and stroked her hair. "Alma, dear. What is the matter?"

"Nothing . . . nothing . . ."

"Mr. Sands is here, Alma. I thought he might be able—we might be able—"

But no one was able. With a long shuddering sob, Alma got up and lurched across the room, hiding her blotched face with her hands. They heard her stumble up the stairs.

Sands said, "I'd better be going."

"No, please don't. I—the fact is, I'm scared stiff. Alma's always been so quiet."

"I know that."

"You don't suppose—there's no chance she's losing her mind?"

If they had not been good neighbors Sands might have remarked that Alma had little mind to lose. As it was, he said cautiously, "She might have had bad news, family trouble of some kind."

"She has no family except me."

"If you're worried, perhaps you'd better call your doctor."

"I think I will."

George Tracy arrived within half an hour, a slight, fair-haired man in his early thirties, with a smooth unhurried manner that imparted confidence. He talked slowly, moved slowly, as if there was all the time in the world to minister to desperate women.

Rackham chafed with impatience while Tracy removed his coat, placed it carefully across the back of the chair, and discussed the weather with Sands.

"It's a beautiful evening," Tracy said, and Alma's moans sliding down the stairs distorted his words, altered their meaning: *a terrible evening, an awful evening.* "There's a touch of fall in the air. You live in these parts, Mr. Sands?"

"Next door."

"For heavens sake, George," Rackham said, "will you hurry up? For all you know, Alma might be dying."

"That I doubt. People don't die as easily as you might imagine. She's in her room?"

"Yes. Now will you *please—*"

"Take it easy, old man."

Tracy picked up his medical bag and went towards the stairs, leisurely, benign.

"He's always like that." Rackham turned to Sands, scowling. "Exasperating son-of-a-gun. You can bet that if he had a wife in

Alma's condition he'd be taking those steps three at a time."

"Who knows?—perhaps he has."

"*I* know," Rackham said crisply. "He's not even married. Never had time for it, he told me. He doesn't look it but he's very ambitious."

"Most doctors are."

"Tracy is, anyway."

Rackham mixed a pitcher of martinis, and the two men sat in front of the unlit fire, waiting and listening. The noises from upstairs gradually ceased, and pretty soon the doctor came down again.

Rackham rushed across the room to meeet him. "How is she?"

"Sleeping. I gave her a hypo."

"Did you talk to her? Did you ask her what was the matter?"

"She was in no condition to answer questions."

"Did you find anything wrong with her?"

"Not physically. She's a healthy young woman."

"Not *physically*. Does that mean—?"

"Take it easy, old man."

Rackham was too concerned with Alma to notice Tracy's choice of words, but Sands noticed, and wondered if it had been conscious or unconscious: Alma's a healthy young woman . . . Take it easy, old man.

"If she's still depressed in the morning," Tracy said, "bring her down to the clinic with you when you come in for your X-rays. We have a good neurologist on our staff." He reached for his coat and hat. "By the way, I hope you followed the instructions?"

Rackham looked at him stupidly. "What instructions?"

"Before we can take specific X-rays, certain medication is necessary."

"I don't know what you're talking about."

"I made it very clear to Alma," Tracy said, sounding annoyed. "You were to take one ounce of sodium phosphate after dinner tonight, and report to the X-ray department at 8 o'clock tomorrow morning without breakfast."

"She didn't tell me."

"Oh."

"It must have slipped her mind."

"Yes. Obviously. Well, it's too late now." He put on his coat, moving quickly for the first time, as if he were in a rush to get away. The change made Sands curious. He wondered why Tracy was suddenly so anxious to leave, and whether there was any connection between Alma's hysteria and her lapse of memory about Rackham's X-rays. He looked at Rackham and guessed, from his pallor and his worried eyes, that Rackham had already made a connection in his mind.

"I understood," Rackham said carefully, "that I was all through at the clinic. My heart, lungs, metabolism—everything fit as a fiddle."

"People," Tracy said, "are not fiddles. Their tone doesn't improve with age. I will make another appointment for you and send you specific instructions by mail. Is that all right with you?"

"I guess it will have to be."

"Well, good night, Mr. Sands, pleasant meeting you." And to Rackham, "Good night, old man."

When he had gone, Rackham leaned against the wall, breathing hard. Sweat crawled down the sides of his face like worms and hid in the collar of his bathrobe. "You'll have to forgive me, Sands. I feel—I'm not feeling very well."

"Is there anything I can do?"

"Yes," Rackham said. "Turn back the clock."

"Beyond my powers, I'm afraid."

"Yes . . . Yes, I'm afraid."

"Good night, Rackham." *Good night, old man.*

"Good night, Sands." *Good night old man to you, too.*

From his study Sands could see the lighted windows of Rackham's bedroom. Rackham's shadow moved back and forth behind the blinds as if seeking escape from the very light that gave it existence. Back and forth, in search of nirvana.

Sands read until far into the night. It was one of the solaces of growing old—if the hours were numbered, at least fewer of them need be wasted in sleep. When he went to bed, Rackham's bedroom light was still on.

They had become good neighbors by design; now, also by design, they became strangers. Whose design it was, Alma's or Rackham's, Sands didn't know.

There was no definite break, no unpleasantness. But the eugenia hedge seemed to have grown taller and thicker, and the concrete driveway a mile away. He saw the Rackhams occasionally; they waved or smiled or said, "Lovely weather," over the backyard fence. But Rackham's smile was thin and painful, Alma waved with a leaden arm, and neither of them cared about the weather. They stayed indoors most of the time, and when they did come out they were always together, arm in arm, walking slowly and in step. It was impossible to tell whose step led, and whose followed.

At the end of the first week in September, Sands met Alma by accident in a drug store downtown. It was the first time since the night of the doctor's visit that he'd seen either of the Rackhams alone.

She was waiting at the prescription counter wearing a flowery print dress that emphasized the fullness of her figure and the bovine expression of her face. A drug-store length away, she looked like a rather dull, badly dressed young woman with a passion for starchy foods, and it was hard to understand what Rackham had seen in her. But then Rackham had never stood a drug-store length away from Alma; he saw her only in close-up, the surprising, intense blue of her eyes, and the color and texture of her skin, like whipped cream. Sands wondered whether it was her skin and eyes, or her quality of serenity which had appealed most to Rackham, who was quick and nervous and excitable.

She said, placidly, "Why, hello there."

"Hello, Alma."

"Lovely weather, isn't it?"

"Yes . . . How is Charles?"

"You must come over for dinner one of these nights."

"I'd like to."

"Next week, perhaps. I'll give you a call—I must run now. Charles is waiting for me. See you next week."

But she did not run, she walked; and Charles was not waiting for her, he was waiting for Sands. He had let himself into Sands' house and was pacing the floor of the study, smoking a cigarette. His color was bad, and he had lost weight, but he seemed to have acquired an inner calm. Sands could not tell whether it was the calm of a man who had come to an important decision, or that of a man who had reached the end of his rope and had stopped struggling.

They shook hands, firmly, pressing the past week back into shape.

Rackham said, "Nice to see you again, old man."

"I've been here all along."

"Yes. Yes, I know. . . . I had things to do, a lot of thinking to do."

"Sit down. I'll make you a drink."

"No, thanks. Alma will be home shortly, I must be there."

Like a Siamese twin, Sands thought, *separated by a miracle, but returning voluntarily to the fusion—because the fusion was in a vital organ.*

"I understand," Sands said.

Rackham shook his head. "No one can understand, really, but you come very close sometimes, Sands. Very close." His cheeks flushed, like a boy's. "I'm not good at words or expressing my emotions, but I wanted to thank you before we leave, and tell you how much Alma and I have enjoyed your companionship."

"You're taking a trip?"

"Yes. Quite a long one."

"When are you leaving?"

"Today."

"You must let me see you off at the station."

"No, no," Rackham said quickly. "I couldn't think of it. I hate last-minute depot farewells. That's why I came over this afternoon to say good-bye."

"Tell me something of your plans."

"I would if I had any. Everything is rather indefinite. I'm not sure where we'll end up."

"I'd like to hear from you now and then."

"Oh, you'll hear from me, of course." Rackham turned away with an impatient twitch of his shoulders as if he was anxious to leave, anxious to start the trip right now before anything happened to prevent it.

"I'll miss you both," Sands said. "We've had a lot of laughs together."

Rackham scowled out of the window. "Please, no farewell speeches. They might shake my decision. My mind is already made up. I want no second thoughts."

"Very well."

"I must go now. Alma will be wondering—"

"I saw Alma earlier this afternoon," Sands said.

"Oh?"

"She invited me for dinner next week."

Outside the open window two hummingbirds fought and fussed, darting with crazy accuracy in and out of the bougainvillea vine.

"Alma," Rackham said carefully, "can be very forgetful sometimes."

"Not that forgetful. She doesn't know about this trip you've planned, does she? . . . Does she, Rackham?"

"I wanted it to be a surprise. She's always had a desire to see the world. She's still young enough to believe that one place is different from any other place . . . You and I know better."

"Do we?"

"Good-bye, Sands."

At the front door they shook hands again, and Rackham again promised to write, and Sands promised to answer his letters. Then Rackham crossed the lawn and the concrete driveway, head bent, shoulders hunched. He didn't look back as he turned the corner of the eugenia hedge.

Sands went over to his desk, looked up a number in the telephone directory, and dialed.

A girl's voice answered, "Tracy clinic, X-ray department."

"This is Charles Rackham," Sands said.

"Yes, Mr. Rackham."

"I'm leaving town unexpectedly. If you'll tell me the amount of my bill I'll send you a check before I go."

"The bill hasn't gone through, but the standard price for a lower gastro-intestinal is twenty-five dollars."

"Let's see. I had that done on the—"

"The fifth. Yesterday."

"But my original appointment was for the first, wasn't it?"

The girl gave a does-it-really-matter sigh. "Just a minute, sir, and I'll check." Half a minute later she was back on the line. "We have no record of an appointment for you on the first, sir."

"You're sure of that?"

"Even without the record book, I'd be sure. The first was a Monday. We do only gall bladders on Monday."

"Oh. Thank you."

Sands went out and got into his car. Before he pulled away from the curb he looked over at Rackham's house and saw Rackham pacing up and down the veranda, waiting for Alma.

The Tracy clinic was less impressive than Sands had expected, a converted two-story stucco house with a red tile roof. Some of the tiles were broken and the whole building needed paint, but the furnishings inside were smart and expensive.

At the reception desk a nurse wearing a crew cut and a professional smile told Sands that Dr. Tracy was booked solid for the entire afternoon. The only chance of seeing him was to sit in the second-floor waiting room and catch him between patients.

Sands went upstairs and took a chair in a little alcove at the end of the hall, near Tracy's door. He sat with his face half hidden behind an open magazine. After a while the door of Tracy's office opened and over the top of his magazine Sands saw a woman silhouetted in the door frame—a plump, fair-haired young woman in a flowery print dress.

Tracy followed her into the hall and the two of them stood looking at each other in silence. Then Alma turned and walked away, passing Sands without seeing him because her eyes were blind with tears.

Sands stood up. "Dr. Tracy?"

Tracy turned sharply, surprise and annoyance pinching the corners of his mouth. "Well? Oh, it's Mr. Sands."

"May I see you a moment?"

"I have quite a full schedule this afternoon."

"This is an emergency."

"Very well. Come in."

They sat facing each other across Tracy's desk.

"You look pretty fit," Tracy said with a wry smile, "for an emergency case."

"The emergency is not mine. It may be yours."

"If it's mine, I'll handle it alone, without the help of a poli— I'll handle it myself."

Sands leaned forward. "Alma has told you, then, that I used to be a policeman."

"She mentioned it in passing."

"I saw Alma leave a few minutes ago. . . . She'd be quite a nice-looking woman if she learned to dress properly."

"Clothes are not important in a woman," Tracy said, with a slight flush. "Besides, I don't care to discuss my patients."

"Alma is a patient of yours?"

"Yes."

"Since the night Rackham called you when she was having hysterics?"

"Before then."

Sands got up, went to the window, and looked down at the

street.

People were passing, children were playing on the sidewalk, the sun shone, the palm trees rustled with wind—everything outside seemed normal and human and real. By contrast, the shape of the idea that was forming in the back of his mind was so grotesque and ugly that he wanted to run out of the office, to join the normal people passing on the street below. But he knew he could not escape by running. The idea would follow him, pursue him until he turned around and faced it.

It moved inside his brain like a vast wheel, and in the middle of the wheel, impassive, immobile, was Alma.

Tracy's harsh voice interrupted the turning of the wheel. "Did you come here to inspect my view, Mr. Sands?"

"Let's say, instead, your viewpoint."

"I'm a busy man. You're wasting my time."

"No. I'm giving you time."

"To do what?"

"Think things over."

"If you don't leave my office immediately, I'll have you thrown out." Tracy glanced at the telephone but he didn't reach for it, and there was no conviction in his voice.

"Perhaps you shouldn't have let me in. Why did you?"

"I thought you might make a fuss if I didn't."

"Fusses aren't in my line." Sands turned from the window. "Liars are, though."

"What are you implying?"

"I've thought a great deal about that night you came to the Rackhams' house. In retrospect, the whole thing appeared too pat; too contrived: Alma had hysterics and you were called to treat her. Natural enough, so far."

Tracy stirred but didn't speak.

"The interesting part came later. You mentioned casually to Rackham that he had an appointment for some X-rays to be taken the following day, September the first. It was assumed that Alma had forgotten to tell him. Only Alma *hadn't* forgotten. There was nothing to forget. I checked with your X-ray department half an hour ago. They have no record of any appointment for Rackham on September the first.

"Records get lost."

"This record wasn't lost. It never existed. You lied to Rackham.

The lie itself wasn't important, it was the *kind* of lie. I could have understood a lie of vanity, or one to avoid punishment or to gain profit. But this seemed such a silly, senseless, little lie. It worried me. I began to wonder about Alma's part in the scene that night. Her crying was most unusual for a woman of Alma's inert nature. What if her crying was also a lie? And what was to be gained by it?"

"Nothing," Tracy said wearily. "Nothing was gained."

"But something was *intended*—and I think I know what it was. The scene was played to worry Rackham, to set him up for an even bigger scene. If that next scene has already been played, I am wasting my time here. Has it?"

"You have a vivid imagination."

"No. The plan was yours—I only figured it out."

"Very poor figuring, Mr. Sands." But Tracy's face was gray, as if mold had grown over his skin.

"I wish it were. I had become quite fond of the Rackhams."

He looked down at the street again, seeing nothing but the wheel turning inside his head. Alma was no longer in the middle of the wheel, passive and immobile; she was revolving with the others—Alma and Tracy and Rackham, turning as the wheel turned, clinging to its perimeter.

Alma, devoted wife, a little on the dull side . . . What sudden passion of hate or love had made her capable of such consummate deceit? Sands imagined the scene the morning after Tracy's visit to the house. Rackham, worried and exhausted after a sleepless night: *"Are you feeling better now, Alma?"*

"Yes."

"What made you cry like that?"

"I was worried."

"About me?"

"Yes."

"Why didn't you tell me about my X-ray appointment?"

"I couldn't. I was frightened. I was afraid they would discover something serious the matter with you."

"Did Tracy give you any reason to think that?"

"He mentioned something about a blockage. Oh, Charles, I'm scared! If anything ever happened to you, I'd die. I couldn't live without you!"

For an emotional and sensitive man like Rackham, it was a perfect set-up: his devoted wife was frightened to the point of hysterics, his good friend and physician had given her reason to be frightened. Rackham was ready for the next step . . .

"According to the records in your X-ray department," Sands said, "Rackham had a lower gastrointestinal X-ray yesterday morning. What was the result?"

"Medical ethics forbid me to—"

"You can't hide behind a wall of medical ethics that's already full of holes. What was the result?"

There was a long silence before Tracy spoke. "Nothing."

"You found nothing the matter with him?"

"That's right."

"Have you told Rackham that?"

"He came in earlier this afternoon, alone."

"Why alone?"

"I didn't want Alma to hear what I had to say."

"Very considerate of you."

"No, it was not considerate," Tracy said dully. "I had decided to back out of our—our agreement—and I didn't want her to know just yet."

"The agreement was to lie to Rackham, convince him that he had a fatal disease?"

"Yes."

"Did you?"

"No. I showed him the X-rays, I made it clear that there was nothing wrong with him . . . I tried. I tried my best. It was no use."

"What do you mean?"

"He wouldn't believe me! He thought I was trying to keep the real truth from him." Tracy drew in his breath sharply. "It's funny, isn't it?—after days of indecision and torment I made up my mind to do the right thing. But it was too late. Alma had played her role too well. She's the only one Rackham will believe."

The telephone on Tracy's desk began to ring but he made no move to answer it, and pretty soon the ringing stopped and the room was quiet again.

Sands said, "Have you asked Alma to tell him the truth?"

"Yes, just before you came in."

"She refused?"

Tracy didn't answer.

"She wants him to think he is fatally ill?"

"I—yes."

"In the hope that he'll kill himself, perhaps?"

Once again Tracy was silent. But no reply was necessary.

"I think Alma miscalculated," Sands said quietly. Instead of planning suicide, Rackham is planning a trip. But before he leaves, he's going to hear the truth—from you and from Alma." Sands went towards the door. "Come on, Tracy. You have a house call to make."

"No, I can't." Tracy grasped the desk with both hands, like a child resisting the physical force of removal by a parent. "I won't go."

"You have to."

"No! Rackham will ruin me if he finds out. That's how this whole thing started. We were afraid, Alma and I, afraid of what Rackham would do if she asked him for a divorce. He's crazy in love with her, he's obsessed!"

"And so are you?"

"Not the way he is. Alma and I both want the same things—a little peace, a little quiet together. We are alike in many ways."

"That I can believe," Sands said grimly. "You want the same things, a little peace, a little quiet—and a little of Rackham's money?"

"The money was secondary."

"A very close second. How did you plan on getting it?"

Tracy shook his head from side to side, like an animal in pain. "You keep referring to plans, ideas, schemes. We didn't start out with plans or schemes. We just fell in love. We've been in love for nearly a year, not daring to do anything about it because I knew how Rackham would react if we told him. I have worked hard to build up this clinic; Rackham could destroy it, and me, within a month."

"That's a chance you'll have to take. Come on, Tracy."

Sands opened the door and the two men walked down the hall, slowly and in step, as if they were handcuffed together.

A nurse in uniform met them at the top of the stairs. "Dr. Tracy, are you ready for your next—?"

"Cancel all my appointments, Miss Leroy."

"But that's imposs—"

"I have a very important house call to make."

"Will it take long?"

"I don't know."

The two men went down the stairs, past the reception desk, and out into the summer afternoon. Before he got into Sands' car, Tracy looked back at the clinic, as if he never expected to see it again.

Sands turned on the ignition and the car sprang forward.

After a time Tracy said, "Of all the people in the world who could have been at the Rackhams' that night, it had to be an ex-policeman."

"It's lucky for you that I was."

"Lucky." Tracy let out a harsh little laugh. "What's lucky about financial ruin?"

"It's better than some other kinds of ruin. If your plan had gone through, you could never have felt like a decent man again."

"You think I will anyway?"

"Perhaps, as the years go by."

"The years." Tracy turned, with a sigh. "What are you going to tell Rackham?"

"Nothing. You will tell him yourself."

"I can't. You don't understand. I'm quite fond of Rackham, and so is Alma. We—it's hard to explain."

"Even harder to understand." Sands thought back to all the times he had seen the Rackhams together and envied their companionship, their mutual devotion. Never, by the slightest glance or gesture of impatience or slip of the tongue, had Alma indicated that she was passionately in love with another man. He recalled the games of scrabble, the dinners, the endless conversations with Rackham, while Alma sat with her knitting, her face reposeful, content. Rackham would ask, "Don't you want to play, too, Alma?" And she would reply, "No, thank you, dear, I'm quite happy with my thoughts."

Alma, happy with her thoughts of violent delights and violent ends.

Sands said, "Alma is equally in love with you?"

"Yes." He sounded absolutely convinced. "No matter what Rackham says or does, we intend to have each other."

"I see."

The blinds of the Rackham house were closed against the sun. Sands led the way up the veranda steps and pressed the door chime, while Tracy stood, stony-faced and erect, like a bill collector or a process server.

Sands could hear the chimes pealing inside the house and feel their vibrations beating under his feet.

He said, "They may have gone already."

"Gone where?"

"Rackham wouldn't tell me. He just said he was planning the trip as a surprise for Alma."

"He can't take her away! He can't force her to leave if she doesn't want to go!"

Sands pressed the door chime again, and called out, "Rackham? Alma?" But there was no response.

He wiped the sudden moisture off his forehead with his coat sleeve. "I'm going in."

"I'm coming with you."

"No."

The door was unlocked. He stepped into the empty hall and shouted up the staircase, "Alma? Rackham? Are you there?"

The echo of his voice teased him from the dim corners.

Tracy had come into the hall. "They've left, then?"

"Perhaps not. They might have just gone out for a drive. It's a nice day for a drive."

"Is it?"

"Go around to the back and see if their car's in the garage."

When Tracy had gone, Sands closed the door behind him and shot the bolt. He stood for a moment listening to Tracy's nervous footsteps on the concrete driveway. Then he turned and walked slowly into the living room, knowing the car would be in the garage, no matter how nice a day it was for a drive.

The drapes were pulled tight across the windows and the room was cool and dark, but alive with images and noisy with the past:

"*I wanted to thank you before we leave, Sands.*"

"*You're taking a trip?*"

"*Yes, quite a long one.*"

"*When are you leaving?*"

"*Today.*"

"*You must let me see you off at the station. . . .*"

But no station had been necessary for Rackham's trip. He lay in front of the fireplace in a pool of blood, and beside him was his companion on the journey, her left arm curving around his waist.

Rackham had kept his promise to write. The note was on the mantel, addressed not to Sands, but to Tracy.

Dear George:

You did your best to fool me but I got the truth from Alma. She could never hide anything from me, we are too close to each other. This is the easiest way out. I am sorry that I must take Alma along, but she has told me so often that she could not live without me. I cannot leave her behind to grieve.

Think of us now and then, and try not to judge me too harshly.

Charles Rackham.

Sands put the note back on the mantel. He stood quietly, his heart pierced by the final splinter of irony: before Rackham had used the gun on himself, he had lain down on the floor beside Alma and placed her dead arm lovingly around his waist.

From outside came the sound of Tracy's footsteps and then the pounding of his fists on the front door.

"Sands, I'm locked out. Open the door. Let me in! Sands, do you hear me? Open this door!"

Sands went and opened the door.

Q. Patrick (Patrick Quentin) is a writing team made up of two men. For many years they have maintained an amazingly high level of excellence in both short stories and novels. We present here "Death Before Breakfast," a very short story which shows how simple it is to write a fine story if you know how. Do you love detection? It's here. Human interest? A believable cop? A fair puzzle? All here, and all in a story you can read in less than five minutes.

5

Death Before Breakfast

By Q. Patrick

Lieutenant Timothy Trant of the New York Homicide Bureau followed the sedate waddle of Minnie, his sister's dachshund, through the midwinter bleakness of Central Park. It was 7:30 on a Sunday morning, an unhallowed hour. But Minnie, who was temporarily boarding with Trant, believed in Rising and Shining.

As an Arctic wind slashed around Trant, Minnie paused imperturbably to inspect a sheet of newspaper which had floated to rest at their side. She put her front paws on it and examined an advertisement for the Ice Follies at the Center Theater. Hopefully, Trant kept the leash slack. Minnie, however, merely sniffed at the Obituaries and padded ahead.

The park was almost deserted, but, coming up the path toward them, Trant noticed the now-familiar figure of the blind man with the Seeing-Eye dog. Every morning since Minnie had inflicted these sadistic pre-breakfast hikes on him, he had met this pathetic pair. Minnie had on previous mornings carried on a hopeless flirtation with the German Shepherd. However, between Trant's firm grip on her leash and the Seeing-Eye dog's apparent indifference, Minnie's progress had been halted.

Sometimes the blind man and his dog were accompanied by a pretty, Gallic-looking girl and sometimes they were alone. Today they were alone, and as the dog steered his master between a bench and a large clumsily boarded excavation in the path, Trant glanced sympathetically at the blind man. His youngish face with its dark glasses looked harsh and hostile. But suddenly he bent to pat his dog's head and his tenderness touched Trant's heart.

"I wonder," he reflected dubiously, "whether I could ever get that fond of Minnie."

It seemed unlikely, unless Minnie made a drastic change in her pattern of life. She dawdled to peer down into the perilous depths of the excavation hole; she inspected a bench nearby and yawned. Then, as if she hadn't a care in the world, she tugged Trant into a skittish gallop.

When Minnie's business was finally completed more people were about and, as Trant hurried homeward toward the life-preserving prospect of hot coffee, he noticed that an excited group was gathering around the excavation hole.

Congenitally curious, he picked up Minnie and walked to the brink of the excavation. In the bottom of the deep pit, sprawled across pipes and jagged fragments of rock, lay the body of the blind man, and the Seeing-Eye dog, moaning despairingly, crouched at his side.

One of the onlookers, a blond young army sergeant, was trying to lower himself into the pit, but each time he tried the dog leaped upward, snarling with bared fangs.

Trant called: "I'll go down, Sergeant."

The sergeant jostled toward him, his open overcoat revealing an Eisenhower jacket impressively hung with foreign and domestic decorations. "Are you a policeman? Listen, I saw it all. I was coming up the path. This guy was sitting on that seat." He pointed to the bench Minnie had inspected earlier. "The dog was off having its run. The guy got up to call his dog. I saw him headed for the pit. I yelled and ran toward him but he didn't hear and went over the edge. The dog rushed up, snarled at me, and jumped down."

"Get a cop," put in Trant.

As the sergeant hurried off, Trant squatted at the edge of the pit with Minnie in his arms. It was improbable that the German Shepherd would co-operate with Minnie but the improbable happened. Lowering demure lashes, she gazed down at the police dog and yelped coyly. The police dog cocked its head attentively. Trant called to it and it did not growl. With Minnie under one arm, he swung recklessly down into the pit. The police dog did growl then, but Minnie pranced toward it with great coquetry. While she charmed it, Trant examined the blind man. He was dead. The skull was crushed and a jagged lump of rock nearby was thickly spattered with blood.

Feeling a kind of cosmic sadness, Trant slipped the wallet from the dead man's pocket and examined its contents—twelve dollars in cash, two ticket stubs for the Center Theater, an identification card giving the name of Andrew Stiles, and a battered photo. Trant peered at the photo. It showed Stiles in sergeant's uniform with the same pretty girl whom Trant had noticed in the park. They were standing in front of an ancient broken bridge, with a little chapel at its center.

Suddenly, as Trant fingered these objects, he experienced a thrill of astonished excitement. The idea was fantastic and proof was at the moment practically nonexistent, but instinct screamed that he was right. If he could bluff it out . . .

Above, two policemen and the blond sergeant were standing at the pit's edge, lowering ropes. Trant supervised the lifting of the corpse. He coaxed the police dog into letting itself be pulled up, too. Finally, with a smug Minnie under one arm and the blood-stained rock under the other, he was hauled up himself. A policeman, recognizing Trant, hovered respectfully. "Okay, Lieutenant, we take over now. Guess there's nothing special you want us to do?"

"I'm afraid there is." Trant turned to the army sergeant, intimidated by his own daring. "Arrest this man for murder."

The sergeant's jaw sagged.

"Murder!" gasped a policeman. "But he saw the blind guy fall . . ."

"He didn't." Inexorably committing himself, Trant held up the rock and indicated the evergreen bushes behind the bench. "He was hiding behind those bushes. He waited until the dog was off on its run, sprang out, hit Andrew Stiles on the head with this rock, and dumped the body and the rock into the excavation."

The sergeant's face was grayish green. "Lieutenant, you're crazy."

"That's what all murderers tell me. But we'll dig up your motive." He pointed to one of the sergeant's decorations. That's the *Croix de Guerre*, isn't it? So you fought in France. Stiles did too."

In spite of the cold, beads of sweat were forming on the sergeant's forehead. Trant produced the photograph from the dead man's wallet. "Look at this snapshot. There's only one broken bridge like that with a chapel in the middle. That's at Avignon. The Pont d'Avignon. And the girl—she's a cute little mademoiselle, isn't she? I've seen her right here in the park with Stiles. He stole her from you, didn't he? The two of you never got on overseas. Then, on top of it all, he snitched your girl and married her. Was that the way it happened?

The sergeant stood as though stunned. Then, with a look of sheer panic, he spun around and started to run like a madman. As the policemen dashed after him, Trant's exultation welled up. *He's cracked*, he thought. *I've done it.*

In a few moments the policemen had dragged the sergeant back. Trant surveyed the young man's guilt-scared face. "Yes, I can see the whole picture. One of these mornings here in the park, quite by chance, you ran into Stiles and his wife and the Seeing-Eye dog. Suddenly, there he was—the guy you'd sworn to get, the guy who'd stolen your girl. And he was blind. What a temptation! All you had to do was to wait in ambush some morning when he came alone with the dog. With the excavation hole, it was a cinch. Blind man, left a few minutes without Seeing-Eye dog, stumbles into pit. A cut-and-dried accident case. And, in due course, what was to stop you showing up out of the blue and courting his widow?"

He shook his head. "Fine, but you shouldn't have stuck around. I see the advantage, of course. With you as a phony eyewitness, there'd be no embarrassing investigations. But, unfortunately, you overlooked one rather important point. Blind men trip and fall into excavations in broad daylight—yes. But *only* blind men. Not men who can see." He paused. "And Andrew Stiles could see. Oh, he'd been blind. Probably one of those shock blindnesses. But he'd regained his sight. We can easily check with his doctors and his wife. But there's no real need. We've got proof enough."

From the wallet Trant produced the theater stubs. "Two tickets to the Center Theater, Radio City. Thanks to my dog's interest in reading the newspapers, I happen to know that the Center's current show is an Ice Follies. A man who can't see might go to the movies, to a concert, to a theater. But never in a million years would a blind man, however much he loved his wife, take her to the Ice Follies. It isn't worth anything to someone who can't *see* it."

The sergeant, completely broken, gasped: "But the dog . . . !"

"Oh, the dog." Trant shrugged. "Stiles undoubtedly thought that Seeing-Eye dogs pine away when they feel they're no longer useful to their masters. Stiles loved his dog. For the dog's sake, it wasn't much of a hardship, when he took it walking, to pretend for a while at least that he was still blind."

Minnie was gazing at the Seeing-Eye dog now with entranced adoration.

Her tail was thumping while she squeaked her delight. Slowly the German Shepherd lowered its head and made a dab at her nose with its tongue.

Trant patted his head. "Okay, boy," he said resignedly, "if Mrs. Stiles doesn't want you now, I guess Minnie and I have house room for another boarder."

The late Craig Rice was a woman of infinite variety. No mystery writer has ever been so consistently funny as she was when she wished to be; very few have ever equalled her in suspense; and as for simple, sensitive, sympathetic delineation of character, how many crime stories approach "A Quiet Day in the County Jail"? When Craig Rice died, not only mystery writing but all literature suffered an irreparable loss.

6

A Quiet Day
in the County Jail

By Craig Rice

"She was so beautiful and pale,
    She seemed so young, too fair to die
    As she sat on her cot in the jail
    With a tear in her lovely eye—"

"Cut that singing out, Artie," the girl's voice called.

Artie, the head trusty, put down his guitar and walked into the cell that was half of what had been named the Presidential Suite. It was unlocked, because its tenant was only being held in protective custody as a material witness.

"What's the matter, Red?" he asked gently. "You nervous?"

She was beautiful, and she was pale, and she did seem too young and too fair to die. She was sitting on the edge of her bunk, wrapped in a green chenille bathrobe. The hair that had given her her nickname was loosed over her shoulders. A cigarette blazed between her trembling fingers.

"Shadow fell over my tombstone, I guess," she said. "Forget it."

He patted her awkwardly on the shoulder and said, "You'd better get some sleep while you can." Right away he knew that had been the wrong thing to say, but it was too late to do anything about it now.

She looked at him with eyes that, for a moment, were bright with fear. "You don't need to remind me. They can't let me get back to Detroit alive."

"Shut up, Red," he said, even more gently. "That isn't what I meant." His voice managed to get back to normal. "I mean they're bringing in Aggie."

"Hot damn!" A smile and a little color came back to her face. "Well," she said thoughtfully, "the jail does need a good cleaning." She crushed out her cigarette in the fruit jar top that served as an ash-tray. "Artie, is there a drink anywhere in the house?"

"Need one?" He looked at her, a mixture of admiration, brotherly affection, sympathy, and a touch of fear. "We confiscated a pint of gin off a guy. Most of it's left. I'll get it."

Her lower lip was trembling almost as much as her pale fingers.

"Red, kid," he said softly, "you're in the safest place in the world. Jail, that is. Everything is going to be all right."

He grinned at her reassuringly, paused at the door, and burst into song again.

> "The sheriff spoke in a quiet tone,
> She seemed so beautiful and so young,
> As he said, 'tonight you're all alone,
> And tomorrow you must be hung—' "

He dodged the folded magazine she threw at him and said, "Take it easy, Red. Even the President doesn't have a better bodyguard. I'll be right back."

The Santa Maria County Jail was as informal as a Sunday School picnic, and on weekends and holidays, twice as noisy. Small, and fitted only with the essentials, it filled the second floor of the police station. The Presidential Suite consisted of two cells in a far corner, reserved for women, juveniles, and special prisoners.

Right now, Red had it to herself.

Because she wasn't strictly speaking, a prisoner, and because she had her bankroll with her, the cell had sheets, a pillow and pillow case. Her expensive clothes were carefully placed on hangers. And because Red was a friendly person, a bunch of blue flowers smiled from a jelly glass on the improvised table that had been made of two suitcases and a length of board.

Artie came back, his hand under his tan jacket. The cell was in semi-darkness, Red was still sitting on the edge of the bunk. He picked up the white enameled cup from the washstand, poured in a generous drink, added a little water, and handed it to her.

"Dirty trick," Red said. "Toss a guy in the can and then take all his gin away."

"He won't miss it," Artie assured her. "He's the Mayor's second cousin, and he's got eighteen dollars on deposit downstairs." He added. "You'd better keep the bottle."

"I may need it," she said. She looked up at him, six foot if he was an inch, crew cut blond hair, a deeply lined face. She slid the bottle between the mattresses of the bunk across from her, downed the contents of the cup fast, choked, and gasped, "*Water!*"

Artie rushed it to her. "Next time, hold your breath." He paused. "Red, you aren't really scared, are you?"

"Who, me?" she said, turning her eyes away. Her hands shook as she gulped the water, and half of it spilled on the floor.

"Red, kid," he said, taking the cup from her hands. "All you got to do is wait till they take you back to Detroit, just for you to testify. Then you're in the clear."

"They'll never let me get to that courtroom," she said, very quietly.

"Don't talk silly," Artie said. "You'll be protected. You'll be safe."

Their eyes met. They were both lying, and they both knew it.

She turned away first, punched up her pillow, lit a cigarette and said, "Let's talk about you. What happens? I saw your lawyer come up here yesterday."

"The case comes up week after next," Artie said. "If the judge gets well, that is. The county's only got two judges, and one of 'em's sick. Two thousand cases were ahead of me, but they got it down to one thousand nine hundred and forty-four. When this other judge gets over his tonsillitis, or ulcers, or beri-beri, or whatever it is, I'm first on the calendar. It'll be a short trial. They reduced the charge to manslaughter, and my lawyer's charging self-defense."

He blew his nose, lit a cigarette. "Red," he said, "I love my wife. She wrote me every day I was in the South Pacific. I love my kids. She brings them to see me every Sunday. I have a nice little ranch, I'm building up a trucking business. I met this guy, he came over to my house, the wife and kids were up visiting her mother, we had a few beers. He went wild and pulled a gun on me. I tried to take it away from him and it went off."

Red reached between the mattresses for the bottle, poured a generous two inches into the cup and handed it to Artie. She had a hunch it was he who needed moral support now.

"You'll get off," she told him. "They may even give you a bounty."

That got a laugh out of him, which was what she wanted. He flicked the ash from his cigarette and said, "Hell, it hasn't been too bad here, these eleven months. Since I been a trusty, I got the run of the place. I go out and do marketing, run errands, eat good and sleep good. Could be worse."

She said with a tired quietness, "I'd rather be here than dead in the streets."

"Red, you quit that kind of talk."

"They got to get me before I can testify," she said.

"I told you before, you're in the safest place in the world."

Suddenly the jail seemed to shake. There were sounds from downstairs, just a little louder than the Bronx Zoo at feeding time, and at about the same pitch.

"That would be Aggie," Red said.

"Couldn't be anyone else," Artie grinned. He rose, locked her cell door and said, "Sorry I have to do this, but it's only for a few minutes." He called, "Hey, Pablo!"

Red settled down on her bunk and listened to the rumpus. Aggie was resisting arrest in two languages, and from the sounds, it was taking both trusties and Fred, the night jailer, to hold her.

Aggie was probably the best cleaning woman in Santa Maria. She was also probably the loudest drunk. She was happy with a bottle, she was just as happy with a pail of soap and water and a mop. Periodically when the jail needed a thorough scrubbing, the word went down the line: "Tour the bars and pick up Aggie."

Aggie always was brought into the jail sounding like a combination of a major riot and a bomb landing in the next block. Next morning the judge invariably sentenced her to six days, which could be worked out in three, and Aggie, cheerful if slightly hung over, filled a pail with soap and hot water and reached for the nearest mop.

Red put her fingers in her ears as Aggie was shoved into the next door cell and locked in. Aggie went right on shouting.

Artie unlocked the metal grill door to Red's room and said, "You asleep?"

"Slept right through it," Red said cheerfully.

The other trusty, the small, sad-eyed Pablo, came in with Artie. "This we take from Aggie," he said gravely.

The bottle was passed around solemnly. Red shuddered. "Can't these cops ever arrest anybody with champagne?"

"Me, I like scotch," Artie said.

She passed the bottle to him. "Shut your eyes and pretend that it's scotch."

There was more noise from the cell next door.

"That Aggie, she makes with the yell," Pablo said.

"I make with the yell myself," Red said grimly. She raised her voice. "Shut up!"

There was a moment's silence, and then an answering yell. "You're who, and what'cha here for?"

"I'm the axe killer you been reading about in the papers," Red called. "And I've got the axe right here, the one I chopped up seven people with. The police let me keep it because I know the Mayor. And my cell door is unlocked, and I've got a key to yours, and I like it quiet when I sleep."

This was at four A.M.

By eight o'clock in the morning, the sun had been turning the heat on for an hour and a half. Red stirred restlessly, felt a hand pat her shoulder gently, turned over and opened her eyes.

It was Fred, the night jailer. "Going off duty now, Red. Just came by to say good-bye and wish you luck."

Suddenly wide awake, she sat up, pulling the blankets around her shoulders. "What do you mean, good-bye?"

Fred looked embarrassed. "I thought they were moving you out today."

"Nobody's told me yet," she said. She didn't need to look in a mirror, she could feel her face turning pale.

"Well," he said, "well, in case they do. Good luck. Don't worry, Red. Come back and visit us when it's all over."

"Sure will," she said heartily. "I'll do just that little thing."

He knew she'd never be back in Santa Maria, and so did she.

They shook hands. She said, "Fred, please thank your wife for sending me the flowers." Flowers for a corpse that was still walking around and talking. "Wait a minute, will you."

She reached for her robe, wrapped it around her, slid off the bunk and rummaged through the suitcase that was under the bed, until she pulled out what looked like a handful of tissue paper. She sat on the edge of the bunk, untangled the tissue paper, and pulled out a brooch. It blazed green, yellow and white fire in the early morning sunlight.

"Please give this to her. It's a phony, just a hunk of costume jewelry, but I think it's pretty. The one thing that isn't phony is the thanks to her that go with it."

"Gosh, Red," Fred said. He choked for a minute, rewrapped the brooch in the tissue paper, and stuck it in his pocket. "Gosh." He paused again. "She wanted to send you some more flowers."

"Tell her to save them for my wake," Red said, managing to keep her voice light. She walked over to the window and stood looking out.

Fred stood for a moment, uncertainty drawn on his broad red face. Finally he walked over and put a hand on her arm. "Red," he said, feeling for words, "if—I mean, if something happens to you—I mean, well, I got friends, we'll find out who did it—"

She turned around, smiling. "Thanks. Now beat it, bum. I've got to get some sleep."

There was something she vaguely remembered from High School. She fished for it in her mind, and all that came to her was "There is a time to sleep, and a time to stay awake." She knew that wasn't right, but it didn't matter now.

She paced up and down the cell. She scrubbed her face and put on fresh make-up. She combed her lovely red hair until it was smooth and shining. She brushed on lipstick and tended to her eyebrows. She put on a pair of dove-gray slacks, a pale green sweater, and darker green sandals.

Eight-thirty. She remembered Aggie with a sudden sense of guilt. She raced for the main room and yelled for Artie.

"Honey, open up Aggie's door. She's got to be in court by nine, and I've got to wash her face."

"Will do," he said, reaching for the keys. He looked at her appreciatively. "You're going to be missed, Red."

Again she could feel the color drain out of her face. "Who says?"

Artie avoided her eyes as he unlocked the door to Aggie's cell. After a moment of inspection and thought, Red went next door and collected a comb, make-up, powder, a lipstick, a big fluffy towel, mouthwash and the remains of the gin. Five vigorous shakes woke Aggie.

"Come on, kid," Red said. "You've got to be in court in half an hour."

Aggie began moaning. An inch of gin in the enameled cup took care of that. She got her eyes open enough to stay that way on the fourth blink, and said, "Red! You still here?"

"Haven't thrown me out yet," Red said, with false cheerfulness. "Babe, do yourself proud in court. Wash your face, and I'll put your make-up on for you and fix your hair." She looked at Aggie's dress and shook her head sadly.

Well, there was one of her own that just might fit. She was as tall as Aggie, and the dress would stretch sideways.

At two minutes to nine, Aggie was on her way downstairs, hair combed, face made up, smelling slightly of mouthwash and Daphne Cologne, and wearing a blue jersey dress that would never shrink back into shape again.

At ten minutes after nine, Aggie came back up the stairs, beaming. "Six to three," she shouted. "Artie, where's the mop?"

Red called from her cell. "Artie! Pablo! Somebody!"

It was Artie who came to the door. "A mouse?" he asked.

"I want breakfast," Red said.

"Breakfast is served in this jail at six-thirty," Artie said. "But since you slipped Frank a buck yesterday to buy eggs, I think we can oblige you." He winked at her. "He's got a dozen eggs stashed away in the refrigerator. And the coffee's good this morning."

It was Pablo who brought in the tin tray. The eggs were cooked just right, the toast was the right color of tan, and the coffee was as good as advertised.

She smiled at Pablo. She always smiled at Pablo. Today she had an extra one.

Pablo was short and slender and black-haired, and he was almost a permanent prisoner. Frank, the day jailer, had confided in Red that Pablo had been serving a thirty-day drunk charge for almost two years. It had become almost a regular routine. Sentenced to thirty days. Made a trusty the next day. Released. Arrested the next day, or even sooner.

Artie swore, and Red believed him, that Pablo had once made the round trip from the jail and back in exactly three hours.

It was Artie who'd told her how Pablo's wife had run away with another man, how he'd lost his job, and seen the bank take away his home, all in one month.

"Señorita Red," Pablo said, "would you like I should go and buy you cigarettes?"

She looked at him with pretended sternness. "The last time I gave you a quarter to buy me cigarettes you were gone for two days, and the judge tacked on an extra thirty days on you when they did find you."

"It was a mistake," Pablo said with great dignity. "Perhaps you could lend me twenty-five cents. Believe me, it is for a good purpose."

She looked at him and her eyes softened. After all, Pablo had only two homes. The jail, and the Frisco Bar and Grill. She pulled her change purse from under her pillow, took out a fifty cent piece, and said, "I hope you have a lot of fun with the good purpose."

That was at ten o'clock in the morning.

The routine daily cleaning was going on, plus Aggie throwing a mop around the kitchen. Red stood looking out the window at the roof of the bowling alley next door. She lifted her eyes to the mountains that ringed the little city and saw a tiny speck of silver racing across the blue. Would they take her out by plane, or train, she wondered.

She could hear Artie going through the big cabinet in the main room, sorting out files. She could hear a prisoner rattling tin trays in the kitchen sink. This will be going on long after I'm gone, she thought. Artie will go on sorting files, then his case will come up in court and chances are he'll be freed; the guy in the kitchen will go on washing dishes and serve his sentence and be on his way. But she would be gone before that, far away from here.

A voice said, "Hey, Red."

She turned. It was Frank, the day jailer. He was a deceptively gentle-looking man with a friendly face, white hair, and a deadly right when he had to use it. He was one more person in the world she would have trusted with her life.

"Chief's on his way up to see you. Thought I'd tell you, case you wanted to powder your face."

"Bless you, Frank." At that moment she heard the buzzer that announced someone was coming up the stairs.

She was sitting on the edge of her bunk, face powdered, when Chief of Police Sankey came in, Frank close behind him.

"Red," he said. "I mean, Miss—"

"That's all right," she said.

He sat down on the bunk across from her, a worried, fretful little man with reddish hair and rimless glasses.

"Well," he said, "we finally got the word. They're taking you on a plane this afternoon. Papers all signed, everything set."

She opened her mouth to speak, shut it again, and finally managed to say, "I'll be ready."

He looked embarrassed. He said, "You'll be well protected, naturally. So there's nothing for you to worry about." He paused and added, "Well, good luck."

After he'd gone, Frank patted her shoulder and said, "Everything's going to be all right, Red."

"Oh, sure." She forced a smile to her face. "It's just that I like your jail so well I hate to leave it. Besides, I feel safe here."

He cleared his throat, started to speak and changed his mind. He patted her shoulder a second time.

"Frank, I saw the whole thing. I was standing right in the doorway of the Blue Casino. Louie did the job himself, and I was right there. All I could think of was to beat it, fast. Threw some stuff in a couple of suitcases, got the first plane to Kansas City. That's where I bought the car and headed south. I could have made it across the border into Mexico easy, but you guys picked me up."

"Maybe it's just as well," Frank told her reassuringly. "This guy would have had you followed. This way he'll get convicted and then you won't have a thing to worry about."

"Oh, sure," she said again. She sighed. "It's just luck that some goon was coming down the sidewalk and saw what was going on. He didn't get close enough to recognize Louie, but I was standing there with the light smack on my face, and he spotted me. The Detroit cops picked up Louie on general principles and started looking for me."

She ran a hand through her shining red hair. "I'm their only witness. 'Course I could get on the stand and swear I didn't see a thing, or I could swear it wasn't Louie."

"You could," Frank said. "But—"

"But I wouldn't," she finished for him. "That is, assuming I ever get to the witness stand."

Artie came in, lit a cigarette, and lounged against the wall.

"This Louie," Frank asked, "was he your boy friend?"

That brought a laugh from her, the first one that day. "I didn't have a boy friend. I ran the Blue Casino. A gambling joint. I ran that end of it, and my partner ran the night club end." She grinned at them. "I came by these diamonds honestly, pals."

"So that's why you've been able to take us at blackjack," Artie said lazily.

"Well," Frank said, getting up, "you'll be protected on the way to the plane, and you'll be protected on the plane, and you'll probably be taken off it in an armored car."

Artie pinched out his cigarette, dropped it on the floor. "Pablo'll clean up in here when he gets back. He's got the car out now, getting potatoes."

At that moment, all hell broke loose in the yard outside. Red and Artie were tied getting to the window. Artie gave a loud whoop and raced for the stairs, yelling for Frank to work the buzzer.

Outside, Pablo was having troubles. The car used by the jail for general errands was parked directly under Red's window, and the trunk compartment was open. What appeared to be about a hundred white chickens, but were actually only six, were creating the disturbance. Pablo was trying to move them from the trunk compartment to a burlap bag, and the chickens were resisting arrest. The scene was beginning to draw a fair-sized audience when reinforcements, in the person of Artie, arrived.

Between them, the chickens were shoved unceremoniously into the bag and tossed, still protesting loudly, in the car. Artie and Pablo got in and drove off.

Frank, who had watched the last act from Red's window, sighed deeply and said, "Sometimes I think they give these trusties too many liberties."

"None of them give you any trouble, though," Red reminded him.

"That's right," he said, "except sometimes Pablo." He looked at her searchingly. "Did you give him any money?"

"I gave him fifty cents," Red confessed. She added, as though in defense, "After all, Frank, it's my last day here."

Frank shook his head sadly. "Another thirty days. Well, he's got to sleep somewhere."

That was at eleven o'clock.

It was sometime later when Artie and Pablo came in triumphantly, Pablo carrying a large paper-wrapped bundle. The chickens were not only silent now, but in addition to losing their voices, they had lost their feathers and a few other odds and ends, and were candidates for the frying pan.

"Farewell party!" Artie called happily, heading for the kitchen.

Red looked at her suitcases, at the clothes hanging against the walls, at the make-up carefully arranged on the improvised table, and started a half-hearted effort toward packing. But there was plenty of time for that later. She flopped down on the bunk, picked up a magazine and tried to read. The words seemed to run together and made no sense at all.

Pablo came in the door. He was completely sober, and walking with great dignity. He carried a package which he presented to Red with even greater dignity.

"For you," he said. "For a going-far-away present."

She unwrapped it. It was a bottle of what was probably the worst wine in the world. This was the important purpose for which Pablo had needed money. She felt tears hot in her eyes.

"Pablo, I thank you," she said with dignity that matched his. She put the package under the bunk, reached between the mattresses for the last of the gin. "For farewell, will you have a drink with me?"

Pablo's dark eyes brightened. "Since you insist upon it."

She rinsed out the enameled cups and divided the gin equally into them. They saluted each other solemnly and silently.

"We will miss you," Pablo said simply.

That was at twelve o'clock.

It was Artie who brought in her lunch, sometime later.

"No stew?" she said, looking up and sniffing. "No pinto beans?"

Artie grinned at her as he set the tray down. "Fried chicken." He shook his head thoughtfully. "That Pablo. It isn't enough that he goes out and steals chickens. But he has to steal the chickens from the Chief of Police."

He went on. "He was going to bring them here and clean them, but I had an idea. We took them to a restaurant where I know the kitchen help. Result, no evidence."

It was one o'clock when he came to take the tray away, and lock Aggie's door. She was, after all, a prisoner, and even in the Santa Maria County Jail, rules were rules. He paused in Red's cell.

"I'll help you pack, after siesta."

She turned her face away. "I can manage, thanks, Artie."

He sat down on the other bunk. "Red, listen. You'll be protected. There's nothing to it. When you get to Detroit, they'll put you up in some expensive hotel, with a bodyguard. You'll testify, and it's all over. There's nothing for you to be scared."

"Who's scared?" she scoffed, managing to keep her voice steady.

"Red," he said slowly, "Red. Will you let me kiss you, once?"

She stared at him.

"I been here eleven months, Red. I'd just like to kiss a girl again."

She smiled and lifted her face to him. He kissed her very gently, almost a little boy kiss.

"It won't seem like the same place without you, Red."

The county jail became silent. Frank had gone out to lunch and everyone else was asleep. Everybody except Red. She lay on her bunk, her eyes closed, wondering if she would ever sleep again. Finally, she gave up. Might as well pack and get it over with.

Mid-afternoon sunlight was streaming in the windows of the trusties' room when the sound of the big door clanging shut and footsteps on the stairs woke Artie. He swung his long legs off the bed and walked into the main room.

That was at three o'clock.

Frank and a stranger had just reached the top of the stairs.

"Detective Connelly, Detroit police," Frank said, puffing, and nodding toward the stranger. "Red all packed and set to leave?"

"I'll see," Artie said.

Red was sitting on the bunk, her suitcase beside her. She had on a light beige suit and a small green hat. Her face was very pale. Artie picked up the suitcase. She rose and followed him into the main room.

Pablo had come out of the trusties' room. Aggie, mop in hand, was watching. Everyone was silent.

Red managed a wan smile at the Detroit detective.

"All set?" He tried to smile but didn't look as though he relished this job. She nodded.

Frank said heartily, "Now remember, Red, don't you worry about a thing. He'll take you back, you testify, this Louie will go to jail or the chair, and that's that."

"Sure," Connelly said, with false confidence. "That's the way."

"And you will come back to visit us," Pablo said. "I will still be here."

That eased the tension a little.

There was nothing left to say but good-bye. Then Red went down the stairs without looking back, Connelly and Frank on either side. The two trusties stood looking after her.

At last they walked to her cell and looked in. There was a faint odor of cigarette smoke, gin, and expensive perfume. Artie straightened a wrinkle in the blankets.

"It seems so quiet," he said.

Pablo looked under the bed, pulled out the package. "She forgets and leaves it behind," he said sadly, unwrapping it. "I buy it for her, a going away present." There were tears in his eyes.

"You're a bad boy, Pablo," Aggie said from the doorway.

Pablo looked wistfully.

"I think she wanted you to open it," Artie said, very gently.

Pablo ripped off the cap. The bottle of the worst wine in the world was passed around in silence.

7

Proof of the Pudding

By Lawrence Treat

Peppery little Flannagan looked like a cross between a cherub and
a featherweight champ, but he felt like a man trying to chop down
a tree with a penknife. The case was two days old and stale, washed
out.

He had come up to the north-woods village of Smyrna because
Barton Seely had sent for him. Seely, broad-shouldered, with round
handsome features under his dark hair, looked out of place in the
tiny cell behind the sheriff's office. Too big for it. Too prosperous,
too well-fed, too healthy despite the worry in his deep brown eyes.

But he was dangerously close to hysteria as he shouted through
the rusty bars of the jail. "You got a wire from me? Then you're
Flannagan. Listen—you know why they have me here—assault
with intent to kill. They can give me ten years for it. Realize what
that is? Know what it means to a man like me? Ten years. It's
crazy. But even Tannick—he's my lawyer, came all the way up

from New York—even Tannick says they can get away with it if I don't run."

Flannagan screwed up his sharp squirrel of a face. "You're going off the deep end, Seely. I never saw you before in my life. You send for a first-class investigator and when I get here you put on a scene like a chorus girl in a jam. Want me to sit down and have a good cry with you or what?"

Seely shook his head. "I'm all up in the air—anybody would be. But you're right, I guess. I'm acting like—like a—"

"Like an idiot," supplied Flannagan pleasantly. "And that's charitable. Suppose you tell me what happened. You and Warren Lamport were on a hunting trip. Who's Lamport?"

"Manages some of my properties, but promotion of high-class real-estate developments is his specialty. Best man at it in the country."

Seely's jaw snapped with the first decisive words he'd pronounced since he was jailed. Flannagan drawled, "So?" in a soothing tone.

"So we came up here. Just the pair of us and my man Glidden. I have a hunting shack that I use every year or two. I shouldn't have taken Warren. We'd been disagreeing about things. It's no secret, Flannagan, so I may as well tell you. He's got a sharp temper in him and I guess I have too. We scrapped on the way up, scrapped in the woods, and scrapped when we got back for the night. We even scrapped over the pudding."

"This a nursery tale?"

"The pudding," went on Seely, as if he hadn't heard. "There's no stove in the shack and Glidden did the cooking over an open fireplace. Makes it more like a camp. Glidden claimed you couldn't cook desserts on it, and Lamport said he was an ass and he'd show him. So Lamport mixed stuff in a bowl and called it a pudding. I was cleaning my gun. I got sarcastic and we had unpleasant words. Glidden went to chop wood and I went outside to cool off. Lamport put his pudding on to cook and— What's the use, anyhow?"

Little Flannagan snapped like a dog herding a steer into the corral. "I come six hundred miles and now you're scared I'll get the goods on you instead of fixing up a phony case. Listen, Seely —you know who I am or you wouldn't have sent for me. I go after the facts, and if you're clean on this I'll get you free. But so help me, if you shot Lamport I'll nail it on you so tight you can't squirm out with a crowbar. Or with a million dollars. Want to tell me what happened or want me to take the next train back?"

Seely shrugged wearily. "You may be able to help—you're the only hope I have left—but my story's so feeble I'd be better off if I shut up. But here it is anyhow. I was standing outside and I'll swear nobody could have gone in or out without my seeing or hearing him. I heard the shot inside. Not loud, not as loud as it should have been, but I knew what it was. So I came in on the run, and there was Warren lying on the floor. No gun in sight, none we could ever find. Mine was in my pocket. No reason to shoot himself. The bullet glanced off his forearm and went into his side. You are not likely to shoot yourself in your own forearm, and you certainly can't do it without a gun. But there he was anyhow, lying on the floor, and as soon as he came to he started groaning about my not meaning it. He really believes I shot him."

"Right forearm? Maybe he was left-handed. You can hide guns."

"He wasn't left-handed and he wasn't ambidextrous either. There was no gun and he's not the suicide type, Flannagan. You'll see for yourself."

Flannagan saw. A tall sinewy man lying on a hospital bed, telling feebly how his best friend had tried to kill him. Deliberately. Then Flannagan had to go out. Lamport was weak and wouldn't talk much. Doctor's orders.

As for the man Glidden, all he could do was shake his head and say nothing with a butler's accent. He'd been chopping wood. He hadn't heard anything. When he came back, Lamport was lying there and telling Seely he shouldn't have done it.

The gun? None except the one in Seely's pocket. Seely had cleaned it, oiled it, and loaded it, standing next to Lamport, who was measuring his ingredients for the pudding.

Pudding again. Little Flannagan let loose a few pounds of steam and marched out to the shack. Seely had called it a shack, anyhow. It had all the modern conveniences except a stove. Seely had funny ideas about roughing it.

Sightseers had messed up most of the evidence, if there'd been much in the first place. Flannagan found merely a couple of dried bloodstains and then the ashes in the fire. He shoveled the ashes into a paper bag and took them back to the sheriff's office to study under a portable microscope. Ashes and the bullet that Sheriff Reveneau had locked in his safe in a carefully labeled envelope.

Reveneau, big and grizzled and matter-of-fact, sat on the edge of the desk and nursed his bewilderment. Flannagan stared at the bullet for a long, long time. He had to believe it, and at the same time it was almost impossible. A smooth-bore pistol. A modern bullet without rifling marks.

After a while Reveneau couldn't keep it to himself any more. "Of all the gosh-darned foolishment," he growled. "They all of 'em admit there wasn't nobody else around, so Seely must have done it. And one bullet missing from his gun. You can't worm out of it, fella, no matter how much money ye git."

Flannagan held the little lead pellet in his hand, flipped it thoughtfully, and caught it. Reveneau was six inches higher and five inches wider, but a man is as big as the inside of his head.

Flannagan said, "Let's iron this out. Who do you think I am, anyhow?"

"Reckon you're asking for it. Seely, he's got more money than'd fill this here room, so he hired you to twist things round his way. Trouble is, you can't twist. This shooting happened in my jurisdiction and you can't buy me neither. Seely goes up for it next court. Gimme back that bullet. Doc Jervis dug it out'n Lamport's side and I don't feel right 'bout lettin' you nor anybody else handle it."

Flannagan dropped it on the desk. "You have me wrong, Sheriff. Neither Seely nor anybody else hired me."

"Come up for the fun of it, hey?"

Flannagan beamed amiably and looked like the bright boy of the class. He had his favorite cue. "In a way, yes. The university has a police school—the Academy of Police Science, it's called—and my job is to tackle the tough ones and show that the scientific methods get results where the old ones don't. Then I send a line in to the papers to the effect that the Academy cracked another one. I'm paid for getting publicity, but my job is to find the truth regardless."

"Science," muttered Sheriff Reveneau slowly. "Ain't nothin' wrong with it if you use your plain common sense. Only when you use your common sense, ain't no need for science."

"I'll make a bet with you, Sheriff. I'll bet Seely didn't shoot Lamport and that Lamport didn't do it himself either, and I'll prove it with this sort of thing." He tapped the microscope. "If I'm wrong, I'll come up here and work under you for three months. But if I'm right, you come down to the Academy and take a three months' course in police work. Is it a bet?"

Reveneau scratched his head thoughtfully, then extended a great bearlike paw. "My hand on it," he said. "But I'll tell you one thing. Even if you proved somethin' with this scientific stuff o' yourn, they wouldn't believe it up here. You got to show a jury what a man instead of a microscope tells."

Paul Flannagan gripped the hand and hardly listened. He was already building up the publicity in his head. "County Sheriff Comes Out for Science." The papers would eat it up.

Arthur Tannick went down on the train with Flannagan. Tannick took care of the legal end of the Seely interests and made enough out of it to have to juggle his own income tax. He was tall, smooth, with a nose that looked as if it were made for his pince-nez glasses rather than the glasses for it.

Tannick lit a cigar that smelled of tobacco and perfume. "I told Seely as soon as he got out on bail to hop the jurisdiction. There's no case unless Lamport takes the stand, and I can persuade him not to."

"I told Seely if he jumped bail he'd practically admit he was guilty."

"Well, isn't he?"

"How do I know? About this Lamport—he's a lawyer?"

Tannick nodded. "Doesn't practice, though. More of a promoter than a lawyer."

Flannagan said, "Seely and Lamport came up for some shooting, and now they got a shooting and they don't like it. I could feel sorry for that pair. All alone in the woods with nothing between them and the cold except a five-thousand-dollar shack, and nothing between them and starvation except Seely's valet. Think of it, Tannick—two men and only one valet. The way I look at it, they should have brought along the chef from the Waldorf and then there wouldn't have been any trouble."

"No need of being facetious. They had angry words over a pudding, and though the statement sounds ludicrous, it was merely the excuse, the *casus belli*. If Lamport goes on the stand they're bound to bring in a verdict of guilty. Even Lamport couldn't explain how he shot himself and then disposed of the gun. Seems to me that's the strongest point against Seely."

Flannagan shrugged. "One point in Seely's favor balances everything else you can possibly say."

"What's that?"

"Why in hell would he call *me* in if he were guilty? He knows I'll get the truth, no matter what it is."

"Maybe you overrate yourself, Flannagan."

And little Flannagan snapped back, "Impossible!" and looked vastly pleased with himself.

But it was sheer bravado. The same bravado with which he'd talked himself into his job three months ago. The university had had a million dollars' worth of police school and laboratory equipment but no pupils and no prestige. Flannagan had erupted with the idea that practical work, practical success was the answer. Solve a few murders, make the world know the Academy was cracking cases, and the Academy was made. He'd wrangled a trial for his scheme, with himself as publicity director.

Maybe it was luck, maybe it was little Flannagan's liberal sprinkling of Academy funds, but the next important murder case was an Academy triumph. The papers stated that the police had arrested the murderer "in cooperation with the Scientific Academy of the University" and the police commissioner admitted he had had "invaluable help." Thereafter Flannagan was made.

But it was a precarious making. One boner and the opposition would be on his neck. The jealous police officials who didn't like to divide credit; the reactionaries who believed in the old-fashioned methods; the crooked politicians who were secretly connected with crime.

As soon as Flannagan reached the city, he walked into the Academy laboratory and put down the bag of ashes he'd collected from the fireplace of Seely's cabin.

"Have a look at this stuff," he said, "and let me know what you find."

Stettinus, the laboratory wizard, tall, stooped, with a yellow wrinkled face and a mouth wide enough to grace a cartoon, said, "What'll I look for?"

"Anything in general, pudding in particular. Bread pudding, prune pudding. Maybe even cordite pudding. You never know these days."

Stettinus sniffed. "Cordite?" he said, and went to work.

There was no cordite, of course. Pine ash, hickory ash, paper ash. Traces of prune pudding. A twisted cartridge case, unmarked. But no cordite. Flannagan read the report and did nothing—yet.

The newspapers interviewed Lamport as soon as he came out of the hospital. He indicated that a high sense of ethics and his feeling of responsibility as a citizen would compel him to appear at the Seely trial next month. As for Seely, he got out on bail, jumped the jurisdiction and persuaded the local authorities to do nothing except hope he'd show up at the proper time. Unusual? Sure. But the answer was Tannick and unlimited money.

Flannagan waited until Lamport had recovered and was back at work. Then Flannagan made an appointment, marched into Lamport's luxurious office and said, "I want to talk to you about the Seely case."

Lamport appraised him with sharp, calculating eyes. "Nothing I know of to talk about."

"Oh, yes there is. I've uncovered an extraordinary piece of evidence, Lamport. About an automatic pistol you own." Flannagan consulted a slip of paper and read off some serial numbers. "That's yours, isn't it?"

"Yes, but I don't see what bearing—"

Flannagan interrupted. "Of course you don't. The strongest point against Seely is that his gun was the only one on the scene and that one bullet was missing. A ballistic expert could prove the bullet that wounded you didn't come from Seely's gun, but a country jury would say, 'If it didn't come from Seely's, then were the devil did it come from?' And they'd disregard the evidence."

"I'm not a ballistics expert and I saw who shot me. That should settle the matter."

"Exactly. Except that I found a cartridge shell near the fireplace and I wondered whether I couldn't hook it up to another weapon. So the other night I took the liberty of entering your apartment and borrowing your gun. I fired a few test shots and compared the ejector marks on the cartridge case with the marks on the cartridge from the fireplace."

"And they didn't match," said Lamport, leaning forward with a shrewd expression.

"And they didn't match," agreed Flannagan genially. "But that, of course, is only between the two of us."

"I don't get you."

Flannagan shrugged. "A simple matter to exchange the cartridge case from the fireplace for one of my test samples. Now, you see, they do match."

"It's a frame-up!" snapped Lamport.

"Sure it is."

Flannagan studied the effect of his words. They produced not outraged morality nor even a sense of being duped, but admiration and a cool, calculating appraisal of how best to handle the situation.

Flannagan said quietly, "I think we understand each other."

"I'll have to think it over." Lamport pressed a switch and spoke into the dictaphone connecting with the receptionist in his outer office. "Will you call Durcher? I'll be wanting him later on." Lamport left the switch connected so that the remainder of the conversation could be heard outside.

"What are you after?" demanded Lamport angrily. "Money?"

"Oh, no. Something far more elemental. Justice."

"What's that?"

"I'll try to explain, though you could best start with a dictionary. Then, if it's still beyond you, I could submit a bibliography. Some very great minds have examined the subject."

"As I understand it, Flannagan, you're deliberately framing me with false testimony. You're claiming that a gun which I left in New York was actually in Smyrna."

"Oh no. I'm claiming that your gun was in Smyrna because I can prove it."

"And just what do you want out of this?"

Flannagan did something rare with him. He repeated himself. "Justice," he said. "When I was in Smyrna, I found a case against Seely that looked practically airtight, except for one little thing. But the alternative was too fantastic, assumed too fast and facile and fertile a brain behind it, so I kept the idea to myself. When I brought my evidence to the laboratory my hunch was confirmed, with a delicate piece of scientific analysis that nobody would believe. Certainly not a Smyrna jury. I needed you to help me and you did." Flannagan heard a door slam in the outer office. The rumble of voices sounded vaguely. He stood up.

"And so," he said, "I found that the marks on the cartridge case prove the gun is yours."

"You lie!" thundered Lamport. "I never even took my gun with me."

"Difficult to prove."

Lamport cleared his throat and spoke in a loud voice. "So your proposition is that if I pay you enough you won't frame me on the

Seely case."

Flannagan, in an equally loud tone, replied, "My proposition is this: I want you to do just one thing." He moved casually toward the side door. "To go to hell!"

He yanked open the door and dived. Lamport yelled, "Get him —cover the back!"

Flannagan dashed to the left, saw a door marked, "Lewin Office Supply," and opened it. A girl was sitting in front of a typewriter. She had dark hair and brown eyes and a long, delicate face. Flannagan peeled off his coat, pulled a gun, and barked, "Don't get scared and you'll be all right. I'm in a jam—cops'll be here—take this letter down on your machine—and so help me, if you give me away—"

His mouth tightened and his eyes shot fire. Then he hopped on one corner of her desk, gun still drawn but concealed by his body so that he was half sitting on it.

Her face went chalk white and she stared with her large, appealing eyes. Flannagan smiled. "Steady," he said. "Now take this: 'According to our records the goods were delivered on the fourteenth of the month and—' "

The typewriter was clicking steadily. Flannagan jerked his head around as two cops punched open the door and strode in.

"What do you want?" demanded Flannagan.

They hesitated. One said, "A little guy, your build—seen him anywhere?"

"Not in the last fifteen minutes. I've been dictating. What happened?"

The cop glared. "How the hell do I know? Maybe nothing. But if he shows up, yell."

"Yell my head off," grinned Flannagan. "Hope you find him, officer."

The door slammed shut. Flannagan drew a deep breath. The girl said, "It was too fast for me and I didn't have time to think. I don't believe you'd shoot me. I'm going to scream."

"Of course I wouldn't shoot you, and you won't scream either. At least not until you know what it's all about. Let's go downstairs and have a soda. I'll tell you how I was framed, and if you think the cops ought to have me, then you can scream your head off. Want my gun for a guarantee of good faith?"

He held her with his eyes, with their clear steady blueness, with their frank liking for her, and with the vague, dreamy, humorous quality in them.

She said, "Yes, I'll take your gun." Flannagan held it by the barrel and waved it casually. "It's a wild, excitable, crazy kind of world, isn't it? You're a stenographer in a—what kind of an office is this?"

"Office supply. Weren't you going to give me the gun?"

"Yes. Fascinating work. Fascinating despite the drudgery, because any minute of any day somebody can walk through that door and change the entire course of your life. Two minutes ago you could have opened your mouth and ruined me. You can still do it. A half-hour ago I kept a routine appointment and a man framed me. The police wouldn't hold me a half-hour, but my name would come out and a very worthy enterprise be damaged with the laughter heaped upon it." He calmly pocketed his revolver. "I wish I could do something to thank you for using your head."

"You could tell me exactly what this is all about and see if I believe it."

He looked thoughtful as he put on his coat. "My name is Flannagan. Paul Flannagan. And yours?"

"Elizabeth Dean."

"May I use your phone, Miss Dean?"

He dialed Lamport's number. Into the mouthpiece he said, "This is Flannagan speaking. I'm in a phone booth around the corner and thought I'd tell you to call off the police hunt. A waste of time, now. I knew what you were doing as soon as you told your receptionist to call Lieutenant Durcher. An unusual name, Durcher, and I happen to know him. I doubt whether he'd have arrested me under any circumstances, but the story would have reached the papers and made me a laughingstock. My attempt to compel you to withhold testimony. My reputation's a vulnerable point, in view of my work. You tried a neat trick but it was obvious that you didn't switch off your outer-office communication. The only obvious thing you've done thus far. And thanks for an interesting afternoon. You enabled me to meet an extremely attractive young lady, and that doesn't happen every day."

He hung up. "I think I can go in safety now, Miss Dean. As for the explanation I was going to give you—suppose we postpone it till dinner this evening. Say the lobby of the Astor, about seven o'clock. Will that suit you?"

It did, but the meeting between Paul Flannagan and Elizabeth Dean is no part of this story, except that as a result she changed her job from the Lewin Office Supply to the publicity office of the Academy of Police Science.

About a week before Seely was due to stand trial in Smyrna for assault with intent to kill, Lamport came to see him by appointment. It was the first time the two men had spoken at any length since the shooting. Seely, embarrassed, older and more haggard than when Lamport had last seen him, offered cigars and a highball before he came to the point of the interview.

"I've been thinking about this, Warren. You claim I shot you. I can't find it in me to doubt your word, even though I have no recollection, no consciousness of the act. They say that men can do things automatically, without volition or realization of the nature of what they're doing. Maybe. If it's possible, maybe that's what I did. A kind of temporary insanity. That's the plea Tannick advises me to make."

"I'd like to think that was the reason, Bart. Even so, it's tough on me."

"On you? You're not threatened with jail—how is it tough on you?"

"To be the means of sending you to prison," said Lamport steadily. "If there were some way out—"

Seely stared at the ash of his cigar. "Unless you give your testimony, there's no case against me. But Tannick made you an offer and you turned him down."

Lamport leaned back in his chair and studied the ceiling. "Suppose, instead of shooting a man—shooting me, to be exact—you'd done something else. Some other crime. Were driven to it by necessity, by circumstances you couldn't control. Suppose you took money which you were handling in a capacity of trust."

Seely sat up suddenly. "The CPA's been going over my books. He hinted at a shortage which he hadn't checked yet. You mean you've been defrauding me?"

Lamport was staring at Seely now, staring with that sharp penetrating look. "I wouldn't care to admit that. But if you found you could lodge a charge against me, and if instead of doing it you made good the money and dropped the charge, then it might be worth my while to keep away from Smyrna." Lamport swallowed. "Pure coincidence that I have this means of defending myself."

Seely said, "How much?"

"Two hundred and fifty thousand. Say another two hundred and fifty to set me up."

Seely broke into a broad grin. "For half a million you'll drop the Smyrna charge? I'll have the money in three days."

"Cash," said Lamport.

"Cash," repeated Seely. "And now that we have it settled, how did the shooting really happen?"

Lamport shrugged. "If I told, my position would be considerably weakened."

The door opened and little Flannagan walked in. "Got it on the dictagraph, Seely. It worked the way I told you. Here are the warrants against Lamport for false imprisonment, malicious prosecution, and extortion."

Lamport leaped to his feet. "Say, what is this?"

"The showdown," replied Flannagan. "The evidence was nothing to get. All I wanted was your admission of Seely's innocence."

Lamport stiffened. "That's something you'll never get!"

" 'If I told' " quoted Flannagan, " 'my position would be considerably weakened.' Wouldn't convince the Smyrna woodsmen, but it'll convince a New York jury, and that's where the actions for false imprisonment and malicious prosecution will be brought. There won't be a trial in Smyrna."

Lamport shrugged. "You have some evidence? Or are these purely obstructive tactics?"

"Judge for yourself. When Seely cleaned and loaded his gun, he dropped one of the bullets without realizing. Dropped it in the prunes and left an empty chamber in his gun. The laboratory can prove it because the cartridge case, despite the heat, still had a minute coating of sugar and syrup and prune particles.

"What happened was that when you poured the prunes into your pudding, you poured the bullet too. Whether you dropped it, whether you spilled the pot or it boiled over, I don't know. But that bullet landed in the fire and the heat discharged the bullet. *No gun ever fired it!*"

"You're crazy!" thundered Lamport.

"That's what I thought at first, when I found a bullet without rifling marks and a cartridge case without any marks at all. It took too clever and quick-thinking a man to engineer. But after my interview with you the other day, I learned not only how quick-thinking you were, but also how worried. There was no reason to try to frame me on an extortion charge, but you saw a chance to force me out of the picture and you grabbed it. The gambler mind taking a long chance. Same thing as at Smyrna.

"A bullet dropped in the fire and then exploded, wounding you. You saw a chance to get something on Seely. You needed that because you'd been embezzling his fund. You held off until now, though you had this in mind right from the beginning."

Lamport laughed. "Sure I did!" His hand whipped from his coat and leveled the automatic. "But the only real evidence you have is that dictagraph, and you're getting the record for me right now and smashing it to bits!"

Flannagan narrowed his eyes. "It's in the next room."

"Put your hands up and stand next to each other. Now walk ahead, slowly. You're both covered."

Flannagan smiled. "That's right, but so are you." He backed slowly toward the door. "By ten or fifteen reporters. I asked them here because I live for publicity." Without turning, he kicked the door open and called out. "Come in, gentlemen."

The babble of voices and the march of feet surged up behind him, and Lamport gaped and slowly lowered his gun.

It was not the first time in history that the pen had proved mightier than the sword, but it was doubtless the only time that a pudding had shot a man. And confessed.

Jean Potts is a writer of great sensitivity and honesty. In "The Withered Heart," there is no sensationalism, nothing extraneous to the main business of the story, which is getting deep into the soul of a man under pressure. There is no real outside action, only the interior conflict between nearly forgotten values and the instincts of self-preservation. Miss Potts has given us a story in the best tradition of modern psychological suspense.

8

The Withered Heart

By Jean Potts

At the sound of the car turning into the driveway, Voss was instantly, thoroughly, awake. Not even a split second of fuzziness. His mind clicked at once into precise, unhurried action, just as it had last night. He sat up on the edge of his bed—Myrtle's, of course, was empty—and reached for his watch. It was only a quarter to eight. Already? he thought, as the car stopped in the driveway. He had not expected anyone quite so soon. Not that it mattered; he was ready any time.

He waited for the next sound, which would be someone knocking on the screen door of the veranda. The bedroom seemed to wait too, breathlessly quiet, except for the whir of the electric fan, tirelessly churning up the sluggish air. The heat—the relentless South American heat—shoved in past the flimsy slats of the window blinds. Even now, in the early morning, there was no escape from its pounding glare. He ought to be used to it; he had been here long enough. More than ten years stagnating in this unspeakable climate, in this forsaken backwater where nothing ever happened except the heat . . .

There. Someone was knocking. In his pajama pants and scuffs, Voss shuffled out to the veranda. Frank Dallas—good old Frank—was waiting at the screen door, peering in through the swarming purple bougainvillea. He looked fresh and hearty. His white linen suit had not yet had time to wilt; his thinning hair still showed the marks of a damp comb.

"Rise and shine, you lazy bum! Top of the morning to you!"

Was there perhaps a hollow ring in Frank's voice? Voss could detect none. Nor any trace of trouble in Frank's open, beaming face. Relax, he told himself; it's too soon—he's come for some other reason.

"Hi. What's the idea, rousing the citizenry at this hour. . . ." Yawning, Voss unhooked the screen door. "What the hell hour is it, anyway?"

"Quarter of eight. Time you were up. Look, Voss"—Frank lowered his voice to a conspiratorial whisper—"Myrtle's gone, isn't she?"

"Sure." He said it automatically, without hesitation. "She's gone up to her sister's for a couple of days. Left early, before six this morning."

"Yeah. She told me she was planning to. That's why I figured it was safe to stop by. I've got this letter that Enid wanted me to give you. She was all upset yesterday, poor kid, resigning the way she did. Well, it kind of threw me too. Anyway, this letter, I promised to see that you got it . . ."

Poor old Frank had never gotten over being nervous about his role as go-between. He was as jittery—and, Voss supposed, as secretly thrilled—today as he had been six months ago, when Voss and Enid started their clandestine affair. Happily married himself, Frank had the romantic, inquisitive disposition of a maiden aunt. Besides, as American consul, he was Enid's boss. Very natural, very convenient for him to get into the act. Fun for everybody. Great fun at first. Lately—well, it was over-simplification to say that Enid was too serious, too impetuous, too intense. Those were the very qualities in her that made this affair different from the others, that made Enid herself such an irresistible magnet to Voss.

Only he couldn't respond to them any more. He did not want to be a philanderer; he wanted to be a true, star-crossed lover—and he had lost the power. It was as if Myrtle had withered his heart.

This envelope in his hand, addressed in Enid's headlong writing —her farewell note, or so she must have thought when she wrote it—even this could not penetrate his benumbed and crippled soul. To be losing, through his own inertia, a love like Enid's, and to feel nothing more than a kind of guilty weariness. . . .

He had felt something more last night, all right. Sudden and vivid as lightning, Myrtle's face flashed into his mind. Alive with malice, as it had been last night—the vulgar, coarse, knowing face of his wife. "So your girl friend's leaving," she said. "I hear she's resigned. My, my, I never thought you'd let this one get away. . . ."

Gloating over her own handiwork—because it *was* her doing; the deadly years of being married to Myrtle had very nearly destroyed in him the capacity for feeling anything. Very nearly. But not quite; last night proved that. Hate was left. And if he could hate, he could also love. So Enid need not be lost, after all.

It was going to take time for the numbness to wear off. Voss was still stunned by the impact of release—which, considering everything, was really very fortunate. This morning, if ever in his life, he needed a mind uncluttered by emotion—a mind as cool and accurate as a machine.

"You're all right, aren't you, old man?" Frank was asking anxiously.

"I'll be all right." He paused, conscious of his own pathos as he placed Enid's letter, tenderly, on the wicker table. "It's just that—well, I guess you know how I feel about Enid."

"I know. It's rugged."

Frank was brimming with sympathy. It would be unkind— more than that, it would be indiscreet—to deny him the chance to spill over. "Have a cup of coffee with me," said Voss. "We'll have to make it ourselves. Myrtle always gives the maid time off when she's going to be away. I'd rather eat at the club than up here alone. The maid's a lousy cook, anyway, but we're lucky to get anybody to come this far out." Their house was set off by itself, on the outermost fringe of the American colony. What a break that had turned out to be, last night!

Voss felt a spasm of nervous excitement rather like stage fright, as he led the way to the kitchen. Here was where it had happened, right here by the sink. . . . Another break—the tiles had been a cinch to clean. But might there be some telltale sign?

There was none. Not the smallest. He breathed easy again.

Back on the veranda, with the coffee tray between them, Frank launched into earnest, incoherent speech. The way he looked at it, it was just one of those things. Not that it was any of his business. But look at it one way, and it was the best thing all around—for Enid to pull out, that is. She was really too young for Voss, so she'd get over it. And there was this much about it, a man just couldn't walk out on a wife like Myrtle, not if he had any conscience.

"No," agreed Voss with a wan smile. "I couldn't walk out on Myrtle." But not on account of his conscience, he added to himself. He thought about last night, probing for some tiny qualm, some flicker of remorse. There was none. This extraordinary lack of any kind of feeling . . .

"Myrtle's a good egg, too, you know." Frank took out his handkerchief and mopped his moist red brow. "I've always liked Myrtle."

Oh, sure! Myrtle was more fun than a barrel of monkeys. Everybody said so. The life of every party. Suddenly the memory of the endless chain of parties, monotonous, almost identical, pressed down on Voss like a physical weight. He used to sit and drink steadily, with every nerve stretched rigid in protest against Myrtle's raucous voice, against the flushed, blowzy looseness of her face. For some reason—maybe because it was her lushness and vivacity that had attracted him in the beginning—her antics had a kind of excruciating fascination for Voss. Your wife, he used to tell himself; look at her, listen to her—she's all yours.

"What I say is," Frank floundered on, "when two people have made a go of it like you and Myrtle for this many years, why, they can't just throw it away at the drop of a hat. Myrtle doesn't know, does she?"

Unprepared for this particular question, Voss hesitated. But it took him only a moment to see the danger in assuring Frank—as he would like to have done—that of course Myrtle did not know. Only a romantic innocent like Frank could imagine that the affair had been a secret; in all likelihood Myrtle herself had unloaded to everybody she knew. Much better to play it safe, just in case the question should arise later. "She probably suspects," he said slowly. "But I don't think she has any idea that it's serious. You know how it is in a place like this—flirtations going on all the time."

"Sure, I know," said Frank, very much the man of the world. "Well, one thing, with her away for a couple of days, you'll have a chance to kind of pull yourself together. She couldn't have picked a better time."

"She certainly couldn't," said Voss sincerely. As Frank stood up to leave, he added, once more conscious of his own pathos, "Many thanks for bringing me the letter, Frank. And for the moral support."

Things couldn't have gone more swimmingly, he was thinking. With his mind clicking away in this admirable, mechanical way, there was no reason why he shouldn't breeze through the rest of the morning without turning a hair. All it took was careful planning and a cool head. He had the cool head, all right. And—thanks to Myrtle—the withered heart that would nevertheless come back to life, all in good time.

It was at this self-congratulatory moment that Frank dropped his bomb. Casually, as an afterthought, a final pleasantry that occurred to him when he was halfway out to his car. "I suppose Myrtle took Pepper with her, didn't she?" he called back. "Of course. I never knew her to go half-a-block without that dog."

Voss himself remained intact. The world around him reeled, and then, with a stately, slow-motion effect, it shattered. Except for Frank, who still waited out there, smiling expectantly.

"Oh, yes." Voss's voice rang, remote and dreamy, in his own ears. "Of course she took Pepper. Myrtle never goes anywhere without Pepper."

"In his traveling case, I suppose? Only dog in the country with his own specially-built traveling compartment." Another cheery wave, and Frank was gone.

It was incredible. Only gradually was Voss able to grasp the magnitude of his blunder, the treachery of his own mind, seemingly so faultless in its operation, which had remembered every other detail and had forgotten—of all the ignominious, obvious things—Pepper.

For Pepper and Myrtle were devoted to each other. She referred to herself as his "Muvver." He was a small, beagle-type dog, a cheerful extrovert whose devotion to Myrtle did not prevent him from indulging in an occasional night out, and he had chosen last night for one of these escapades.

Voss closed his eyes. The veranda seemed to echo, as it had last evening, with Myrtle's strident summons: "Here, Peppy, Peppy!" But they had waited in vain for the sound of Pepper tearing through the shrubbery and up the driveway, for his joyful voice proclaiming that he was home. Ordinarily, Myrtle would have kept on calling, at intervals, until Pepper showed up—as he always did, sooner or later—looking ashamed and proud in equal parts. Ordinarily, it wouldn't have mattered that he was still not back.

But there was nothing ordinary about last night and this morning. That was just the point: Voss had to make this extraordinary, deranged, secret stretch of time *seem* ordinary. He had to. And it was impossible, because all his calculations had been made minus Pepper.

A current of panic ran through him. He willed himself to stand still and think. Now was no time to lose his head, or to dissolve in futile self-recrimination. He must think, the way he had thought last night, with that beautiful, unhurried precision. . . .

Pepper at large, perhaps galloping around the neighborhood calling attention to himself, was a shocking hazard. But to call the little beast would only advertise more fatally the fact that he was not where he ought to be, and furthermore that Voss knew it.

There was nothing to do, then, but wait.

He rubbed his clammy hands against his pajama pants. His knees threatened to buckle under him. But it was somehow unthinkable to sit down. He stood in the middle of the veranda, staring at the screen door, where the bougainvillea climbed, trying to get in. It was the personification of Myrtle, that burgeoning vine. Its harsh purplish flowers were her color, and the way it swarmed over everything, its boundless vulgarity—it was Myrtle to the life.

There was nothing to do but wait. . . .

Then all at once Pepper was there. He barked, in an apologetic way, as if he were anxious to make clear that he was only suggesting—by no means demanding—that he be let in. And when Voss tottered to the screen and opened it, the dog swaggered in with an uneasy attempt at bravado.

Trembling all over, Voss collapsed in one of the wicker chairs.

He could hear the little dog clicking off in search of a more demonstrative welcome. And in spite of all he could do, memory re-enacted for him last night's whole flawless (almost) project, after— Well, just after. It had seemed to work itself out with such magical accuracy. First of all, the heaven-sent circumstances of Myrtle's visit to her sister, who lived (bless her heart) in an inland town, the road to which was infrequently traveled, curving, and in spots precipitous. Ideal for Voss's purposes. Who was likely to be abroad at three-thirty in the morning to see him, either when he left the house—with Myrtle's body and the bicycle bundled in the back seat of her car—or when he returned, alone on the bicycle?

The answer was, no one. He had had the whole moonless, empty world to himself; he had managed the crash—like everything else —with dreamlike precision.

And when Myrtle's body and her car were found smashed to bits at the bottom of the gorge, who was going to pry too much? Accidents happened all the time, and Myrtle was a notoriously rash driver.

He had thought of everything, including Myrtle's suitcase which, obligingly enough, she had already packed, and the new hat she had bought for her trip. It had a red veil, not quite the same shade as the flower trimming. Trust Myrtle. He had been very proud of remembering about the hat.

Only he had forgotten Pepper. She never went anywhere without him; she would as soon set out stark naked as without Pepper. She did not trust him to ride on the seat beside her; the possibility that something in the passing scene might prove too much for his inquiring temperament terrified her. So she had had a special traveling case built for him. The case, with Pepper inside, was placed on the floor of the front seat, during even the shortest trips.

When not in use, the case was stored in a corner of the garage. That was where it was now, along with Voss's own car, the one he used to drive back and forth to work. If only, last night, he had happened to glance in that particular corner . .   He must get rid of it. And he must get rid of Pepper.

At least Pepper was here, under his control, no longer prancing around in public. Perhaps he had already been noticed? Perhaps. Voss answered himself grimly. In which case it would simply be his word against someone else's. All right, his word. But there was no way whatever to account for a hale and hearty Pepper here in the house; or for the telltale case, sitting undamaged in the garage. Voss recalled his own remote voice, replying to Frank: "Oh, yes. Of course she took Pepper." That was his story, and to make it work, both Pepper and the traveling case ought to be in the car at the bottom of the gorge.

Well, he could get them there. He had his own car. He saw, with a flash of excitement and renewed hope, that there was time, that he still had a chance. A much chancier chance than the one he had taken last night, when no one had been around to notice his coming and going. It was broad daylight now. Even so, he would be safe enough, once he (and Pepper, and the case) got on the road that led to the gorge. Getting there was the tricky part; to reach the turn-off he would have to drive through one stretch of the American colony—dark and silent last night, but buzzing with activity now that morning was here. Someone would be sure to hear Pepper, who invariably barked his head off the minute he was put in his case, and kept it up until he reached his destination. No, it was a risk that simply could not be taken. Pepper must be disposed of, silenced forever, before he set off on his final trip.

How to do it? This was the problem, stripped to its basic bones.

As if on cue, Pepper appeared in the doorway between the veranda and the living room. His expression was one of friendly inquiry. If this turned out to be a game of hide-and-seek, his manner seemed to convey, they could count on him; he was always ready for fun and games; if, on the other hand, his favorite human being had actually gone away and left him—

Well, Pepper was no dog to brood. You would never catch him stretched out on somebody's grave, or refusing to eat and moping himself away to a shadow. Love came easy to this sturdy, lively little creature.

Voss eyed him, and Pepper, mistaking speculation for interest, trotted over, all sociability. My God, thought Voss, he'd even get attached to *me*, given time. Which of course was precisely what Pepper was not going to be given. He did not know this, however. He did not know that Voss's heart had all but withered, that he was not capable of the tiniest flicker of sympathy for any living thing. In cheerful ignorance, the dog sat down beside Voss's feet —tentatively, with his tail thumping and his spotted head cocked upward. He seemed to be smiling.

"Go away," said Voss coldly.

Pepper could take a hint; still smiling amiably, he ambled over to the living-room door.

A gun would be the easiest way. One neat shot—it would sound like a car back-firing, in case anyone happened to hear it—and a quick, unobtrusive burial. No problem there, with a body as small as Pepper's. But Voss did not own a gun.

Well, there was gas. Except that there wasn't. Everything here was electric.

Where did you stab a dog? That is . . . Voss glanced toward the door, where Pepper sat, alert for the smallest sign of encouragement. His anatomy must be roughly like that of a human being. But somehow his front legs became, in Voss's mind, a hopeless complication. Pepper wasn't large, but he was strong and wiry. And he loved life; he would hang on to it with all his might.

Voss turned away from Pepper's trustful gaze, and, as he turned, his eye fell on the bougainvillea. One strand had thrust its way inside the screen door, probably when he let Pepper in; it swung there, searching for a toe hold. He went over, shoved it out savagely, and hooked the screen door against it.

From time to time Pepper left his post to make another fruitless tour of the house. After each trip he looked a little less debonair, a little more anxious. Now he pattered over to Voss's side and uttered a series of barks. Not loud, but insistent.

He would have to be kept quiet until the method of permanent disposal had been decided upon. Food would do it. Voss stood up. Here at least was something he could handle. And anyway, Pepper, being condemned was entitled to a hearty breakfast. The dog bustled out to the kitchen ahead of Voss, all eagerness and good humor again.

The business of opening a can of dog food and filling Pepper's water bowl was calming. But Voss was startled to see that it was now nine-thirty; he should have been at the office an hour ago. He phoned at once, with the first excuse that occurred to him.

His secretary, a flip type, said sure, she understood about his headache, and had he tried tomato juice? Or a hair of the dog?

He had a perilous impulse to laugh and laugh. "I'll see you after lunch," he said icily, and hung up.

Meanwhile Pepper, full of peace and breakfast, had retired to his favorite spot under the dining-room table for a nap. His round stomach rose and fell rhythmically. Now and then his forehead puckered, or his paws flicked busily, in pursuit of a dream-rabbit. Watching him, Voss felt a drowsiness, almost like hypnosis, creeping over him.

The jangling of the telephone jerked him to his feet, wild-eyed and suddenly drenched in cold sweat. After three rings, however, he had collected his wits and was able to answer in a normal, deliberate voice.

"Is that you, Voss? Is something wrong? Why aren't you at the office?" Myrtle's sister sounded flurried. But then she always did.

She always interrupted, too. He had barely begun to explain about his headache when she broke in. "But, Voss, what I called about—what's happened to Myrtle? I thought she was going to get an early start. I've been expecting her for hours."

"You mean she's not there yet?" He paused, just long enough. "But I don't understand it. She left here before six—"

"Before six! But it's ten-thirty now, and it's only a three-hour drive—at the very most!"

"I know," he said, aware that the slight edge of irritation in his voice was a convincing touch: worry often made people snappish. "She certainly should be there by now. I don't understand it. I'd better— What had I better do? I can check with—"

"Now keep calm. There must be some simple explanation."

"I don't know what," he said bleakly. "Thank God you called me. I'll get in touch with Frank Dallas right away. He'll know what to do. In the meantime, if you hear anything—"

"I will. Of course I'll call you." Her voice quavered.

This was according to schedule. He had expected the call from Myrtle's sister; the only change was that his next move—to report his problem to good old Frank—must now be delayed until Pepper was dead and at the bottom of the gorge.

Pepper strolled in, pausing at the doorway to yawn luxuriously and stretch each leg in turn. The sight of him chilled Voss; he had a moment's sharp, appalling view not only of his own peril but of his own irresponsibility in the face of it. How could he have let so much of the morning slip by in weak hesitation? What kind of tricks was his mind playing on him, that he could draw an easy breath with Pepper still here to blow his story to smithereens?

It's Pepper or me, he thought. Life or death. Dog eat dog.

In a frenzy now that time was so short, he rushed to the sideboard in the dining room and snatched the carving knife from the drawer. Pepper capered at his heels, making little jumps toward his knee. How easy it would be to grab him by his muzzle, force his head back, and, quickly, with one stroke of the knife . . .

Only not in here. In the kitchen. Tiles, instead of rush matting.

But at that moment it came—the phone call that exploded what was left of his original carefully planned schedule. It was Frank, and his voice was even heartier than usual, in a transparent effort to hide his concern. "Look, Voss, I just had a long-distance call from Myrtle's sister. Seems Myrtle hasn't shown up yet . . ."

Damn the woman, damn her! But damn himself, too, for not foreseeing that she would jump the gun and call Frank herself, instead of leaving it to him. He made a desperate snatch to salvage what little he could. "I know, I've been trying to get you, but your line was busy."

"Now don't get in a sweat, Voss. Like I told her sister, there are any number of simple explanations. Pepper might have gotten carsick. He does sometimes, you know. I'll get right on it and call you the minute we've found out."

Abandon the idea of getting Pepper and the traveling case out to the gorge. Scrap it—there was not time. There was just time, now, to kill him, hide his body and the case temporarily, and hope that his absence in the wreckage might at first be overlooked. Then later . . .

It came to him then—the best way, the obvious method that he should have thought of right away. He could put Pepper to sleep, the way a veterinary would. Giddy with relief, Voss hurried into the bathroom and flung open the door of the medicine chest. Both he and Myrtle had prescriptions for sleeping pills. A handful of these . . .

There was one lonesome capsule rattling around in his own prescription bottle. Myrtle had evidently packed hers. They were nowhere to be found. It was hopeless, but he could not bring himself to stop searching. Not until the phone rang.

This time Frank's voice, drained of its usual heartiness, was all hushed gravity. "Voss, I'm afraid you've got to prepare yourself for some bad news . . . There's been an accident, a bad one . . . I'll be with you in ten minutes, old man."

Ten minutes, and Pepper still here to give the lie to the whole "accident" story. For his presence would surprise Frank. It would set him to wondering, set him to investigating what wouldn't bear investigating. Pepper stood at Voss's knee, the question—"What can I do for you, sir?"—on the tip of his cordial pink tongue.

"You can die," whispered Voss.

Ten minutes left—probably only nine by now. Voss cast an agonized glance around the room, with its jumble of tawdry color and design, its clutter of Myrtle's gimcracks.

The paperweight was right there on the table beside him. Heavy; a solid, ugly chunk of onyx that fitted suggestively in his hand. One stunning blow aimed at the brown spot between Pepper's ears, and the rest would be easy.

Clasping the paperweight, Voss sat down and patted his lap invitingly. "Here, Peppy," he said.

Pepper leaped up at once; he was used to being held and petted. Snuggling the little dog's head in the crook of his left arm, Voss slowly raised the paperweight, poised it, focusing eye, hand, and will for the one smashing blow.

But he could not bring himself to do it. Now, at this untimely, this fatal, moment, he felt his withered heart stir and come to life—as it should have done for Enid.

His arm sagged, the paperweight thudded to the floor. He grabbed Pepper's warm, sturdy body between his two hands and glared down into the trustful eyes. He did not really like the foolish, friendly creature any more than he ever had. But it was as if he were holding here, in Pepper's compact person, an engine of life. It set up in him a responsive current, melting away the numbness, throbbing all through him in a triumphant flood of warmth.

Yes, triumphant—although he was lost and he knew it, although he could hear the sound of Frank's car already turning into the driveway.

His hands tightened convulsively on Pepper, who had heard too, and was struggling to free himself. Then Voss gave a helpless laugh—or maybe it was a sob—and let go.

Bursting with his tidings of welcome, Pepper rushed out to the veranda. After a moment Voss followed him to the screen door and waited there—waited for Frank.

Short story writers are inclined to look down on novelists, saying that "with all that room to roam around in, anybody can tell his story!" Matthew Head is primarily a novelist; he writes here, at short story length, a complete and satisfying drama with enough character, setting, action, and analysis to fill a couple of books. Perhaps a writer is a writer. Mr. Head is, in any case.

9

Three Strips of Flesh

By Matthew Head

The body of Gérôme de l'Andréneau, with the neck broken and three strips of flesh peeled off the back of the shoulders, was found at the tip of a spectacular promontory near the limits of the Congo-Ruzi station. Although there was other money on the body, the murderer or murderers had robbed it of exactly one franc.

The Congo-Ruzi was a private agricultural experimental station in a remote part of the Kivu, in the Belgian Congo, and it was in a hell of a bad way even before the murder of its director. I happened to be there because I was making an inspection of the station in connection with an American government loan they had applied for during the war.

I had rather liked this Gérôme de l'Andréneau—a tall, still good-looking man of the fading matinée-idol type, who was utterly lost in the Congo, and so lousy a manager that he had reduced the station to such an extremity that there wasn't a chance of giving them the loan.

Gérôme was survived by several people who for one reason or another might have liked the idea of his being dead, including his wife and her lover, and his assistant manager who did all the work for half the salary, and a very large group of natives. As for the wife, Jacqueline, from the minute I met her I knew that if she wasn't a nymph she was close to it, and although she obviously didn't bite her nails, which were about an inch-and-a-half long, she was pretty well chewed up inside. You couldn't help feeling sorry for her in a way, since it can't be much fun being a woman who has never lived for anything but her looks and the pleasure of attracting men, when she finds herself on the verge of middle age isolated a hundred miles from the nearest village and a couple of thousand miles from a really first-rate cosmetics counter. With Gérôme dead she could have sold the station for what it was worth, which was still something, and got back to the source of supply of men and war paint.

I've no way of being certain that Jacqueline had a lover at the station, a big handsome young fellow named Henri Debuc, except that Jacqueline and Henri were both people of tremendous sexual vitality, that neither one of them gave any indication of being particularly strait-laced, that they had an awful lot of spare time on their hands, and that the isolation of the Congo-Ruzi station was just one step beyond the old cast-up-on-a-desert-island-together deal. And although I personally wouldn't have killed a jack rabbit for the privilege of running off with Jacqueline, I could see how Henri might have looked at things differently, especially if the setup involved a release from the desperate ennui of his position.

Gérôme gave a party for me the night I arrived at the station, with all the white population of the station—six—there, plus two white visitors. I arrived late, with Henri, since I was being put up at his cottage, and after we had said polite things in the hallway to Gérôme and Jacqueline we went on into the living room. This was two days before the murder. They were talking about a killing which had occurred some time before, when a local tribe, the M'bukus, had done away with a white overseer. A large, carroty-haired plain-faced woman about fifty years old was gesturing with a pair of big freckled hands and speaking in English with a strong Middle-Western accent.

"My God, César," she was saying, "I don't see how you can say it. You saw him as well as I did, lying there with his throat cut from ear to ear and half the flesh stripped off his back. If it wasn't for my medical oath, I wouldn't touch another of your goddam M'bukus with a ten-foot hypodermic."

Jacqueline interrupted to introduce me around; she was dressed in a slinky kind of hostess gown that was threadbare in spots, but in her own affected way she had a certain amount of style. The carroty-haired American, I learned, was Dr. Mary Finney, a medical missionary who had hit the Congo-Ruzi the day before on her semiannual visit to the native village near by.

"Don't let us interrupt you, Miss Finney," I said. "What's a goddam M'buku?"

"Have I been swearing again?" asked Miss Finney.

"You know you have, Mary Finney," said a small mousy woman at her side. This was her partner, Miss Emily Collins. Miss Finney always said that since Emily ran the soul and hymn department, the two of them represented the flesh and the spirit between them.

"Every time I swear, Emily bursts into tears," said Miss Finney.

"I do not," said Emily.

"You do too," said Miss Finney, and Miss Collins gave it up.

Henri stepped into the breach. "My houseboy's a M'buku," he said to me, "the one who took care of your things. They're the leading tribe around here. Miss Finney hasn't much to say for them."

"They're the meanest blacks in the Congo, I'll say that much for them," Miss Finney told him.

"But that boy doesn't strike me as being mean," I said. I felt sorry for Miss Collins, who was fiddling nervously with the hem of her skirt and looking pretty well squashed. She had a pallid, grainy face with light brown eyes and scanty hair crimped in some kind of patent waver. "Oh, yes, I know that boy," she said. "Albert. Albert Nkodio. He's a member of the village mission. Albert's been a very faithful boy."

Miss Finney grunted.

"He's been a very syphilitic boy," she said. "You needn't worry, though, Henri—I gave him that examination this morning and you just keep on giving him the injections."

Miss Collins coughed daintily and nervously, took the tiniest sip of her drink, set it down on the table by her side, and pulled at her hem.

"Emily," said Miss Finney, "if you pull that damn skirt one

more time you're going to have it right down off your neck. After the things we've done the last twenty-five years I should think you could take a little reference to syphilis without fidgeting. You've got a chronic case of New England girlhood, that's what you've got." She added as an afterthought, "I'd rather have syphilis."

Miss Collins coughed again and glanced meaningfully at somebody I haven't mentioned yet, an extraordinarily pretty young girl named Gabrielle.

"Oh, that," said Miss Finney. All this had been in English. She said in French, "Gaby, did you understand what we were saying?"

Gaby said in English, "Not very much of it." She had a very strong and very delightful accent. She was, I'd have guessed, only about sixteen, perhaps at most a year or two older. She had naturally that wonderful combination of tawny skin and blond hair that the girls in California work toward with sun and chemicals. Her father was the assistant manager who did all the work for half the salary, César Boutegourde, such a short fat bald little typical *père de famille* that I always thought of him as Papa Boutegourde, and his plump wife, with nothing left of what must have been real beauty except her great luminous eyes, as Mama. They were sitting protectively on either side of Gaby. Papa was a violent Walloon, but Mama's family were Flemings, so Gaby had learned at home to slip easily from French to Flemish. She spoke French to Gérôme and Jacqueline and Henri, and English to Miss Finney and Miss Collins and me, and later I heard her chatter in Lingala to the natives, and she used all of these, shifting from one to another without any difficulty or hesitation. She had grown up doing it.

There was a short silence, and I realized that I was looking directly across the room at Gabrielle's breasts where they began to swell above the low, square-cut neckline of her dress, and that everybody else in the room was looking at me doing it.

I said quickly, "These M'bukus. I've heard of them somewhere."

Miss Finne‧ grinned at me and said, "Maybe you've heard of the M'buku Rebellion."

I hadn't, but I said I had. Miss Finney grinned at me again and said, "César thinks of it as his own little rebellion. It was on one of the station's fields, not forty miles from here."

Papa Boutegourde opened his mouth, but Miss Finney said, "Let *me* tell it. It's a fine bloody story. You see, Mr. Tolliver," she said to me, and then, "Oh, for goodness' sake, what's your first name?"

"Hooper."

"Well, Hoopie, you see, this nasty little Duclerc was subadministrator or something, and after the natives had worked out their road tax—they all pay a road tax in labor—he kept them working on his own plantation, and no pay."

"And a gun and whip to back him up, remember that," said Papa Boutegourde.

"All right, a gun and whip to back him up. I guess there was a lot to be said for the natives," admitted Miss Finney. "But he made his mistake when he hired a couple of Kitusis to stand guard."

Papa Boutegourde interrupted. "The Kitusis had always warred on the M'bukus, but even in the old days the M'bukus wouldn't eat Kitusi flesh because they regarded the Kitusis as inferiors, but when Duclerc hired—"

"*I* started this," Miss Finney broke in. "I know you know everything about native history and customs, César, but I'm trying to get to the bloody part. Hoopie's a tourist. *Well*," she said with relish, "it was the most excitement this place ever saw. Three M'bukus got the Kitusis, then they went on and got Duclerc. Damn fool, if he hadn't hired the Kitusis he'd have got away with it. White men are still sort of demigods out here, but not when they play with Kitusis. They dragged Duclerc out of his house into the bush and cut his throat and took three strips of flesh off the back of his shoulders. I suppose," she said, "they cut his throat first. I know they ate the flesh."

Miss Collins moaned faintly. "*Mary!*" she breathed.

"That's all," said Miss Finney. "It's a nice story for tourists and happens to be true into the bargain. They got one of the M'bukus alive and hanged him right there on the plantation."

"They did?" I said. "In a place like this, who acts as hangman?"

There was an uncomfortable pause. Then Papa Boutegourde said hesitantly, "They—asked me to, but I couldn't bring myself to do it." He paused again, then said, "Gérôme was—brave enough."

"I hanged him," Gérôme said, with a smile. He indicated a coin that hung on his watch chain. "A souvenir," he said. "Perhaps a rather grim souvenir. One franc. My fee. They paid me one franc, to make it legal." He smiled again, not at all uncomfortably, and said, "It was only a native, of course, but still, I can say I hanged a man."

Jacqueline said sharply, "If you have quite succeeded in ruining our appetites—" then she pulled herself together, smiled at us around the room, and said to me, "Mr. Tolliver, will you take me in to dinner?"

By rights Papa Boutegourde should have sat at Jacqueline's left, but Henri was there instead, and Jacqueline was so much more interested in him than in me that I paid my attention mostly to Gaby on my other side. Sitting close to her I looked for a single flaw in her skin; it wasn't there. She had on some lipstick and I think a little darkening on her eyelashes, but beyond that she wasn't made up, and didn't need to be. We talked about nothing much, but always knowing what we really would have liked to talk about, then all of a sudden she said to me,

"Do you like my dress?"

"I do. It's a very pretty dress."

"I made it myself. We have to do so many things for ourselves out here." She looked directly at me and smiled and said in a lower voice, "Before I came tonight I cut the neck lower. Mama is furious. But you like it, don't you?"

She took me so by surprise that I stammered like a fool. She smiled again and turned calmly from me with a faint air of dismissal and said to Henri, across the table, "I haven't seen you for so long, Henri. You are not looking well." Jacqueline looked at her with hatred, then turned to me and began talking about New York. Gaby kept her calm air all through dinner, but I noticed something else. Under the shield of the table she would clench her napkin or twist it in her fingers. Then she would stop, but before long she would be at it again, her hands twisting and clenching until the napkin was moist and crumpled all over.

Two days later I had finished my inspection of the station, and I was sitting up late with Papa Boutegourde in the Boutegourdes' house (the houses on the station were separated as much as half a mile, in the interest of some kind of privacy), and we were winding up the checking of some figures I had to take with me when I left the next morning. It must have been nearly two; Mama and Gaby had excused themselves long ago, and I was afraid that Gaby would get sick of waiting for me out on the promontory, where we were going to say goodbye.

Papa and I were in a small room, a kind of study, or we would have heard Jacqueline as she came stumbling and gasping across the station grounds. We heard her burst into the living room and ran in there; she was horrible to see and hear. She was trying to talk in a strange, thickened voice, but a kind of idiot laughing or sobbing would break through and she would go off into hysterics. There were remains of make-up smeared over her face, and her hair was sticking out in every direction. She had on something that looked like red crepe lounging pajamas; they were ripped and snagged all over, and spotted with dust and stains of moisture. We got her onto the sofa and she lay there looking thin and slippery-boned, writhing like an eel and twitching, and clutching at Papa Boutegourde's bathrobe while she screamed with laughter or choked with sobs.

"You'll have to hit her to get her out of that," I said. Jacqueline sat straight up. "*Rape!*" she screeched, and fell flat on her back again and went into peal after peal of laughter, twisting her fingers together until you would think they would never straighten out again.

"They hurt me!" she whimpered. She began screaming again. "Oh, Gérôme, my poor Gérôme! Where's Gérôme? What did they do to you, Gérôme? Oh, Gérô-o-o-ome!" and her voice went off into a long howl. Then she collapsed and lay there heaving, with hiccoughs jerking out of her.

Mama Boutegourde appeared in the room in bathrobe and pigtails, wild-eyed. "*Brandy!*" yelled Papa Boutegourde, and Mama disappeared. She reappeared with a glass and a bottle, and Papa pressed the glass of brandy against Jacqueline's lips, but she moaned and made bubbly and snuffly noises into the glass so that the brandy spilled over.

"If she won't drink it, throw it on her," I said.

Jacqueline whimpered and downed the brandy in a couple of gulps.

"You've got to find Gérôme," she said, fairly normally, but still in that strange, thick voice. It gave me the feeling you get when the dentist stuffs the little wads of gauze under your lip while he's working on you. Jacqueline was quiet enough now so that I could see that her mouth didn't look funny only because the lipstick was smeared. It was bruised and swollen on one side, and the bluish flush spread on up into her cheek.

"Regardez-ça!" cried Madame Boutegourde suddenly. She had lifted one of Jacqueline's hands to chafe the wrist, and the loose sleeve had slid back to the elbow. Her wrist was bruised. You could see the finger marks, and when Madame Boutegourde pushed the sleeve on up to the shoulder, there they were again, on the upper arm.

"They hurt me," Jacqueline moaned. "Gérôme! Oh, please, they've got him; go find him, César!" Now she lay back on the pillow and began crying in a helpless, despairing kind of way that would have been heart-rending in anybody else. "You all hate me," she said, "and you won't help me. Oh, Gérôme, Gérôme!"

When we finally got the story out of her, it went like this:

She had gone to her room to change into the pajamas earlier that night, and had expected Gérôme to follow her. When he didn't appear she had gone back into the living room. Gérôme was standing petrified, facing two natives she had never seen before. She had not heard them come in, she had heard no sound at all; they had simply appeared out of thin air, and she had entered to face the terrifying tableau. Gérôme spoke to the natives in French, asking them what they wanted. They had answered briefly in their own tongue, but neither Jacqueline nor Gérôme could understand a word.

Jacqueline remembered Gérôme's pistol in their bedroom. She turned to leave the room but one of the natives was upon her in an instant, grabbing her from behind by the arms near the shoulder and making the bruises we had seen. Gérôme had turned to attack the native. The second native jumped across the room and felled Gérôme with a blow. Gérôme lay still on the concrete floor. Jacqueline had screamed. The second native stepped over Gérôme's body and grabbed both her wrists in one hand. "He was big, big! A great black brute of a thing—" and she displayed to us her two small bruised wrists that he had clamped in his one great hand. He had put the other over her mouth. She had fainted.

When she came to, both natives had Gérôme's body and were carrying it out of the room. She had crawled across the floor toward them on her hands and knees. Then rising to her knees she had beat at one of them with her fists. He freed one hand and hit her in the mouth, saying something in his language. She didn't know how long she was unconscious this time. When she came to she was alone. She was half crazy with terror; she hadn't even remembered that she could have driven the car. She had run all the way to the Boutegourdes', falling down, running into bushes. She remembered it only as one remembers a nightmare. The rest we knew.

Mama Boutegourde went to get towels and water for some kind of repair job on Jacqueline, but instead, we heard her shriek from the other end of the house. She appeared in the doorway looking like the last acts of all the Greek tragedies rolled into one. "She's gone!" she screamed. "She's not there! Her bed—her window—" Mama Boutegourde fell into a chair and began giving a good imitation of what Jacqueline had just been doing.

I said to Papa Boutegourde, "I know where Gaby is. I'll go get her." Papa Boutegourde looked as if the last semblance of reason had been snatched from his universe. I went out, to keep—in a way—my late date with Gaby.

You reached the promontory through a bush path that was used as a short cut between points on the station. I had been along it before, with Gaby, but tonight I kept going off the path and into the thick masses of foliage which bounded it. I had a flashlight, and in any case you couldn't stray far, simply because of the thickness of those foliage walls, so I blundered through at a good rate of speed, with things swishing and crackling around and under my feet, and my face and hands getting scratched; but I didn't have to go far before I found Gaby there, cowering as far off the path as she could press herself into the tangled growth. My light picked her out, half crouching and pressing herself backward, her eyes wide and her lips drawing back from her teeth. She was so still that she looked like one of those night photographs of wild animals, where the animals trip off their own flash.

Her voice came out in a croak. "Don't touch me," she said. "Don't touch me." She kept saying it.

"It's Hoop, Gaby," I said. She didn't move or change expression. I turned the light up into my own face, so she could see.

I heard her cry come out like something giving way under pressure. Before I got the light back onto her she had flung herself on me, both hands clutching the front of my shirt. I put both arms around her to keep her from falling, and she let go of my shirt and flung her arms around me too. We stood there pressed close together and I could feel the current of her fear, like an actual emanation from her body. She tried to talk but I couldn't get the words, then she began to relax and tremble, and finally she stopped trembling and let her head drop against me and began to cry. I could feel her going limp and I knew she was all right now.

She told me what I could hardly believe, that he was there; then she led me along the path until we came to the clearing on the promontory where we had been supposed to meet. I remember how he looked in the beam of the flashlight. I could see the gash in his throat and I saw his shirt ripped half off his back and his back dark with blood, but it wasn't until I had taken Gabrielle home and Miss Finny had come back and examined him that we saw how the strips of flesh had been peeled off his shoulder.

I won't go into the embarrassment of seeing Papa and Mama Boutegourde and having to admit that I was meeting Gabrielle on the promontory. As far as good Belgian parents are concerned, murder is a less heinous crime. But I will summarize Gaby's story as she told it to her mother and father and Miss Finney:

She had gone out to the promontory and waited there for me, she didn't know how long, until she had heard the sound of someone coming. Since she couldn't be certain it would be me, and since the footsteps seemed oddly slow and heavy, she had run back into the edge of the bush, and had seen one figure come out onto the promontory, bent over under the weight of what he carried on his back. He had thrown his weight onto the ground. The body was long and thin and in white pants and shirt; she had recognized it as Gérôme's. She could see the other figure in not much more than silhouette, but she could tell it was a native. She had shut her eyes when she saw that he had a knife, and what he was doing to the body, after ripping off the shirt; she was afraid she would faint, and concentrated everything on staying conscious and quiet. She didn't know how long it took until the native left, going down the path into the valley toward the native village; she didn't remember how long it had taken her to go back along the path when she saw my light in the distance. She thought it was a native, with a light he had stolen; either a native concerned with Gérôme's murder, or the same native she had seen, doubling back. She had told him not to touch her, and then had recognized me when I turned the flash on myself. She showed me Gérôme's body, as I have told, and I took her back to her house.

Miss Finney listened to this story of Gaby's that night. It was close to dawn when we left the Boutegourdes' house, because among other things Miss Finney had had to administer sedative injections to Mama Boutegourde and Jacqueline.

As we drove along the station roads to her guest house, Miss Finney said to me, "Hoop—what exactly did Gaby say, when you flashed that light on her?"

"Just what she said she said," I told her. "She just kept saying, 'Don't touch me, don't touch me,' over and over again."

"Those her exact words?"

"You asked me, I told you. Yes."

"Strange," said Miss Finney. "If she didn't know it was you, why did she speak in English?"

I felt myself flushing in the dark. "Sorry," I said. "She did say it in French, now that I think of it."

"Goddammit," said Miss Finney, "when I say exact words I mean exact words."

"All right then, her exact words were 'Ne me touchez pas.'"

"Exactly," said Miss Finney. "According to her story she thought you were a native, so she said to you 'Ne me touchez pas.'"

"Get to the point," I said.

"Lord Almighty, Hoop!" said Miss Finney. "She spoke in French! In *French!* Gabrielle never spoke to the natives in French. She was one of those Congo babies who have black boys for nurse-maids and have to be spanked into speaking French. They always pick up Lingala first and they'd rather speak it, it's easier. She translates back and forth like a breeze. It's second nature to her to speak their own tongue to the natives. Most of them wouldn't understand anything else anyhow. She didn't think you were a native—she thought you were a white man, a French-speaking white man. She didn't see a native out there with Gérôme's body —she saw a white man. She didn't see him go down the path to the village, she saw him go back in the direction of the station, the way he had come. When she saw that light bobbing through the bush she thought he was coming back for something, taking the short cut. When the light flashed on her she thought there was a murderer behind it—a white man! She didn't think it was a native. If she had, do you know what she'd have said? She'd have said 'Koba! Koba-du-bai! Koba-du-bai!' My God, does that sound like 'Ne me touchez pas' to you?"

"All right, all right," I said, feeling sick about what was coming next.

"But then she pops up with this rigmarole about a native," Miss Finney went on, "because she saw that white man and what he was doing to that body and she knew why he was doing it, and why he was laying him out on the path to the village like that, to make it look like a fancy M'buku revenge on Gérôme for that hanging job he did. But she loved Henri. She might not have wanted him to touch her, not there in the bush or ever again, but she couldn't bring herself to give him away. If you don't know she loved Henri you're blind. What else could happen—a young healthy girl who never sees any man at all, stuck out here, and Henri as handsome as he is? If he hadn't been tied up with Jacqueline—and I guess you think he is just the way I do—they might have fallen in love. Of course, she loved him."

"All right, she loved him," I said, "but this white man she saw. It happens I've been with Mr. Boutegourde all evening so he's out, but you didn't know that and you jump at Henri right away. Why couldn't you suspect Boutegourde?"

"Oh, my God, Hoop," Miss Finney said in despair, "why wouldn't I suspect Santa Claus? And anyhow, she'd have spoken in Flemish if she'd thought it was her father."

"I'm finished," I said meekly enough. "And what are you going to do now?"

Miss Finney was quiet for a moment. She sighed heavily, and said, "I don't know exactly. I know from the bruises on Jacqueline's arms and wrists and mouth that she was being beat up pretty badly. I don't think those bruises were planted on purpose. It's hard to do something like that to yourself or to someone else deliberately, even to conceal a murder. The only man around here I can think of who'd have reason to beat Jacqueline up was Gérôme. The only reason Gérôme would beat her up right now, with you, an important stranger on the place, would be that something unexpected had happened that cracked him up. And the most unexpected thing that could happen to Gérôme, poor dope that he was, would be to find Jacqueline and Henri together. I think he did. I think he grabbed her, hit her in the face, and so on, and I think Henri tried to stop him and killed him by accident. His neck was broken. And I think it was Jacqueline's idea to fake this native vengeance on the body. Then by the time she had run half a mile and fallen down a few times and showed up bruised and genuinely half-hysterical at the Boutegourdes', she could put on a pretty convincing show. And all Henri has to say is that he slept through the whole thing. Do you think that holds water?"

It held a little too much water. Henri's suicide, some weeks later, was accompanied by a written confession.

Miriam Allen deFord is one of those rare writers who can build almost unbearable suspense without using the conventional techniques of the suspense story. In "Walking Alone," there is no mystery, no question of "whodunit?"; there is no frantic action, no atmospheric locale. Using ordinary people in an ordinary setting, Miss deFord has created an interior drama of character which is likely to haunt your thoughts long after you have forgotten more usual stories. *Who was the real criminal anyway?*

10

Walking Alone

By Miriam Allen deFord

John Larsen stood waiting for the bus to take him to work. It was only the middle of March, but spring had sent out a feeler; the air had a hint of warmth in it and the sky was a deeper blue than winter had known. Across the street little green spikes of leafbuds dotted the poplar trees flanking a billboard.

All at once he remembered sharply springlike mornings in his boyhood, thirty years ago. He would wake and see a sky like this through the open window, and his heart would be filled with a strange, nameless emotion, made up of a yearning for something unknown, a longing for something not yet experienced.

The bus was not in sight. If it was late, he would be late too, and Sims would put on his sour face and say, "Busy day, Larsen. Can't you ever get here on time?" But it wouldn't be a busy day—

it seldom was. People don't buy rugs and carpets the way they buy vegetables and paper napkins.

"Fed up," Larsen muttered to himself, waiting alone on the dreary corner. "Just fed up." His mind went back to the hour before and Kate's peevish voice. "For heaven's sake, John, wake up! You want to be late for work? Next thing you know, they'll fire you, and then where'll we be? Hurry up! Think I like having to get up at all hours to cook your breakfast? Least you can do is eat it when I make it."

It was the same old monologue. When he'd left she would crawl back into bed, in her unappetizing curlers, and goodness knew when she'd crawl out again to dawdle through the day. He could fix breakfast himself in half the time she took, but then she wouldn't be a martyr to an inefficient, dreamy failure of a husband.

He shivered in his worn topcoat; it wasn't as springlike as he first thought, although the sun would warm things soon. His mind flitted to the woods and fields of his childhood, to the freedom and irresponsibility of those far-off years. He peered down the street; there was no sign of the bus.

Abruptly he crossed to the corner drug store, before common sense could change his mind. He fished for a dime in his pocket and went into the phone booth.

"Mr. Sims? This is Larsen. Look, I'm awfully sorry, but I just can't make it today. It's my back; I'm going to the doctor about it. I'll be there tomorrow, no matter how I feel. No, I couldn't hold out till lunchtime—my back's like a toothache. Yes, I know, but— Well, thanks, Mr. Sims. I'll do that, yes, sir. I'm sorry too."

Sims would wonder why he hadn't had Kate phone for him, if he felt so bad. Maybe he'd say it took a younger man to handle the job. Oh, to hell with it; it was too late now to reconsider.

He stayed on that side of the street, and the bus he took was one going in the other direction, away from the city. He rode to the end of the line.

Just to be alone—it was wonderful. Nobody nagging at him, no need to watch the time. He'd never been in the suburb where the bus landed him. For a while he just walked around, admiring houses and gardens—the sort of places he'd once dreamed of living in himself, when he and Kate were first married. Perhaps if they'd had any kids to be ambitious for, or if Kate hadn't turned into the slatternly shrew she'd become—

By noon he was tired of walking. He went back to the little business district and had a hamburger and coffee at a half-deserted lunchroom. While he was there he asked about the bus schedule. Just so he got back home at the regular time, Kate would never know and have something new to yell at him about. No danger she'd phone him at the store; she knew they wouldn't call him off the floor except for an emergency. He bought a pack of cigarettes and a magazine and struck off along a promising road leading beyond the town.

It was more than an hour before he found what he wanted—a friendly little wood with a brook running through it and a sunny clearing by the side of an unfrequented road where he could sit on a fallen tree-stump and read and smoke and let the peace and silence seep into his nerves. Dotted around in the near distance were the tops of tree-hidden houses on the hill, but none of them was near enough to matter. Only an occasional car passed in either direction, and nobody noticed him in his snug sanctuary. It was very quiet; presently he dozed off.

He awoke with a start, and looked first at the sun and then at his watch. It was 4:40; he had plenty of time to catch the bus. He stood up and stretched, debating whether to walk on a bit farther or turn around and saunter slowly back to the bus stop.

Up the road, in the silence, he heard a shuffling in dry leaves. He peered out, and saw a girl in her early teens coming toward him on the opposite side of the road. He stood back, waiting till she had passed; it might scare the kid to see a strange man suddenly emerge from the woods. Leaning against a tree, he stood watching her.

She was a pretty girl, with long golden hair falling over the collar of her red sweater. She wore a dark blue skirt, red socks, and brown leather scuffs, and under her arm were a few schoolbooks. She was singing to herself as she walked, in a clear, thin, childish voice. Pretty late for her to be coming home from school, but she might have stayed for some student get-together. Probably she lived in one of the houses whose roofs showed above the trees; there must be short cuts up to the hill to them.

She passed him now and he waited for her to go out of sight around a curve in the road. Then he heard a car coming, slowly, from behind them, in the same direction she was walking.

It was a rattletrap old black coupe, with only the driver in it.

Larsen caught a glimpse of him—a heavy-set man of about his own age, with a shock of dark hair, and no hat. The car passed him too, and Larsen stepped out onto the road and turned toward the town. Belatedly he thought he could have hailed the car and perhaps got a lift to the bus stop.

The girl was now about a hundred feet away, just nearing the curve. The car had caught up with her. It stopped.

Everything happened so suddenly Larsen could not collect his wits, which were dulled from his unaccustomed nap.

The driver jumped out, said something to the girl, and she shook her head. He grabbed her by the shoulder, hustled her toward the car. She struggled and started to scream; he clamped one hand over her mouth. He dragged her in, got in after her, slammed the door. She jumped up—perhaps she saw Larsen now, where he stood paralyzed with bewilderment—reached for the door handle, tried again to scream. The man struck her twice, knocking her to the floor. Then he took the wheel and drove rapidly away. By the time Larsen, shaking himself from his stupor, had run to the curve, the car and its occupants were out of sight. He had not noticed the license number.

All the way back to the suburban town he pondered what he should do. It was his duty, he knew, to hunt out whatever police the town possessed and report what he had seen. But that would involve explaining why he himself was there, giving his name and address, appearing later as a witness if he had seen a crime committed and the man were caught. Then Sims would know he had lied about his absence from work. Kate would know too. Sims would probably fire him. Kate would make his life an even worse hell on earth. He might never get another job, even one as poor as this one, at his age. He had no money saved, and they were in debt for half the things in the house.

John Larsen had a clear, horrifying view of what he would be letting himself in for if he reported the incident.

He didn't really know the circumstances. The man might even be the girl's father. She might have been playing hooky, just as he had done, or have been disobeying some parental command. What he had witnessed might have been only severe but lawful punishment for some youthful misdemeanor.

Besides, what good could he do? He couldn't actually identify the man—he'd caught just a passing glimpse of him, could never pick him out in any assortment of heavy middle-aged men with thick dark hair. He would only be getting himself into a mess he'd never get out of, and for nothing at all.

He reached the town with time to spare, without catching sight or sound again of the black car; there were byroads all the way, any of which it could have taken. To pacify his conscience, he looked around for a policeman in the business district, but there was no sign of one. Stifling his uneasiness, he took the next bus, found it would land him in the city too early, got off about half-way, and waited for the following one. He reached home at the usual time, and, as usual, found that Kate didn't have dinner ready. He sat grumpily reading the evening paper, while she complained and scolded at him from the kitchen. They never asked each other for news of their day; there was never anything to tell that would interest either of them.

He had sense enough the next morning to tell Sims that the doctor had said it was merely a touch of lumbago, and that the rest had about fixed it. When he saw Sims's eyes on him he remembered occasionally to grimace and rub his back. By luck he sold a woman a big length of old-fashioned stair-carpeting they'd been trying to get rid of for months. Sims showed his gratification by saying good night and hoping Larsen's back would be better soon. He didn't, however, forget to dock him for the day off. That meant Larsen would have to skip lunches all next week; he couldn't let Kate know his pay was short.

When he stopped to get the paper, two evenings later, there was a picture on the first page. *Have You Seen This Girl?* the caption said. He recognized her instantly. The clothing they described was the same she had worn.

Her name was Diane Morrison, and she was the daughter of the principal of Belleville Consolidated Junior High School, where she was a first-year student. Usually her father drove her to and from school. On Tuesday she had waited for him till half-past four, then he found he would be tied up for another hour at least; so, as had sometimes happened in the past, the father told her she'd better walk the mile or so home and tell her mother he'd be late. When he got there about six she hadn't appeared. She was a reliable child who would have phoned if she had stopped off anywhere. Her parents had searched all the way back to the school and had called all her friends. But nobody had seen Diane. And nobody had seen her since.

Because there was a possibility of kidnaping, the F.B.I. had come into the case. They and the State and county police were combing the woods and hills around Belleville. So far they had found no trace or clue.

"For mercy's sake," Kate snapped, "can't you open your mouth except to eat? Never a word out of you, just wool-gathering. Here I am, cooped up all day long, and you come home and act like I was a piece of furniture or something. How do you think I—"

He let her rave. He was trying to decide. Should he or shouldn't he? Would it help at all if he did? They might spot the man if he described him. But then where would John Larsen be? In the worst trouble of his life.

He glanced at Kate and almost considered telling her the truth and asking her advice. Then he reconsidered, quailing at how she would take it. And he knew what her advice would be—keep out of it and don't get us into an even deeper jam than you've risked getting us into already. Let the police do their own work—that's what they're paid for.

He began buying a morning paper as well as an evening one, forcing himself, with a cold fear at the pit of his stomach, to search them for news.

A week later, under a covering of gravel in an abandoned quarry, they found her body. Her skull had been fractured in three places by some heavy instrument like a tire iron. She was covered with cuts and bruises, and she had been violated. Clutched in her right hand was a man's handkerchief, red-and-white checked.

John Larsen lay awake all night, with Kate breathing heavily beside him. By the time the window was turning gray, he had decided to let it go a while longer. He recalled crime stories he had read; there would be fragments of flesh under the girl's fingernails, the scientific cops would find minute threads and hairs on her clothing, they would go over the cars of all possible suspects for fingerprints. In a little place like Belleville they would soon get on to the dark-haired man, unless he was a stranger from some other place.

It was the purest chance that Larsen had witnessed the abduction. Suppose he *hadn't* been there—then they would have had to investigate just as they were doing now. He saw himself trying to explain to some incredulous F.B.I. man just what he was doing on a road near Belleville when he ought to have been at work in the city. Looking back now, his whole day of playing hooky seemed unbelievable childishness. Nobody would understand; they'd be sure he was lying. Why, they might think he'd made up the story just to protect himself. They might put him through a third degree. Lying there in bed, his flesh crawled. And he'd be ruined. The only thing to do was to pretend to himself that that day had never happened. They'd find the man soon, anyway—they always did. And then he'd be glad he'd had the sense to let bad enough alone.

When, three days later, he saw the headline, *Morrison Suspect Captured*, his relief was so great that tears came to his eyes. Standing in the bus, he read the story avidly.

The man arrested was an assistant janitor at the high school. His name was Joseph Kennelly. He had been under suspicion from the beginning, the story said. He knew the girl by sight, of course. He was unmarried, and lived alone in a two-room shack near the quarry where the body had been found. And he had a police record —not involving sex crimes, but a long series of arrests for disorderly conduct and for driving while drunk. He had spent part of his boyhood in a home for retarded children.

The police theory was that he had seen the girl leave school late, when his own hours of duty were over. There was no question that he had shown an unwholesome interest in her; now, when it was too late, boy students related how Joe had made vulgar cracks about Diane's golden hair and budding figure. He was a slipshod worker, on bad terms with the school principal, and had been in trouble more than once drinking on the job; Mr. Morrison had threatened to have him fired. So the motives for the crime were clear—revenge and lust.

And the handkerchief was his—a laundry mark proved it. Moreover, he had a deep scratch, a week or two old, on the left side of his jaw.

He denied everything heatedly, of course. He had driven home that day as always, he said, and hadn't left his shack till he went to work the next morning. He hadn't even seen Diane—or anyone else. A nearly empty bottle of whiskey was found in the broom closet at the school, and Kennelly acknowledged he'd been feeling pretty high by the time he left. At home he'd gone on drinking, had passed out about ten o'clock, and hadn't wakened till dawn.

Nobody could be found who had noticed him, at the school or elsewhere, between four o'clock Tuesday afternoon and nine Wednesday morning.

As for the handkerchief, he admitted it was his, but he claimed he had lost it somewhere, weeks before. The murderer must have been the one who found it. The scratch? Why, the morning after that big drunk he had been so shaky that he had done it himself while he was trying to shave.

So far, so good: John Larsen read the account with thankfulness that he had let things take their course. Then his heart plummeted like a cannon ball.

Joseph Kennelly was twenty-six years old. His picture showed a tall, skinny young man with lightish hair receding at the temples. And his car was a dark blue sedan.

Larsen reached his home, walking from the bus like an automaton. He threw the paper and his hat on the nearest chair, went into the bathroom, and locked the door: it was the only room in the house where he could be alone to think. "That you, John?" Kate called; then she saw where he had gone and returned to the kitchen. Dinner was just begun, as usual; he often wondered what on earth she did with herself all day. Sat glued to the TV set, probably, just as she used to sit glued to the radio.

Perched on the toilet seat, Larsen wrestled with his conscience. There was no use telling himself any more that his evidence didn't matter. He had seen Diane Morrison kidnaped, he had seen her kidnaper, and it was not Joseph Kennelly.

He couldn't phone from home—Kate would be on his neck at once. He must make some kind of excuse to call from outside. He played again with the idea of telling her. No, that was hopeless; he knew Kate.

She tried the doorknob.

"For gosh sake," she called, "what you got the door locked for? You sick or something?"

"I'm all right," he mumbled, and turned the key.

"I never saw such a man! Never a word out of you when you come home—you might think you didn't have a wife. I'm just a servant around here, to make your meals and look after you. Locking yourself in, like I was a stranger! Here I am, all day alone, working my fingers off—"

"What do you want me to talk about? I'm tired."

"And maybe *I'm* not, huh?"

"Let's not fight, Kate," he said easily. An inspiration came to him. "I've got a fierce headache. If dinner isn't ready, I think I'll walk down to the drug store and get something for it."

"Wait till you've eaten," she said, placated. "That'll make you feel better." She made a conscious effort to achieve a friendly tone. "I was just looking at the paper. Gee, that's awful about that kid, isn't it? I'm glad they got the man. People like that ought to be fried in oil."

"How do you know he's the right one?" he couldn't keep himself from asking.

Kate flared up instantly.

"Well, so I guess you know more than the police, Mr. Smarty! If he wasn't the one did it, why'd they arrest him? They don't arrest anybody till they've got the goods on 'em—anybody can tell you that."

"I guess so," he said feebly, and started to set the table before she told him to.

He did have a headache, and no wonder. Kate's words started him thinking again. She was wrong; they *had* arrested an innocent man. But by that very token, they could never convict him. His mind flitted to the police laboratories he had read about. The hairs and fibers from the girl's clothing would belong to another man, burly middle-aged man with thick dark hair, whoever he was. There were doubtless lots of other scientific findings he knew nothing about, and they'd all point away from Kennelly. The janitor might be indicted by the grand jury on what they got, but he'd never come to trial—they were sure to find the man who really did it.

And without John Larsen's sticking his fool neck out, to no end but his own ruin.

He didn't go out to phone.

The grand jury did indict Kennelly, and he was held without bail in the county jail. Larsen thought about him a good deal, though the sharp impact of that terrible day was growing dimmer. Tough luck for the guy, to be in prison all this time for something he didn't do. But from all acounts he was no good anyway, and a good scare might straighten him out. Any time now they would find they didn't have enough to try him on, or something would turn up that would lead them to the real criminal—though Larsen realized they wouldn't be looking very hard for any other suspect while they thought they had the guilty man.

Kennelly had a good lawyer—a prosperous uncle had turned up from somewhere and was paying the bill. Lawrence Prather, the lawyer's name was; he'd been defense attorney in a number of local murder cases and nearly always got his client off. Kennelly would be sure to be acquitted, if he was ever tried.

The date was set for the trial.

Larsen persuaded himself that if there had been the slightest doubt in his mind of the man's acquittal he would have sacrificed himself and gone to Prather with his story. But there wasn't any doubt. He heard the fellows talking about the case in the store, heard people sometimes in the bus; it was exciting a lot of interest. Everybody predicted Kennelly would go free, though everybody took it for granted he was guilty. Some of them were just cynical about justice; some of them thought you couldn't get a conviction on circumstantial evidence alone.

Sometimes, shivering, John Larsen imagined his interview with the defense lawyer. There would be no point in his going to him if he weren't willing to be a witness. And he could hear the prosecutor cross-examining him at the trial.

"And just how did you happen to be at that particular spot at that particular moment, Mr. Larsen?"

There'd be nobody to back him up; it would be just his word against everybody's. The prosecution might make it out that he was a friend of Kennelly's, or had been bribed to toss in this red herring; that he'd made the whole thing up. They might even suspect or pretend to suspect, that he was covering up not for Kennelly but for himself. The people in that lunchroom could identify him; he'd been in Belleville that afternoon. He'd be cleared, of course; but by that time, with all the notoriety, his goose would be cooked.

He stayed away from Prather's office. Kennelly's trial began in October.

Larsen couldn't go, naturally; he had to work. But he followed every word in print. He couldn't keep his mind on anything else. Sims caught him talking about it to a customer, and got angry. "We want people to think about rugs in here, not murders," he said. "If you can't attend to your work, Larsen—" Larsen apologized humbly and watched his step.

He was amazed and frightened by the public excitement. It took almost a week to get a jury. Kennelly was booed and yelled at as he was taken to and from court. The sex murder of a young girl was the worst crime imaginable, and people wanted somebody punished for it. Larsen shuddered at the thought of daring to deprive them of their prey. It wasn't safe even to say aloud that he believed Joseph Kennelly might be innocent.

As the trial progressed, Larsen began having nightmares. He couldn't eat and was losing weight. Even Kate noticed and nagged him about it. Like everyone else, she was following the trial closely, and every night she wanted to talk it over. She *knew* Kennelly was guilty, and the electric chair was too good for him. If he went free, he ought to be lynched.

"Oh, shut up!" her husband finally shouted at her.

"I suppose you're sorry for him!" she retorted. "Maybe you wish *you* could do something like that and get away with it!"

Larsen went into the bathroom to keep from answering her.

He waited in vain, during the prosecution, for any mention of hairs or textile fibers; apparently either none had been found or they were being ignored because they did not implicate Kennelly. Nobody said anything about fingerprints or bloodstains in the car, either—doubtless for the same reason. An expert witness did prove that fragments of gravel taken from the seams of the defendant's shoes had come from the quarry, but then Kennelly had often visited the place, which was near his own home. If there were no witnesses to prove Kennelly's alibi, neither were there any to disprove it. The boys from the school who testified to his remarks about Diane had only vague generalities to offer. Larsen began to feel the load lifting from him.

But the defense was little more than a formality. Kennelly himself was his only witness, and he made a poor one—confessedly drunk all through the crucial period. No attempt was made to claim Kennelly was insane, as Larsen had hoped for. Prather gave a strong closing speech, pointing out the lack of direct evidence, pleading that no testimony had actually proved his client's guilt.

But then District Attorney Holcombe pulled out all the stops— denouncing the janitor, exposing his sorry record, calling him "a creature in human form, a vile, vicious rat." The most damning thing of all was that handkerchief. "I just don't believe in coincidences like that," said Holcombe sarcastically. "I'll tell you what

I do believe—I believe that poor girl pulled the handkerchief out of Kennelly's pocket while she struggled with him for her honor and her life. And I believe she scratched his face in her feeble attempt to fight back, to escape from the monster who was attacking her."

The audience in the courtroom applauded, and had to be threatened with eviction.

In his charge to the jury Judge Stith tried to be neutral, but the jury could see which way he leaned. They leaned the same way; they remembered vividly the photographs of Diane's pitiful little corpse. Many of them had daughters of their own. Somebody had to be punished for the fiendish crime.

They brought in a verdict of guilty on both counts, kidnaping and murder. It took only three ballots, the foreman told reporters afterward, to bring to their senses a couple of sentimental old fools holding out for a reasonable doubt.

But the judge *can't* condemn him to death, Larsen thought wildly. He can't, just on circumstantial evidence. The man will be given a life sentence at the most, and that means he'll be out on parole eventually. That much won't hurt him, a ne'er-do-well like him.

The judge sentenced Kennelly to the electric chair. He had daughters too.

But there's always an appeal, thought Larsen desperately. The appeal would be granted. Kennelly would have another trial, and by that time the truth would surely have come out.

"For heaven's sake, stop *fussing!*" Kate said a dozen times an evening. "What on earth's the matter with you lately? And you're smoking too much, John. I won't have it—you're spending a fortune on cigarettes!"

The appeal was denied.

The District Attorney told the papers he was pleased. "Death is too good for a human snake like Kennelly," he said.

Prather did not carry the appeal to the State Supreme Court. "No grounds," he explained.

There *were* grounds. Larsen could furnish them.

Twice he got as far as starting to dial Prather's office. Then he realized all that it would mean, and hung up. Wait and see, he told himself. These things drag on for years, one reprieve after another.

"And why have you delayed so long in bringing me this information, Mr. Larsen?" he could hear the defense lawyer saying.

It would be useless to throw himself on the man's mercy, to beg him to follow up the clue and leave John Larsen out of it. Without his testimony the new evidence would mean nothing. It might mean nothing now, anyway. At the very beginning, when Kennelly was first arrested—or before that—it would have been of use. Now he would only involve himself, he kept telling himself, with small chance of helping Kennelly.

If only there were somebody—anybody in the world—to whom he could tell everything, who would advise him and protect him and make things come out right!

Kennelly was in the death row at the State penitentiary. The date for his execution was set for three months away.

Then it was two months.

Then one.

Prather took Kennelly's uncle, his only relative, to the governor. The governor was running for re-election the next November. He wasn't reprieving a man convicted of the sex murder of a teen-age girl.

Then it was one week.

Then it was two days.

John Larsen had lost twenty pounds. He was afraid to sleep; once he screamed in a nightmare and woke Kate. He hardly noticed her nagging any more.

"If you're sick, go to a doctor."

"I'm not sick."

"You think I'm a fool? There's *something* wrong with you. What have you been doing, John?" She cast about for possibilities. "John, you tell me!" Suddenly she burst into tears. "I know what it is, and I ain't going to stand for it. You've got some other woman on your mind! If you think, after twenty-seven years, I'll let you—"

Larsen laughed. It wasn't a pretty sound.

Crazy plans flitted through his brain. He would go to Belleville, he would hunt until he found the dark-haired man, he would force the murderer to confess.

All nonsense.

There was no last-minute reprieve. In his heart Larsen knew he hadn't really expected one. Kennelly went to the chair on schedule, shouting his innocence with his last breath.

Reading every painful word of the newspaper story, John Larsen stood at last face to face with the bare truth.

Perhaps he could not have prevented the murder of the girl—though he might have if he had acted at once. But he had done enough.

He had let a man die, in order to hold on to a job he loathed and a wife he hated. He, John Larsen, had murdered Joseph Kennelly, whom he had never seen, as surely as that unknown man had murdered Diane Morrison.

He was a murderer, and murderers ought to die. But he hadn't had the courage to save Kennelly, and he didn't begin to have the courage to die himself. All he could do was to endure, to the last limit of endurance.

At the sight of his face that evening, Kate's words froze on her lips. He picked at his dinner in silence. Immediately after he went to bed. He slept the clock around in the heavy, dreamless sleep of an exhausted animal.

In the middle of the next morning he was displaying a rug to a customer. Suddenly he dropped it and stiffened.

He began to scream: "I did it! I did it! I did it!"

It took two men to subdue him until the ambulance came . . .

And near Belleville a heavy man with a shock of dark hair, a harmless "character" whom everybody knew and nobody ever noticed, prowled the lonely country roads in his old black car, his eyes alert for a good-looking girl walking alone . . .

Every editor of the previous MWA anthologies was asked to recommend three stories for inclusion in this book. Every editor who had one available recommended a story by Stanley Ellin. We chose "Robert," but we might have chosen any of several others which have become classics in our field. If Mr. Ellin has a problem as a short story writer, it is that his work is so sought after by anthologists and award givers that it is almost impossible to find an Ellin story that a mystery fan does not already know almost by heart.

11

Robert

By Stanley Ellin

The windows of the Sixth Grade classroom were wide open to the June afternoon, and through them came all the sounds of the departing school: the thunder of bus motors warming up, the hiss of gravel under running feet, the voices raised in cynical fervor.

"So we sing all hail to thee,
District Schoo-wull Number Three . . ."

Miss Gildea' flinched a little at the last high, shrill note, and pressed her fingers to her aching forehead. She was tired, more tired than she could ever recall being in her thirty-eight years of teaching, and, as she told herself, she had reason to be. It had not been a good term, not good at all, what with the size of the class, and the Principal's insistence on new methods, and then her mother's shocking death coming right in the middle of everything.

Perhaps she had been too close to her mother, Miss Gildea thought; perhaps she had been wrong, never taking into account that some day the old lady would have to pass on and leave her alone in the world. Well, thinking about it all the time didn't make it any easier. She should try to forget.

And, of course, to add to her troubles, there had been during the past few weeks this maddening business of Robert. He had been a perfectly nice boy, and then, out of a clear sky, had become impossible. Not bothersome or noisy really, but sunk into an endless daydream from which Miss Gildea had to sharply jar him a dozen times a day.

She turned her attention to Robert who sat alone in the room at the desk immediately before hers, a thin boy with neatly combed, colorless hair bracketed between large ears; mild blue eyes in a pale face fixed solemnly on hers.

"Robert."

"Yes, Miss Gildea."

"Do you know why I told you to remain after school, Robert?"

He frowned thoughtfully at this, as if it were some lesson he was being called on for, but had failed to memorize properly.

"I suppose for being bad," he said, at last.

Miss Gildea sighed.

"No, Robert, that's not it at all. I know a bad boy when I see one, Robert, and you aren't one like that. But I do know there's something troubling you, something on your mind, and I think I can help you."

"There's nothing bothering me, Miss Gildea. Honest, there isn't."

Miss Gildea found the silver pencil thrust into her hair and tapped it in a nervous rhythm on her desk.

"Oh, come, Robert. During the last month every time I looked at you your mind was a million miles away. Now, what is it? Just making plans for vacation, or, perhaps, some trouble with the boys?"

"I'm not having trouble with anybody, Miss Gildea."

"You don't seem to understand, Robert, that I'm not trying to punish you for anything. Your homework is good. You've managed to keep up with the class, but I do think your inattentiveness should be explained. What, for example, were you thinking this afternoon when I spoke to you directly for five minutes, and you didn't hear a word I said?"

"Nothing, Miss Gildea."

She brought the pencil down sharply on the desk. "There must have been *something*, Robert. Now, I insist that you think back, and try to explain yourself."

Looking at his impassive face she knew that somehow she herself had been put on the defensive, that if any means of graceful retreat were offered now she would gladly take it. Thirty-eight years, she thought grimly, and I'm still trying to play mother-hen to ducklings. Not that there wasn't a bright side to the picture. Thirty-eight years passed meant only two more to go before retirement, the half-salary pension, the chance to putter around the house, tend to the garden properly. The pension wouldn't buy you furs and diamonds, sure enough, but it could buy the right to enjoy your own home for the rest of your days instead of a dismal room in the County Home for Old Ladies. Miss Gildea had visited the County Home once, on an instructional visit, and preferred not to think about it.

"Well, Robert," she said wearily, "have you remembered what you were thinking?"

"Yes, Miss Gildea."

"What was it?"

"I'd rather not tell, Miss Gildea."

"I insist!"

"Well," Robert said gently, "I was thinking I wished you were dead, Miss Gildea. I was thinking I wished I could kill you."

Her first reaction was simply blank incomprehension. She had been standing not ten feet away when that car had skidded up on the sidewalk and crushed her mother's life from her, and Miss Gildea had neither screamed nor fainted. She had stood there dumbly, because of the very unreality of the thing. Just the way she stood in court where they explained that the man got a year in jail, but didn't have a dime to pay for the tragedy he had brought about. And now the orderly ranks of desks before her, the expanse of blackboard around her, and Robert's face in the midst of it all were no more real. She found herself rising from her chair, walking toward Robert who shrank back, his eyes wide and panicky, his elbow half-lifted as if to ward off a blow.

"Do you understand what you've just said?" Miss Gildea demanded hoarsely.

"No, Miss Gildea! Honest, I didn't mean anything."

She shook her head unbelievingly. "Whatever made you say it? Whatever in the world could make a boy say a thing like that, such a wicked, terrible thing!"

"You wanted to know! You kept asking me!"

The sight of that protective elbow raised against her cut as deep as the incredible words had.

"Put that arm down!" Miss Gildea said shrilly, and then struggled to get her voice under control. "In all my years I've never struck a child, and I don't intend to start now!"

Robert dropped his arm and clasped his hands together on his desk, and Miss Gildea looking at the pinched white knuckles realized with surprise that her own hands were shaking uncontrollably. "But if you think this little matter ends here, young-feller-me-lad," she said, "you've got another thought coming. You get your things together, and we're marching right up to Mr. Harkness. He'll be very much interested in all this."

Mr. Harkness was the Principal. He had arrived only the term before, and but for his taste in eyeglasses (the large, black-rimmed kind which, Miss Gildea privately thought, looked actorish) and his predilection for the phrase "modern pedagogical methods" was, in her opinion, a rather engaging young man.

He looked at Robert's frightened face and then at Miss Gildea's pursed lips. "Well," he said pleasantly, "what seems to be the trouble here?"

"That," said Miss Gildea, "is something I think Robert should tell you about."

She placed a hand on Robert's shoulder, but he pulled away and backed slowly toward Mr. Harkness, his breath coming in loud, shuddering sobs, his eyes riveted on Miss Gildea as if she were the only thing in the room beside himself. Mr. Harkness put an arm around Robert and frowned at Miss Gildea.

"Now, what's behind all this, Miss Gildea? The boy seems frightened to death."

Miss Gildea found herself sick of it all, anxious to get out of the room, away from Robert. "That's enough, Robert," she commanded. "Just tell Mr. Harkness exactly what happened."

"I said the boy was frightened to death, Miss Gildea," Mr. Harkness said brusquely. "We'll talk about it as soon as he understands we're his friends. Won't we, Robert?"

Robert shook his head vehemently. "I didn't do anything bad! Miss Gildea said I didn't do anything bad!"

"Well, then!" said Mr. Harkness triumphantly. "There's nothing to be afraid of, is there?"

Robert shook his head again. "She said I had to stay in after school."

Mr. Harkness glanced sharply at Miss Gildea. "I suppose he missed the morning bus, is that it? And after I said in a directive that the staff was to make allowances—"

"Robert doesn't use a bus," Miss Gildea protested. "Perhaps I'd better explain all this, Mr. Harkness. You see—"

"I think Robert's doing very well," Mr. Harkness said, and tightened his arm around Robert who nodded shakily.

"She kept me in," he said, "and then when we were alone she came up close to me and she said, "I know what you're thinking. You're thinking you'd like to see me dead! You're thinking you'd like to kill me, aren't you?"

Robert's voice had dropped to an eerie whisper that bound Miss Gildea like a spell. It was broken only when she saw the expression on Mr. Harkness' face.

"Why, that's a lie!" she cried. "That's the most dreadful lie I ever heard any boy dare—"

Mr. Harkness cut in abruptly. "Miss Gildea! I *insist* you let the boy finish what he has to say."

Miss Gildea's voice fluttered. "It seems to me, Mr. Harkness, that he has been allowed to say quite enough already!"

"Has he?" Mr. Harkness asked.

"Robert has been inattentive lately, especially so this afternoon. After class I asked him what he had been thinking about, and he dared to say he was thinking how he wished I were dead! How he wanted to kill me!"

"Robert said that?"

"In almost those exact words. And I can tell you, Mr. Harkness, that I was shocked, terribly shocked, especially since Robert always seemed like such a nice boy."

"His record—?"

"His record is quite good. It's just—"

"And his social conduct?" asked Mr. Harkness in the same level voice.

"As far as I know, he gets along with the other children well enough."

"But for some reason," persisted Mr. Harkness, "you found him annoying you."

Robert raised his voice. "I didn't! Miss Gildea said I didn't do anything bad. And I always liked her. I like her better than *any* teacher!"

Miss Gildea fumbled blindly in her hair for the silver pencil, and failed to find it. She looked around the floor distractedly.

"Yes?" said Mr. Harkness.

"My pencil," said Miss Gildea on the verge of tears. "It's gone."

"Surely, Miss Gildea," said Mr. Harkness in a tone of mild exasperation. "This is not quite the moment—"

"It was very valuable," Miss Gildea tried to explain hopelessly. "It was my mother's." In the face of Mr. Harkness' stony surveillance she knew she must look a complete mess. Hems crooked, nose red, hair all disheveled. "I'm all upset, Mr. Harkness. It's been a long term and now all this right at the end of it. I don't know what to say."

Mr. Harkness' face fell into sympathetic lines.

"That's quite all right, Miss Gildea. I know how you feel. Now, if you want to leave, I think Robert and I should have a long, friendly talk."

"If you don't mind—"

"No, no," Mr. Harkness said heartily. "As a matter of fact, I think that would be the best thing all around."

After he had seen her out he closed the door abruptly behind her, and Miss Gildea walked heavily up the stairway and down the corridor to the Sixth-Grade room. The silver pencil was there on the floor at Robert's desk, and she picked it up and carefully polished it with her handkerchief. Then she sat down at her desk with the handkerchief to her nose and wept soundlessly for ten minutes.

That night when the bitter taste of humiliation had grown faint enough to permit it, Miss Gildea reviewed the episode with all the honesty at her command. Honesty with oneself had always been a major point in her credo, had, in fact, been passed on through succeeding classes during the required lesson on The Duties of an American Citizen, when Miss Gildea, to sum up the lesson, would recite: "This above all, To thine ownself be true . . ." while thumping her fist on her desk as an accompaniment to each syllable.

Hamlet, of course, was not in the syllabus of the Sixth Grade whose reactions over the years never deviated from a mixed bewilderment and indifference. But Miss Gildea, after some prodding of the better minds into a discussion of the lines, would rest content with the knowledge that she had sown good seed on what, she prayed, was fertile ground.

Reviewing the case of Robert now, with her emotions under control, she came to the unhappy conclusion that it was she who had committed the injustice. The child had been ordered to stay after school, something that to him could mean only a punishment. He had been ordered to disclose some shadowy, childlike thoughts that had drifted through his mind hours before, and, unable to do so, either had to make up something out of the whole cloth, or blurt out the immediate thought in his immature mind.

It was hardly unusual, reflected Miss Gildea sadly, for a child badgered by a teacher to think what Robert had; she could well remember her own feelings toward a certain pompadoured harridan who still haunted her dreams. And the only conclusion to be drawn, unpleasant though it was, was that Robert, and not she, had truly put into practice those beautiful words from Shakespeare.

It was this, as well as the sight of his pale accusing face before her while she led the class through the morning session next day, which prompted her to put Robert in charge of refilling the water pitcher during recess. The duties of the water pitcher monitor were to leave the playground a little before the rest of the class and clean and refill the pitcher on her desk, but since the task was regarded as an honor by the class, her gesture, Miss Gildea felt with some self-approval, carried exactly the right note of conciliation.

She was erasing the blackboard at the front of the room near the end of the recess when she heard Robert approaching her desk, but much as she wanted to she could not summon up courage enough to turn and face him. As if, she thought, he were the teacher, and I were afraid of him. And she could feel her cheeks grow warm at the thought.

He re-entered the room on the sound of the bell that marked the end of recess, and this time Miss Gildea plopped the eraser firmly into its place beneath the blackboard and turned to look at him. "Thank you very much, Robert," she said as he set the pitcher down and neatly capped it with her drinking glass.

"You're welcome, Miss Gildea," Robert said politely. He drew a handkerchief from his pocket, wiped his hands with it, then smiled gently at Miss Gildea. "I bet you think I put poison or something into that water," he said gravely, "but I wouldn't do anything like that, Miss Gildea. Honest, I wouldn't."

Miss Gildea gasped, then reached out a hand toward Robert's shoulder. She withdrew it hastily when he shrank away with the familiar panicky look in his eyes.

"Why did you say that, Robert?" Miss Gildea demanded in a terrible voice. "That was plain impudence, wasn't it? You thought you were being smart, didn't you?"

At that moment the rest of the class surged noisily into the room, but Miss Gildea froze them into silence with a commanding wave of the hand. Out of the corner of her eye she noted the cluster of shocked and righteous faces allied with her in condemnation, and she felt a quick little sense of triumph in her position.

"I was talking to you, Robert," she said. "What do you have to say for yourself?"

Robert took another step backward and almost tumbled over a school-bag left carelessly in the aisle. He caught himself, then stood there helplessly, his eyes never leaving Miss Gildea's.

"Well, Robert!"

He shook his head wildly. "I didn't do it!" he cried. "I didn't put anything in your water, Miss Gildea! I told you I didn't!"

Without looking Miss Gildea knew that the cluster of accusing faces had swung toward her now, felt her triumph turn to a sick bewilderment inside her. It was as if Robert, with his teary eyes and pale, frightened face and too-large ears had turned into a strange jelly-like creature that could not be pinned down and put in its place. As if he were retreating further and further down some dark, twisting path, and leading her on with him. And, she thought desperately, she had to pull herself free before she did something dreadful, something unforgivable.

She couldn't take the boy to Mr. Harkness again. Not only did the memory of that scene in his office the day before make her shudder, but a repeated visit would be an admission that after thirty-eight years of teaching she was not up to the mark as a disciplinarian.

But for her sake, if for nothing else, Robert had to be put in his place. With a gesture, Miss Gildea ordered the rest of the class to their seats and turned to Robert who remained standing.

"Robert," said Miss Gildea, "I want an apology for what has just happened."

"I'm sorry, Miss Gildea," Robert said, and it looked as if his eyes would be brimming with tears in another moment.

Miss Gildea hardened her heart to this. "*I apologize, Miss Gildea, and it will not happen again,*" she prompted.

Miraculously, Robert contained his tears. "I apologize, Miss Gildea, and it will not happen again," he muttered and dropped limply into his seat.

"Well!" said Miss Gildea, drawing a deep breath as she looked around at the hushed class. "Perhaps that will be a lesson to us all."

The classroom work did not go well after that, but, as Miss Gildea told herself, there were only a few days left to the end of the term, and after that, praise be, there was the garden, the comfortable front porch of the old house to share with neighbors in the summer evenings, and then next term a new set of faces in the classroom, with Robert's not among them.

Later, closing the windows of the room after the class had left, Miss Gildea was brought up short by the sight of a large group gathered on the sidewalk near the parked busses. It was Robert, she saw, surrounded by most of the Sixth Grade, and obviously the center of interest. He was nodding emphatically when she put her face to the window, and she drew back quickly at the sight, moved by some queer sense of guilt.

Only a child, she assured herself, *he's only a child,* but that thought did not in any way dissolve the anger against him that stuck like a lump in her throat.

That was on Thursday. By Tuesday of the next week, the final week of the term, Miss Gildea was acutely conscious of the oppressive atmosphere lying over the classroom. Ordinarily, the awareness of impending vacation acted on the class like a violent agent dropped into some inert liquid. There would be ferment and seething beneath the surface, manifested by uncontrollable giggling and whispering, and this would grow more and more turbulent until all restraint and discipline was swept away in the general upheaval of excitement and good spirits.

That, Miss Gildea thought, was the way it always had been, but it was strangely different now. The Sixth Grade, down to the most irrepressible spirits in it, acted as if it had been turned to a set of robots before her startled eyes. Hands tightly clasped on desks, eyes turned toward her with an almost frightening intensity, the class responded to her mildest requests as if they were shouted commands. And when she walked down the aisles between them, one and all seemed to have adopted Robert's manner of shrinking away fearfully at her approach.

Miss Gildea did not like to think of what all this might mean, but valiantly forced herself to do so. Can it mean, she asked herself, that all think as Robert does, are choosing this way of showing it? And, if they knew how cruel it was, would they do it?

Other teachers, Miss Gildea knew, sometimes took problems such as this to the Teacher's Room where they could be studied and answered by those who saw them in an objective light. It might be that the curious state of the Sixth Grade was being duplicated in other classes. Perhaps, she herself was imagining the whole thing, or, frightening thought, looking back, as people will when they grow old, on the sort of past that never really did exist. Why, in that case—and Miss Gildea had to laugh at herself with a faint merriment—she would just find herself reminiscing about her thirty-eight years of teaching to some bored young woman who didn't have the fraction of experience she did.

But underneath the current of these thoughts, Miss Gildea knew there was one honest reason for not going to the Teacher's Room this last week of the term. She had received no gifts, not one. And the spoils from each grade heaped high in a series of pyramids against the wall. The boxes of fractured cookies, the clumsily wrapped jars of preserves, the scarves, the stockings, the handkerchiefs, infinite, endless boxes of handkerchiefs, all were there to mark the triumph of each teacher. And Miss Gildea, who in all her years at District School Number Three had been blushingly proud of the way her pyramid was highest at the end of each term, had not yet received a single gift from the Sixth-Grade class.

After the class was dismissed that afternoon, however, the spell was broken. Only a few of her pupils still loitered in the hallway near the door, Miss Gildea noted, but Robert remained in his seat. Then, as she gathered together her belongings, Robert approached her with a box outheld in his hand. It was, from its shape, a box of candy, and, as Miss Gildea could tell from the wrapping, expensive candy. Automatically, she reached a hand out, then stopped herself short. He'll never make up to me for what he's done, she told herself furiously; I'll never let him.

"Yes, Robert?" she said coolly.

"It's a present for you, Miss Gildea," Robert said, and then as Miss Gildea watched in fascination he began to strip the wrappings from it. He laid the paper neatly on the desk and lifted the cover of the box to display the chocolates within. "My mother said that's the biggest box they had," he said wistfully. "Don't you even want them, Miss Gildea?"

Miss Gildea weakened despite herself. "Did you think I would, after what's happened, Robert?" she asked.

Robert reflected a moment. "Well," he said at last, "if you want me to, I'll eat one right in front of you, Miss Gildea."

Miss Gildea recoiled as if at a faraway warning. *Don't let him say any more*, something inside her cried; *he's only playing a trick, another horrible trick*, and then she was saying, "Why would I want you to do that, Robert?"

"So you'll see they're not poison or anything, Miss Gildea," Robert said. "Then you'll believe it, won't you, Miss Gildea?"

She had been prepared. Even before he said the words, she had felt her body drawing itself tighter and tighter against what she knew was coming. But the sound of the words themselves only served to release her like a spring coiled too tightly.

"You little monster!" sobbed Miss Gildea and struck wildly at the proffered box which flew almost to the far wall, while chocolates cascaded stickily around the room. "How dare you!" she cried. "How dare you!" and her small bony fists beat at Robert's cowering shoulders and back as he tried to retreat.

He half turned in the aisle, slipped on a piece of chocolate, and went down to his knees, but before he could recover himself Miss Gildea was on him again, her lips drawn back, her fists pummeling him as if they were a pair of tireless mallets. Robert had started to scream at the top of his lungs from the first blow, but it was no more than a remote buzzing in Miss Gildea's ears.

"Miss Gildea!"

That was Mr. Harkness' voice, she knew, and those must be Mr. Harkness' hands which pulled her away so roughly that she had to keep herself from falling by clutching at her desk. She stood there weakly, feeling the wild fluttering of her heart, feeling the sick churning of shame and anguish in her while she tried to bring the room into focus again. There was the knot of small excited faces peering through the open doorway, they must have called Mr. Harkness, Mr. Harkness himself listening to Robert who talked and wept alternately, and there was a mess everywhere. Of course, thought Miss Gildea dazedly, those must be chocolate stains. Chocolate stains all over my lovely clean room.

Then Robert was gone, the faces at the door were gone, and the door itself was closed behind them. Only Mr. Harkness remained, and Miss Gildea watched him as he removed his glasses, cleaned them carefully, and then held them up at arm's length and studied them before settling them once more on his nose.

"Well, Miss Gildea," said Mr. Harkness as if he were speaking to the glasses rather than to her, "this is a serious business."

Miss Gildea nodded.

"I am sick," Mr. Harkness said quietly, "really sick at the thought that somewhere in this school, where I tried to introduce decent pedagogical standards, corporal punishment is still being practised."

"That's not fair at all, Mr. Harkness," Miss Gildea said shakily. "I hit the boy, that's true, and I know I was wrong to do it, but that is the first time in all my life I raised a finger against any child. And if you knew my feelings—"

"Ah," said Mr. Harkness, "that's exactly what I would like to know, Miss Gildea." He nodded to her chair, and she sat down weakly. "Now, just go ahead and explain everything as you saw it."

It was a difficult task, made even more difficult by the fact that Mr. Harkness chose to stand facing the window. Forced to address his back this way, Miss Gildea found that she had the sensation of speaking in a vacuum, but she mustered the facts as well as she could, presented them with strong emotion, and then sank back in the chair quite exhausted.

Mr. Harkness remained silent for a long while, then slowly turned to face Miss Gildea. "I am not a practising psychiatrist," he said at last, "although as an educator I have, of course, taken a considerable interest in that field. But I do not think it needs a practitioner to tell what a clear-cut and obvious case I am facing here. Nor," he added sympathetically, "what a tragic one."

"It might simply be," suggested Miss Gildea, "that Robert—"

"I am not speaking about Robert," said Mr. Harkness soberly, quietly.

It took an instant for this to penetrate, and then Miss Gildea felt the blood run cold in her.

"Do you think I'm lying about all this?" she cried incredulously. "Can you possibly—"

"I am sure," Mr. Harkness replied soothingly, "that you were describing things exactly as you saw them, Miss Gildea. But—have you ever heard the phrase 'persecution complex'? Do you think you could recognize the symptoms of that condition if they were presented objectively? I can, Miss Gildea, I assure you, I can."

Miss Gildea struggled to speak, but the words seemed to choke her. "No," she managed to say, "you couldn't! Because some mischievous boy chooses to make trouble—"

"Miss Gildea, no child of eleven, however mischievous, could draw the experiences Robert has described to me out of his imagination. He has discussed these experiences with me at length; now I have heard your side of the case. And the conclusions to be drawn, I must say, are practically forced on me."

The room started to slip out of focus again, and Miss Gildea frantically tried to hold it steady.

"But that just means you're taking his word against mine!" she said fiercely.

"Unfortunately, Miss Gildea, not his word alone. Last week end, a delegation of parents met the School Board and made it quite plain that they were worried because of what their children told them of your recent actions. A dozen children in your class described graphically at that meeting how you had accused them of trying to poison your drinking water, and how you had threatened them because of this. And Robert, it may interest you to know, was not even one of them.

"The School Board voted your dismissal then and there, Miss Gildea, but in view of your long years of service it was left for me to override that decision if I wished to on my sole responsibility. After this episode, however, I cannot see that I have any choice. I must do what is best."

"Dismissal?" said Miss Gildea vaguely. "But they can't. I only have two more years to go. They can't do that, Mr. Harkness; all they're trying to do is trick me out of my pension!"

"Believe me," said Mr. Harkness gently, "they're not trying to do anything of the sort, Miss Gildea. Nobody in the world is trying to hurt you. I give you my solemn word that the only thing which has entered into consideration of this case from first to last has been the welfare of the children."

The room swam in sunlight, but under it Miss Gildea's face was gray and lifeless. She reached forward to fill her glass with water, stopped short, and seemed to gather herself together with a sudden brittle determination. "I'll just have to speak to the Board myself," she said in a high breathless voice. "That's the only thing to do, go there and explain the whole thing to them!"

"That would not help," said Mr. Harkness pityingly. "Believe me, Miss Gildea, it would not."

Miss Gildea left her chair and came to him, her eyes wide and frightened. She laid a trembling hand on his arm and spoke eagerly, quickly, trying to make him understand. "You see," she said, "that means I won't get my pension. I must have two more years for that, don't you see? There's the payment on the house, the garden—no, the garden is part of the house, really—but without the pension—"

She was pulling furiously at his arm with every phrase as if she could drag him bodily into a comprehension of her words, but he stood unyielding and only shook his head pityingly. "You must control yourself, Miss Gildea," he pleaded. "You're not yourself, and it's impossible—"

"No!" she cried in a strange voice. "No!"

When she pulled away he knew almost simultaneously what she intended to do, but the thought froze him to the spot, and when he moved it was too late. He burst into the corridor through the door she had flung open, and almost threw himself down the stairway to the main hall. The door to the street was just swinging shut and he ran toward it, one hand holding the rim of his glasses, a sharp little pain digging into his side, but before he could reach the door he heard the screech of brakes, the single agonized scream, and the horrified shout of a hundred shrill voices.

He put his hand on the door, but could not find the strength to open it. A few minutes later, a cleaning woman had to sidle around him to get outside and see what all the excitement was about.

Miss Reardon, the substitute, took the Sixth Grade the next day, and, everything considered, handled it very well. The single ripple in the even current of the session came at its very start when Miss Reardon explained her presence by referring to the "sad accident that happened to dear Miss Gildea." The mild hubbub which followed this contained several voices, notably in the back of the room, which protested plaintively, "It was *not* an accident, Miss Reardon; she ran right in front of that bus," but Miss Reardon quickly brought order to the room with a few sharp raps of her ruler, and after that, classwork was carried on in a pleasant and orderly fashion.

Robert walked home slowly that afternoon, swinging his school-bag placidly at his side, savoring the June warmth soaking into him, the fresh green smell in the air, the memory of Miss Reardon's understanding face so often turned toward his in eager and friendly interest. His home was identical with all the others on the block, square white boxes with small lawns before them, and its only distinction was that all its blinds were drawn down. After he had closed the front door very quietly behind him, he set his schoolbag down in the hallway, and went into the stuffy half-darkness of the living room.

Robert's father sat in the big armchair in his bathrobe, the way he always did, and Robert's mother was bent over him holding a glass of water.

"No!" Robert's father said. "You just want to get rid of me, but I won't let you! I know what you put into it, and I won't drink it! I'll die before I drink it!"

"Please," Robert's mother said, "please take it. I swear it's only water. I'll drink some myself if you don't believe me." But when she drank a little and then held the glass to his lips, Robert's father only tossed his head from side to side.

Robert stood there watching the scene with fascination, his lips moving in silent mimicry of the familiar words. Then he cleared his throat.

"I'm home, mama," Robert said softly. "Can I have some milk and cookies, please?"

Nedra Tyre has accomplished something seemingly impossible in "Reflections on Murder." She has interwoven a penetrating critical essay on mystery fiction and a frightening tale of death and destiny in a remarkable, and remarkably short, story. This has been done with a magic that retains both her authority as a critic and the suspense and horror of her story.

12

Reflections on Murder

Nedra Tyre

Since you are reading this it is not unlikely that murder interests you. It fascinates me, I confess, and although I can no longer trace the origin of my predilection for death in print it may have begun when I first confronted *The Murder of Roger Ackroyd*. Do you remember the first time that detective fiction held you in thrall and that you realized forever after you would follow it down its labyrinthine ways?

How I wish we might sit facing each other, perhaps in front of a fire and over a glass of wine, and talk of murder as literature and figuratively smack our guilty lips over the classics of the genre and stop to disagree or even to spar over preferences.

All addicts of fanatical proportions—and I am one of them—have their heresies and I would parade mine and, even in this curious and arid predicament in which I find myself, welcome your ripostes however prejudiced I might secretly find them. Would this statement shake you? If you share most of the conventional opinions about detective fiction it may, so brace yourself. I have always found *Trent's Last Case* a bore. While I have no taste for Heard's *A Taste for Honey* I do not think that his *The Black Fox* has ever received its due; to me it is one of the unmistakable masterpieces. As for Josephine Tey, I consider her *The Daughter of Time* unsurpassed, but the rest of her work, except for *Miss Pym Disposes*, I find, in spite of critical raves, no better than the good average that is maintained by most mystery writers.

Are you one of the apostates who denigrate *The Moonstone* and say it is no detective story at all? Then may the briars and thorns of Sergeant Cuff's roses prick and scratch you!

In recent years I have deplored the decline of the nice person murder and have grown concerned over the ascendancy of the private eye, but then you may agree with a reviewer with whose opinion I usually concur and always respect who says that the private eye of detective fiction has become the folk hero of our present-day culture. Puzzles have piqued my interest but have not ever satisfied it, so on the whole I do not care for this type of mystery. And instead of police procedure in its minutiae which now floods the field I have wanted to read of the guilt that the murderer feels. It is his reactions I hunger after rather than his pursuit by detectives.

All of this is opinionated, I admit, and if only you were here to talk with me your exchange might help me to modify my ideas on murder, but I do not think that I would ever alter them to any considerable extent.

I have often wondered over the appeal of fiction dealing with death by violence. A certain school of analysts may be corrected in its hypothesis that it is our guilt that is catered to and our sadistic tendencies that are fed and momentarily satiated. I think there may be other reasons. We are all threatened by disaster. Death may approach us at any time—a flight of steps, a street crossing, even the bath is filled with hazard. Illness or ruin may confront us at any moment. This sense of doom can haunt us. Detective fiction, on the other hand, gives us a feeling of peril which has form and shape to it; its peril has cause and effect, it is not the blind, idiotic, unnamed anxiety that stalks us in everyday living. Or something like that.

Yes, I wish someone with a passion like mine for this art form of the detective story could be with me to recite the names that are music and that I can scan as if they were meters of a poem:

Collins, Iles, Christie, Sayers, Queen, Chandler, Innes, Crispin, Daly, Poe, Hammett, all these and dozens more.

And—like you, I'm sure—I've often thought after reading a mediocre piece of mystery fiction that I could write one just as good with one or both hands tied behind my back. So I began one, only to find that even the least of them required more than was apparent to the reading eye.

And of course in my unconscious as in everyone's there is down some unlit corridor in some dark and secret room the thought of actual murder; it is undoubtedly a remnant of our childhood, of the megalomania of the infantile mind in which lurks the wish of death for everyone that stands in its way. Perhaps it is a refinement of those early feral impulses that is in a calm contemplation of potential murder and of a dispassionate speculation on such a question as: what murder would create good? The death of what public figure would have the most felicitous result? Or since many of us are not of a political turn, this question can center on the death of which person of our acquaintance would be most fortunate —perhaps a nagging wife, but the more logical of us would counter that no one has to put up with a nagging wife, a man has chosen such a wife out of some valid need for her. Surely a fit object of murder would be a possessive mother who will not release her child to marriage, but a child in his torturous progress toward adulthood must have effected his own release or he could not use the freedom provided by a fortunate murder. What then? Who then? Perhaps a person hopelessly ill suffering the continuous torment of pain. Call it humane or inhumane, as your conscience prescribes, but I have found the thought untenable that a person doomed to invalidism and to constant pain should have an indeterminate stay on this earth.

All these random thoughts and more I jotted down in what I call my commonplace book on murder. It has been a pleasant exercise of the mind to consider and reconsider such reflections, to argue with myself, or to put aside the suspense or detective novel I had in my hand and parry the point of view presented, not that many writers choose the philosophical aspects of murder; with most of them it is simply a matter of crime and punishment or the tracking down of a criminal.

I would like to keep my reflections on murder general but they must now become specific. I must present myself to you but I should like to do so without reference to my name or my age or my profession. I may even try to keep my sex out of it, and if I am successful I might make a feeble joke about this being one of the rare modern instances where sex in murder is minimized. Well, to begin: I am, or I was, a reasonably satisfied person, and though I have neither talents nor gifts and very little competitive spirit I have considerable application and conscientiousness and I have had a fair share of what is called success.

I should mention that my profession requires a great deal of traveling so that I am out of town much of the time. My work is such that I have had few friends. No one can count on me for a fourth at bridge because too often I have to go away unexpectedly, and I have left too many last minute gaps in seating arrangements to be a welcome dinner guest. Almost two years ago my head-quarters were moved to this city and I have not formed anything resembling a friendship, though I am glad to say that my job, which is one of responsibility, presupposes that I can establish immediate rapport with persons of all classes and positions.

The place where I live is for persons of fairly substantial means or at least for those who for one reason or another can afford rather steep rents. In my particular section of the building there are only two apartments, both of identical size, but for a while I knew nothing at all about my neighbor. I had not ever had even an accidental contact, such as being on the elevator at the same time, or happening to answer the door just when he or she entered or left.

This interpolation is necessary: a fondness for flowers is another passion with me, perhaps not so marked as my attachment for detective fiction, but keen and intense. I would like to have a garden but my life being what it is I cannot, and since I am away from my apartment so much of the time even pot flowers are beyond me. For a while I tried to keep them and entrusted their care in my long absences to the elevator boy and the janitor or the assistant superintendent, but I would return only to find the flowers drowned or parched, killed by too much or too little attention. Since I was in no position then to indulge my taste for flowers I was delighted with the remarkable arrangements on a long low table in the hall which I shared with the tenant about whom I had no knowledge. I had thought at first that the flowers were supplied by the management and were a recompense for the high rental we paid and I commented once on their beauty to the elevator operator; he shrugged and told me that she did it, and he pointed to the apartment across from mine.

Talent and care and thought invariably went into the arrangements; sometimes they were pot flowers, sometimes they were leaves, and very often they were cut flowers and these were not allowed to stay beyond their first beauty. Shortly before Christmas there appeared an especially attractive display; this consisted of one of those interesting wooden figures, a primitive carving, Mexican I believe, some two feet high, painted in rich dark colors, and beside it there was a huge brass container filled with cedar boughs. My description is shamefully inadequate and does not in any way suggest the taste and artistry that went into the piece.

At Christmas time I count my blessings and my obligations and I thought how during the four months I had so far lived in the apartment house the flowers had been a constant joy to me, and I did not know at all how to show my appreciation of them. I realized that it was not usual for people living on the same floor to make calls on a newcomer, or even necessarily to know when there was a newcomer, but I felt that if any advance were made it should issue from the person already there when a new tenant arrived. So it appeared obvious to me that whoever lived across the hall wanted to be left alone. Still I was most eager to show my gratitude. At last I thought that a gift of a bottle of wine at the door might be acceptable, but then I had misgivings that the tenant might be abstemious, in which case she would resent my offering. Then I decided on brandy instead of wine and that I would write a brief ambiguous greeting that the brandy might be used for cooking or fruit, so that my neighbor if a teetotaler would not think I was plying her with spirits. Somehow this idea confused me even more and I decided that I would do nothing, that however much I enjoyed the flowers they were of the tenant's doing and had no connection with me. But again I felt like an ingrate not to do something, especially just after I entered or left the hall and my eyes were delighted by the centerpiece; so my dilemma grew more painful.

Here I am reliving my uncertainty on that first Christmas, and it is well that I do because if I had done nothing I might not now have occasion to make some of these reflections on murder.

It was sherry that I settled on after all, an expensive cream sherry. Around the bottle's neck I attached a ribbon and a note. My note was not overly cordial and I purposely said nothing about wishing to thank personally the one who was so generous with her flowers. I remember the message as rather warm but on the whole formal.

On Christmas Eve I placed the wine at the door.

Days went by and there was no acknowledgment at all; not that I wanted or even expected one; I simply hoped the recipient understood my gratitude.

The winter days passed pleasantly, my job was demanding but most rewarding and at night I indulged myself in my usual delight of reading detective fiction. Occasionally I would stop reading and write an observation or so in my commonplace book on murder. I do not now remember the title of the book which I put aside for an instant to write: *The Murder of An Absolute Stranger. Would not the true connoisseur of murder take the most satisfaction in causing the death of someone he did not know, with whom he had no ties at all? No one could ever assign the murder to him, and because he was in no way connected with his victim, he could not know great remorse. Is this perhaps what happens in war? Men who kill in war cannot feel guilt for the unknown persons who are their victims.*

So the months went on and I was satisfied; my job gave me pleasure and my reading in murder and speculations about the subject made as happy a life as one could ever expect when intimate personal relationships are impossible.

The exquisite flower arrangements continued.

There is only one flower to which I am allergic, or rather I should say which I dislike. The lily. It is beautiful but its odor is pervasive and obnoxious to me and I do not care for it. For that reason I was somehow dreading Easter and what might appear in the hall; but when Easter came there was one gigantic pot of white hyacinths in a white wrapping and around it clustered a number of small pots of white and pink and blue hyacinths. My sense of beauty was so satisfied and captivated that again I wanted to do something to show appreciation and once more, but this time with no note of any kind, I set a bottle of sherry at the door.

Again there was no acknowledgment and I wanted none; so spring left and summer came and went and fall blustered in with that suddenness that eternally confounds me.

It was the first of October and I remember being grateful that the heat had been turned on. I did not plan to read that night but intended to devote some time to my fall clothes—pulling them out of mothproof bags, deciding what was usable and what had to be discarded, for no matter how satisfactory clothes may look when they are put away they somehow acquire a shabbiness.

I had just ripped a dangling button from a jacket when I heard a frantic knock at the door. I was expecting no one and in my lonely existence I had few callers. I was somewhat disheveled from working with my clothes, but the knock was so doomladen that I did not take the time to tidy myself.

A woman stood at my door. I knew at once that she was my neighbor. She was in a dressing gown, there was true elegance about her; the gown was black satin, her hair was white and beautifully kept, and her eyes were the only violet ones I have ever seen; her face wore a mask of concern and though it was distorted by worry and consternation I saw that age had only increased its beauty. Voices are apt to be affected by tension and when she spoke hers was, but even in that high, unnatural range her voice had a resonance of remarkable loveliness.

In my early days in statistics and research when I made door to door canvasses I was confronted by extraordinarily varied receptions and I have found that however inwardly I may be concerned or even shocked I can maintain a certain external complacency. I was shocked by her appearance on my threshold and concerned by her obvious distress.

"Good evening," I said. "Won't you come in?"

There was a wariness about her, she took a step forward but stopped as if she could not pass beneath the lintel and I thought fleetingly of witches who cannot cross water or passages that have nails embedded in them.

She turned and went to her own door and then she said: "If you will, please come in here."

I followed her across the hall into a place of matchless taste. My eyes did not have time to particularize the furnishings, I only knew that I was in one of the most gracious series of rooms I had ever entered. She motioned to me to sit beside her on a small sofa upholstered in deep green velvet and I glanced at a Manet and a Berthe Morisot before I concentrated on the woman who was my hostess.

"I've a most unusual request to make of you," she said. "I've no one else to appeal to. You've been so understanding. I couldn't have asked for a more considerate neighbor."

This is what she wanted of me, and she instructed me in deadly earnest. At nine-fifteen I was to ring her doorbell, there would be guests with her, I was to act ill at ease as if I hadn't known she had company, she would insist that I come in and I would agree after some hesitation. I was to mention casually a few times that she had dined with me and refer to several games of bridge she had played with me and some other friends, and I was to leave with the reminder that she had promised to play cards in my apartment on the following Friday and she was not to disappoint me as I was inviting two dear friends who wanted most especially to meet her.

She made no explanation of her request and gave no reason for the need for such fabrications on my part. There was a shyness about her and an absolute goodness. I knew intuitively that my lies would be for an innocent purpose.

It was then eight-thirty. I had a brief rehearsal which quite satisfied her and then I went back to my apartment. I sat down at my commonplace book and I wrote easily and without thought as if it were automatic writing: *Does the victim choose the killer even more than the killer chooses the victim?* I found my question so provocative that I thought of it until nine-fifteen.

When I rang her bell I heard her voice cry out to me to enter. Three persons were present beside herself. I could tell that a conversation of extreme urgency had been interrupted and it took very little acting on my part to offer apologies and try to withdraw, but she insisted that I join them. I was somehow flattered to see that the sherry I had given her was on the table in front of her though I would have thought with the lovely decanter on the sideboard she would have emptied the wine into it; no matter, I began my speech about the dinners and the hands of bridge; she had assigned names to some of the persons supposedly my guests and she said wasn't Charles wonderfully witty and that Frank was a superb bridge player; she thanked me for my kindness in sending her more of the sherry that I knew she liked so well and wouldn't I have a glass; I declined with some reference to claret being the only wine I enjoyed, and then I mentioned the forthcoming bridge game and made my adieux. I was so intent on our dialogue that I did not pay much attention to the other persons there, but it seemed to me that there was a resemblance, not necessarily of the nature of close relatives, but perhaps of cousins; she might even have been the aunt of the two younger men. Their interest in our brief conversation was what I can only term profound and intense.

Since we had been conspirators I thought that when her guests left she might sneak across the hall to smile over our performance and to explain the reason for it, but nothing of the sort happened. Anyway, I hoped the charade in which we acted out a history of social contact was convincing. I did not speculate to any extent as to its purpose. Long since I have taken as a tenet for my conduct this quotation from Henry James: *Remember that every life is a special problem which is not yours but another's, and content yourself with the terrible algebra of your own.* I had no intention whatever of probing or delving into the woman's affairs.

Again time passed and the flowers in their beauty and their variety continued to appear but there was no word from the tenant across the hall.

Another spring had almost progressed into summer when there was another knock on my door. It was she; this time she wore a blue robe and this time there was nothing at all distressful about her appearance; the third time I saw her I realized that she had beauty of remarkable proportions and not even youth had been kinder to her looks than age was, not that I could judge her age, she might have been in her middle forties, she could even have been sixty, and though she smiled I sensed a sadness and a wistfulness about her.

"I didn't think it would work," she said, "but it has. All these months. My dear, I have no right to drag you into matters that don't concern you. Those people whom you saw are my relatives. I feel no real affection for them—nothing but the goodwill I try to feel toward all human beings. But they were trying to manipulate me. Their behavior was monstrous. I can't give you the details of my life—I've been fortunate in many ways and unfortunate in others. I came to mistrust people, to mistrust the world, and all I want is to be let alone, to stay by myself in quietness. But they insisted that I move out in the world. They even wanted me to come live with them. They said my withdrawal was a sign of a breakdown. I thought if they couldn't understand my point of view, then—well, our little hoax—if they could be made to think that I did go out occasionally and that I had friends. I can't thank you enough for what you did. I can't tell you how grateful I am. If I'm made to leave here for any reason I'll die or I'll go into a madness that is worse than death."

Though I found her words melodramatic she spoke quietly. She made no further elaborations and I did not ask any questions; I only know that her thank you to me when she left my living room was the most genuine statement ever directed to me.

Then some weeks later there was the morning when the flowers looked rather wilted and that had not ever happened in our corridor; she did not allow the slightest taint of wilt to touch them, they were removed at the very peak of their beauty. The next day the crisp brownness of death had laid its blight on the flowers and withered petals were strewn on the table. That evening when I returned late from dinner the dead flowers were a desecration to the time of their loveliness and I removed them.

I was concerned over my neighbor but I did not venture to make an inquiry; I remembered her desperate need to be left alone, or I thought that perhaps the dead flowers had left their own message and she had finally been persuaded by her relatives to move in with them. The hall table remained bare and I grew nostalgic for its former beauty.

One night after a particularly trying day at the office I took too long over my after dinner coffee and I was startled to see that I had only moments to pack and to get a plane. I was frantically jerking clothes from the closet and out of drawers when someone knocked on my door.

A woman in a nurse's uniform stood there. I saw that beyond the frame of my door in which she stood the door across the hall had swung open. Even as the nurse spoke she was pulling on a coat. "I must go," she said. "My husband is downstairs waiting for me. The other nurse is late. My patient said perhaps you wouldn't mind coming in for a moment. She belongs in a hospital and no matter how she objects they're going to put her in one tomorrow."

I did not protest my own lateness for the plane, but went at once to the apartment.

My neighbor looked small on the tremendous tester bed; she was ravaged, it seemed to me, not so much by illness as by hopelessness, and beauty that had stayed with her so long was still faithful, it had not deserted her even in this nadir of despair. I looked at her as through bars of a cage, she was of a particular and rare loveliness and deserved nothing so little as the trap in which she obviously found herself, she could exist only in an atmosphere of her own choosing, she could not survive removal from this beautiful retreat. I have wished for many things in my life but I know they were idle wishes with no real intent behind them in comparison with the passionate desire I then had to do something to relieve her suffering and her predicament. We looked at each other and I do not know what there was in the stare that we exchanged, we had lived as neighbors for almost two years in that house and we had seen each other only three times before and those times were moments only, but in those moments she had revealed herself and she had fathomed my nature.

"In the living room, in the top drawer," she said to me in her exquisite voice. I went where her lovely, pathetic gesture indicated. Various objects were there in the secretary but I had not the slightest hesitation when I saw the box. There was no need for words. I knew what she wanted. I knew what she meant. I did not need to read the label or the dosage or the warning. Neither of us faltered as I helped her to a sitting position and handed her the box and a glass of water. Yes, I knew very well what I had done, what we had done together, and then she said: "Please go. I feel I can rest now. I am forever grateful to you."

I saw then that only four minutes had passed since the nurse had summoned me and if I hurried and if I were lucky I could still get my plane. I snatched my suitcase and buzzed continuously for the elevator and shouted down the shaft for service, something I had not ever done before, and I begged the operator to hurry when he made his casual appearance. He later testified as to my hysteria, my frantic and distressed air as I tried to escape from the terrible deed of murder.

We want to question you about the circumstances surrounding the death of so-and-so and you should be warned that anything you say may be taken down as evidence against you. I had read those words a hundred times in detective fiction; I did not know their import until the police in the city where I had flown on the business trip told me that the authorities in the town where I lived wanted to question me in connection with the death of Miss Teresa Covington, and they did not believe me when I said I was not acquainted with any person by that name; you see we had not introduced ourselves, there was no nameplate at her door, and since there was a desk at which we received our mail I had not even seen her name on a box.

The police had found my commonplace book on murder before I returned, they were interested in my various observations, and when I protested that I had not known the dead woman long enough or intimately enough to kill her they produced my speculations about the perfect murder, the murder that could not be solved, that of a stranger. But my protestation that I did not know her well was contradicted by the relatives who testified against me; they had seen me in her apartment and we had exchanged conversation which confirmed many meetings. They described me as fawning, ingratiating. But even now I think that nothing would have come of it if Miss Covington had not left me a small fortune, at least it was a fortune in my estimation. It was not that she disinherited her relatives in my favor, they received handsome bequests, as did many charitable organizations, but a legacy of fifty thousand dollars was enough to convince the most lenient jury that I had motive and to spare for murder.

Yes, yes, yes, I *was* the instrument of her death. I admit it, as I later admitted in testimony. She selected me as her murderer and it was exactly as I had written: does the victim choose the killer even more than the killer chooses the victim? And the answer was yes.

I at last came to that awful, that fateful moment when sentence was pronounced and I almost forgot the despair in her eyes and their terrible pleading for death, and I wished then that she were alive and suffering; I was overcome by the profound intimation that every moment of being, under whatever conditions, is a prize and a premium.

Time that has so often stumbled and stood still is now galloping and my final night is almost gone. I must be detached about what will happen to me early tomorrow and I will turn even now for comfort to what has so often buoyed me. Not even this last predicament can altogether deaden it, though my taste for murder fiction did falter and leave me for a while when the feeling of numbness and puzzlement and bewilderment engulfed me. It is back now, almost as strong as ever, and in the few hours that remain I am wondering what I will ask for to sustain me. My mind has considered many choices; those possibilities have narrowed however; and at the moment I cannot decide between *The Hands of Mr. Ottermole* and *The Two Bottles of Relish*.

Rex Stout, of course, is most famous as the creator of Nero Wolfe, which alone would assure him of a place in any Mystery Hall of Fame, but his contributions to the cause of mystery fiction do not stop there. He has been an unselfish and untiring leader in the writers' battle for a fair share of the fruits of their toil. Here is one of Mr. Stout's rare short-short stories. Nero Wolfe is absent, but the sure hand of a talented professional is, as always, very much present.

13

Cop's Gift

By Rex Stout

"Christmas Eve," Art Hipple was thinking to himself, "would be a good time for the murder."

The thought was both timely and characteristic. It was three o'clock in the afternoon of December 24th; and though the murder would have got an eager welcome from Art Hipple any day at all, his disdainful attitude toward the prolonged hurly-burly of Christmas sentiment and shopping made that the best possible date for it. He did not actually turn up his nose at Christmas, for that would have been un-American, but as a New York cop not yet out of his twenties who had recently been made a precinct dick and had hung his uniform in the back of the closet of his furnished room, it had to be made clear, especially to himself, that he was good and tough, and a cynical slant on Christmas was therefore imperative.

His hope of running across a murder had begun back in the

days when his assignment had been tagging illegally parked cars, and was merely practical and professional. His dear ambition was promotion to Homicide, and the shortest cut would have been discovery of a beaut. It had not gone so far as obsession; as he strode down the sidewalk this December afternoon he was not sniffing for the scent of blood at each dingy entrance he passed; but when he reached the number he had been given and turned to enter, his hand darted inside his jacket to touch his gun.

None of the three people he found in the cluttered and smelly little room one flight up seemed to need shooting. Art identified himself and got their names down. The man at the battered old desk, who was twice Art's age and needed a shave, was Emil Duross, proprietor of the business conducted in that room—Duross Specialties, mail-order dealer in gimcrack jewellery. The younger man, small, dark, and neat, seated on a chair squeezed in between the desk and shelves stacked with cardboard boxes, was H. E. Koenig, adjuster, according to a card he had proffered, for the Apex Insurance Company. The girl, who had pale watery eyes and a stringy neck, stood backed up to a pile of cartons the height of her shoulder. She had on a dark brown felt hat and a lighter brown woollen coat that had lost a button. Her name was Helen Lauro, and it could have been not rheum in her eyes but the remains of tears.

Because Art was thorough it took him twenty minutes to get the story to his satisfaction. Then he returned his notebook to his pocket, looked at Duross, at Koenig, and last at the girl. He wanted to tell her to wipe her eyes, but what if she didn't have a handkerchief?

He spoke to Duross. "Stop me if I'm wrong," he said. "You bought the ring a week ago to give to your wife for Christmas and paid sixty-two dollars for it. You put it there in a desk drawer after showing it to Miss Lauro?"

Duross turned his palms up. "Just a natural thing. She works for me, she's a woman, it's a beautiful ring."

"Okay. Today you work with her filling orders, addressing packages, and putting postage on. You send her to the post office with a bag of the packages. Why didn't she take all of them?"

"She did."

"Then what are those?" Art pointed to a pile of little boxes, addressed and stamped, on the end of a table.

"Orders that came in the afternoon mail. I did them while she was gone to the post office."

Art nodded. "And also while she was gone you looked in the drawer to get the ring to take it home for Christmas, and it wasn't there. You know it was there this morning because Miss Lauro asked if she could look at it again, and you showed it to her and let her put it on her finger, and then you put it back in the drawer. But this afternoon it was gone, and you couldn't have taken it yourself because you haven't left this room. Miss Lauro went out and got sandwiches for your lunch. So you decided she took the ring, you phoned the insurance company, and Mr. Koenig came and advised you to call the police, and you did so, and—"

"Only his stock is insured," Koenig put in. "The ring was not a stock item and was not covered."

"Just a legality," Duross declared scornfully. "Insurance companies can't hide behind legalities. It hurts their reputation."

Koenig smiled politely but noncommittally.

Art turned to the girl. "Why don't you sit down?" he asked her. "There's a chair we men are not using."

"I will never sit down in this room again," she declared in a thin tight voice.

"Okay." Art scowled at her. She was certainly not comely. "If you did take the ring you might—"

"I didn't!"

"Very well. But if you did you might as well tell me where it is because you won't ever dare to wear it or sell it."

"Of course I wouldn't. I knew I wouldn't. That's why I didn't take it."

"Oh? You thought of taking it?"

"Of course I did. It was a beautiful ring." She stopped to swallow. "Maybe my life isn't much, but what it is, I'd give it for a ring like that, and a girl like me, I could live a hundred years and I'll never have one. Of course I thought of taking it, but I knew I couldn't ever wear it."

"You see?" Duross appealed to the law. "She's foxy, that girl. She's slick."

Art downed an impulse to cut it short, get out, return to the station house, and write a report. Nobody here deserved anything, not even justice. Perhaps especially not justice. Writing a brief report was all it rated, and all, ninety-nine times out of a hundred, it would have got. But instead of breaking it off, Art sat and thought it over through a long silence, with the three pairs of eyes on him. Finally he spoke to Duross:

"Get me the orders that came in the afternoon mail."

Duross was startled. "Why?"

"I want to check them with that pile of boxes you addressed and stamped."

Duross shook his head. "I don't need a cop to check my orders and shipments. Is this a gag?"

"No. Get me the orders."

"I will not!"

"Then I'll have to open all the boxes." Art rose and headed for the table. Duross bounced up and got in front of him and they were chest to chest.

"You don't touch those boxes," Duross told him. "You got no search warrant. You don't touch anything."

"That's just a legality." Art backed off a foot to avoid contact. "And since I guessed right, what's a little legality? I'm going to open the boxes here and now, but I'll count ten first to give you a chance to pick it out and hand it to me and save both of us a lot of bother. One, two, three—"

"I'll phone the station house!"

"Go ahead. Four, five, six, seven, eight, nine—" Art stopped at nine because Duross had moved to the table and was fingering the boxes. As he drew away with one in his hand Art commanded him: "Gimme." He hesitated but passed it over, and after a glance at the address Art ripped the tape off, opened the flap of the box, took out a wad of tissue paper, and then a ring box. From that he removed a ring, yellow gold, with a large greenish stone. Helen Lauro made a noise in her throat. Koenig let out a grunt, evidently meant for applause. Duross made a grab, not for the ring but for the box on which he had put an address, and missed.

"It stuck out as plain as your nose," Art told him, "but of course my going for the boxes was just a good guess. Did you pay sixty-two bucks for this?"

Duross's lips parted, but no words came. Apparently he had none. He nodded, not vigorously. Then he looked down at the floor.

Art turned to the girl. "Look, Miss Lauro. You say you're through here. You ought to have something to remember it by. You could make some trouble for Mr. Duross for the dirty trick he tried to play on you, and if you lay off I expect he'd like to show his appreciation by giving you this ring. Wouldn't you, Mr. Duross?"

Duross managed to get it out. "Sure I would."

"Shall I give it to her for you?"

"Sure," Duross's jaw worked. "Go ahead."

Art extended a hand with the ring and the girl took it, but not looking at it because she was gazing incredulously at him. It was a gaze so intense as to disconcert him, and he covered by turning to Duross and proffering the box with an address on it.

"Here," he said, "you can have it. Next time you cook up a plan for getting credit with your wife for buying her a ring, and collecting from the insurance company for its cost, and sending the ring to a girl friend, all in one neat little operation, don't do it. And don't forget you gave Miss Lauro that ring before witnesses."

Duross gulped and nodded.

Koenig spoke. "Your name is not Hipple, officer, it's Santa Claus. You have given her the ring she would have given her life for, you have given him an out on a charge of attempted fraud, and you have given me a cross-off on a claim. That's the ticket! That's the old yuletide spirit! Merry Christmas!"

"Nuts," Art said contemptuously, and turned and marched from the room, down the stairs, and out to the sidewalk. As he headed in the direction of the station house he decided that he would tone it down a little in his report. Getting a name for being tough was okay, but not too damn tough. That insurance guy sure was dumb, calling him Santa Claus—him, Art Hipple, feeling as he did about Christmas.

Which reminded him, Christmas Eve would be a swell time for the murder.

Margaret Manners has appeared in several MWA anthologies. Not to choose one of her stories would be unthinkable; to choose only one is difficult indeed. "Mr. Dilby's Timetable" was originally published as "Death on Little Cat's Feet." Like all of Miss Manners' work, it generates an almost unbearable suspense by delving deeper into character than lesser writers would dare, or be able, to go.

14

Mr. Dilby's Timetable

By Margaret Manners

No one looking at Horace Dilby would ever have supposed that he was engaged in a struggle with Time and the Universe. Horace had a round face, a stiff nervous smile, a chubby figure and thinning hair. His outer existence was a simple pattern of dull and trivial routine. A timetable. His inner existence was a rather more complicated pattern of equally trivial eccentricities. Another timetable.

Horace was obsessed by what he called *patterns*. Life was a chaos of intermingling patterns like the designs in an oriental rug. But there was one difference. If you stared at a rug you could often penetrate its meaning, find its order. In life you were part of an unfathomable design. You never knew where you were, nor when the patterns would whirl you into complete confusion. Horace allowed himself to be haunted, terrified, by this idea.

He had a system for keeping his fear at bay. A poor, contrived little system, perhaps, but it carried him safely from minute to minute. And if it had the rigor of a strait jacket, that rigor was welcomed for the security it afforded. For Horace made his own pattern and followed it with only occasional mishaps, day after day. How could you be a blind pawn in the hands of chance if you were running like a train on familiar tracks, stopping at designated stations, leaving and arriving on time?

Since childhood he had been a step-counter, a fence-toucher, a pavement crack-skipper. It was only natural that step-counting and minute-watching should be the basis of his timetable, since Space and Time are of the essence in all timetables.

So it went. He left the house at precisely the same minute every morning. Knew the shortest route by steps to the subway station; this was quite a trick, a hurrying crowd could throw you out in no time. He always crossed the threshold of his bachelor apartment at the same time every evening.

Then there was the feat of picking up a newspaper on the way home. It had to be a *Tribune* and one had to pick it up without being noticed from the subway seat and carry it off quite casually. He threw it away afterwards. This was just a test that added the element of risk, copies of the *Tribune* were not always available at that hour.

Since Horace was afraid of strangers he would force himself to speak to one stranger a day and exact a smile from the chosen face. This usually took the tame form of bumping into someone, apologizing and receiving the acknowledgment of this civility. But you couldn't just bump anyone who conveniently offered. You had to decide on your quarry in advance, stalk him, bump him, and get the formula in return. "That's all right," or "Quite all right!" and, of course, the smile.

Then there was the routine identified by Horace as "Smith and the Water Cooler." He had worked out the shortest route to the office cooler and it was his custom to beat Smith to it every time. He always stacked the cards against himself. Smith had to be on his feet in motion before Horace could rise from his place, and then without the least appearance of hurrying and without giving Smith any reason to suspect what he was up to, he had to beat him.

When Horace accomplished his daily quota of patterns he felt safe, or at least he felt that he had paid in advance for a margin of safety. When he failed life was empty and frightening.

Tonight life was empty.

In the first place it was Saturday. Horace dreaded Saturday nights. Monday was followed by Tuesday, Tuesday by Wednesday. But after Saturday came that break in routine, that space that had to be safely filled before the next Monday.

Besides Saturday nights were unpleasant in his apartment. The woman upstairs almost always gave a party, and, while generally speaking, it was all right to have a little fun on Saturday nights, the woman upstairs went too far. She started early and ended early, early in the morning. The noise and vibration gave Horace a headache, but he never had the courage to complain. He longed to call the police and he often planned what he would say, but his indignation froze in a solid lump in his throat before his hand even touched the telephone.

But this Saturday night was the worst that he remembered. Everything had gone wrong all day. That morning he had been jostled into the greatest number of steps from subway to office that he had ever taken. The man he had planned to bump had escaped in the crowd. And *twice* Smith had beaten him to the water cooler. He had been so shaken by these failures that he had made an error in his accounts, and had worked overtime finding it.

When he left the office at last the heavy fall dusk was already shrouding the city. The world seemed an alarming and hostile place. There was only one thing to do. He had to try to undo or redeem the day before it was lost. He knew from experience that one could sometimes balance a failure, but for this particular case strong measures would be needed. It was necessary to accomplish something especially distasteful and difficult within a given time.

He decided to allow exactly thirty-seven minutes for his home journey. And to complicate the timing he would walk part of the way. He would also stop at a pet shop and buy some catnip for Ginger. Ginger was a large and very dignified cat who visited him by means of his bedroom fire escape every evening at exactly the same time. Ginger was intelligent and had been easy to condition.

Horace often wondered if it had not been Ginger who had conditioned him. The saucer of milk and the liver had certainly been Ginger's idea. Catnip, however, was an intoxication that Horace allowed only on rare occasions. Ginger under its influence lost all dignity and became a clawing, rolling, chewing, frankly inebriated cat. Tonight was definitely a night for catnip, Horace thought. One

of them was entitled to an intoxicant and as he did not drink—
Anyway it would go very nicely with the party upstairs.

But all that seemed too easy. There must be something . . .

Finally, he made up his mind. He would leave the subway three
stops ahead of his station and walk home through the park along
the river. He chose it because he was timid and did not like dark
lonely places. If he could manage all that within the given time he
felt that honor would be satisfied. With a glance at his watch
Mr. Dilby left the starting post.

Buying the catnip took more time than he intended. The woman
in the pet shop was a chronic talker and she rattled on, her words
an avalanche of pebbles rolling down an endless hill. He felt the
minutes ticking away, the beat of his heart, the pulse of life itself.

When he got away almost ten of his precious minutes had leaked
into the past.

As soon as he entered the subway car he saw the newspaper, a
Tribune, neatly folded, and an empty seat beside it! He almost lost
the seat to another passenger, but slid into it with a desperate
wriggle and a sheepish smile. After settling himself he glanced
around and let his hand steal out toward the paper. At that instant,
without a word or a glance, the man who was seated on the other
side of the paper reached out and took it. Horace had to clench
his hand to keep from tearing it from the despoiler and beating him
over the head with it.

He regretted now that he had attempted the paper at all. It had
not, properly speaking, been included in his improvised plans for
the evening. To have ignored the temptation would have been
better than to succumb and fail.

Much disheartened, he left the train three stations ahead,
crossed the street and walked the few blocks toward the river.
The idea of giving up the whole idea and just going home presented
itself and was quickly rejected. That would be cheating and Horace
never cheated.

It was dark now, a chilly evening, heavy with damp. The park
loomed in mist like an etching in a Victorian Gothic novel. The
lamps along the paths were dimmed by the thick atmosphere into
golden globules of haze floating overhead. Dark shadows crouched
everywhere.

Horace remembered his Aunt Henrietta, the spartan, bosomless
woman who had raised him. She had never permitted a night light

and he had been afraid of the dark. It was no small act of courage to plunge into the park remembering the night terrors of his childhood.

The air was cooler there. He forced himself not to walk too quickly. It was almost as bad to be ahead of time as to be late. His footsteps sounded lonely and strange echoing on the path so he stepped on the edge of the turf and walked there.

Suddenly he was exasperated with himself. Why couldn't he be like other people and just go home? Why did he have to . . . ?

He was walking in the massed shelter of a line of trees when he heard the approaching footsteps. A few feet ahead the path was clear and treeless. There was a lamp and beneath it a wire refuse basket. Then abruptly the path turned and disappeared into more trees.

The man appeared suddenly at the turn of the path and paused. Horace could see him like a figure on a stage caught in the soft spotlight of the lamp. He was tall and seemed to be well-dressed. His hat brim shaded his face and he carried a rolled up newspaper. As Horace watched, the man glanced around and dropped the newspaper into the refuse basket. Then he came on.

Horace stepped forward and onto the path quickly. Better pass in the open under the light. It would look funny walking on the grass.

They met and passed each other a few yards from the trees. Horace kept his eyes down. Was the other watching him? He glanced sideways and caught the needle-flash of sharp eyes probing. What *was* the matter with him tonight? Why should he think that there was something sinister about the man?

He glanced back nervously but the unknown had already been swallowed up by the trees. Directly beside him was the wire basket. The rolled up newspaper lay on top. And it was a *Tribune!* Impossible to resist the impulse. Horace grabbed it and walked on.

He felt foolish and slyly triumphant. But as he glanced at the thing he carried his fastidious nature was offended. The paper seemed to have something in it, a piece of string had been wound round it to hold it together. He ought to throw it away at once. It might contain any number of ignominious bits better left hidden. Perhaps, the remains of a meal prepared in a nonhousekeeping room and smuggled out past a suspicious landlady.

Really! This was the silliest thing he had ever done. Suppose

the man had seen him? Horace blushed. Yet he could not let the
thing go. The mechanism of a day's thwarted patterns was working
against reason. He clutched the paper defiantly. He would carry it
as far as his house and then dispose of it.

And then he remembered, or thought he remembered, that
after the man had reached the trees he had heard no footsteps.
That might mean that he had been standing there in the shadows
watching. Horace caught his breath and walked faster. Was he
being followed? He told himself that the idea was ridiculous and
almost believed it.

With passionate relief he saw the exit path that would bring him
out closest to his street and plunged along it toward the lights and
the traffic.

The park and its fears had been defeated.

He looked at his watch. Four and one half minutes left. He
walked very fast indeed.

Several houses before his own he fumbled for his keys. By the
time he reached the vestibule he had the mailbox key ready. This
was part of the ritual, to skip it would be to cheat. No letter. Now,
up the stairs. He sighed. The newspaper was still tucked under his
arm. If he went out into the street again he would be late but he
didn't want the thing in his apartment.

At the back of the hall where the stairs went up there was a
door into the back area. It took him a split second to open the door
and deposit the paper in one of the empty ash cans that were lined
up there.

He crossed his threshold exactly one minute late. It had all
been for nothing.

Crossing the tiny foyer he entered the living room and flipped
the switch on the standard lamp in the corner. To his annoyance
it did not go on and he had to light others. Of course, he had
unplugged the lamp yesterday because the cord was so badly frayed.
He'd have to fix that. A good task for that evening. The party was
in progress upstairs and he knew reading would be out of the question.

As he looked round the simple comfortable room he felt tired
and defeated. The upholstered chair, the secretary, the huge bookcase, the vase of water plants on the small table—tonight it looked
cold and unfriendly, less like a sanctuary than a prison. The light
perhaps. Not having the tall lamp made all the difference. He'd

have to fix it tonight.

Before he could remove his hat or coat the doorbell rang.

A mistake, of course. He was not expecting anything. Children, perhaps.

The bell rang again, long and hard.

With a sigh Horace pressed the buzzer, opened his door and waited.

The man who mounted the stairs came straight toward him. "Mr. Dilby?"

"I'm afraid . . ." Horace began.

And then he was pushed, *pushed* back into his apartment. The door shut behind them. He opened his mouth to protest, and stood there, frozen. A gun! Pointing at him!

He was too dazed to dodge the hand. It swept his hat to the floor in one contemptuous movement and then struck him across the face.

His topcoat was opened. A hand went inside, patted his pockets, felt around the belt of his trousers, slapped his legs.

A voice said, "Where is it? You didn't have much time. Where is it?"

Horace tried to understand what was happening. The face thrust itself at him venomously. It was a sharp face, a thin wedge, two profiles stuck together. Pale blue eyes, feverishly bright, flickered with anger. It was—it was the man from the park!

Horace's knees melted under him.

"Sit down!" He was pushed into a chair. "We'll talk first, then you can give me what I came for."

But that could only be the newspaper! And why was the man looking up at the ceiling that way? Oh yes, the party, it was getting noisier.

The intruder seemed to be pleased. "That racket will help," he said. "Did you know that a cushion properly used will muffle the sound of a shot? Tell me, Mr. Dilby, why did Harlan hire you to wait there in the park?"

"I wasn't hired," Horace stammered. "It . . . I was just coming home."

"I'm not an idiot." The voice was sharper now. "I saw you. I followed you."

"How . . . I mean, how do you know my name?"

"I saw which mailbox you opened. I'm not a professional gunman, Mr. Dilby, but I can shoot and I'm desperate. I am not sentimental about humanity and I am not easily fooled. Try to understand what I'm saying. Are you listening? Do you follow me?"

Horace nodded.

"When I came in just now I was rough with you; that was nothing, just an introduction. I want you to know I'm the boss. I need what you took in the park, and I need it quickly. I also intend to find out what you have to do with Harlan."

"Nothing—I assure you," Horace said quickly. A fierce look silenced him.

"I know Harlan didn't need you to watch me. He already had the proof he wanted. That's why I had to . . . arrange for his silence. Another day or two and the money would have been replaced, the books fixed up, but he found out. He was going to hand me over to the police."

The blue eyes glistened unpleasantly. "I was his superior in every way, but I had to work for him. He had everything and did not know how to use it . . . a miser. Even his wife had to beg for every penny. He treated me like dirt. I had it all worked out. She was as bad as he was in her own way. She deserved no consideration. Why did you interfere? Why were you there? Harlan couldn't have known."

One thought struck Mr. Dilby. He was filled with horror. He couldn't tell where the *Tribune* was. As long as it was hidden the man would be reluctant to kill him, but after . . . He tried to think of something to say.

"I wasn't waiting for you," he protested. "I wasn't. It was just chance." Just chance! And to Horace Dilby chance represented all unknown peril and chaos. He shivered violently.

"Cold, Mr. Dilby?" There was mockery and contempt in the voice. "Never mind. I have the answer. Though I certainly would never have picked you as a man to spy on other men's wives."

Horace was stupefied. "Other men's wives?"

"It's obvious. Harlan didn't need to have me watched. He didn't know I'd be in the park or why. If he had he would have safeguarded himself against . . ." There was a short pause. "But he did know that his wife walked the dog there every evening. He sent you to watch her. He was jealous. Everyone knew it. When I showed up you thought I was leaving a warning for her. Perhaps you thought that I was the man she was to meet."

"Oh, no! You're wrong. I did not know who you were."

"Didn't you? Harlan had a few snapshots of me taken last summer. I can just see him showing them to you. 'That's my secretary, Willet. My wife may even be meeting him.' He didn't trust me. He didn't trust anyone. Oh, you recognized me all right."

Willet stood up and pushed back his chair. "No matter. You took what I left there. You came between me and my safety. Now you can give it back to me. Where is it?"

Horace was silent.

"Fool!" Willet said. "I'll find it. It's here somewhere. Stand up!"

Horace stood up. It did not occur to him to fight, to throw himself on the hand that held the gun. He was only too painfully aware of his limitations.

"Face the wall! Keep your hands above your head! If you move I'll kill you."

Horace did as he was told and the search began. What would happen when bedroom, kitchen, everything had been searched? His arms started to ache and he thought of physical pain and his cowardice when faced with a visit to the dentist. He didn't realize that Ginger was there until he felt the soft rubbing against his ankle.

"Meow!" Ginger said loudly.

Willet stopped opening drawers. "What's that?"

"Just the cat," Horace said. "He came through the bedroom door. He always comes at the same time and I . . ."

Ginger complained again.

"He wants his milk. If I could just go to the kitchen, please?"

"The kitchen, Dilby? Lead the way, then."

But he wasn't permitted to give Ginger his milk. He had to stand as before, facing the wall, his hands high.

The cat meowed bitterly. Horace felt the inexorable push of his timetable but dared not move. He heard the pots and pans being knocked about, drawers opened, cupboards rifled.

Stillness. And then a soft hissing. A small explosion as the pilot on the stove ignited the gas.

Willet's voice reached him, quiet, even, without anger, without pity. "You can use a stove for more than cooking, my obstinate hero. I can easily make you tell me. Why not save time and spare us both a very shocking experience."

It had come at last. The threat of pain. Cold sweat covered his body. The moisture ran down his raised arms. He swayed.

"Rest your arms a minute," Willet said.

Horace lowered them and turned, facing Willet across an opened drawer of the cabinet. He tried to bring the swimming haze into focus. Odds and ends. A few tools. A flashlight. Horace stared at them. The thought of darkness came to him. Not the darkness of death, but the darkness of power failure. If only— But he must say something. Must seem to be willing to—

"Suppose," he said shakily, "that I had taken something you left in the park."

Willet smiled.

"But *if* I had, you understand? If I gave it back to you you'd kill me before you left."

"Don't be foolish," Willet said impatiently. "I have no particular wish to kill you."

Horace was not fooled. He knew the difference between wish and necessity. But if Willet thought he was weakening perhaps he would let him feed Ginger. He did not know why feeding Ginger was important or how it would help. He only knew that to perform the accustomed task would perhaps wipe out some of the fear, help him to think.

"But tomorrow or the next day a crime would be discovered. I'd know when I read the papers. How can you overlook that? If you could convince me that I'd still be alive after . . ."

"I'll tie you up." Willet was eager to deceive him. "Before you were found and released I'd be out of the country using another name."

"I don't know," Horace said weakly. "How can I trust you?"

Willet's eyes narrowed. "You have to take that chance," he said.

Ginger meowed plaintively.

"May I feed him?" Horace begged, reaching toward the refrigerator.

Willet's hand shot out, opened the refrigerator. He inspected everything, even the ice cube trays. Then he slammed it shut again.

"It will only take a second," Horace pleaded. "Just a little milk."

"No!" the bright fanatic eyes were like polished stones.

"But why not? It can't do any harm."

"You can't feed the cat because this gun says you can't. You do what I say, only what I say. Understand?"

"But that's ridiculous!" Horace couldn't control himself. He had submitted to terror because there was nothing in him to oppose to terror. Now every nerve in his body was exasperated by this senseless prohibition.

"You're fond of that cat, aren't you?"

"Not particularly," Horace said quickly, too quickly. "He's not even my cat. It's just habit. I feed him every night."

Ginger stalked between them his tail held high, eager for the saucer which always followed the opening and closing of the refrigerator.

Without any change of expression Willet kicked the cat.

Horace's cry was an echo of Ginger's.

"How could you?" Tears of rage blinded him. "He trusts me. He's conditioned to expect kindness here. Don't you realize . . . ? It's bewildering, worse than frightening for a conditioned animal to be faced with the unexpected. It's more cruel than physical pain . . . it's . . ."

"How well you understand that cat," Willet said. "Well, how about it? Do you give it to me? Or is Ginger to get some more of the unexpected?"

"Give me one minute," Horace heard himself say.

He bent and coaxed Ginger to come out from under the chair where he had crawled. With an unsteady hand he petted and soothed the shocked animal. His mind was suddenly a hard and unfamiliar instrument that worked by itself unaffected by the fear that shook his body. He thought of the opened drawer behind him and what it contained. Under his hand Ginger began to purr again.

"All right. I'll show you where it is," he said in a level voice.

With the gun behind him he led Willet back to the living room and faced the corner where the disconnected lamp stood. Against the wall was the enormous mahogany bookcase, near it was the small table with the water plants.

That was all. And it was in this corner that he had to convince Willet that the thing was hidden.

"I'll have to move the bookcase away from the wall," he said. "It's quite heavy. Will you help me?"

Willet was suspicious as he had hoped he would be. "Not me,

I'm holding the gun, remember? Anyway you didn't have time to move it before I came up here. What's the idea?"

"I didn't have to move it." Horace's voice was surprisingly steady. "I threw it up over the top when the bell rang. It fell down behind. I can manage it myself, I guess. But I'll need more light."

He pressed the lamp switch. "Now what is the matter with . . . Oh yes." He bent down and plugged the cord in. The light went on.

"I'd better move this little table out of my way." He lifted it with care, balancing the vase of water plants on it. "Now, Ginger, keep out of my way," he said gently, hoping that Ginger would understand the tone and not the words.

Ginger obligingly came to him rubbing against Horace's legs. Horace lifted one foot and gently pushed him away. As he did so the table top tilted just enough. The vase crashed to the floor. There was a lot of water. The frayed lamp cord lay in a little puddle, but nothing happened.

"Oh dear, I'm sorry. I'll have to wipe that up . . . there's a cloth in the . . ."

"Move the bookcase and don't be a fool," Willet snapped.

"Of course . . . I . . ."

With a loud *sphut* the lights went out.

As Willet swore, Horace moved toward the foyer. A minute, only a minute . . .

He stumbled against a soft body, scraping the floor in his effort to keep on his feet. The noise wasn't loud but it was enough. Instantly the gun was between his shoulder blades pressing cruelly so that he felt the hard mouth through topcoat and suit as if it were biting into naked flesh.

Sick with despair he realized that Ginger's curiosity had betrayed him. The cat after his leap away from the falling vase had returned to investigate and Horace had stumbled over him.

"You asked for it!" Willet's voice was as empty and metallic as the snap of a trigger. And now that he thought the thing was behind the bookcase, he *would* kill, he would . . .

"The landlady!" Horace cried. "She's coming up here. If I don't answer she'll let herself in with the pass key."

"What? You're lying. Why should she?"

Horace improvised wildly. "A stupid arrangement . . . only temporary . . . until they rewire the house . . . Fuse box in my foyer controls her apartment too . . . Her lights out as well . . .

I'll have to let her in."

The gun pressed less hard. And he knew that although Willet doubted, he was afraid to act on that doubt.

"You won't let her in, Dilby. I saw fuses in the kitchen. I'll hold the flashlight while you change them. Come on."

He groped his way to the kitchen and the gun never lost contact with his back.

"How long before she gets up here?" Willet demanded hoarsely.

"Right away if she was in her apartment when the lights went out. But she might be in the cellar or in the yard, then she might take a few minutes."

Horace fussed over the kitchen drawer. It was ridiculous, a silly idea, but he had to try, and the slightest distraction might help. The flashlight dazzled him making him feel even more defenseless. He prayed for courage. But he was despicably afraid. Afraid of the gun, afraid of the light, afraid of the thin vicious face, afraid, most of all, of the impersonal cruelty of life.

"I'll have to carry out the stepladder," he explained. "The fuse box is up over the door."

He put the fuses in his pocket and caressed the tight little cellophane package of catnip. Catnip and fuses against a gun! He giggled hysterically.

Willet swore. The gun pushed him toward the ladder.

He set it up in front of the door in the foyer, tested its steadiness, mounted two rungs, and then came down again.

"What the hell's the matter now?" Willet whispered.

"I almost forgot. If I don't disconnect the lamp first the fuse may blow all over again."

It was unanswerable. Willet had to take him back to the lamp.

Horace tugged at the plug, pretending. "Bring the light closer, please. It seems to have stuck."

While one hand pulled at the cord the other was in his pocket. His fingernail slit the cellophane.

"What's that?" Horace lifted his head, listening. "I think she's coming in!"

"If she does," Willet said, "I'll kill her."

Horace called out, "Don't come in, Mrs. Forest. I'm on the ladder changing the fuse. You'll knock me down."

He allowed the plug to come out suddenly and sat down heavily on the floor. His hand pushed catnip into Willet's trouser cuff.

Calling another reassurance to the nonexistent landlady he went back to the foyer and mounted the ladder.

He yanked open the fuse box. *Ginger, Ginger!* Hadn't he smelled it yet? Had that one kick from Willet so discouraged the cat that even the scent of catnip could not tempt him?

The beam of light pointed upward steadily, too steadily. Slowly he unscrewed the fuse. Willet's face was there below him, looking up, a pale featureless blob behind the light. The gun and the light.

He shivered.

Then he heard Willet's startled exclamation, heard the foot trying to shake off the claws. A sharp cry of pain.

The flashlight swung erratically down the wall away from Horace. He poised his foot and kicked out from the ladder with all his strength. It caught the point of Willet's chin. The head snapped back, but it was the light not the gun that fell to the floor. Horace jumped.

They were on the floor. He had the hand, twisting it in a blind passion of exertion. Then he bit the flesh hard, Willet squealed like an animal, and the gun was his. He swung the butt in a fierce arc and heard it crack on Willet's skull. He waited anxiously, but there was no movement, only a hoarse deep breathing.

Moving as in a dream he picked up the light, found picture wire in a drawer and trussed the unconscious man. Then he replaced the fuse and put away the ladder. He brought out milk and liver, but Ginger wasn't interested. He was happily at work on the intoxicating trouser cuff.

These tasks finished he had to think what to do next. Surely they had made a great deal of noise. Wouldn't someone come to see if he had had an accident? Reflecting bitterly that a man could be murdered in his own apartment and no one care, he threw an angry glance at the ceiling.

Laughing and dancing! Callous indifference! If he'd been shot they wouldn't have heard it, or been interested if they had heard. His rage mounted like a rocket and he went to the telephone.

He found himself complaining to the policeman who answered his call about the noise of the party.

"I know it's not very late," he said hysterically, "but that is no reason they can't be a little quieter . . . I've had a very trying evening . . ." And suddenly he was calm, very calm. "Please send someone." He gave his name and address. "I have a man here, he's been holding me at the point of a gun . . .

"No, I'm not upset! Yes, of course I am. Wouldn't you be? His name's Willet. I think he murdered someone called Harlan . . ."

Now the official voice was interested. Harlan's body had been found.

"No, I'm all right. He's tied up. I'm a bit confused about the facts, but I've got him for you."

With a sigh he cradled the phone and waited for them to come. Willet was still unconscious when they removed him.

Horace listened to the police and answered their questions. Really, they knew more than he did about the whole business. The body had been discovered when Mrs. Harlan came back from walking her dog in the park. Knocking on her husband's study door and receiving no answer she had gone in to find him murdered. Willet was not suspected because she was sure her husband had been alive when the secretary left the house at the end of his working day. She had heard them saying good night.

"He must have gone back in through the study window," the police lieutenant said. "It's a private house with a garden."

They found the *Tribune* in the ash can where Horace had thrown it. Inside the paper was a blood-stained knife, an ornate monogrammed knife.

"Those are Mrs. Harlan's initials," the lieutenant said. "She used it on her desk. It didn't look good that it was missing. She was the only one who had left the house. That was Willet's idea. We were supposed to find it in the park where she walked the dog. They didn't get along. The cook said they had violent quarrels. It didn't look good." He eyed Horace curiously. "Just what made you pick it up?"

Horace flushed. "The way he looked," he said weakly. "I just had a feeling."

That seemed to satisfy the lieutenant who expressed a great respect for hunches. "But how did you get the gun away from him?"

Horace was aware that the policeman's eye was traveling over his dumpy figure, it was not a complimentary glance.

"Well . . . Ginger helped by . . . er . . . creating a diversion. Then I kicked him in the jaw."

There was a brief silence. Horace added no explanation. He had never been one to say more than was necessary.

Sunday was a busy day. What with the newspaper reporters and the people in the house, Horace hardly had a minute to himself.

It was quite touching to see how concerned his neighbors were. The lady upstairs was quite upset.

"And there we were enjoying ourselves without any idea . . ."

"Yes," Horace said dryly, "I heard you."

She smiled. She was really a very nice-looking woman. "Next Saturday won't you join us? A party's more fun if you're not underneath it."

Monday Horace went to work. He blushed when he read the papers. *"Courage, Catnip and Kitty,"* was one heading. Really! But he was pleased.

It wasn't until he reached his office building that he realized he had not counted a single step, hadn't once looked at his watch, hadn't even thought of bumping anyone. For a moment he was shaken. Freedom, that terrible, unpredictable burden was his!

He couldn't, of course, expect to play the hero, and then go back to safety and a timetable. He understood that. But to be emancipated so soon! And then the feeling of alarm faded. He straightened his shoulders and went up to the office.

Smith and the rest would want to ask questions too, that was only natural, he would try not to disappoint them. He smiled happily. Smith would never know that henceforward the water cooler would be his without competition.

Michael Gilbert refutes forever the myth that a writer needs the peace and quiet of an ivory tower to write. He has produced his novels, plays, and many short stories while commuting from the suburbs to his practice as a London solicitor. Granted that the British Railroads are not the IRT, still!

No one handles the English policeman nearly so well as Mr. Gilbert. Here we have the imperturbable Hazlerigg perturbed.

15

Modus Operandi

By Michael Gilbert

Chief Inspector Hazlerigg reserved his most intolerant criticisms for what he called "pinch of dust" detectives.

I think the expression originated in his mind when I told him of a story I had read in a magazine about a detective whose only clue to the identity of a felon was a sample of dust from the turn-ups of his trousers—the felon's trousers, I mean. Microscopic analysis revealed that this dust was composed in equal parts of a green chalk, of grains of sand of a type found only at Bognor Regis, and of particles of powdered granite belonging to a geological stratum which, surprisingly enough, approaches the earth's surface at Bickley. It was then child's play to deduce, look for, and arrest a billiard marker of Bickley who took his summer holidays at Bognor.

"Why?" said Hazlerigg. "Why not an enthusiastic snooker-player from Bognor with relatives at Bickley?"

"Or," suggested Inspector Pickup, "a man who lived at Orpington but worked in a shop at Bickley and had in his back garden a sand-pit that his predecessor had stocked with sand from Bognor."

"Or a man who had bought a pair of trousers second-hand from a chap who had exchanged *his* trousers for—"

"All right, all right," I said. "We yield the point. You mean, I take it, that it's no good using these scientific analyses to catch your man."

"Oh, there's nothing wrong with science," said Hazlerigg, broad-mindedly. "Once the prisoner's in custody, let science have its head. So long as it's the sort of science a jury will swallow," he added. "It's taken them fifty years to believe in fingerprints."

"Then if you don't catch them by science—?"

Hazlerigg observed the bait, but appeared to accept the hook.

"That's what you've been leading up to all along, isn't it?" he said. "All right, I'll tell you. There's no terrific secret about it. Take burglars. Apart from the ones which may actually be caught on the job—and the British householder perpetually amazes me by his willingness to tackle anything up to twice his own weight in armed housebreakers—out of every hundred who eventually get caught, I should say that fifty, at least, run into trouble trying to dispose of the proceeds."

"Well, it's a sad reflection on human nature," went on Hazlerigg, "but the next biggest group are those who are given away by informers."

"And the rest?"

"Miscellaneous. Hard work and concentration on the M.O. files."

"I've never really understood that," I said. "I mean, I know the principle of *modus operandi*. You are called to a burglary in Hampstead and you find that the pantry window has been forced with a bricklayer's trowel and that the burglar has helped himself to a cup of tea before leaving by the back door. You then trot back to Scotland Yard, turn up the index, and discover that the only man on your books who habitually uses a bricklayer's trowel *and* gains access by pantry windows *and* helps himself to a cup of tea is Smokey Joe. So you send someone off to pull Joe in, and if Joe can't explain his movements last Friday evening, then ten to one he's for it. That's about it, isn't it?"

"More or less."

"Then what I don't understand is why doesn't Joe take the trouble to change his habits? He's only got to open, say, the library window with a pick head, or even wait till he gets home before he has his cup of tea, and he's safe as houses."

"You might think so," said Hazlerigg. "It doesn't work out that way. First, because a lot of the items in the M.O. index are things that he *can't* change or, at least, would be very unlikely to change. The type of stuff he steals—well, that'll depend on what facilities he has for getting rid of it, doesn't it? If his receiver gives him top prices for fur coats, then fur coats he must have. The demand creates the supply. Again, take the question of whether he works alone or not. Now, that's a matter of temperament. He's born with it—"

"In fundamentals, I agree; but what about the little things?"

"Look here," said Hazlerigg. "If I told you that it was vitally important that you shouldn't hitch up the knees of your trousers before sitting down in a chair—as I've noticed once or twice is a habit of yours—if I told you that your life depended on your not doing it, could you *guarantee* that you wouldn't do it again—say, next week?"

"Well—no. Perhaps not. But I don't think that's a fair analogy."

Hazlerigg grinned and looked at Inspector Pickup, who mouthed a word that sounded like "Copley," and they both laughed.

That was all I got out of them, at the time. The story was still in the top-secret drawer. I heard the rest of it some time later.

During the aftermath of the late war, at a time when all the crime charts were rocketing, Scotland Yard started to become conscious of the activities of a new burglar. All criminals whose work is both distinctive and successful—successful, I mean, from the criminal's point of view—are apt to acquire simple nicknames and this burglar was known to the police of the Metropolis and Home Counties as the Flat Man (because he specialized in flats) or more commonly as the Neat Man, because he never left many traces of his visit, unless you can call the absence of the owner's silver, jewelry, and clothing a trace. He was also called the Neat Man for another reason which will presently appear.

"He works single-handed," said Hazlerigg, when he was presenting an analysis to the Assistant Commissioner (the Neat Man had become that important). "And either he is the most marvellous lock-picker alive or else he has the art of selecting the right key for the right door. He never forces a catch. He never goes through a window. So far as we know, he enters like a gentleman, by the front door, which he opens, as I said, with a key or in some other painless manner."

"Catch locks?" said the Assistant Commissioner.

"Oh, no, sir. Everything. Mortice locks and all. Then there's another thing. He seems to know his way about so uncannily. We can usually pick up his footprints. He has an exceptionally small neat foot and often wears dancing pumps. Many of these expensive flats have floor-to-floor carpets, and when we arrive on the scene before it's been too trodden over, we can follow his progress there and back. It's always the same story. He comes in the front door; he goes straight to the room he wants; he takes what he can find—I mean, he never breaks open cupboards or desks, he just lifts whatever comes handy; then he goes straight back again to the hall—and then there was something used to puzzle us. You'd see his footsteps going straight up the hall. Suddenly, for no reason, they'd stop, there'd be a mark where he'd turned, and a pair of prints pointing sideways, toward the wall, if you follow me. Usually with the toe prints clearer than the heels."

"It sounds quite mad to me," said the Assistant Commissioner. "What did you make of it?"

"We made nothing of it at first," said Hazlerigg. "But when we did spot it, well, it was perfectly obvious. He was a tie-twiddler."

"A what?"

"A tie-twiddler or a hair-smoother, or a lapel-brusher—I mean, he was the sort of man who couldn't pass a looking glass without stopping for a moment to peer at himself. Probably did it quite unconsciously. Being on the small side—as his footprints indicate —he usually had to stand on tiptoe. Hence the marks."

"So all we've got to do," said the Assistant Commissioner, "is to search London for a small man who admires himself in looking glasses." He didn't say it unkindly. He appreciated the difficulties.

Inspector Hazlerigg had found himself in charge of the Neat Man investigation in the fortuitous way that things sometimes happened at Scotland Yard. The Neat Man seemed to specialize in stealing good clothes. Good clothes were a strong black-market proposition. Hazlerigg was known to be an expert on black-market offences—it was, in fact, his chief occupation. Therefore, the Neat Man was handed to him. Hazlerigg was neither pleased nor grateful. He had a good deal on his plate already. Nevertheless he made the routine investigations in the same thorough way that he did all his work. All the relevant reports were brought to him and he studied them and analysed them and cross-indexed the results and hoped for a break. Then, one night, the job ceased to be routine.

Hazlerigg was living, at that time, in a furnished flat toward the Highgate end of Hornsey Lane. He came home to it at a quarter to midnight after a long day. He felt very tired. When he got in he went to the sideboard for a tankard of beer and found, to his surprise, that the cupboard was empty. There had been some table silver in it as well as the tankards; also a pair of rather nice small Georgian candlesticks. They were gone, too. With a sudden sinking feeling he made for his bedroom and opened the wardrobe. "Both suits and my dinner jacket," he said, "curse him!" He reached for the telephone.

"It's Mr. Neat all right," said the Divisional Detective Inspector. "It's got all the trade marks. Here's where he stopped to take a look at himself"—he pointed to a barometer that had been hanging on the wall predicting *Wet to Stormy* ever since Hazlerigg had come into the flat. "No marks of forcing on the door, either. Did you turn the lock when you went out, sir?"

Hazlerigg had the grace to blush. "No," he said. "I forgot."

From that moment he really started putting his back into the job.

First thing next morning he summoned Sergeant Brakewell to his room. What Sergeant Brakewell didn't know about locks could hardly be classified as knowledge.

"How do burglars set about picking locks?" Hazlerigg asked. "In particular, the locks on the doors of flats."

"Well, sir," said Sergeant Brakewell, "it's a big subject. But roughly speaking—"

At the end of three quarters of an hour he paused for breath and Hazlerigg said: "As I understand it, catch locks are easy. You push the tongue back with a stiff bit of talc, or gum the works up with liquid paraffin, and use a plain key. Mortice locks are more difficult, but most real experts have such a fine collection of basic keys—what people call skeleton keys—that they can usually find one to fit. And if it won't quite fit they cover it with lampblack, push it in, look at the scratches, file it down a trifle, and bob's your uncle."

"That's about it," said Sergeant Brakewell.

"Right. Now, here are the records of more than forty house-breakings. We're pretty certain they are the same man. I'll let you have them to study and I'll arrange for you to see the actual lock itself if you think it'll be helpful—and if you want a recent and untouched specimen," he added grimly, "I have the very thing for you at home."

"So I've heard," said Sergeant Brakewell with a discreet grin.

A week later he made his report.

"I think, sir," he concluded, "that there's no reasonable doubt. In every case the door was opened with a copy of the actual key. As I explained, where the lock's new, a copy key will make very much the same marks as the regular one. But where it's an old lock, one that has developed play, a copy, however careful, will leave marks."

He enumerated them, and Hazlerigg listened a little absent-mindedly.

When Sergeant Brakewell had gone, he opened the classified directory and searched under the house agents until he found the firm he wanted. Then he turned to the records of the cases and went through them again, copying down details.

To Inspector Pickup, two days later, he confided the results of his inquiries.

"I think we're on to something," he said, "though I'm blessed if I can quite see how it works. If Brakewell's right about the keys—and I'd back his judgment in that line against anyone in England—then it means that this burglar must at some time or other have had his hand on the original keys. But then you're up against a difficulty. House keys are things people are apt to be a bit careful with. I mean, they don't leave them lying about or entrust them to perfect strangers. I didn't anyway. I don't think my door key was ever out of my possession."

"But the house agent—"

"Exactly," said Hazlerigg. "So I took the trouble to find out who had acted in the renting of all these flats."

"And it was the same firm?"

"Not quite," said Hazlerigg. "It was three firms. All North London firms, it's true. But not connected with each other, so far as I know. Start & Baxter of Hornsey, Croppers of Highgate, and Shaw, Shaw, Shaw & Shaw of Hampstead. I'm on my way to see Croppers now."

Messrs. Croppers (*If You Want a House of Character Come to Croppers*) have their estate agency on Highgate Hill. It possesses a low entrance, a step down from the pavement, and black beams alternating with cream plaster: all of which are well-known to be signs of Character in a House. Even Mr. Cropper, who wore a Victorian frock coat, had a certain old-fashioned grace about him.

Inspector Hazlerigg introduced himself and explained a small part of what was in his mind. Mr. Cropper said: "We are always very friendly with Start & Baxter—a very nice little firm. But as for Shaw & Shaw, well, you know, Inspector, they're hardly in our line. In fact, they're hardly the sort of firm I'd care to—"

"Of course."

"I should describe them," said Mr. Cropper, "as modern. We here at Croppers have certain old-fashioned traditions, certain prejudices as to what is fair dealing—"

Half an hour later Hazlerigg was seated in the chromium and art-leather interior of Messrs. Shaw, Shaw, Shaw & Shaw's estate office in Hampstead. The senior partner, after glancing cautiously at the Chief Inspector's card, said: "Yes, I know Croppers very well. We have as little to do with them as we can. This is an up-to-the-minute business and we try to run it on up-to-the-minute lines."

He glanced complacently at the six huge olive-green steel filing cabinets. "I can't think of any possible—er—line of connection between us. I don't even recollect that we've ever taken on one of their employees. Nor, so far as I know, have any of our employees stepped—er—down to join them."

Mr. Baxter, of Start & Baxter, a little sandy-haired man who worked in a three-room office in Hornsey, proved the most helpful and the easiest to deal with: and in return Hazlerigg told him a great deal more of the truth than he had exposed to either of his rivals.

"Let me see," said Mr. Baxter. "We got your flat for you, didn't we? I thought I recognized you—yes—well, now about those other firms. I don't really have a great deal to do with them —now."

Hazlerigg looked up sharply.

"It used to be different—just after the end of the war, when everybody wanted flats and houses, and people were lining up for anything and everything. There used to be a certain amount of splitting commissions, among the established firms, and I worked in with the Shaws and Croppers on one or two deals. The idea, from our point of view, was to keep the mushroom business out of it—and it suited the public too. It meant that they could use two or three different firms to sell their houses without the risk of having to pay two or three commissions."

"But you didn't work together over all these jobs—" Hazlerigg pointed to his list.

"Oh, Lord, no," said Mr. Baxter. "In fact, I don't think any of those were joint jobs. That arrangement was really mostly confined to outright sales."

"I see," said Hazlerigg. "Now about the keys—"

"Well, you're quite right there, too, of course. House agents do hold the keys in nine cases out of ten. It's one of the risks you have to take. We're as careful as we can be in picking our assistants. I've just got my son here and one other, and I'd go bail for both of them. But in a big firm like—well, never mind names. In a big firm, I don't say you mightn't get a bad 'un."

"But so far as you know," said Hazlerigg, "no one person, principal or employer, could have had all the keys on that list."

"You can bet your life on that," agreed Mr. Baxter.

And yet the idea was there.

It was based on something that he had seen or heard when he was completing arrangements for the lease of his own flat. Hazlerigg knew better than to try to force these ideas. Instead, he went home early and had a good night's rest.

It was on the top of the bus, on his way to Scotland Yard next morning, that it clicked.

As soon as he reached his office he got on the telephone to Mr. Rumbold of Wragg & Rumbold, Solicitors.

"Can you tell me," he said, "when you acted for me in the lease of my flat—what did we get?"

"What do you mean?" said Mr. Rumbold cautiously.

"What papers did we get? I seem to remember signing a document of some sort which had to be handed over. Did we get anything in exchange?"

"You signed a counterpart lease," said Mr. Rumbold, "and

received the original lease for yourself."

"Have you got it there?"

"It's in my strong-room," said Mr. Rumbold.

"Then get it out, please," said Hazlerigg. "I'm coming round to see you."

Half an hour later he was in Mr. Rumbold's office in Coleman Street, and he and his solicitor were examining an engrossment.

"Is there anything that strikes you as unusual about this lease?" asked Hazlerigg.

Mr. Rumbold picked up the four pages of heavy parchment, folded bookwise, and ran a conveyancer's eye over them.

"No," he said at last. "There's certainly nothing irregular about it, if that's what you mean. In fact," he went on, "it's rather a conscientious piece of work."

"Rather unusually conscientious?"

"By present-day standards, perhaps, yes. It has a large-scale plan, showing each individual room—that is perhaps a little uncommon in a lease of house property."

"And that schedule thing?"

"Most leases of furnished flats have schedules of contents," said Mr. Rumbold. "Then if any question of dilapidations arises—"

Hazlerigg ran his eye down the schedule.

"One sideboard with two drawers and two cupboards (locked)," he saw. This appeared to decide him.

"Look here," he said. "Can you get hold of some of the other leases of flats on this list?"

"Well—yes. I might," said Mr. Rumbold. "I think I acted for Mrs. Frobisher myself—and Colonel Davenant goes to Lathoms'—they'd lend me the lease if I gave some reason."

"Make up anything you like," said Hazlerigg. "I promise you your professional reputation won't be compromised. But collect as many of them as you can."

"It'll take a bit of time."

"One other thing," said Hazlerigg. "When you'd actually completed the arrangements for my lease, you yourself handed me the keys. That was the fact that stuck in my memory. Now, how did you get them? What was the routine? Who gave them to you?"

"The solicitors on the other side, I should imagine," said Mr. Rumbold. "They handed them over at completion."

"Is that usual?"

"In the sale of a freehold property, yes. In the lease of a flat it's more usual, perhaps, for the house agent to hand them direct to the incoming tenant."

"But a solicitor is perfectly within his rights in asking for them, so that he can hand them over himself?"

"Certainly, yes. I should say that was the proper way to do it."

"I see," said Hazlerigg. As, indeed, he was beginning to.

Mr. Rumbold was better than his word. Two days later he had six leases spread out on his desk when Hazlerigg called. He was examining them with the beginnings of a frown on his plump face.

"There's no doubt about it," he said, in answer to the Inspector's first question. "They were all drawn by the same man. As you know, a solicitor doesn't actually put his name on an engrossment, but there are so many points of similarity. You see—the same large-scale plan. The same detailed schedules of furniture. But it isn't only that. Look at that last clause—"

When Hazlerigg had deciphered the script he threw back his head and laughed aloud.

"Genius," he said. "That's genius—the genuine unmistakable tough. Now for it. Who drew these leases?"

"That's an easy one to answer," said Mr. Rumbold. "If the same firm acted for all the landlords, I can find them by turning up your file. Incidentally, that explains the agents, too. If we're dealing here with only two or three groups of landlords or estate corporations who employ the same solicitor, they would naturally use the same two or three agents—there's usually some sort of professional tie-up." He was opening the file as he spoke.

"Henryman & Bosforth," he said. "I don't know much about them. Their office is just off Bedford Row."

A little later that morning Inspector Hazlerigg was shown into the outer office of Henryman & Bosforth. Inspector Pickup was just behind him, and Sergeant Crabbe loitered unobtrusively on the opposite pavement.

"It's about the lease of my flat," he said to the girl. "Start & Baxter of Hornsey are the agents. They told me—"

"Oh, yes," said the girl. "That'll be our Mr. Copley. He does all that. Would you wait in here for a moment? I'll send him down. Are you—?"

"The other gentleman is with me," said Hazlerigg vaguely.

They sat in the small waiting room. Five minutes passed.

"You don't think he's walked out on us, do you?" said Pickup anxiously.

"Crabbe will pick him up if he has," said Hazlerigg. "There's only one way out. No, here he comes."

There was the sound of light footsteps tripping down the stairs and a little man came almost dancing in. Just inside the door hung a huge framed advertisement of the Consequential Insurance Company, its glass shining. As he passed it the little man paused for a moment to straighten his perfectly straight tie.

"Gentlemen," he said, "I am Mr. Copley. I am very glad to see you."

"Mr. Copley," said Inspector Hazlerigg, "you are not nearly as glad to see me"—Pickup slid unobtrusively between him and the door—"as I am to see you . . ."

I heard the whole story from Inspector Hazlerigg some time later.

"What was it you spotted in the leases? What did they all have in common?" I asked.

"Well, it wasn't a pinch of dust," said Hazlerigg.

"All right," I said, "don't rub it in. What was it?"

"They all had a clause," said Hazlerigg, "forbidding the tenant' to have any sort of pet. Wouldn't have kept the premises neat, you see . . ."

Cora Jarrett is now, unfortunately, no longer writing mysteries. "The Little Dry Sticks" which we publish here is an almost perfect example of the tale of true detection with the plus value of deeply realized characters. Unfortunately again, this type of story is not being written very often today. Perhaps it never was. But if some of our younger writers would learn Miss Jarrett's secret of painstaking construction and simplicity in telling, they, we, and the mystery story would all benefit.

16

The Little Dry Sticks

By Cora Jarrett

It was the bitterest of winter afternoons. The earth was iron, the fierce wind had an unearthly acrid keenness that was like an actual smell in our flinching nostrils as they drew it in. The deserted roads and fields—for the day was Sunday—were desolate beyond the natural desolateness of the day and hour. "Fine day for a tramp," grunted our host sarcastically, and yet with a trace of amusement in his deep pleasant voice. Pelham and I, with our heads hunched against the blast, grunted back, but without the amusement; after all, these people over the hill were his friends and not ours. And until Danby's small car balked and refused to start in the cold, we had expected to drive. "And to think," wheezed young Pelham, between his attempts to blow upon stiffening fingers, "that the three of us would be sitting this minute in front of a blazing fire if Danby weren't such a ladies' man."

Danby, well-known as the most considerate of hosts, and certainly not a ladies' man at all, would have had a right to resent this saucy speech from anybody but Pelham. Pelham spent his young life ragging his elders, in the most affectionate way in the world, and as if nobody, however honored and famed, however gray-haired or otherwise reverend, was a day over twenty-five years old; and in consequence he was scolded and loved and invited everywhere. He was, in those happy days, of which that day of our winter walk was the very last, the delight of us all. And his own particular delight and admiration was Danby.

Danby now said, with his habitual lazy amusement, "I told you both to stay at home, you young cub."

"And we rejoined," said Pelham, "that we were better men than you, and would prove it, if we froze our ears off." This contingency really seemed not unlikely to me, as my numbed feet stumbled on the bars of the gate we were climbing. "Moreover," said Pelham, as he followed, "when it's a case of beauty in distress—"

"She's not a beauty, and she's not in distress," retorted Danby.

"About the beauty, that's as it may be," said our young friend, "and as I still hope to see the lady, please heaven, before my eyeballs are totally congealed, I'll judge of that for myself. But any lady is in distress, whether she knows it or not, who calls for practical advice upon a scientific man."

Danby, the eminent scientist, grunted.

"The scientific mind," declared young Pelham, skipping from frozen clod to clod in that wicked cold, as we cut across the field, "functions without the human touch. No link with life. And it's always spilling the beans."

"The links of life," said Danby coolly, "are all scientific. Every darn one of 'em."

"You don't follow me, really you don't," said Pelham. "It distresses me, Danby, to see how you're losing your grip."

Danby's eye, turned indulgently on the audacious youth, was the eye of an adult police dog taking in a Sealyham pup. But deep down in it glimmered the look of a childless man at the youth he would have liked for a son. Danby was not married. Women liked the superficial brutality of his face, men loved the sensitiveness, seldom glimpsed, under his disillusioned ways. Pelham worshipped him. His days at Danby's tiny place in the country, to which so few of us were ever asked, were the happiest days of his life. Danby was celebrated to the world's ends, and poor as only a very celebrated scientist can be poor. His delightful shabby sitting room, his one manservant, his plain food and wonderful cigars, remain in my mind as part of a time that was too good to last. We wished for his invitations; if we got one we bragged. "Down at Redoaks, Sunday. Danby's place, you know. Yes, *the* Danby. The chemist."

There were seldom any women, young or old. But women liked Danby; they always invited him, and sometimes he went. He could be a good friend to women.

That this was so, our present bleak expedition was proof. We were taking it because a certain Mrs. Elderson, unknown to either of us, had asked our host to advise her, and he had not refused. I was prepared to find her a disagreeable woman; any woman who would drag a man out in such a wind as this—for the day and hour were of her own choosing—must have, if there was any justice in heaven, a sharp voice and a number nine shoe. Decidedly, our course across the fields was not improving my temper. The short cut, chosen to avoid the sweep of wind on the bare highroad, was certainly no warmer, and was devilish rough underfoot. Pelham, however, was undepressed.

"Our honored host," he said, "is in a bad way. Can't follow a train of thought. Let's see if I can put it in words of one syllable. You saw that play, *Interference?*"

We had all seen it.

"The hero is a doctor. You remember, after the murder, how all the clues are faked to save the suspected person?"

We remembered.

"And just then, when the police and everybody have been put quite off the scent—when the plant is within a hair's breadth of working like a charm—the scientific mind observes, and tells the police, that the supper tray of the left-handed lady has been set the wrong way round! Great work! And it brings suspicion down instantly—bang!—on the very person whom the doctor wants to protect."

Danby smiled maliciously; Pelham had made one slip. "The unidentified faculty used by journalists in those crises when other people employ their minds," said Danby, "seems in your case to function quite normally. You've got everything right except the single detail that makes the whole thing wrong. The person who spills those particular beans in that play, by pointing out the discrepancy to the police—I'm sorry, Pelham—is the newspaper man. And here, thank the Lord, is the gate!"

The gate was a wooden affair, gray for want of paint; it hung between handsome stone posts grown over with vines. The edges of the drive were furred with brittle skeletons of weeds. The air of almost cynical neglect that overhung Mrs. Elderson's acres of ground did not prepare me for the aspect of the house, which rose above us on its knoll; as we approached it, the whole effect of it, even in that winter twilight, was clear and bright. Even the leafless vines of the porch were vines that had been tended and trimmed. It had been painted—not indeed very lately, but lately enough. Its broad low roof, unlike the roof of the summerhouse on the lawn, had an unpatched and perfect sweep. The glass of its front windows, not yet lighted, was polished glass; it was not dull, it gleamed. And having already confessed my feeling against the instigator of our comfortless walk, I will further own that by this time my prejudice went farther; I began to get a distinctly unpleasant impression from this contrast between the house and its grounds. That smiling house, rising out of an unkempt lawn and a ruined garden, looked to me like a callous castaway on a tiny raft, leaving everything around it to drown.

Meantime, as we mounted the drive, Danby himself lamented the state of the grounds, outward sign of a restriction of income that he had already mentioned to us. It was his particular reason for wishing to help this lady. Her husband, stricken in years, had lately muddled away a lot of money; she was taking things over in the hope of saving what remained.

"I hope," said Danby, "that the house won't have to be sold. Mrs. Elderson planned it herself, and it's charming. Just look at this end."

He led us to the right, round the corner, to a side that was invisible from the drive, and even to my chilled senses the house was all that he said. Every aspect of it had charm and character. Suddenly he shivered loudly in my ear. "Brrr! Trust a woman to be ventilating something, even if it's in Greenland! This temperature must be close to nothing at all—and look at that window. Wide open!"

"Women," said Pelham, shivering in sympathy as we followed our host up the steps to the front door, "don't realize that air is no good in winter till it's aged in the wood." And till it is warmed, I thought, bringing up the rear. Well warmed. Steam heat—wood fires—hot whisky punch—

Such were my thoughts when, before we had time to ring, the door opened. A lady, becomingly hatted and wrapped, stood on the threshold. But my first pleasant impression was submerged in shocked dismay when she stepped outside the door and closed it behind her. There were introductions and handshakes and compliments on our promptness. We already knew that we were to inspect a field where she was asked to allow the passage of a transmission line. We now learned that she had forestalled our ringing of the bell that her husband might not be disturbed; she had listened for steps on the porch. Mr. Elderson, who was far from strong, was having his afternoon nap in the library; he would see us when we came back again for tea. And while we stood there, I for one almost ready to cry with cold, Mrs. Elderson stepped down from the porch.

Now for his own somewhat heartless feeling about the events of that afternoon, Pelham, even in his deepest distress, could account quite naturally afterward. "To think," he said, "that if Danby's car had been running that day I might have liked her from the first!" The boy is right. If we had alighted warm from a snug car we should have welcomed the notion of getting our short cold walk over before we settled down to tea and a fire. But even a short walk, on top of a long cold one, was an appalling prospect. Sullenly we followed her. Only the thickness of a door between us and a warm room—even the hall—even three minutes in a warm hall— As Pelham says, not even Danby should have expected us to sympathize with the misfortunes of a lady who had made on us, however innocently and thoughtlessly, such a painful first impression. "Consideration for husbands is all very well," growled Pelham to me, "but even the unmarried male is human. What harm would it have done her to lend me a blanket?" He hunched himself in his thin overcoat.

Danby, striding along, vigorous and glowing, in the big rough canvas-and-sheepskin coat that he used for winter walks, seemed to think that the blood coursed just as freely under our inadequate city clothes. We were all for haste, and he hardly hurried at all; he seemed to think that we enjoyed his friend Mrs. Elderson as much as he did himself. And heaven knows that under a more propitious star I, too, might have liked her very well. Clearly, she was younger than her husband, whom Danby described as elderly if not old. She was slim and erect and still blonde—I judged: not artificially, or very discreetly so. Her dress was the dress of a lady quite capable of designing such a charming house.

I thought her nervous and a little hard, but she had fascination; that I could feel it at all that day proves that it was great indeed. We reached the site of the proposed transmission line, and over this business she was kind enough not to linger, and I began to bless her. By this time the wind was like a knife. After all, she needed only to be assured that the line would not injure the property, which she might yet be obliged to sell; and we reassured her with one voice. The spot was ten minutes' walk from the house; she had brought us round by a rather longer way, to show us the winter sunset from the hill, but by the very shortest path—so Danby told us—the distance was a ten-minute walk, if you walked rapidly. We agreed that Mrs. Elderson might grant the easement, for the sum that was offered her, with no misgivings whatever.

"Thank you," she said heartily, adding with almost violent frankness. "I have many uses for the money. Too many." There was a queer little silence. I was surprised that she did not now without delay turn our steps toward the house and tea. Instead, she stood for a moment without saying anything; she might almost have been thought to hesitate. She broke a little stick that she held between her hands.

"I would take a bet," said Danby, who was watching her with a more indulgent smile than was natural to his rather saturnine features—or indeed, I remember thinking rather testily, to the features of any man whom the lady regarded was keeping out-of-doors in a very cold wind—"that you have at some time in your life done a great deal of camping."

She looked surprised, but nodded. "At one time I spent many months of the year in that way. With my first husband." She spoke briefly; her first marriage had been a failure; we knew that she spoke of it very seldom. "How did you guess?"

"In the way that Pelham says a scientist never guesses." He chuckled cheerfully at Pelham. "Through interest in the human life about me." Pelham opened his mouth and shut it again. Of course this was not what he had said at all, but he did not want a discussion out here in the fields; he wanted a speedy start for a warm room and some tea. So he held his peace. Danby went on. "On several occasions when I have walked with you I have noticed that you have a habit of picking up very small sticks, and carrying them in your hand as you walk. Sometimes when I have parted from you I have noticed you walking away from me still holding the little stick you have chosen; sometimes I have even seen you with two or three sticks at a time—holding them, playing with them. You pick up sticks at all times, as if it were a habit, but the ones that you keep and carry in your hand are always very short and very dry. And this unconscious principle of choice I attribute to your experience in the woods. You have the eye of the practiced woodsman choosing sticks for a quick fire."

She said quietly, "You are perfectly right,"—said it even with the thin ghost of a smile. But she was very pale. Clearly he had reminded her of something that she did not like to remember. "It is a good thing," she said, "that on this bitter day we do not need to depend on anything I may pick up. A fire of logs is waiting for us at the house, and you must want your tea—which very carelessly I failed to order. Let us lose no more time." But in the same moment, just turning toward the way by which we had come, she stopped. "I hate to ask—but if you would do me one more favor, all three of you! Would you follow the surveyor's stakes to the corner of our land and tell me if I must consent to sacrifice the big elm? If it's absolutely necessary?"

Her voice was pleading. Her face, still pale in the dim light, was pleading too. Obediently we turned back, but Mrs. Elderson did not turn with us. "I must see about the tea. You'll forgive me? The stakes are quite plain; I'm sure you'll be no more than twenty minutes after me." I told myself grimly that we should be less than twenty if I had my way. . . . all the more that the lady herself, vanishing between the cedar hedges on her way back to the house, was walking very slowly indeed as she disappeared. Almost strolling. What right had a lady, when three of her fellow creatures were freezing in her service, to feel warm enough to walk as slowly as that?

As for us, our pace was anything but leisurely. We walked as fast as freezing men, eager for shelter, would naturally walk, and our inspection of the threatened elm was brief indeed, for the tree seemed to us not to be threatened at all.

An old negress of a cook-like appearance opened to us and spoke to Danby by name; one inferred the waitress's afternoon out. The hall was warm and bright, and the welcoming voice of Mrs. Elderson descended to us from above. She stood by the railing of the wide gallery upstairs, and over it she looked down at us, still holding her hat in her hand. "I'm ashamed not to be ready; I should have walked faster. Will you join my husband in the library?" She indicated the still unlighted room on the right of the hall. "I haven't been in to wake him, but it's time he was waked. If you'll just switch the light on—Mr. Danby knows the place. I'll be down—" Her voice trailed away into sanctuaries of the toilette, and we opened the library door. Out of the dark, we were met by a wave of heat. My thought was: "The old chap must be very old indeed if he likes it like this." For even to my ill-used frame, still craving warmth, the room was unpleasantly hot. Danby found the button, he touched it. We saw a small, comfortable room with deep chairs. A very low fire, burned down to redness, was before us on the hearth, and in front of it, in the deepest chair of all, an old man in such a strange attitude that I think I knew instantly he would never change it. Mr. Elderson, fallen over sideways in his comfortable chair, was dead. He had been robbed, and stabbed through the heart.

We were still at the gruesome business of establishing these primary facts, with no thought of how we should tell his wife, when an appalling screech and a crash of china from the door behind us testified to the sensitiveness of the cook. She fled in howling hysterics. Danby rose with a heartfelt curse; he had just time to catch Mrs. Elderson in the hall, rushing down. We heard him murmur something, then something else. Presently, over the ruins of the tea tray, he brought her in.

That was the time when I began to be ashamed of not having admired her before. Frightfully shaken, ashen-white, with trembling lips and hands, she was still plucky and cool. She told us how to get the Sheriff and the doctor; when they came she helped us to check up the indications—unhappily so few—of how the deed was done. Her husband had been stabbed with a knife, and his pocketbook and watch were gone. Anyone might have entered the house; though the front door was locked, and the back door under the eye of the cook, the side door was unlocked. No footprints could be traced on the frozen ground; the dusk was deep enough to have hidden completely an intruder's escape. And apparently not a clue of any kind had been left behind.

We had got as far as this when Mrs. Elderson interrupted us with an uncontrollable cry. "It's my fault. I shouldn't have left him. You must tell me, I've got to know—surely he wasn't dead before I left the house?"

No. No indeed. The doctor could assure her of that.

"But then—if instead of dawdling—instead of walking home slowly, I had hurried—if I had even come straight to him when I got back, might I have been in time?" Her suspense, waiting for his answer, was very moving to see. "How long has he—" Her voice failed suddenly and sank away, but her look kept on asking.

The doctor was evidently moved. "Mr. Elderson has been dead more than half an hour. He was dead sometime before you entered the house." He took courage. "Your husband's body is cold, it is even beginning to be stiff. From its temperature and rigidity, I should say that life has been extinct for not less than thirty and possibly for forty minutes. And in a room heated, as this is, almost to eighty degrees, the coagulation of blood from a wound is slow; that also gives us a measure."

She gasped. "Then, even if I had hurried—" I thought again of her composed figure, turning in between the cedars.

He shook his head. But she was somber again, and shivering. "If I hadn't gone. If only I hadn't. Think, Doctor Greene! At twenty minutes past four I left the house—I saw the kitchen clock when I went out to tell Agnes that my husband mustn't be disturbed—and these gentlemen came just after. At two minutes of five I came in again by the kitchen door, in order to tell Agnes at once about tea; I went up the back stairs, straight from the kitchen, in such haste that I was still giving directions as I went up, all the way to the top—and only a few minutes later Mr. Danby and his friends were back. Here we all were, I mean, in the house with my husband—before—and after. And such a short time between! I can never forgive myself." Her agitation choked her.

But the next moment, fortunately, she was in better hands than those of tongue-tied dumbly sympathizing males: two women neighbors arrived. Shedding tears at last—we noted it thankfully —she was borne away and we were left to grind our teeth over the riddle on our hands.

We found nothing. Nothing. Pelham telephoned the facts to

his newspaper, but there was little to say. The old negress was of course above suspicion; the other servants, chauffeur and maid, were in town for the day, and their movements could be checked. The sum of money taken was not large, and there was no reason to think that Mr. Elderson was believed to keep large sums on hand. The thing had the look of an impulsive crime, done on the spur of the moment when opportunity served, perhaps by a passing tramp. But no tramps had been seen passing.

A farmer, rattling homeward, had seen a car turn in at somebody's gate, in the dusk; it might have been the Eldersons' gate. A car could have come up unheard by the cook—bandits roamed in cars. The police also heard that the cook had been expecting a visit from her husband; but she swore—and telephone inquiries partly confirmed this—that he had never come at all. The investigators—by this time there were several—were more at a loss than ever. And the doctor rose to go.

"You don't think," Danby asked him, as we stood with him in the hall, "that Mrs. Elderson will worry herself ill?"

The doctor shook his head. "She'll feel better about it presently." He eyed us briefly. "There's a special reason why she will stop worrying—as soon as she thinks of it. As soon as the shock passes, and she remembers. I dropped a word to her only a month ago, rather doubting my own wisdom at the time, but now I'm glad I did. Mr. Elderson had a progressive and quite incurable, though painless, disease; he was actually a doomed man, though of course he might have lived for years. And that—bad enough, you'll say, for him—would have been a hundred times worse for her. In cases like his, of course, every treatment is tried; a devoted wife like Mrs. Elderson couldn't have failed to try every one. The thing would have left her broken in health, and quite certainly impoverished. I understand their means have been reduced—in fact," said Doctor Greene, "candidly, I'm sorry it happened this way, but I'm thankful it happened!"

Pelham said to Danby, "I'm not going home with you. I'm staying here." To the officers he said, "I'm on the *Inquirer*. You don't mind?" It was news.

So we were to leave him there. We looked round the room.

"Foolish, I know," said Danby, in the involuntary hushed voice we were using, "but aren't you glad the old fellow was so comfortable when it—happened? Maybe he never knew at all, perhaps he was asleep. He was comfortable, he was warm, he had pulled his chair just where he wanted it—see? Only a man whose wife was out would have pushed up the rug like that."

A rueful smile was our tribute to the truth of this bit of observation. The chair, dragged or pushed along, had carried the rug with it in great careless folds over the smooth wood of the floor, in its approach to the fire. Yes, old Elderson had settled himself just where he wanted to be.

Danby and I had our dinner alone. It was useless, of course, but we talked and speculated and guessed till our tongues and our minds were tired, on and on—till we heard the slam of the gate. Then, in a moment, Pelham was in the room.

We didn't need to ask him; success was written on him. "You're too smart, you two," he said, but he was pleased. "You've guessed!"

"We've guessed that you think you have some news. Spill it!" I said.

"Did you say *some* news? I've got *the* news—the big news, all the news there is. And the credit," he said to Danby, "is yours." Then, as Danby stared, "My hat's off to the scientific mind, Danby. You pulled your stuff without a notion of what you were doing, of course. You've proved my case for me, there," he put in with irrepressible mischief, "up to the hilt. But it was your darned uncanny gift of observation that did the trick."

"What trick?"

"Ran the thing down. Caught the criminal—redhanded."

"*My* observation?" stuttered Danby.

"From the minute when you noticed the window—mind if I stop to light?" He struck a match, he puffed, the cigar was off. "I say—let me tell it my own way, will you?" But Danby had to ask one question: "The window?"

"The one that was open—you remember? You noticed it, you pointed it out. Well—it was the library window!"

"You don't mean some one got in—had got in—*then*. But the doctor said—"

"No one got in—there. Lord, no! It isn't so simple as that. See here—do let me tell it my way!" We kept still.

"This is just how it happened: Elderson's murderer entered by the side door when the old man was of course alone in the house except for the cook dozing in the kitchen. Entered the house, entered the room where Elderson was sitting, and took him into the library."

"But Elderson was already," I cried, "in the library!"

"No. That's a mistake. He was napping by the dining-room fire."

"Then he was killed, and taken—"

"No. First taken, then killed." My mind had a picture of an old man gagged and struggling. "But why?"

"I'm coming to that. We got the reason why from the very first clue you gave us, Danby. The rug! You remember the rug—how it was all pushed up in folds?"

"But just as any rug would be," said Danby, as puzzled as I, "if a man drew his chair toward the fire."

"Excuse me. *Not* just as any rug would be. Those folds were not in front of the chair. They were on one side. The chair had been moved sideways, and not forward in the direction of the fire, at all. The chair had been moved toward the middle of the room from a position somewhere near the window. And at the time when it was moved—there was a heavy weight in it."

"Elderson?"

"Elderson, alive or dead. But most probably—in fact, certainly—quite dead."

"But, there's no sense in any of it," said Danby, pulling at his pipe.

"That's what we thought," said Pelham. "No sense at all. We thought we had not a clue in the world, not the ghost of one—and all at once, there at our feet, was something that cried aloud to be explained. Why had the chair moved sideways, and in a direction that brought it no nearer to the fire? And of course that made us look at the fire."

Pelham looked with shining eyes at Danby. "That's where your real stroke of genius came in! You'll get full credit. For that wasn't an ordinary fire at all, and after we had had a good look at it we looked around for what I remembered your mentioning out in the field—the little dry sticks that Mrs. Elderson habitually picked up to start her fires with. At last, not by the wood box, but by a deep cupboard to one side, we saw some dust of very dry bark, and we opened the cupboard door. Well—the murderer of Mr. Elderson had opened it before us."

"Fingerprints?" I said.

He shook his head. "We didn't need them. The cupboard had apparently been quite full of Mrs. Elderson's little sticks. And almost every one of them was gone."

"Gone?"

"Of course, burned. You remember that the room was hot? I'll tell you why. The reason flashed on me when I suddenly thought of your third clue, Danby—the window. When Elderson was stabbed, that little library was like Greenland. Elderson's body was left by an open window in a chair, in a room that was freezing cold, for—well, we'll say for as long as Elderson's murderer dared. Then a fire was lighted—a roaring fire, that would bring the temperature up with a run, and fall to ashes—look like a burnt-out fire of logs. And at the last moment Elderson's chair was pushed away from the window into a plausible position in the middle of the room; and as the chair was too heavy to lift, the rug was pushed before it in folds. In folds on one side. That's the story, corroborated by confession, of Elderson's murder."

"The murderer's really caught?" I said. "And confessed?"

"Confessed. After we found the knife."

"But hold on! Hold on!" cried Danby. "What criminal in his senses would fool around with fires and windows after the thing was done?"

"You haven't realized," said Pelham, "the effect of extreme cold on a dead body. I mean, in the first moments of its being dead. A very short time under an open window in a temperature like that would coagulate blood. A body exposed like that would seem, if you came on it just afterward in a very warm room, to be the body of a person who had been dead longer than was actually the case."

"I see," said Danby. "By Jove, that's clever; it confuses the time, doesn't it? A man seen leaving a house at a certain moment wouldn't be connected with a crime—" Suddenly he stopped. "But see here, it works backwards! And it ought to work forward to do any good. For an alibi, I mean. The crime should have been made to look as if it happened later, not earlier.

"Say a man leaves a house at five. You don't connect him with a crime that occurred, or seems to have occurred, at five-ten. But you are darn likely to associate his movements with a murder committed at four-fifty five! Let's see how it works out, by the clock.

"Why, why—Pelham," Danby stammered, with a look of new and sharp distress, "that puts the old chap's death a lot closer to the time when we might have saved him! Suppose we hadn't gone to look at that damn tree—why, from that spot in the field where

Mrs. Elderson left us—left us going the wrong way, three able-bodied men who would have made short work"—Danby sat forward in the chair—"from that spot, Pelham, a good runner could have made it in four minutes!"

I thought Pelham looked strange. He said, "A good runner *did* make it. In three. We found the knife in her bureau drawer."

In the unnatural, stunned silence I heard myself say, "In *her*—?"

"With the pocketbook and the watch. She felt as safe as that."

I saw the horror and stupefaction of Danby's face.

"She sent us on a fool's errand, to look at that tree; and as soon as she was out of our sight she ran. She went in by the side door; she waked the old fellow up from his nap by the dining-room fire, where she had left him; she hustled him into the library and knifed him! The open window did the rest. Her chimneyful of little dry sticks was ready beforehand, she had seen to that! But she hadn't known that you would speak of her little dry sticks in my hearing. I tell you, she thought she was as safe as a church! She cut the time as fine as she dared before she shut the window and lighted the fire and slipped out by the side door again. Then all she had to do was to go in through the kitchen, making sure that the old negress noticed the clock. She had it all planned— and it clicked."

"But *why*? Why did she do it?" I cried. "Haven't you heard Danby talk about her devotion to that old man?" Danby's shocked face, even in the gloom, was white. These people had been his near neighbors for several years.

"I think," said Pelham's stern young voice, "that she just didn't want to be poor. She might have waited for him to die if she hadn't feared that by the time he was gone, the money would be gone too. You see, I haven't a doubt there's another man somewhere. Another man . . . a liaison, I'm sure of it. But no money! Doesn't it fit in? Wouldn't it account for her amiable willingness to carry on, as long as her precious personal future wasn't threatened? I guess she had all she wanted! But when she saw poverty ahead . . ." It was Pelham's turn to sit forward in his chair. For all his disclaiming the mood of an avenger of blood, it was like an avenger of blood that he spoke. "Think of it! Can't you picture it, can't you see it? Think of how she must have tested it out, over and over again, with that poor old devil asleep in his bed upstairs. So many minutes with a fire of little dry sticks, piled probably halfway up the chimney, to raise the temperature of that room . . . you remember it's a small one . . . so many degrees! As to the actual effect of the cold, and the open window, of course she had to guess. Just guess, and pick the coldest Sunday afternoon she could find, when the waitress and the man were out of the way. And it worked, it worked to a charm. It fooled the doctor, it fooled the police, it fooled everybody but Danby. Your name is going to be in the headlines tomorrow, Danby, as the champion sleuth of the ages! What do you think about that?"

"I think," said Danby in a sudden firm loud voice, "that we all need a drink." He rose from his dark corner, he got out the makings, he mixed us three of the stiffest glasses it was ever my lot to drain. And by the time that I got mine down, I was to realize that I needed it indeed. But we did not drink for a moment yet, because Danby said, "I must get something," and stepped away from us into his little laboratory behind the living room. As he came back, we heard his voice, "Get ready. We'll drink to a good night's sleep."

"That be hanged," said Pelham. "I'm a newspaper man. A good night's sleep is more than I shall get!"

But Danby said, "I'll sleep all right." For the first time I saw that he was holding a small brown bottle, he was dropping a liquid into a glass. From a dawning wonder at seeing Danby, of the iron nerves, feel the need of any drug, I was distracted by his voice. "You win, Pelham. You've made me prove your case against the scientific mind."

"What rot! It's all the other way," cried Pelham eagerly and anxiously, afraid he had offended Danby whom he liked so much, and whose voice all at once sounded so very queer.

"The case against the mind that never knows what it's doing till it's done. . . . I guess I've proved *that*. I've brought suspicion down, landed it square. . . ." He stopped.

"But she. . . . But Mrs. Elderson. . . ." I stammered, "she isn't. . . . Is she. . . ."

"My mistress," said Danby, and drank.

Of course he was stone dead before he struck the floor. My hardest job was making Pelham believe it.

If there is one name which is responsible for the present high status of the mystery short story, that name is Ellery Queen. Two who share the name are many things: writer, editor, anthologist, historian of the genre, founding member and Past President of MWA, teacher, and, perhaps above all, discoverer of new talent (at this writing, some two hundred thirty "Firsts" have appeared in EQMM). The third Ellery Queen is a detective in the Grand Tradition. No collection of the Cream could be complete without him.

17

Diamonds in Paradise

Ellery Queen

Maybe Lili Minx was THE GIRL of your dreams, too. It's nothing to be ashamed of. Lili caused more insomnia in her day than all the midnight maatjes herring consumed on Broadway and 51st Street on all the opening nights put together since Jenny Lind scared the gulls off the roof of Castle Garden.

It wasn't just Lili's face and figure, either, although she could have drifted out on a bare stage before a two-bit vaudeville flat and stood there for two hours and twenty minutes just looking at you, and you'd have headed for your herring mumbling "smash hit." It wasn't even her voice, which made every other set of female pipes on Broadway sound like something ground out of a box with a monkey on it. It was the trick she had of making every male within eyeshot and mike range feel that he was alone with her in a dreamboat.

Of course there was a catch, as the seven yachtsmen she married found out. With all her wonderful equipment, Lili was a mixed-up kid. She was a hopelessly incurable gambler, and she was hipped on diamonds. And the two things didn't seem to go together. Let the psychologists explain it, but the fact is money didn't mean a thing to her. She could drop ten grand at the roulette wheel and yawn like a lady. Diamonds were another story. Let her temporarily mislay a single chip from her jewel box and she went into hysterics. Her press agent swore that she checked her inventory every night before going to bed like a kid casing his marbles.

Naturally, Lili's collection was the target of every itch-fingers out of the jug. But Lili was no push-over. When it came to her diamonds, she was like a Javert in the sewers of Paris; she never gave up. The police were kept busy. They didn't mind. With La Minx on the broadcasting end of a complaint, every cop with a front porch and asthma felt like No-Hips Lancelot, the Terror of the Underworld.

Lili's favorite gambling hell, while it lasted, was Paradise Gardens. Those were the days when New York was wide open and everything went, usually before you could come back for more. Paradise Gardens had a longer run than most. It operated behind a frowsy old brownstone front of Fifth Avenue, in the Frolicking Fifties.

The ceiling was a menace to healthy eyesight, with its glittering stars and sequinned angels; you swallowed your buffalo steaks and cougar juice among tropical flowers under papier-mâché trees with wax apples tied onto them; and you were served by tired ex-show-girl-type waitresses wearing imitation fig leaves. So it was a relief to go upstairs where there was no mullarkey about gardens or Edens —just nice business décor and green baize-covered tables at which the management allowed you to lose your shirt or bra, as the case might be.

On this particular evening Lili Minx, being between husbands, was alone. She drifted in, pale and perfect in white velvet and ermine, unapproachable as the nearest star and tasty-looking as a charlotte russe. On each little pink ear glowed a cold green fire, like a radioactive pea, La Minx's only jewelry tonight. They were the famous mumtaz green-diamond earrings, once the property of Shah Jahan's favorite wife, which had been clipped to Lili's lobes by the trembling hands of an Iraqi millionaire, who was running hard at the time in the sixth race of La Minx Handicap. Lili prized her green diamonds at least as highly as the ears to which they were attached.

Everything stopped as Lili posed in the archway for her usual moment of tribute: then life went on, and Lili bought a stack of hundred-dollar chips at the cashier's cage and made for the roulette table.

An hour later, her second stack was in the croupier's bank. Lili laughed and drifted toward the ladies' lounge. No one spoke to her.

The trim French maid in the lounge came forward swiftly. "Madame has the headache?"

"Yes."

"Perhaps a cold compress?"

"Please."

Lili lay down on a chaise longue and closed her eyes. At the cool touch of the wrapped ice bag on her forehead she bestowed a smile. The maid adjusted the pillow about her head deftly, in sympathetic silence. It was quiet in the deserted lounge, and Lili floated off into her own world of dreams.

She awoke a few minutes later, put the ice bag aside, and rose from the chaise. The maid had discreetly vanished. Lili went to a vanity and sat down to fix her hair. . . .

And at that exact moment the gambling rooms of Paradise Gardens went berserk. Women shrieked, their escorts scuttled about like trapped crabs, the housemen struggled with their nefarious tools, and the massive door gave way under the axheads of the police.

"Hold it!" An elderly man with a gray mustache hopped nimbly onto a crap table and held up his arms for silence. "I'm Inspector Queen of police headquarters on special gambling detail. This is a raid, ladies and gentlemen. No sense trying to make a break; every exit is covered. Now if you'll all please line up along the walls while these officers get going—"

And that was when Lili Minx burst from the ladies' lounge like one of the Furies, screaming, "My diamond earrings! I been robbed!"

So immediately what had begun as a gambling raid turned into a robbery investigation. La Minx was in top form, and Inspector Queen did her bidding as meekly as a rookie cop. She had often enough disturbed his dreams, too.

As the axes rose and fell and the equipment flew apart, the Inspector was crooning, "Now don't worry your pretty head, Miss Minx. We'll find your earrings—"

"And that creep of a maid!" stormed La Minx. "She's the only one who touched me, Inspector Queen. I want that maid clobbered, too!"

"She can't get away, Lili," soothed the Inspector, patting the lovely hand. "We've had the Paradise surrounded for an hour, getting set for the jump, and not a soul got out. So she has to be here . . . Well, Velie?" he barked, as the big Sergeant came loping from the ladies' lounge, furtively feeling his tie. "Where is the woman?"

"Right here," said Sergeant Velie, looking at Lili like a homesick Newfoundland. And he thrust into Inspector Queen's hands, blindly, a maid's uniform, a starched cap and apron, a pair of high-heeled shoes, two sheer stockings, and a wig. "Dumped in the broom closet."

"What does this mean?" cried Lili, staring at the wig.

"Why, it's Harry the Actor," said the Inspector, pleased. "A clever character at female impersonation, Lili—he's made his finest hauls as a French maid. So Harry's tried it on you, has he? You just wait here, my dear," and the Inspector began to march along the line-up like a small gray Fate, followed by La Minx, who waited for no one.

"And here he is," said the Inspector cheerily, stopping before a short slender man with boyish cheeks which were very pale at the moment. "Tough luck, Harry—about the raid, I mean. Suppose we try this on for size, shall we?" and he clapped the wig on the little man's head.

"That's the one," said Lili Minx in a throbbing voice, and the little man turned a shade paler. She stepped up to him, and looked deep into his eyes. "You give me back my diamond earrings, or—" She mentioned several alternatives.

"Get her away from me, get her out of here," quavered Harry the Actor in his girlish treble, trying to burrow into the wall.

"Search him, Velie," said Inspector Queen sternly.

A half hour later, in the manager's office, with the drapes drawn before the window, Harry the Actor stood shivering. On the desk lay his clothes and everything taken from his person—a wallet con-

aining several hundred dollars, a pocketful of loose change, a ball
f hard candy, a yellow pencil, a racing form, a pair of battered old
lice, a crumpled cigarette pack and a booklet of matches, a tiny
ial of French perfume, a lipstick, a compact, a handkerchief
meared with make-up and a box of Kiss-Mee, the Magic Breath-
weetener. Everything in parts had been disassembled. The cig-
rettes had been shredded. The hard candy had been smashed.
Harry's clothing had been gone over stitch by stitch. His shoes had
been tapped for hidden compartments. His mouth and hair had
been probed. Various other indignities had been visited upon his
erson. Even the maid's outfit had been examined.

And no green-diamond earrings.

"All right," muttered the Inspector, "get dressed."

And all the while, from the other side of the manager's door,
Lili's creamy voice kept promising Harry what was in store for him
as soon as she could get her little hands on him.

And it drove the thief at last to a desperate folly. In the midst
of stuffing his belongings back in his pockets, he leaped over the
desk, stiff-armed the officer before the window, and plunged head-
first through the drapes like a goat. It was a hard-luck night for
Harry the Actor all around. The railing of the fire escape was rotted
through with rust. His momentum took him into space, carrying
the railing with him.

They heard the railing land on the concrete of the back yard
three stories below, then Harry.

The officers posted in the yard were shaking their heads over the
little man when Inspector Queen and Sergeant Velie dropped off
the fire-escape ladder, followed—inevitably—by Lili.

If the thief had had any hope of cheating his fate, one glazed
look at the furious beauty glaring down at him destroyed it. Either
way he was a goner, and he knew it.

"Harry," said Inspector Queen, tapping the swollen cheek gently. "You're checking out. If you want a fair shake Upstairs, you'd
better talk fast. Where did you stash 'em?"

Harry's eyes rolled. Then his tongue came out and he said
thickly, "Diamonds . . . in . . . the Paradise . . ."

"In the Paradise *what*, Harry?" asked the Inspector frantically,
as Harry stopped. "In the Paradise *where*?"

But Harry had had it.

Ellery always said that, if it wasn't his greatest case, it was certainly his shortest.

He first learned about it when his father staggered home at breakfast time. Ellery got some coffee into the old man and extracted the maddening details.

"And I tell you, son," raved the Inspector, "we went back into that joint and tore it apart. It was rotten luck that Harry died before he could tell us just where in the Paradise Gardens he's hidden Lili's diamonds. They had to be in the building somewhere, either in something or on someone. We still hadn't let anyone go from the raid. We not only took the Paradise apart piece by piece, we body-searched every mother's son and daughter on the premises, thinking Harry might have passed the earrings on to an accomplice. Well, we didn't find them!" The Inspector sounded as if he were going to cry. "I don't know what I'll say to that lovely child."

"Diamonds speak louder than words," said Ellery briskly. "At least—from all I hear—in the case of Lili Minx."

"You mean . . . ?" said his father. "But how *can* you know where the Actor hid them?" he cried. "You weren't even there!"

"You told me. Harry was putting his belongings away in his pockets when he made his sudden break. Where is Harry now, Dad?"

"Harry? In the Morgue!"

"Then the Morgue is where Lili's earrings are."

"They were *on* him? But Ellery, we searched Harry outside and —and in!"

"Tell me again," said Ellery, "what he had in his pockets."

"Money, a dirty handkerchief, women's cosmetics, a hard candy, a racing form, cigarettes, a pair of dice, a pencil—"

"I quote you quoting the late Actor's dying statement," said Ellery. " 'Diamonds—in Paradise.' "

"Paradise . . ." The Inspector's jaw wiggled. "*Pair o' dice!* His dice were just shells—*they're in the dice!*"

"So if you'll phone the Morgue property clerk, Dad—"

Inspector Queen turned feebly from the phone. "But Ellery, it did sound just like the Paradise . . ."

"What do you expect from a dying man," asked Ellery reasonably, "elocution lesson?"

A few years ago, MWA published an anthology called *The Lethal Sex*. It was restricted to work by women writers. You might expect that a great many of the stories would be "had I but known" "maiden in distress" operas. Wrong! The stories, almost without exception, were shockers, hard, lean, and chilling. A good example is Carolyn Thomas' "A Matter of Ethics." Somewhere women may be turning out reams of trite "feminine" rubbish, but not our members! Not Miss Thomas!

18

A Matter of Ethics

By Carolyn Thomas

Although Trinidadians, native or transplanted, grow bored with hearing their island described as the Crossroads of the Caribbean, there remains enough truth in the cliché to keep it going. Sooner or later, it seems, everybody you've ever known is apt to turn up in Trinidad. Especially is this true of the Queen's Park Hotel in Port of Spain where I encountered Barton Wentworth again after the long years.

It was a sweltering afternoon in mid-May and the cocktail lounge at the Queen's Park is air-conditioned. As a medical man I am aware that there are certain objections to sudden, extreme changes of temperature, but as a mere sweaty human being the vision of a rum punch, slowly sipped in delectable coolness, was irresistible. Moreover, I told myself virtuously, Ellen, my secretary and girl-of-all-work, was looking drawn and pallid from the heat and from having transcribed notes since early morning. She deserved a refresher. In any case, we weren't going to finish the book that day or even the next. One of the pleasant things about having an independent income is the release from pressures.

While we waited for our punches I glanced briefly at our reflections in one of the mirrors paneling the big room. I saw myself, a man of fifty-four, with smooth brown hair flecked by gray, with deep-set gray eyes that held few illusions and a high-cheekboned, almost ascetic face. Although I am only a respectably average five feet ten, I looked very tall beside Ellen who is a tiny little thing, barely five feet and slim. Just twenty-two and fresh out of business college, she has curly dark hair and her face with its intelligent brown eyes has an elfin quality, piquant rather than pretty. But she looks pretty when she smiles, for her smile is an exceptionally sweet one. She has, as is so common in the West Indies, just a touch of the tarbrush, although I wouldn't have guessed it if she hadn't told me.

We might, I thought, from the disparity in our ages, have been taken for father and daughter. And I was aware of a fleeting pang at the thought, not because of my advanced years which don't oppress me unduly, but because I have never had a daughter and I would have liked one. For that matter, I will say, at the risk of inspiring bawdy remarks, that I take a fatherly interest in Ellen. She is a bright girl and a hard worker and I admire her determination to lift herself above an unfortunate home situation. I also like her young man, Leon, who is studying to become an architect. He is an extremely handsome lad, no darker than many of the tourists off cruise ships, and completely devoted to Ellen.

Despite what I have said about people turning up in Trinidad, I was startled when, midway through our drinks, I glimpsed Barton Wentworth at a table not far from ours. Perhaps instead of startled I should say shaken. I had known Wentworth fairly well at one time and seeing him reminded me of events I preferred not to dwell upon. He was with a woman, naturally—nobody I knew—and I observed that his technique had, if anything, improved with the years. Ten years it would have been and they had dealt kindly with him. He was eight years my junior, of course, but if there was any gray in his thick black hair I couldn't see it. Nor could I detect marks of age or dissipation on his bronzed face. It wasn't an especially handsome face and I had often puzzled over what made Bart Wentworth so undeniably attractive to women. It must have been a kind of animal vitality that emanated from him, and, possibly, his own conviction that he was irresistible. He was a big man—six feet two—and brawny, but he thought too much of his body to allow it to become fat. I wondered whether he still took cold showers and hiked five miles before breakfast and gobbled vitamins by the handful.

He may have felt my gaze, for, while I was debating whether to get up and leave without speaking, he glanced our way. The years must not have changed me too much either, physically, because his recognition was immediate. And following recognition, just for a second, an odd expression crossed his face. It might have been doubt, if one could imagine Bart Wentworth's ever being unsure of himself; it could have been apprehension, except that would have been beneath his manly vigor and he knew of no reason to fear me. Whatever it was, the expression vanished almost at once to be replaced by a genial smile. We were, I knew, in for it now and I slowly got to my feet as he came toward me, his hand outstretched.

"Heffner! Paul Heffner! Well, I'll be damned! If you'll pardon the expression, imagine meeting you here!"

"Hello, Bart," I said, shaking his hand as briefly as possible.

He still took a childish glee in crushing one's fingers in his grip and his sheer looming bulk still made me feel dwarfed when I stood beside him.

I forced cordiality into my voice as I presented him to Ellen, adding, "Bart is the Barton Wentworth whose by-line you've seen in the paper. Pretty widely syndicated now, aren't you, Bart?"

Ellen's eyes grew round with respect, which spurred him to greater heights of good fellowship.

"Sure am," he agreed. "I've just been in Venezuela on a yarn. Aren't they always having a hell of a time about something? So then I got this brilliant thought of stopping here a few days—maybe get a story on how the new West Indies Federation is panning out. Say, what are you doing here, Doc? Just playing around?"

He grinned meaningly at Ellen.

"I live here. I've lived here about eight years now."

"The hell you do! Knew you'd dropped out of sight, but didn't think much about it—I've lost touch with so many of my old friends."

I felt sure he was speaking the truth. Bart Wentworth would lose touch with his old friends as he mounted the ladder. I murmured something, wishing he would leave. Bart, however, had always had all the sensitivity of an ox.

"Say, this is great running into you, Heffner. I'll bet you can give me a lot of tips on the local situation. I came in from Caracas this afternoon and haven't got to work yet." He glanced quickly toward the table where his companion waited, impatiently, I imagine. And he added, with his old insinuating smile, "Not real work."

"I'm no authority on the Federation," I said. "But I'll be glad to give you any help I can. I might be able to arrange some introductions—that sort of thing."

While we talked he had been scrutinizing Ellen with that bold, suggestive stare, and the poor girl was more flustered than I had ever seen her. Averting her eyes and blushing, she drained her punch in a gulp. I felt my fingers tighten on my own glass.

"Here's the deal," Bart said. "I'll ditch this babe I've got in tow and you and your—ah—secretary have dinner with me. I'll give you all the latest news flashes on the good old U.S.A. and you can fill me in on What Every Young Boy Should Know in Trinidad. Okay?"

The last thing I wished was to have dinner with Barton Wentworth, who would almost certainly want to make a night of it, but I saw no graceful way of bowing out. And also, something that could have been the beginning of an idea was stirring in my unconscious.

I said, "Why, thanks, Bart, I'll be delighted. Unfortunately, I believe Ellen has a date with her fiancé and won't be able to join us."

Noting his alerted look, I regretted the slight emphasis I had given the word fiancé. Learning that another man had a prior claim had always whetted his interest. I'm sure that at first he had assumed that the prior claim was mine, but I'm not that particular kind of fool. Except for his poaching instincts, I doubt that Ellen would have appealed very much to Bart Wentworth, lacking as she does that flamboyance he usually went for. Not always, but usually. The woman who still waited at the other table, for instance, a spectacular blonde, was much more his type.

While he returned to the blonde to make whatever glib excuses came to his tongue, I laid down the law to Ellen. She was wistful;

I suppose having dinner, and perhaps a series of luncheons and dinners, with a well-known newspaper correspondent appealed to her young imagination as romantic. But I was too fond of Ellen and I liked her Leon too well to let Barton Wentworth mess up their lives as he very likely would, given half a chance. Ellen pouted a bit and pointed out that she wasn't married yet, but she didn't really want to hurt Leon so she took my advice and left to keep her date.

Bart came back, looking well satisfied with himself, and the first thing he said was, "Hey, where's little cutie-pie?"

"I told you she had a previous engagement."

"Aw, she could have busted it. You always were a selfish bastard, Paul. I'll bet you scared her off with stories about the big, bad wolf."

He would have guffawed if I'd explained that Ellen was like a daughter to me, so I forbore argument.

He demanded, "How come you need a secretary, anyway? Is she a nurse?"

I shook my head.

"I'm not practicing here." I paused, then added quietly, "I sold my practice in the States after my wife's death. Losing Cynthia hit me pretty hard, you know."

"Uh, sure, must have been tough." He had always shied away from the thought of death or suffering and now he looked uncomfortable, casting about for a change of subject.

I said, "Fortunately I've found a project of absorbing interest and, I hope, one that will be of real value. I'm working on a book about tropical diseases, using an approach that's quite unique."

"God!" he grimaced. "Don't see how you can stand even to think about such things, much less write about them. So far as that goes, I don't see how you can stand living in a place like this where you must be exposed to all kinds of gruesome germs all the time."

"Your theory being that some germs are more gruesome than others?"

"You damned well know they are. Well, I took precautions. Before this trip I got shot for everything from yellow fever to the plague. Say, Paul, those inoculations are sure-fire, aren't they? I mean, once you've had 'em you're one hundred per cent guaranteed not to catch anything, aren't you?"

I smiled. "Now, Bart, you must understand that such sweeping generalizations are distasteful to the scientific mind. Let us say that the inoculations are effective *virtually* always."

"Virtually!" He flagged a passing waiter. "Boy, bring us another round." He fumbled out a filter-tip cigarette and lighted it with hands that were almost steady.

I smiled again. "You should have been a writer of fiction. You have an inflamed imagination."

"It's all very well for you to be casual. You're a doctor and used to all kinds of unpleasantness. But it gives me the willies just to visit anybody in the hospital. I've never been sick a day in my life, except when I broke my leg and that doesn't count, and I think I'd shoot myself before I'd submit to a lingering illness. Especially one of those horrible diseases you've got down here."

He meant it too. I studied him thoughtfully. Perspiration glittered on his forehead and he wiped the back of his neck.

"You're unbalanced on the subject, Bart," I said slowly. "It's not healthy. You ought to take hold of yourself. You know what would be good for you? Let me take you on a visit to the leper colony at Chacachacare. You'd be amazed at how happy many of those people seem. It's still a living death, of course, but someday we may even find a cure for it. Meanwhile, you'll be impressed by the difference between the old days when a leper had to ring a bell and call out, 'Unclean, unclean,' and our modern leprosariums. I should think it would give you good material for a story too."

"God damn it, Heffner, you're needling me! Leper colony! Will you cut it out or shall I slug you one?"

"Why, of course, if you're that unreasonable, we won't continue the discussion. I was only trying to help you out of a bad mental state. Let's forget it. Where shall we eat dinner?"

"What's the matter with right here? Big hotel like this, run by the British, ought to have some notion of sanitation in their kitchens."

When I raised my eyebrows in ever so faint derision, he flared, "All right, God damn it, laugh at me! But don't give me any more of your so-called clinical observations or I'll feel like going up and taking another bath."

As I had drearily anticipated, Wentworth insisted on making a night of it. Quite late that evening we were having a drink on the terrace of the Belvedere high on Lady Chancellor Hill with all of

Port of Spain and the harbor twinkling below. It was a pleasant spot, with frangipani and hibiscus scenting the soft air and night birds swooping around the lanterns. We had stopped at several other places before this and Bart was again in great good spirits. As usual, when he got a little high, he started telling an interminable succession of off-color stories. His attitude was "I don't care whether it's funny or not, just so it's dirty."

I was pretty bored and glanced at my watch, preparatory to breaking it up. He seemed not to notice the gesture, but abruptly broke off his ribald laughter and leaned across the table, lowering his voice.

"Say, Paul, you mentioned earlier about arranging introductions for me. How's about fixing me up with one of these native girls? I understand they're hot little numbers."

I frowned. It was not, of course, quite the sort of introduction I'd had in mind, although, knowing him, I should have anticipated such a request. But I wasn't enthusiastic about acting as procurer for Barton Wentworth.

"Oh, come off it, Paul," he said. "Don't pull that lily-pure stuff on me. You haven't lived here all these years without learning your way around. Don't be so damned selfish all the time."

While I hesitated, still frowning, he said, "I don't care what color she is, just so she's lively. And clean." His tone was suddenly anxious. "You know? I want to be sure about that."

That nameless something stirred in my unconscious again.

"Maybe," I said slowly, "I can arrange something. But you'll have to promise me, Bart, to use the utmost discretion. I have my reputation to think about, you know, and if I do you this favor, you'll have to agree to my conditions."

"Why, hell, discretion is my middle name. Let's get going."

"You wait here a few minutes," I said. "I'll have to make a telephone call."

When I returned and nodded to him that it was all set, we called for the check.

In the parking lot, climbing into my MG, he demanded, "Now this mystery woman, whoever she is, is clean, isn't she? You're sure of that? I don't want to pick up VD down here—or anywhere else, for that matter."

"Bart," I said, with exaggerated patience, "I absolutely guarantee you on my word of honor as a doctor that this girl doesn't have

VD. Does that satisfy you?"

"Well, you don't need to get huffy about it. A fellow can't be too careful."

We wound down the long hill, skirted the north edge of the savannah, and turned into the hills again toward my place in the Maraval section. It's a modest enough colonial bungalow, but nicely situated to catch the night breezes and with sufficient ground to insure privacy. In the rear is a luxuriant tropical garden and at the very end of the garden, far from house and street, a small building which started out in life as a summer house and which I converted into a sort of studio apartment to accommodate any house guests I may have. They are fairly infrequent, but I cannot endure having people underfoot.

Lights still burned in the bungalow and, as I turned off the motor in the drive, I said, "I believe my housekeeper is still up. We'd better go in and have a nightcap—let her know I have a guest."

Mrs. Johnson was just leaving my study after having placed there the tray with whisky, ice and soda which she left for me every night. I introduced Wentworth to her, mentioning that he would be leaving after a drink or two. She is a tall spare woman in her sixties, with that gentle dignity which is characteristic of the West Indian Negro and with that equally characteristic grave courtesy. After a brief chat with Wentworth she retired while I busied myself with highball glasses.

Bart was full of questions and impatience, but I ignored his eagerness, painstakingly giving him my impressions of the West Indian Federation, which was what he was supposed to be interested in. At last, draining my glass, I rose and picked up a flashlight.

"Mrs. Johnson should be asleep. Now I want it understood, Bart, that this is one amorous exploit you will boast of to nobody. Nobody. Not even mention it obliquely. Also, you must promise to be off these premises by daylight. Call a cab, but don't have it come here—have it stop down at the intersection and wait. Agreed?"

He grumbled a bit, but promised. Actually, there was no reason why he couldn't have stayed as long as he liked—Mrs. Johnson would not have been surprised if he had spent the night in the studio. But I thought that part about being off the premises by daylight was a nice dramatic touch. And it amused me to think of

Wentworth, tired and bleary-eyed, creeping back to his hotel in the predawn bleakness. Also, I knew what he didn't: that Trinidad cab-drivers doubled their charges in the small hours. Oh, granted, that was a trifling thing, but gratifying.

I handed him the flashlight and showed him the path leading back through the garden.

"She's waiting for you there, Bart. She's expecting you. Just remember the conditions."

"Well, uh, this is sure great of you, Paul. You're a real pal. I'll give you a buzz tomorrow. Okay?"

"Do that," I said. "I'm in the book."

I stood there a minute, smiling in the darkness as the flashlight's beams receded. I knew that Anna Marie would be there, as she had promised, and I felt sure Anna Marie wouldn't disappoint him. She was the youngest of Mrs. Johnson's ten or twelve children, although I hadn't told him that. Whether she had been a house child or a yard child, I didn't know, but I suspected the latter, for Anna Marie was so light she could have passed. She was twenty-five, very pretty, very charming and very promiscuous. That was important because, while I'm sure Wentworth would have preferred the seduction of a virgin, I would have suffered compunctions about collusion in such an affair.

Nor had I lied to him about the VD. Anna Marie lived with her mother in the servants' quarters at the back of the bungalow. She worked as a maid and when I gave one of my occasional small dinners to repay the generous hospitality always shown to an unattached male she waited on table very nicely. If for no other reason than to protect myself and my guests, I had some time ago had a heart-to-heart talk with Anna Marie, and I also took the precaution of running a blood check on her periodically. Anna Marie knew the facts of life all right, including, I imagine, a few of which even Barton Wentworth was unaware.

I didn't see much of Wentworth from then on till he left Trinidad. He had called me next day, full of enthusiasm about Anna Marie. I repeated my warnings about discretion, but he swore he was calling from a public booth and couldn't be overheard. At his insistence and feigning reluctance, I agreed that he could use the studio to meet her again that night if he would take every precaution against being observed. I believe he met her every night while he was in town.

Then one morning he called and announced that he was taking the two-thirty Pan Am flight back to New York. He would like, he said, to buy me a farewell lunch for what he called auld lang syne and in appreciation of all I had done to make his stay in Trinidad so pleasant. I accepted, suggesting that I drive him out to Piarco where he could get weighed in early and we could then eat at the Bel Air Hotel which has excellent food. It is almost twenty miles from Port of Spain to Piarco Airport and I thought it a gracious gesture on my part. He agreed cheerfully and we arranged that I should pick him up at eleven-thirty.

Probably I should not have taken Ellen along. But she had been very sulky ever since that first night and I hoped to placate her. Also, possibly, to educate her. Bart, of course, was delighted when he came out to the car and found Ellen sitting there, looking so sweet and fresh in her dimity dress and tiny white hat. A seasoned traveler, he carried only a two-suiter and a briefcase, but even so we were crowded in the little car, a fact of which he took full advantage.

By one o'clock he had finished all the formalities including his currency declaration and we were seated in the cool cocktail lounge of the Bel Air with ample time for Daiquiris and a leisurely lunch. If Wentworth felt any pangs about leaving Anna Marie, with whom he had been so smitten, he didn't show it. He was bringing all his charm to bear on Ellen and the poor child was eating it up. Occasionally she spared me a reproachful glance which plainly said, "See how much fun I could have had if you weren't such an old fussbudget?"

I didn't allow Ellen's attitude to ruffle my composure. I was engaged in thinking over what I wanted to say to Barton Wentworth. But I waited till two-fifteen when we were standing near the gate beyond which only embarking passengers were allowed. Then I said quietly, "Remember the other evening, Bart, when I mentioned how broken up I was by my wife's death?"

He looked surprised and wariness crept into his pale blue eyes.

"Sure I remember, Paul. Uh—I don't blame you. Cynthia was a pretty girl. Sweet, too."

"You liked her, didn't you, Bart?"

"Why, hell yes, I thought a lot of Cynthia. I couldn't believe it when I heard about—uh—about her accident. It was an awful shock."

"I'm sure it was," I said. "But you see, Bart, it wasn't an accident. That's just the story I gave out. She took all those sleeping pills on purpose."

His wariness increased.

"No! I can't believe it! Why in hell would she have done such a thing?"

"Because she was in love with another man, Bart. He played around with her for a while and then ditched her for somebody else. She just couldn't take it."

His face flushed and his manner turned blustery.

"How do you know that? Did she tell you?"

"She left a note, begging my forgiveness for the pain she was causing me and naming the man. I suppressed the note and gave out the accident story for two reasons. The first was Cynthia's reputation and the second was my hope that someday I would meet again the man who had been her lover. When that happened I didn't want him to realize that I knew the whole story. That man killed my wife, Bart, just as surely as if he had put a gun to her temple."

Over the loudspeaker a voice with a marked British accent was making the first announcement of the Pan American flight for San Juan, Jamaica and New York. Wentworth glanced at his watch.

"Well," he said slowly, "that's all a long time ago, isn't it?"

"Yes," I said. "Ten years. The mills of the gods, you know. But that's all right. Slow, slow. If it didn't sound melodramatic, I would say that mine will be a slow revenge. Let's call it instead slow justice, shall we?"

He looked nervously at his watch again.

"How do you mean?"

"You'll probably feel all right for three or four weeks," I said. "Maybe longer. I've heard of cases where a person harbored the *Mycobacterium leprae* for almost ten years before the fatal signs began to appear—the white patches, the gradual deformity of the joints and so on. Slow, slow."

It was interesting to watch his big, hearty, extroverted face change; interesting to observe how his eyes seemed to sink into their sockets, how his mouth hung slack and his skin took on the color of old parchment.

"For God's sake, Heffner," he said, and his voice cracked. "What are you saying?"

"Anna Marie is a leper," I told him. "You never would have guessed it, would you? She's isolated in my studio while I study the progress of the disease."

"You're lying," he said desperately.

I shrugged.

"Will all passengers for Pan American Flight Number 361-A kindly extinguish their pipes and cigarettes and proceed at once to the aircraft," said the British voice.

"You'd better run along, Bart. Make the most of whatever time you have."

He grabbed my arm. "Tell me you're lying. Good God, I'll never go through— Anything but that!"

"Wasn't Anna Marie worth it? You've always thought your little adventures were worth whatever they cost, haven't you, Bart? Cost other people, that is."

The loudspeaker was growing impatient. "Will passenger Barton Wentworth for Flight Number 361-A kindly board the aircraft at once? You are delaying the take-off."

I shoved Bart through the gate.

"Get going, old man. If you stay on the island, I'll have to report the matter to the Board of Health. I'm just giving you a break out of old friendship."

He shook his head groggily, like a punchy fighter, and in a quiet, hoarse voice he said, "You son of a bitch." Then he turned and made his way across the field toward the plane, walking like a very old or a very drunk man. Going up the steps he stumbled.

Smiling, I turned to Ellen whose dark eyes were shooting sparks.

"I think you're horrible!" she said. "I won't work for you another hour. I don't care why you're getting even with him. Only a monster would deliberately expose anybody, even his worst enemy, to— to—that."

"Dear child," I said, "save your indignation. Anna Marie no more has leprosy than you do or I do. How could I, a doctor, willfully allow a fellow human being to become infected? It wouldn't be ethical."

"But—"

"Of course, he will undoubtedly develop some very interesting symptoms, even if they are all psychosomatic. He may even," I added quietly, "shoot himself."

Since the founding of MWA, Larry Blochman has been one of our hardest working, most devoted, and most valued members. He has served the organization in every capacity from sandwich-maker in the old days of our youth and poverty to President. His first mystery was published in 1930, and since that time he has produced stories which reflect the richness of his life as foreign correspondent, medical expert, gourmet, and observer of all things human. This story is set in the Far East, and by the authority of its telling, you know that Mr. Blochman has been there.

19

The Dog that Wouldn't Talk

By Lawrence G. Blochman

Farnsworth, the district officer, saw the stranger and his dog sitting in the mail tonga as it rattled past his verandah. He watched with only mild curiosity until he saw the tonga go on down the hill, past the bazaar, to stop in front of the *dak* bungalow.

The stranger got out, holding his dog on a chain-leash that flashed in the late afternoon sun. He was traveling without servants.

Farnsworth clapped his hands and sent one of his bearers scurrying down the hill, to open the *dak* bungalow, while another went off to find the *khansama* who usually looked after it. Few travelers used the Government of India's rest house at Gandapur. There were so many lonely tea planters in the district, only too eager to furnish hospitality in exchange for the rare pleasure of looking at a new face, that the *dak* bungalow was closed most of the time.

The district officer waited a decent interval to give the stranger a chance to clean up, then with an effort hoisted his massive frame from the fan-backed chair and went down the hill to propose a drink and perhaps dinner. He had scarcely walked through the cobwebby door of the *dak* bungalow when he knew he had made a mistake.

The stranger, bending over a valise as he came in, slammed it closed, straightened up instantly, and fixed Farnsworth with a challenging stare. He still wore the khaki shorts, white shirt, and khaki topee in which he had arrived. He was very thin, which made him seem much taller than he really was.

The dog came out from under the bed to growl at Farnsworth. It was a bowlegged brindle bull, with an underslung jaw. It was off its leash.

"Hello. I'm Farnsworth, the D.O. here," said the district officer. "I thought perhaps you'd like to stop by the bungalow for a chota peg."

"I don't drink," said the stranger coldly.

"Oh, sorry." A shadow of disappointment crossed Farnsworth's round, pink, good-natured face. He began to regret having left his fan-backed chair. He noted that the stranger did not volunteer his own name. "If there's anything I can do, Mr.—"

"The tonga driver said the Gandapur tea garden is quite near here," the stranger interrupted. "Is he right?"

"That's the Gandapur tea garden right over there," Farnsworth said, pointing through the doorway. A succession of hills rolled back from the village, each striped with the green-and-brown plaid of tea plants against tilled earth. "The staff bungalows are just around that first hill, near the factory buildings. The tonga-walla could have driven you right there."

"I didn't want him to drive me there," the stranger said.

"If there's anyone in particular you'd like to see at the garden, I'd be glad to send a chit for you."

"I'd rather you didn't," the stranger said.

"Yes, of course. Well . . . Sorry to have troubled you." Farnsworth backed away awkwardly. The stranger stared at him in silence. The bulldog growled again. "Good night," said Farnsworth.

He hurried back up the hill and had three chota pegs in quick succession.

At ten o'clock that night the *dak* bungalow was afire.

Farnsworth was playing bridge with the civil surgeon, and the forestry officer and public works engineer who were stopping with the surgeon. He had just bid six spades and the civil surgeon had doubled, when a bearer came in with the news.

As they hurried down the hill, the thatched roof of the bungalow was already a roaring torch, hurling scraps of flame against the stars. Farnsworth pushed through the line of bronzed little Gurka guards who were holding off the crowd of open-mouthed natives. Bearded Sikhs were working furiously at the hand pumps of Gandapur's primitive fire brigade. The thin streams of water had no effect upon the conflagration except to add hissing clouds of steam to the twisting column of smoke and flame.

"There is a sahib in the bungalow," Farnsworth panted as he came up to the Sikh in charge of the ineffectual fire-fighters. "A sahib with a dog."

"No, Huzur. The sahib with the dog was seen to leave the bungalow half an hour before the fire."

"Are you sure?"

"Quite sure, Huzur."

Farnsworth breathed a sigh of relief—just as the roof fell in. In twenty minutes the *dak* bungalow was a mass of glowing embers. The stranger's luggage was no doubt part of the smouldering mass; but he so obviously resented any intrusion upon his privacy that Farnsworth thought it best to return home and play the hand upon which he had bid a small slam in spades.

He was set four tricks, vulnerable.

After the civil surgeon and his guests had gone home, Farnsworth sat on his verandah, sipping a nightcap and wondering if he could have made his contract by finessing the queen of hearts. He also wondered vaguely what had set fire to the *dak* bungalow: a carelessly abandoned cigarette, probably—although for a moment Farnsworth thought he had smelled kerosene.

He continued to sip his drink, listening to a jackal howling. Suddenly he realized that he was no longer stationed on the plains, and that there were probably no jackals in the Assam hills. It was a dog howling.

Farnsworth stood up. A drop of cold sweat trickled down his spine. The dog was some distance away, but its dismal howl sounded clearly in the stillness of the night, rising from the depths of animal woe. Farnsworth put an electric torch in his pocket and went out.

He told himself that he was merely taking a brisk walk before going to bed. Deep inside himself, however, he knew he was going out to look for the howling dog.

He passed the glowing ruins of the *dak* bungalow and continued down the road toward the Gandapur tea garden. The doleful lament of the dog was louder now; a hollow lugubrious note that rose to a sustained crescendo of despair and died in a whimper.

The Gandapur tea garden was only a five-minute walk from the village, and the homes of the personnel were a hundred yards beyond the entrance to the estate. They were all dark: the manager's bungalow, now occupied by Dave Bell, the proprietor, who arrived with his blond young wife only a month ago; the assistant's bungalow of Henri Joubert, the factory overseer from Indochina. The coolie lines were near the factory buildings, another few hundred yards further on.

When Farnsworth entered the plantation, the dog stopped howling. He drew his flashlight, shone it ahead of him as he walked up the road. When he had taken twenty steps, a furious barking began at his right. He left the road and advanced cautiously through the tea plants.

The savage barking increased in fury—almost underfoot. He shone his light downward. The luminous circle framed the open, aggressive jaws of the stranger's brindle bull. The chain leash trailed on the ground.

Beyond the dog the stranger himself lay on his back, his lips parted forever in a silent cry of terror. Without touching him, Farnsworth knew that the stranger was dead. The haft of a knife protruded from the crimson bosom of his shirt.

The dog continued to bark.

Lights went on in Dave Bell's bungalow. A screen door slammed and Bell appeared on the verandah steps, a raincoat over his pajamas. He held a flashlight in one hand and a revolver in the other.

"Don't shoot, Dave. It's Farnsworth," the district officer called in a shaky voice. "Come here."

Dave Bell hurried down the road in his slippers. He was a handsome, well-built man with a boyish face that belied his thirty-five years. "What's up?" he demanded. "That damned dog's been keeping us awake for an hour. It is your— Good Lord, who's that?"

"That's what I was going to ask you," said Farnsworth.

"Never saw him before in my life." Bell came as close to the dead man as the dog would permit.

"He came in on the mail tonga this evening," Farnsworth explained. "I saw him for a minute at the *dak* bungalow. He asked the way to your place. I thought you knew him."

"Maybe he was a friend of Rowan's."

"Couldn't have been much of a friend," Farnsworth explained, looking at the knife haft. "The bungalow burned down just after he left it tonight. Didn't you see the flames from your place?"

"We went to bed early," Bell said. "How—"

A scream cut him short—a shrill, chilling cry of terror. Both men whirled. The two flashlights converged on the white, tense face of the blond Mrs. Bell. She gripped a dressing gown of peacock blue closely about her shapely young body. Her hand trembled violently, and her blue eyes were round and staring.

Farnsworth had never seen her without makeup before. He couldn't help noticing that even unadorned, even on the verge of hysterics, she was still beautiful in an elemental, sensuous way.

"Don't look, Mrs. Bell," Farnsworth said.

"I—I've seen. What happened?" Mrs. Bell spoke with difficulty.

"Nothing. An accident. Go back to bed, Linda," Bell ordered.

"He was stabbed. Who killed him?" Her voice faltered, as if she was afraid to hear the answer.

"We don't know. Do run along, Linda. Please," Bell pleaded.

"Did you ever see him before, Mrs. Bell?" Farnsworth asked.

Linda Bell shook her head until her blond ringlets quivered. She did not look at Farnsworth, but stared at her husband with some strange fear in her eyes. She swayed slightly. The district officer had a sudden feeling that her terror was not merely the reaction of a woman to murder in her front yard; it was a deep dread, a personal shock that had wrenched her very soul.

"Here's Rowan," Bell said. "Maybe he knows the man."

The manager of the tea gardens, a well-muscled redhead with big ears, came loping down the road ahead of Joubert, the factory man. He, too, denied knowing the stranger.

"The poor chap's done for, whoever he is," Rowan said. "Friend of yours, Joubert?"

Joubert lazily sauntered up to look at the corpse. He was a round, oily man with a paunch that bulged over the belt of the ragged shorts that were his only garment. He peered through narrow, dark slits of eyes that had something of Asia in them. He shrugged.

"No," said Joubert. He turned away and slouched back toward his bungalow, shaking his head as if to say that he resented being disturbed by such trifles.

The brindle bulldog had stopped barking, but it still snarled menaces whenever anyone approached its dead master. Its eyes were green in the light of the pocket lamps.

"What are we going to do about the dog?" Farnsworth asked.

"He's a fine-looking animal," Bell declared. "Be a shame to destroy him. I'll try to handle him."

"Good," said Farnsworth. "Then I'll make arrangements to have the gentleman removed right away. I'll see you all later to ask the usual questions."

The first thing that the district officer did when he returned to the village was to get the telegraph operator out of bed, to open a line to Gauhati so he could send a message to the deputy police commissioner. While Farnsworth represented full police authority at Gandapur, he saw he was going to need help on this case.

He was worried—or as nearly worried as possible for the most easygoing D.O. in the Indian Civil Service. This was the second mysterious death in Gandapur in a month.

Just a month ago, on the day that Dave and Linda Bell came to Gandapur, a young tea planter named Green was found dead with a bullet in his head and a gun in his hand. Green had been assistant to Rowan, who told Farnsworth that the boy was terribly homesick and probably killed himself while half-crazy with loneliness.

Farnsworth had believed the story; although Green left no suicide note, it was quite possible that loneliness had affected his mind. Farnsworth knew that loneliness did strange things to tea planters. Some tried to escape in drink; plenty quit; and once in a while some youngster would go balmy.

The strange events of tonight, however, made Farnsworth think he had perhaps been too gullible. Two deaths on the same estate within a month might be a coincidence; again they might not be. And the fact that Green had died on the day the Bells arrived, coupled with Mrs. Bell's complete terror at the death of the mysterious stranger—she had not been at all upset over Green's death —decided Farnsworth to seek the help of a more expert investigator than he.

Late the next afternoon an official-looking motor car stopped in front of the district officer's bungalow. A dynamic little man in white ducks, black alpaca coat, and khaki sun helmet sprang out and went up the steps with quick, determined strides.

"You're Farnsworth, of course," he said when the district officer greeted him. "I'm Prike of the C.I.D."

"Indeed. You're more than welcome, Inspector." Farnsworth beamed. He knew Inspector Leonidas Prike by reputation. The deputy commissioner must have been impressed by last night's telegram to have sent the Criminal Investigation Department's ace detective. "I hardly hoped to meet you in this forsaken corner of the Assam hills, Inspector."

Prike removed his topee from an amazingly bald head. "I was en route to Shillong for a short holiday," he said. "The burra sahib suggested I might break my journey and your murder case at the same time. Tell me about it."

"Certainly. You'll have a chota peg first?"

"Brandy, if you don't mind."

Farnsworth clapped his hands and gave orders to the red-turbaned bearer who appeared.

As the district officer began his story of the arrival of the stranger, Inspector Prike listened with the abstract attention of a mild-mannered scholar. But when Farnsworth told of Linda Bell's reactions to the discovery of the stranger's body, and of the coincidental death of the young planter on the day the Bells arrived in Gandapur—then a gold, hard glint came into Prike's steel-gray eyes, and the muscles of his strong jaw tightened in sharp, resolute lines.

"You found no marks of identification whatever, Mr. Farnsworth?" he demanded.

"None. There was nothing on the body or in the clothing he wore. The rest was destroyed in the *dak* bungalow fire."

"Deliberately, of course." Prike sipped his brandy. "We'll make photos of the corpse and ultimately our men will run down the man's identity. If possible, however, I should like very much to clean up the case in a day or two, so I can get along with my holiday. Have you the weapon?"

"Right here," said Farnsworth.

Inspector Prike put down his brandy and took the knife. He glanced at it casually, then screwed a jeweler's glass into one eye and examined it again. "Made in Haiphong," he said. "Is there any Tonkinese labor at the tea garden?"

"Joubert, the overseer of the factory, comes from French Indochina. Matter of fact, I wouldn't be surprised if he is part Tonkinese. He certainly seems to have a touch of the tarbrush. I say, that's important, isn't it, Inspector?"

"Possibly," said Prike. The glint faded from his eyes. He stood up, fondled his brandy glass, and stared out at the woolly pattern the tea plantation made on the hills. For a long moment he was lost in thought.

"Too bad the only eye-witness was a dog," Farnsworth said. "You could leave Shillong in ten minutes if the dead man's dog could talk."

Inspector Prike turned abruptly. "Perhaps we can get the dog to talk," he said.

Farnsworth started to laugh, but checked himself when he saw that the inspector was not joking.

Before he could say anything, he saw the red-headed Frank Rowan getting off his bicycle in front of the bungalow. Rowan ran up the steps, calling excitedly: "Mr. Bell wants you to come right over, Mr. Farnsworth. Something— Sorry. I didn't know you were busy."

"Inspector, this is Rowan, manager of the tea garden," said the district officer. "Rowan, meet Inspector Prike of the C.I.D."

"You're just in time, Inspector," Rowan panted. "Joubert is gone."

"Gone?" Farnsworth glanced triumphantly at Prike, and nodded toward the factory overseer's knife. "Where did he go?"

"Nobody knows. Nobody saw him leave. He stole a rifle out of my bungalow and disappeared."

"That's an admission of guilt, isn't it, Inspector?" Farnsworth asked.

Prike reached for his topee. "I suggest we drive over and have a few words with that dog," he said.

Rowan held his bicycle on the running board of Prike's car as they drove through the thickening dusk toward the Bell plantation. Prike, sitting next to the redhead, asked him:

"What part of Australia are you from, Mr. Rowan?"

Rowan grinned. "You caught the accent all right, Inspector. I'm from Melbourne."

"And how long have you been manager at Gandapur tea garden?"

"About five years," Rowan replied.

"Five years without a break?"

"Right. Except for a yearly holiday, of course."

"Where do you go for your holiday, Mr. Rowan?"

"Calcutta, mostly. Last year I went to Singapore."

"And the missing overseer—Mr. Joubert, is it—how long has he been working with you?"

"About four years. He came the year after I did," Rowan said.

"From Indochina?"

"Yes. He always said he was from Haiphong."

"Do you know if he's ever been back there on holiday?"

Rowan laughed. "He never arrived anywhere on holiday," he said. "Joubert always started out for Calcutta, but the farthest he ever got was Dacca. He usually woke up broke and sober in Gauhati."

Prike nodded. The car pulled up in front of the Bell bungalow. Dave Bell came down the steps to greet them, his usual boyish good nature clouded by worry. Linda Bell remained on the verandah, standing beside a lamp. She received the men with a cosmetic smile.

Farnsworth thought she was more lovely and less panicky than she had been the night before, yet she was still obviously upset. Her lips trembled as she said, "I hope you've sent your constables looking for Joubert, Mr. Farnsworth."

"Inspector Prike is taking over, Mrs. Bell."

"We'll all join in the hunt," Rowan said. "Just tell us what you want us to do."

"I suppose we'd best wait until morning, since the man is armed," Bell volunteered.

"Before organizing a hunt," said Inspector Prike, "it is always good to know exactly what is to be hunted. I should like to talk to the dead man's dog, Mr. Bell."

"Oh, the dog. He's been raising a frightful row all day," Mrs. Bell volunteered.

"He's in the lumber room," Bell said. "This way, Inspector."

Prike and Farnsworth followed Dave Bell to a small room at

the back of the bungalow. Mrs. Bell held a lamp above her head as Prike opened the door. An outburst of savage sound and a baring of fangs greeted him.

"Stop it, boy," Prike called. "Be a good dog. Lie down now, old chap. Good dog."

The brindle bull continued barking.

"*Kutta, kutta, kutta.*" Prike tried the vernacular. "*Idhar ao, kutta-ji. Umdu kutta.*"

The barking increased in fury.

"He doesn't understand Hindustani," Bell said. "We've been trying it on him all day."

Prike next spoke to the dog in Tamil, Punjabi, and Pushtu. The dog showed no recognition of any of the Indian dialects. He tried French; the dog only barked the louder.

The inspector returned to the front of the house, frowning. "How long has Joubert been missing, Mr. Bell?" he asked.

"He probably left during the night," Bell said.

"Why did you not notify Mr. Farnsworth earlier?"

"Well, we weren't sure . . ." Bell sat down uneasily.

"I told Mr. Bell at noon that I hadn't seen him around this morning," Rowan volunteered. "But that's not unusual. Joubert sometimes went on solitary drunks. It was only when I found this afternoon that he'd taken my rifle from my bungalow that we thought something was wrong."

"I see." Prike turned to Bell. "How long have you owned this estate, Mr. Bell?" He asked casually.

Bell squirmed. "Well, it's not exactly mine," he admitted. "The title is in my wife's name. Linda inherited the plantation from her brother who died in Calcutta three years ago."

"This was before your marriage to Mrs. Bell?"

"After. We were married in Bombay four years ago."

"And this is your first visit to Gandapur?"

"Yes. We'd never been in eastern India before." Bell looked at his wife. "The plantation hasn't been doing very well the last two years, and when we actually lost money last year, we thought we'd better come up and see if we couldn't pull our chestnuts out of the fire. Our tea, rather."

"And are you succeeding, Mr. Bell?"

"Well, I'm not much of a tea planter myself," Bell said. "But Rowan, my manager, seems to think the soil may be played out.

What about it, Rowan?"

"We haven't been getting a very good grade of leaf," Rowan said. "I told Mr. Bell that perhaps we'd better wait until after the third picking and then have the soil analyzed. We—"

Linda Bell screamed. She was standing near the door, staring across the verandah with wide-eyed dismay.

Chairs scraped the floor as the four men sprang up. Farnsworth turned to follow her gaze. Several hundred yards away he saw long tongues of flame licking at the darkness.

"Another fire!" Linda wailed.

"The tea factory!" Bell exclaimed, starting for the door. "You stay here, Linda."

"No, no!" Linda seemed to grow suddenly older as she gave her blond head a terrified shake. "Not alone. I—I'd die!"

She joined the men already going down the verandah steps.

One end of the tea factory was blazing furiously. Men and women were streaming from the coolie lines nearby. The reflection of the fire gleamed on their black Tamil faces, flashed on the gold jewelry in the ears and noses of the women tea pickers.

While Bell and Rowan began organizing a bucket brigade, Inspector Prike marched straight into the smoke-filled gloom of the sorting and grading sheds, which had not yet caught fire.

"I say, Inspector." Farnsworth ran after him. "Isn't this dangerous, Inspector? Those corrugated-iron roofs—"

"They won't fall on us for at least half an hour," said Prike, glancing casually upward. "There is an obvious connection between arson and homicide in this case of yours, Mr. Farnsworth, and if there is a possibility of discovering any evidence in the few minutes still left to us—"

The inspector stopped to scoop up a handful of fragrant leaves from the withering trays. He smelled them, examined them carefully by the lurid flicker of the crackling flames.

Farnsworth coughed and tied his handkerchief about his face as he followed Prike through the acrid haze. The inspector was quite deliberate as he walked through the rolling and fermenting rooms, taking his time to run his fingers through the half-processed tea whenever he found any. He seemed even intent on going for a look at the firing ovens, although the blaze, which had obviously started at that end of the factory, was fiercest there. A flaming timber fell across the doorway, however, before he reached it.

"Inspector—don't you think we've seen enough?" Farnsworth coughed, as Prike seemed to be considering means of surmounting the new hazard.

"No," Prike replied, "but I'm afraid we've seen all we possibly can. Do you know which is Joubert's bungalow?"

"Yes." Farnsworth groped through the smoke for Prike's arm.

"Then take me there, while Bell is still busy with his fire."

Farnsworth lost no time in getting out of the factory. He filled his lungs with fresh air, shook his head violently as if trying to get the roar of the flames out of his ears.

"This way," he said.

They pushed through the lines of Tamils passing buckets, and stepped over the pitifully inadequate hose of the Gandapur fire brigade which was just getting into action. They did not see either Bell or Rowan.

Farnsworth led the way to Joubert's bungalow and climbed the steps. He tried the door. It was unlocked. He pushed it open—and immediately stepped back into Inspector Prike's arms. Two huge luminous eyes were staring at him from the darkness.

The ghostly, greenish blobs of phosphorescence shimmered from above the eye level. The unearthly animal, whatever it was, must be of tremendous size.

Inspector Prike's pocket lamp flung its cone of light into the darkness and the shining eyes disappeared. In their place was a glass jar on a shelf. The jar contained two lumps of some waxy, translucent substance immersed in a colorless liquid. A second bottle stood next to the jar.

Prike pushed Farnsworth aside and walked quickly to the shelf. He removed the cork from the bottle. A strong odor of rotten eggs immediately permeated the room.

Prike grunted with satisfaction. "Here is the explanation of your two fires," he said. "Phosphorus and carbon disulphide. The arsonist dissolved one in the other. When the carbon disulphide evaporated, the phosphorus burst into flame spontaneously. By the time the evaporation was complete, the arsonist was far away."

"But I thought I smelled kerosene at the *dak* bungalow last night," Farnsworth said.

"Probably you did. It could have been poured from a lamp, to help spread the fire quickly after the spontaneous combustion of the phosphorus."

"But why did Joubert set fire to the tea factory?" Farnsworth asked.

Prike replaced the cork in the bottle of carbon disulfide. "That is something we must discover," he said.

He lighted a lamp and carefully went through the three-room bungalow. He found nothing to interest him until he came to a pair of heavy shoes under an unmade bed. The shoes were caked with a clay of a peculiar yellow color.

"Do you know any place in the vicinity where mud of this color might be found, Mr. Farnsworth?" Prike asked.

Farnsworth did not know. He had never noticed the color of the soil about Gandapur.

"We shall have to wait for daylight to make certain," Prike said, "although my impression is that the soil of the plantation is sandy, darker, and not at all yellow." He probed the muddy crust with his finger. It was damp and soft underneath.

Suddenly he straightened up. An ominous sound beat upon the air. Farnsworth looked quickly at Prike and saw in the lamplight that the detective's jaw muscles were taut, his whole body rigid.

The sound came again: a sharp explosion that rolled off the hillside in a deep-throated echo.

Before Farnsworth could say, "Pistol shots?" the detective was already on his way out of Joubert's bungalow, running away from the dying fire of the tea factory, toward the bungalow of Dave Bell; and Farnsworth loped after him.

Linda Bell was standing on the verandah, a kerosene lamp in her hand. She was deathly pale, and trembling from head to foot. Prike took the lamp from her quaking grasp and put it on the table.

"Well?" he demanded.

"I just got here," she whispered. "I heard the shots. They seemed to come from out back."

Frank Rowan came charging up the verandah steps, followed from another direction by Dave Bell.

"What happened?" Rowan demanded.

Prike looked puzzled for an instant. Then, "The dog!" he exclaimed. He whipped out his automatic. "Bring the light, Mr. Farnsworth."

The district officer followed Prike to the back of the house. He held the lamp above his head as Prike opened the door to the lumber room. The night wind blew through a shattered window. There were fresh blood stains among the broken glass on the floor. The bulldog was gone.

All eyes were on Inspector Prike as he looked at the broken window, examined the shattered glass. He did not tarry long. Thoughtfully he returned to the living room. Farnsworth, Rowan, Dave and Linda Bell followed him. None spoke as the little detective paced the floor in silence.

Suddenly Prike stopped in front of the fireplace—winter evenings are cool in the Assam hills—bent down, and ran his fingers through a small pile of ashes in the grate. Farnsworth saw him pick out a few unburned scraps of paper—one of them the corner of an envelope with a tiny fragment of postage stamp on it—and drop them again. He straightened up, brushing his fingers against the palm of his other hand.

"Who has been burning paper here, Mrs. Bell?" he asked.

"I'm sure I don't know," Linda replied. She did not look at Prike.

"The ashes were not here earlier in the evening," Prike said quietly. His keen eyes scanned the faces about him. No one spoke. "Come, Mr. Farnsworth," he said after a tense pause. "I think I shall retire for a few hours' sleep before resuming work tomorrow."

"Aren't you going to hunt for Joubert, Inspector?" Bell protested. "Evidently he's still in the neighborhood."

Prike's eyebrows raised slightly. "Is he?" he countered.

"He's about, all right," Rowan said. "He did for the bulldog."

"I'm not certain Joubert has anything to do with the dog's disappearance," Prike said, looking squarely at Mrs. Bell. "The dog did not understand French. Goodnight, everyone."

Inspector Prike was up before dawn. Daylight was just beginning to gray the east when Farnsworth heard him stirring. The district officer bathed and dressed quickly. He barely had time for a cup of tea before joining the inspector. They drove directly to the plantation.

They found the bulldog just as the sun was coming up over the hills. It was lying among the tea plants, not far from the road, a few yards from the spot where its master had been murdered. It was covered with dried blood from a long gash that split one shoulder and furrowed its flank.

As Prike bent over it, however, the dog lifted its head, bared its fangs and snarled savagely. It tried to get up, but sank back weakly on its haunches.

Suddenly a curious look came into Prike's steel-gray eyes. He addressed the dog in Malay. "*Mari sini, anjing,*" he said softly.

The animal stopped growling and pricked up its ears.

"*Bat anjing,*" Prike continued. "*Branji anjing.*"

The dog wagged its tail feebly.

Prike picked the dog up in his arms, passed it to Farnsworth. "Take it to the Bell bungalow and have Mrs. Bell bandage its wounds," he said. "On second thought, don't. Jump in my car and take the dog to your own place. Do you know Malay?"

"No."

"Then just say '*bai*' from time to time. That means 'good dog.' Have the pup bandaged, and post someone to stand guard. We must save our only witness. Luckily the person who shot him last night was an atrocious marksman. You'll find me on the plantation."

Farnsworth followed instructions. When he drove back to the plantation from the village, he left the car opposite the still-smoking ruins of the tea factory. Then he asked several tea pickers which way the inspector had gone, and set out across the garden.

He had walked for hours, it seemed to him, without catching sight of the man. He was puffing badly by the time he had trudged to the northernmost limit of the plantation and found himself facing a wall of jungle.

"Inspector Prike," he called.

There was no answer. He hurried along the edge of the forest, stopping every few minutes to call again, hearing only the deafening hum of cicadas in reply.

"Inspector Prike!"

"Hello, Mr. Farnsworth." Prike emerged from the undergrowth, his white trousers muddy, his alpaca jacket torn, his khaki topee decorated with wet, clinging leaves. "I've just been following an outcropping of rock. I wanted to make sure it was crystalline limestone."

"Really?" Farnsworth blinked his amazement.

"You probably think I've gone mad," Prike said, "but you must admit that establishing a motive is sometimes quite useful in a murder investigation. I believe we're getting somewhere, Mr. Farnsworth."

"Are we, indeed? Where, Inspector?"

"Look at this, Mr. Farnsworth." Prike led the way to a narrow pit that had been dug into the plantation, near the edge of the undergrowth. It was only about two feet deep, but it extended for a considerable distance. The soil was of a peculiar yellowish color—like the mud that had caked on the shoes under Joubert's bed. "They're all over the place, these pits," Prike continued. "I noticed one half a mile back. There's another right over there."

Prike stooped to pick up a handful of the yellow-brown clay. He held it out, asking, "Mr. Farnsworth, wouldn't you say this might be byon?"

"Byon?"

"That's what they call ruby earth in Burma. And the Mogok ruby fields are surrounded by crystalline limestone formation. Shall we go back now?"

Farnsworth had longer legs than the inspector, but he also had a longer waistline, and he had some difficulty keeping up. When they had walked for half an hour between the rows of tea plants, Prike stopped to let him catch up. Breaking off the end of a slim branch, he held it out and asked, "What do you make of this, Farnsworth?"

Farnsworth said, "I'm new to the tea country."

"Look at the end leaves," Prike insisted.

Farnsworth looked. He saw only leaves.

"You will notice," Prike continued, "that the white terminal buds—the buds which yield the flower pekoe if picked while the down is still on the young leaves—have been allowed to open and develop."

"Have they, Inspector?" Farnsworth tried to register intelligent surprise.

"They have. And as a consequence the next picking is going to yield considerably more souchong than pekoe."

Prike was off again, saying no more until he had reached the Bell bungalow. He went directly to Linda Bell, who was having her morning tea on the verandah.

"The time has come, Mrs. Bell," he said crisply, "for you to tell the truth."

Linda put down her cup. "I have told you everything."

"The bulldog was not killed last night, Mrs. Bell. And the dog speaks Malay."

Linda's lips parted but she said nothing.

"The letter which was burned in the grate last night," Prike went on, "bore a Straits Settlement stamp; it was probably mailed from either Singapore or Penang. Since the dog obviously comes from somewhere in Malaya, I am assuming that his dead master also came from there. Am I also to assume that Mr. Bell burned the letter to conceal the fact that he corresponded with the murdered man?"

"Dave didn't burn that letter!" Linda Bell sat up very straight. "I did."

"Then you knew the man?"

"Yes." Linda's voice was barely audible. "His name was Hugh Walter."

"Why didn't you say so last night?"

Linda took a deep breath and looked Inspector Prike squarely in the eyes. "Because I knew that Dave would be suspected of killing him—although Dave never saw the man in his life."

"That doesn't make sense, Mrs. Bell."

"Oh, but it does. Dave has always been terribly jealous of Hugh Walter. He knows I nearly married Hugh once—when I thought I was in love with him. Hugh was a friend of my brother, and he once owned an interest in Gandapur tea garden. My brother bought him out several years before he died. Hugh left Bombay to go to Singapore—to get rich, he said. He did, too, but while he was gone I married Dave.

"Hugh had written me regularly ever since, saying he was going to take me away from Dave. I've never answered, never seen him since, but just the other day he wrote that he knew the plantation was in trouble, and that he was coming up to buy it—for my sake. That was the letter I burned.

"Until I saw him lying dead, I didn't know he was in Gandapur. I swear it. But I was panicky, naturally, because Dave had always threatened to kill Hugh if he ever showed up. I—"

She stopped. Dave Bell was coming up the steps.

"Morning, Inspector," he said. "Any trace of Joubert?"

"I think we shall find Mr. Joubert later today," Prike said, "just as soon as the corrugated-iron roof cools off enough so that we may lift it off the embers of the tea factory."

"Good Lord!" Bell exclaimed. "You don't think Joubert is dead?"

"I'm convinced of it," Prike said, grasping the back of a chair. "I—"

"Up with your hands! All of you."

The red-headed Rowan stood in the doorway, white-faced, grim-lipped, a gun in each hand. He had come through from the back of the house.

Prike was the first to raise his hands—flinging the chair across the verandah into Rowan's face.

Rowan's two guns exploded. The verandah was loud with shouts, screams, and the roar of gunfire. Before the echoes had died away, Rowan was on the floor, and Prike was astride him, with a tight body scissors grip about his middle. Farnsworth disarmed him.

Prike stripped Rowan's shirt from his back, and jerked a small chamois bag from the string around his waist.

"Keep the gun on him, please, Mr. Farnsworth," said Prike as he got up. "He's your man from now on. I suggest you ask him why he killed Joubert."

"I've got nothing to say," Rowan declared sullenly.

"I'm not sure whether Joubert objected to having his knife used in a murder, or whether he had been too curious about the ruby-earth at the far edge of the plantation. I would appreciate your correcting me, Mr. Rowan, as there are several points on which I am forced to guess. You knew, of course, Mr. Bell, that your manager has been deliberately depressing the value of your tea crops?"

"Rowan? How—"

"By sending the pickers out too late, after the higher-priced leaves had already grown into lower-grade tea. By making the plantation seem unprofitable, he hoped you would be willing to sell it cheap."

"But why?" Bell asked.

Prike tossed over the chamois bag. Bell opened it. Half a dozen dull-red hexagonal crystals ran into his hand.

"Because he has discovered rubies on your plantation. And while he could steal a few as a sideline to managing your estate, rubies are mined in India under Government license, and it might prove difficult to sell stones on which royalties had not been paid. Therefore Mr. Rowan went to Singapore on his last holiday to see a gentleman formerly connected with this plantation. Since this gentleman has become rich in the interim, I assume he was to furnish the capital for buying the tea garden when its present owner had been convinced that it was a liability. His name was Walter."

"Walter?" Dave Bell stared at his wife. "Was the dead man Hugh Walter?"

"Mrs. Bell, I wonder if I could trouble you for a double brandy," Prike said quickly.

When Linda Bell left the verandah Prike went on: "I can't say exactly what caused the thieves to fall out when Walter reached Gandapur the other night. But it is a safe guess to say that Rowan killed him over a matter of greed."

"He asked for it." Rowan spoke at last. "He wanted to freeze me out."

"Or vice versa," Prike suggested. "You might very well have decided to hog the whole business, Mr. Rowan—particularly if Walter arrived here with the purchase price in his pocket. Make a note of that when you search Rowan's bungalow, Mr. Farnsworth."

"You are a cold-blooded individual, Mr. Rowan. Your murder of Walter was carefully premeditated. You stole Joubert's knife for the purpose well in advance. You planted the phosphorus in Joubert's bungalow to tie up with the two fires. But you really should not have left Joubert's shoes, still caked with ruby-earth, where a curious investigator might find them. No doubt you were made bold by the ease with which you escaped detection for the murder of young Mr. Green."

"Green shot himself," Rowan protested.

"I rather think you killed him because of something he was about to reveal to Mr. Bell. It is quite likely that he had discovered the method by which you were causing a first-rate plantation to produce low-grade tea. That, however, is beside the point. The punishment for one murder is the same as for three. . . . This is excellent brandy, Mrs. Bell. Thank you."

Prike drained his glass, then said: "I think we ought to see how the dog is getting on, Mr. Farnsworth. I would like to take him a large, juicy steak. I might not have remembered that Mr. Rowan was in Singapore for his holiday if the dog had not understood Malay."

One might almost say that Lillian de la Torre had
created Dr. Sam Johnson, he has become so much hers.
Dr. Johnson is the subject of perhaps the greatest and
most personal biography in the history of letters; it
would seem nearly impossible to bend such a strong
and well-known character to an author's requirements,
but Miss de la Torre has done it brilliantly again and
again without ever in any way altering the character of
her stiff-necked protagonist.

20

The Disappearing
Servant Wench

By Lillian de la Torre

Elizabeth Canning went from her friends between nine and ten
on *Monday* Night, being New Year's Night; betwixt *Houndsditch
& Bishopsgate*, fresh-colour'd, pitted with ye Smallpox, high Forehead, light Eyebrows, about five-foot-high, well-set, had on a
purple masquerade-stuff Gown, black stuff Petticoat, a white Chip
Hat bound round with green, white Apron and Handkerchief, blue
Stockings, and leather Shoes. Any Coachman, who remembers
taking up such a Person, and can give any Account where she is,
shall have Two Guineas Reward, to be paid by Mrs. *Canning*, in
Aldermanbury Postern, Sawyer, which will greatly satisfy her
Mother.

These lines were roughly printed in the form of a handbill. My friend Dr. Sam. Johnson, detector of crime and chicane, produced the dog's-eared scrap of paper from the accumulations in his untidy book-garret in his house in Johnson's Court. I perused it with care.

"Pray, sir," I ventured, "have you still, in April, hopes of finding the girl? Sure the thing is all too plain. The lass hath been caught up and carried off by some rakish fellow, and now ten to one she plies a shameful trade by Covent Garden, and shames to return to her mother."

"No, sir, there you are out. The girl has returned to her home long since."

"Why then, sir, the girl has told her tale, and there's an end on't."

"Yes, sir, the girl has told her tale indeed, and thence arises the puzzle."

"Pray tell it me."

"Why, thus, sir: 'Twas King Charles's Martyrdom Eve, eight and twenty days after that fatal New Year's Day, and the Sawyer's 'prentice was just upon locking the door for the night, when there comes a faint knocking. 'Tis Elizabeth Canning! She is sodden, and starving, and exhausted and blue, and her clothes are gone. Good lack, cries Goody Canning, Bet, what has happened to you? And Bet tells her tale. Stay, you shall hear it as she told it in Bow Street."

From a mass of old printed papers my bulky friend drew a thin pamphlet, and from it began to read out in his sonorous voice:

"The INFORMATION *of Elizabeth Canning of Aldermanbury Postern, London,* Spinster.

"This Informant, upon her Oath, saith, that on Monday, the First Day of January last past, she, this Informant, went to see her Uncle and Aunt, who live at Salt-Petre Bank, near Rosemary-Lane, in the County of Middlesex, and continued with them until the Evening; and saith, That upon her Return home, about Half an Hour after Nine, being opposite Bethlehem-gate in Moorfields, she, this Informant, was seized by two men (whose Names are unknown to her, this Informant) who both had brown Bob-wigs on, and drab-coloured Great-coats; one of whom held her, this Informant, whilst the other, feloniously and violently, took from her one Shaving Hat, one Stuff Gown, and one Linen Apron, which she had on; and also, Half a Guinea in Gold, and three Shillings in Silver; and then he that held her threatened to do for this Informant. And this Informant saith, That, immediately after, they, the same two Men, violently took hold of her, and dragged her up into the Gravel-walk that leads down to the said Gate, and about the Middle thereof, he the said Man, that first held her, gave her, with his Fist, a very violent Blow upon the right Temple, which threw her into a Fit, and deprived her of her Senses (which Fits, she, this Informant, saith she is accustomed and subject to, upon being frighted, and that they often continue for six or seven Hours. . . .)"

"Stay, stay, sir," I implored, "for here is such a foyson of this Informant, and the said Informant, as carries me back to the Court of Session, whence I am newly a truant; so pray, sir, give me the straight of the story without circumlocution."

"Well, then, sir: Bet Canning told a horrid tale, how these pandours in bob-wigs snatched her up by Bedlam Gate, and carried her off in her fit. They carried her off to a bawdy house in the suburbs, said Bet; and there an old woman took her by the hand, and My dear, says she, will you go our way? For if you do, you shall have fine clothes. No, says Bet. Straightway the old woman takes up a carving-knife, and cuts the lace of the girl's stays, which the men in bob-wigs had overlooked, and takes them from her. Then she feels of the girl's petticoats. These are of no use, says she, I'll give you them. With that she gives the girl a great slap in the chops, and turns her up a pair of stairs, half-naked as she was, into a kind of loft or shuffleboard room. There, said Betty, she found some old mouldy bread and a broken jug full of water; but for which, and a penny minced pye which she happened to have by her, she had starved to death. For eight-and-twenty days no soul came nigh her. On the five-and-twentieth day she ate her minced pye; and on the eight-and-twentieth day she broke out at the window and ran away home."

"Sure, sir," I cried, "these were no Christians, but heathen Turks, so to misuse a poor innocent girl!"

"Yet you will allow, sir, that 'tis an excess of Christianity, thus to suffer for eight-and-twenty days an unnecessary martyrdom; for she who can break out at a window on the eight-and-twentieth day of fasting, might have done so with less fatigue on the first."

"Heathen Turks," I reiterated hotly, "and I heartily wish they may have been laid by the heels."

"As to Turks, Bozzy, you are not so far out; and as to laying by the heels, they were so. And a precious crew they proved to be, being the old bawd, Susannah Wells by name, and a parcel of Gipsies, her lodgers. They carried the girl to the suburbs to identify the people and the place. This is the house, says Bet; this is the shuffleboard room; and these are the miscreants, says she, pointing at the Gipsies. It was the old Gipsy woman cut my stays; and I think, says she, I *think* the Gipsy man her son was one of the men in bob-wigs; while as to the two Gipsy wenches her daughters, though they laughed at me they did nothing to me. As to the old bawd, I don't know that ever I saw her in my life before."

"I hope," cried I, "that the whole precious crew have long since had their just deserts."

"No, sir," replied my friend coolly, "'tis true, the world was once of your mind; Wells was branded in the hand, and the old Gipsy woman was to hang for the stays. But the old woman found friends, who have so managed that she had the King's pardon, and placed the girl in the dock in her stead."

"Upon what charge?" I cried.

"Upon a charge of perjury."

"Monstrous!" I exclaimed angrily. "How mean you, friends? The publican of some ale-house under a hedge?"

"No, sir," replied Dr. Johnson. "I will name but one: the Lord Mayor of London."

I gaped.

"You have wished to see the sights of London," remarked my friend. "Here is one you are not to pass by. The girl takes her trial today."

Now it was clear why my friend had caused me to hear the girl's story. The curtain was about to rise on a new act of the drama.

"Will you come, sir?"

"No, sir. I am too old and too thick in the middle to batter my way into the press at the Old Bailey."

I was young and spry. I clapped on my three-cornered hat and made off down Fleet Street to the Sessions House in the ancient street known as the Old Bailey.

Before I had turned the corner a muttering sound told me of the crowd that was milling uneasily in the paved courtyard. I was not to be daunted. I butted and pushed my way until I stood, half-suffocated, under the balcony and close by the dock.

On the long bench at the front sat the Justices of Oyer and Terminer, the lawyers in robes, the aldermen with their chains of office about their necks. On the floor before them a spry man with his big wig pushed back was talking in brisk tenor tones. But I had no eyes for them.

On the raised platform of the dock, clinging to the rail that fenced it, stood the girl. She was a stocky chit, no higher than five feet, drest in a clean linnen gown. She wore buckled shoes and a decent lawn kerchief, and her plain cap was fastened under her chin. The light fell on her pink, expressionless face. The spry lawyer was describing her in unflattering terms as a liar for profit; but the large blue eyes never flickered. Elizabeth Canning looked at him as if he weren't there at all.

Then her eyes shifted, and I followed her gaze. Seated to one side, in a large armed chair, sat the most hideous old hag I had ever had the misfortune to see. She was bent, and tremulous, and swarthy. Swathing clouts half-hid a face like a nightmare. She had a great frog's mouth smeared all over the lower half of her face. Her chin was aflame with the purple scars of an old disease, and her swarthy hooked nose jutted over all. This was Mary Squires, the Gipsy beldame. She was attended by a sparkling dark girl and a trim-built young Gipsy man.

I could not read the stolid girl's expression as she looked at her enemy. It held neither indignation nor remorse, but something more like puzzlement.

For ten mortal hours I stood on my feet as the Gipsy's witnesses followed one another on the stand.

"How is it with Canning?" asked Dr. Johnson as I supped with him. "Is she cast?"

"No, sir," I replied. "There are prosecution witnesses still to come, spare the defence; for length this trial bids fair to make history."

"Pray, how will it go?"

"Sir," I replied, "ill, I fear. Here have been forty witnesses come up from Dorset to swear an alibi for yonder Gipsy hag. She was strolling, they will stand to it, through the Dorset market-towns peddling such smuggled goods as she might come by in the seaports. Here has been a most respectable witness, an exciseman, who will swear it, that they lay in the excise office at Abbotsbury on the very night. Here have been landlords of inns from Abbotsbury to London to trace them on their way, bar only a four-days' journey from Coombe to Basingstoke. They came to Enfield full three weeks after Canning absconded. How 'tis managed I know not, but the girl is devoted to doom."

A knocking interrupted my discourse. The knocker proved to be a heavy-set red-faced man. He was accompanied by a younger man, a spindle-shanked sandy fellow with a long nose. Between them they supported a weeping woman. The woman was fortyish, and ample to overflowing.

The sandy young man burst immediately into speech.

"Robert Scarrat, hartshorn-rasper, at your service, sir, which I rasps hartshorn on a piece basis for Mrs. Waller of Old 'Change, and her son is tenant to Mrs. Canning here."

The weeping woman snuffled and confirmed the hartshorn-rasper with a nod.

"This here," the nervous strident tones hurried on, "is by name John Wintlebury, as is landlord of the Weavers Arms, and Bet Canning was a servant in his house."

" 'Tis a good wench," rumbled the publican.

"Nevertheless they have contrived her ruin among them," cried the woman, "and will transport her to the plantations—unless you, sir, would undertake to clear up the matter."

"You must tell me," replied my friend, "what they are saying about her."

" 'Tis never true that I hid her for my gain," cried out the weeping mother, smearing her bleared eyes with a thick finger, "for I never had rest, day or night, for wondering where she was. Mostly I thought her dead in Houndsditch, sir, or catched up by some rakish young fellow. I had dreams and wandering thoughts, and I prayed day and night to have a vision of her. But the cunning man said—"

"The cunning man?"

"A mere piece of woman's folly, sir," muttered the innkeeper, but Mrs. Canning paid him no mind.

"The cunning man in the Old Bailey. I went to him to have news of her, he had a black wig over his face."

"What said he?"

"Not a word, sir, only wrote, scribble, scribble, scribble along. He said, an old black woman had my daughter, and she would return soon."

"Ay," chimed in the hartshorn-rasper, his prominent hazel eyes rolling with superstitious awe, "is't not strange, sir?"

Mrs. Canning shuddered, and sobbed harder than ever. The landlord laid his hand on the woman's arm.

"Be easy, ma'am," he said gently, "for we know Bet's a good girl, and Dr. Johnson will soon make the matter clear. No need to take the hystericks over it."

The woman moaned. Scarrat took up the tale.

"Nor 'tis not true," he went on, "that I went off with the girl for my pleasure, for she was unknown to me."

"Ay," seconded the landlord, "for all the time she lived in my house, she was modest and shy, and would scarce so much as go to the door to speak to a man; and though Mr. Scarrat frequented the house, they never exchanged a word."

"And," cried the spindly man, growing hot, "as to my forging this tale, out of revenge against the bawd, 'tis false as Hell, though indeed I owe the creature no kindness."

"A notorious woman," said Wintlebury, "I knew of her infamous brothel when I lived and courted in Hertford."

"Oh, pray, pray, Dr. Johnson," sobbed out the weeping mother, "will not you help us?"

"Do, sir," I seconded. "Could you but see the vile face of the Gipsy hag, you would rush to the girl's defence."

"As to faces," replied my friend, "there's no art to find in them the mind's construction; and as to helping, if I must come down to the Old Bailey, 'twill not do."

The fat woman gave a howl and fell to the floor in a paroxysm. There was instant confusion. The fat friend and the thin one fell to slapping her wrists, while I applied under her snubby nose the hartshorn-bottle which was perhaps the fruit of Mr. Scarrat's endeavours.

When she had gasped and sat up, I turned to my kindly friend.

"Pray give your assistance," I begged. "I will be your deputy to the Old Bailey."

My friend accepted of my offer, and the friends of Canning departed in better cheer.

Only the fame of my companion gained us access to the Gipsy. She sat in the best room of the White Horse, in the Haymarket, and regarded us sardonically with black, beady eyes. She was surrounded by a court of Dorsetshire fishermen, King's landwaiters, and Gipsies in leather breeches. Her pretty daughter sat hand in hand with a tall man in fustian; I recognized with a start one of the principal witnesses for the prosecution, a cordwainer of Dorset. A black-browed little raisin of a man turned out to be the girl's uncle, Samuel Squires, a landwaiter of the customs right here in London and a Gipsy of considerable influence.

Dr. Johnson ran a lowering eye over the motley crew; the men of the customs particularly took his eye. Then he waved them all away, and to my relief they went.

"Now, ma'am," says Dr. Johnson, "out with it. There's more in this than meets the eye."

The beady eyes measured him.

"I will confess," said the rusty voice.

I thrilled to my toes. The girl was saved!

"I'll confess. Though I have passed myself for a strolling pedlar, I am in reality—"

Dr. Johnson leaned forward.

"I am in reality—a *witch*. I can be present at *two* places at one time," whispered the old beldame with hoarse and ostentatious caution, "and though all these people saw me in Dorset, I nevertheless carried Canning to Enfield on my *broom-stick*—"

Dr. Johnson cut short her triumphant cackle by rising to his feet.

"Have a care, ma'am," he said angrily, "I am not to be trifled with."

The old hag leaned back and laughed in his face.

"I know you are no witch," my friend went on grimly, "but I will tell you what you are."

He spoke three words in her ear. Her face changed. She looked at him with more respect.

"Ah," she said, "I see you are in the councils of the great."

"I can see a church by daylight," he replied as we withdrew.

I made off, being engaged to dine with some ladies in St. James's, but Dr. Johnson turned into the tap-room and lingered.

"Alack, Mr. Boswell," he told me when again we met. "Alas for Bet Canning, the rusticks are honest. I had their story over a can of ale, and with such a wealth of detail as can scarce be forgery. The honest cordwainer loves the Gipsy wench; he dallied eight days in their company at Abbotsbury, and when they departed he followed them on the road. There are landlords to swear to them all, and the things they saw and the meals they ate. So rich is the tale, it must be more than mendacious invention."

"Yet who pays," I cried, "who pays the scot of the poor Gipsy pedlar and her forty witnesses at the White Horse in the Haymarket? Who keeps them in victuals and gin?"

"My Lord Mayor, 'tis said," replied my companion. "But come, Mr. Boswell, let me know your mind: shall we push forward and uncover the truth, wherever it lies? Or shall we leave Bet Canning to her luck with the jury?"

"Let us wait," I replied uneasily, "and see."

I filled the days of waiting in the court-room of the Old Bailey, where each day the girl sat in the dock with her wrists crossed before her, and looked on without expression while witnesses called her liar or martyr.

"How goes the trial, Bozzy?" demanded my friend as I returned bedraggled from another day's session.

"Ill, for the girl, ill," I replied dejectedly. "You may know how ill, when I tell you that the Lord Mayor was pelted by the resentful Canningite rabble as he came away from the Sessions-house. The girl has been made to appear a liar. Before the sitting Aldermen, so he has sworn, she described her prison to be little, square, and dark. Then they took her to Enfield; when it appeared that the room she swore to was long and light, with many other contradictions. I know not what to think."

"A starved girl, after long imprisonment, may surely exhibit some confusion," suggested Dr. Johnson thoughtfully.

"There is more," I replied. "From Enfield came many witnesses, who swore that they visited her supposed prison during that month, and saw there no such person as Elizabeth Canning."

"What said the girl to this?"

"Never a word, save once. 'Twas a son of Wells's testified, he stepped into the shuffleboard room to lay by his tools, for he is a carpenter, and there was no soul there save the labouring man that lodged there. Bet Canning leaned forward, and scanned him closely. She frowned, and looked him up and down. *I never saw him before, as I know of,* says she."

"Why did she so?"

"Who can tell? 'Tis a strange wench. Just so, by the evidence, did she comport herself when they took her to Enfield: would not be sure of the Gipsy man, could not be sure she had ever seen Wells. Only the Gipsy woman she swore to without hesitation. They report strange things of the girl, too, in Wells's loft. *Do you remember that six-foot nest of drawers?* says they. *I never saw it before,* says Miss. *Do you remember the hay and the saddles stored up here?* says they. She scratches her head. *I will not swear,* says she, *but there is more hay. As to the saddles, I remember one only. But there was a grate,* says she. *O no,* says they, *look for yourself. There's no grate and never has been: look at the cobwebs. There was a grate,* says she, *and from it I took the rags I wore when I fled. There was never a grate,* says they."

"Is it so!" cried my venerable friend. "Here is no liar, but one trying to speak the truth. Bozzy, we must save this girl!"

I stared. The evidence, that had shaken my faith in the girl, had spoken quite otherwise to him. It had spoken with such clear moral force and conviction that it stirred his great bulk, and brought it next morning into the court-room of the Old Bailey.

He cleared his way through the press like a bailiff, with jerks of his sturdy oak staff. We were in time to hear the defence begin. The crowd murmured in sympathy as Bet's sad story was repeated by her friends as they had heard it from her on that Monday in January. All her natural functions were suspended, related the apothecary in sepulchral tones, the whole time of her imprisonment; she was very faint and weak, and the black-and-blue marks never went off for a month afterwards. My venerable friend shook his head from side to side, and clicked his tongue.

Burning glances of sympathy were levelled at the abused girl where she sat impassive in the dock as the story was told. They changed to looks of triumph as the defence brought aces out of their sleeves—a witness who had seen the girl led past his turnpike, in tears, by a pair of ruffians; three persons who had seen the bedraggled creature returning in the misty evening.

Dr. Johnson, seated on a bench with his chin on his staff, frowned and shook his head.

"How can this help?" he muttered. "The girl swore she was dragged off in a fit. Now we find she walked by the turnpike. Where is the truth to be found?"

The defence rested.

It was three o'clock the next morning when I knocked up my friend.

"The girl is cast!" I told him. "She will be transported."

"Cast!" exclaimed my friend. "What this girl has been, I know not; but she is no perjurer."

A double knock announced a later walker than I. Again it was John Wintlebury and Robert Scarrat.

"You must help us!" cried the hartshorn-rasper. "Can you give us no hope?"

"Only this, that the girl is innocent," replied my friend. "I will do what I can. Where is the girl?"

"Alack," exclaimed the volatile Scarrat, "in Newgate."

"Then we must have her out."

That was easier said than done, but Johnson managed it. Scarrat carried the request. Meanwhile, off went the black boy Francis to the White Horse. He came back with a note:

> "She says she will come, if only to laugh.
> *Ma: Squires*"

The old Gipsy woman herself was not far behind. Next to arrive was Mother Wells. She came supported by the carpenter son. My friend received his curious callers with solemn dignity, and offered them cakes and port. The wrinkled old bawd guzzled hers with coarse greed.

It was still dark night when a sedan-chair turned into Johnson's Court. It was attended by two turnkeys and followed by our friends, once again supporting between them the high-strung matron. All three tenderly extracted from the chair the stocky person of Elizabeth Canning, and so she was assisted up the stair.

Dr. Johnson took her hand.

"Do not be afraid, my dear."

"I am not afraid," said Bet Canning.

She looked levelly at the hideous old Gipsy hag, then at the bawd. The latter wiped a drool of port off her chin. Dr. Johnson handed the girl to a chair, her friends found places, and a hush fell as everyone in the room looked toward my learned friend.

"My dear," said Dr. Johnson, addressing himself to the girl, "there are those who think you are lying. I do not think you are lying."

"Thank you, sir."

The Gipsy beldame, a mere huddle of rags except for her bright black eyes, snorted.

"But, my dear," my friend continued quietly, "there is much that is dark, much that you have not been able to tell us."

"I have told," said Bet Canning clearly, "all that I know."

"We must look further, then. There is one in this cause," said Dr. Johnson, "who seemed a knowledgeable man."

I leaned forward.

"Who?"

"The cunning man," replied my learned friend solemnly. "He knew where Elizabeth was, and he wrote it down, scribble, scribble, scribble along. He was right. I would have consulted him myself, but he is not to be found. There is no conjurer in the Old Bailey."

"I saw him there myself," cried Mrs. Canning. "He had his wig over his face; and when he lighted up the candles, he frighted me, and I could not stay for more."

"Well, well, he is gone away from thence, he is no longer to be consulted. We must make do without him."

He produced a leather case, which being opened revealed a gleaming polished disk of some black substance.

"This," said Dr. Johnson solemnly, "is the famous Black Stone of Dr. Dee the alchemist. I had it of Mr. Walpole against this night's purpose. Into it," he lowered his sonorous voice another pitch, "the alchemist used to call his spirits, and they revealed the truth to him."

Nobody spoke.

Dr. Johnson extinguished the candles, all but one, which gleamed fitfully on the table, accentuating rather than piercing the darkness. For a moment there was dead silence.

"Before the spirits speak," said Dr. Johnson, "has no one a word to tell us?"

I heard somebody gasp. The old Gipsy was shaking and muttering to herself, it might have been a charm or an incantation. Mrs. Canning was crying again, in long shuddering gasps, and the hartshorn-rasper was twitching where he sat. Only the stolid inn-keeper and the cynical old bawd preserved an unbroken calm.

Elizabeth Canning's gaze caught and hung on the gleaming speculum. Her plain face was white as paper.

"Pray, my girl," said Dr. Johnson gently, "look into the magick stone of Dr. Dee, and tell us what you see."

"I see nothing," she faltered.

"You will see the truth," said my friend. "Look well, and tell us what you see."

The girl stared into the polished surface, scarcely seeming to breathe. Her eyes contracted to pin-points. She sat rigid.

"It is the night of January 1," breathed my friend in the silence. "Do you see Elizabeth Canning?"

"I see her."

The voice was tight and high, and seemed to come from a long way off.

"I see Elizabeth Canning. She is walking between two men, and weeping. It is a road, with water in it. Now they turn into a house, there is an old woman there."

"Swarthy and black?"

"No, grey and wrinkled. She takes away her clothes, and puts her into a room."

"Without any furniture?"

"No," replied the trance-like voice. "No, it is the best bedroom. The door opens, and the man comes in. Now Elizabeth can see his face. It is he. It is the same man who wanted Elizabeth to do the bad thing, always and always he was at her elbow saying it to her, and she would not. Now he is here to do it, and Elizabeth cannot help herself."

In a violent shudder the dreaming voice died away. For a moment there was silence in the room.

"Here," muttered Wintlebury finally, "you must stop this, sir, you've bewitched the girl to her hurt. Who knows what she'll say?"

"She'll say the truth," said Dr. Johnson sharply. "Be silent, sir, and listen."

He spoke soothingly to the rigid girl.

"It is the eve of King Charles's Martyrdom. Do you see Elizabeth Canning?"

"I see her."

"Where is she?"

"She is in the loft. The wicked man has left her behind, they have taken away her clothes, she cannot eat for shame. Because she would not do the bad thing with other men, they have beaten her and thrust her into the loft. She wants to go home, but she does not know where home is. She has forgotten her name. She has forgotten everything. She is very wretched."

Again the level voice died away.

"And then?"

The polished disk gleamed in the candlelight. The girl's eyes were like pin-points.

"And then she hears her name spoken, and she knows it is hers. She looks down into the kitchen and sees the ugly-faced Gipsy. She is hungry and cold and afraid. The minced pye is still in the pocket of her torn petticoat; it is stale and dry, but she eats it. She takes an old rag from the fireplace to wrap herself in, and breaks out at the window, and runs away home."

"But the grate?" I struck in.

"A saw across the fireplace," said a quiet voice in my ear. It was the young carpenter. "My cross-cut saw."

"She runs away home. They ask where she has been for four weeks; but she has forgotten. Only it seems to her that she was somewhere hungry and cold, and she has been somehow harmed, the ugly-faced woman must have done it, and her clothes are gone; so she tells them as best she can what must have happened, and they believe her, and are very angry. Even the man who did the bad thing to her, he is angry too, and wants the Gipsy hanged. Elizabeth has forgotten what he did to her; she thinks he is her friend."

"The man," Dr. Johnson leaned forward gently, "who was the man?"

"That's enough of this flummery," came an angry voice. "Can't you see that the girl is mad?"

A rough hand struck aside the magick speculum of Dr. Dee. Elizabeth Canning looked up into an out-thrust face, somehow distorted in the flickering light of the candle from below, and recoiled with scream after scream of terror. Then the candle flame was struck out, and footsteps clattered on the stair.

"Let him go," said Dr. Johnson. "Mr. John Wintlebury is not the first to enforce his desires on a virtuous serving-wench, and I fear there's no law to touch him."

"I'll touch him," cried the hartshorn-rasper violently. "I'll— I'll rasp him!"

He held the shuddering girl tight against his shoulder. He touched her pale hair.

"She's not mad, sir?" he pleaded.

"Not the least in the world," replied my friend, "yet hers is a strange affliction. The learned call it the catalepsy. One so afflicted may preach, or prophesy, or fast without hunger, or cut his flesh with knives, and not feel it; or fall unconscious and lie as the dead; or believe the body's functions to be pretermitted; or they may upon great suffering or shame forget who they are, and wander homeless until they remember. It was Mr. John Wintlebury's good luck that the wronged girl forgot him and the wrong he did her, and even herself, for very shame."

"And my bad luck," croaked the Gipsy crone, "for the story that came from her disturbed mind put me into jeopardy of my life."

"You were never in jeopardy, being what you are," returned Dr. Johnson.

"What are you?" I burst out uncontrollably.

"A customs spy," replied the old witch, "and a good one, young man. Who'd ever suspect the old Gipsy beggar when she came nosing about the barns? I knew every smugglers' lay on that coast. O no, me Lord Treasurer wouldn't have let the old Gipsy woman hang. 'Twas but a few nights lying hard in gaol; he could not move openly in the matter, for fear of betraying me and mine to the smugglers. In the end me Lord Mayor had his orders, and I was enlarged."

"And Mother Wells?" I touched flint and steel to the candle.

"It all happened," my friend replied, "of course, in her house of assignation; it was she who beat the girl when she would not go the way of the house."

I advanced the candle toward the old bawd's corner. The lees of her port were there in the glass, but the old woman was gone.

"Upon her," remarked Dr. Johnson, "justice has been done. You will remember that, although Mary Squires was pardoned, Susannah Wells has been branded on the hand for her part in the work."

Elizabeth Canning's sobs had died away, and she lay in a sleep like death against the hartshorn-rasper's shoulder.

"When she awakes," he asked, "will she remember?"

"I cannot say," replied my learned friend. "Perhaps she will remember everything. If not, you must tell her, gently, over and over, until the two times join into one in her mind and she no longer has those agonizing moments of trying to remember, like the time in the loft, or in the dock when she struggled to remember the young carpenter."

He pulled aside the heavy curtains and let in the dawn.

"Tomorrow," he said, "I will wait upon the Secretary of State."

The sun was up as the sleepy turnkeys roused to help lift the unconscious girl back into the sedan-chair. My benevolent friend followed it with his eyes to the mouth of the court.

"The issue of this night's sitting," he remarked with a half-smile, "has exceeded expectation. I reasoned that someone close to the girl knew where she was, else why the cunning man with the muffled face, who must write his predictions? Clearly his face and his voice were known. I brought her friends together, and produced a conjuration of my own. I hoped that superstition would affright one of them, and even that the girl might take courage and 'see' in the speculum what perhaps she had been frighted from telling. I never guessed that so strange is the mind in a catalepsy that it will see truly, as it were in a sleep, what it has forgotten in waking."

Anthony Boucher is the modern Renaissance Man. At the same time, he is the outstanding critic in the mystery field, a top translator, anthologist, historian, and general authority, and, alas too infrequently of late, a writer. He also interests himself in the affairs of opera and music in general, radio and television. There is much else, but this story stems mostly from an encyclopediac knowledge of music and an unarguable authority on all things criminous.

21

The Anomaly

of the Empty Man

By Anthony Boucher

"This is for you," Inspector Abrahams announced wryly. "Another screwy one."

I was late and out of breath. I'd somehow got entangled on Market Street with the Downtown Merchants' Association annual parade, and for a while it looked like I'd be spending the day surrounded by gigantic balloon-parodies of humanity. But it takes more than rubber Gullivers to hold me up when Inspector Abrahams announces that he's got a case of the kind he labels "for Lamb."

And San Francisco's the city for them to happen in. Nobody anywhere else ever had such a motive for murder as the butler

Frank Miller in 1896, or such an idea of how to execute a bank robbery as the zany Mr. Will in 1952. Take a look at Joe Jackson's *San Francisco Murders*, and you'll see that we can achieve a flavor all our own. And when we do, Abrahams lets me in on it.

Abrahams didn't add any explanation. He just opened the door of the apartment. I went in ahead of him. It was a place I could have liked if it hadn't been for what was on the floor.

Two walls were mostly windows. One gave a good view of the Golden Gate. From the other, on a fine day, you could see the Farallones, and it was a fine day.

The other two walls were records and a record player. I'd heard of the Stambaugh collection of early operatic recordings. If I'd been there on any other errand, my mouth would have watered at the prospect of listening to lost great voices.

"If you can get a story out of this that makes sense," the Inspector grunted, "you're welcome to it—at the usual fee." Which was a dinner at Lupo's Pizzeria, complete with pizza Carus', tomatoes with fresh basil and sour French bread to mop up the inspired sauce of Lupo's special *calamari* (squids to you). "Everything's just the way we found it."

I looked at the unfinished highball, now almost colorless with all its ice melted and its soda flat. I looked at the cylindrical ash of the cigaret which had burned itself out. I looked at the vacuum cleaner—a shockingly utilitarian object in this set for gracious living. I looked at the record player, still switched on, still making its methodical seventy-eight revolutions per minute, though there was no record on the turntable.

Then I managed to look again at the thing on the floor.

It was worse than a body. It was like a tasteless bloodless parody of the usual occupant of the spot marked X. Clothes scattered in disorder seem normal—even more normal, perhaps, in a bachelor apartment than clothes properly hung in closets. But this . . .

Above the neck of the dressing gown lay the spectacles. The sleeves of the shirt were inside the sleeves of the dressing gown. The shirt was buttoned, even to the collar, and the foulard tie was knotted tight up against the collar button. The tails of the shirt were tucked properly into the zipped-up, properly belted trousers. Below the trouser cuffs lay the shoes, at a lifelike angle, with the tops of the socks emerging from them.

"And there's an undershirt under the shirt," Inspector Abrahams muttered disconsolately, "and shorts inside the pants. Complete outfit: what the well-dressed man will wear. Only no man in them."

It was as though James Stambaugh had been attacked by some solvent which eats away only flesh and leaves all the inanimate articles. Or as though some hyperspatial suction had drawn the living man out of his wardrobe, leaving his sartorial shell behind him.

I said, "Can I dirty an ashtray in this scene?"

Abrahams nodded. "I was just keeping it for you to see. We've got our pictures." While I lit up, he crossed to the record player and switched it off. "Damned whirligig gets on my nerves."

"Whole damned setup gets on mine," I said. "It's like a strip-tease version of the *Mary Celeste*. Only the strip wasn't a gradual tease; just abruptly, *whoosh!*, a man's gone. One minute he's comfortably dressed in his apartment, smoking, drinking, playing records. The next he's stark naked—and where and doing what?"

Abrahams pulled at his nose, which didn't need lengthening. "We had the Japanese valet check the wardrobe. Every article of clothing James Stambaugh owned is still here in the apartment."

"Who found him?" I asked.

"Kaguchi. The valet. He had last night off. He let himself in this morning, to prepare coffee and prairie oysters as usual. He found this."

"Blood?" I ventured.

Abrahams shook his head.

"Visitors?"

"Ten apartments in this building. Three of them had parties last night. You can figure how much help the elevator man was."

"The drink?"

"We took a sample to the lab. Nothing but the best scotch."

"Motive?"

"Gay dog, our Mr. Stambaugh. Maybe you read Herb Caen's gossip column too? And Kaguchi gave us a little fill-in. Brothers, fathers, husbands . . . Too many motives."

"But why this way?" I brooded. "Get rid of him, sure. But why leave this hollow husk . . . ?"

"Not just why, Lamb. How."

"How? That should be easy enough to—"

"Try it. Try fitting sleeves into sleeves, pants into pants, so they're as smooth and even as if they were still on the body. I've tried, with the rest of the wardrobe. It doesn't work."

I had an idea. "You don't fit 'em in," I said smugly. "You take 'em off. Look." I unbuttoned my coat and shirt, undid my tie, and pulled everything off at once. "See," I said; "sleeves in sleeves." I unzipped and stepped out of trousers and shorts. "See; pants in pants."

Inspector Abrahams was whistling the refrain of "Strip Polka." "You missed your career, Lamb," he said. "Only now you've got to put your shirt tails between the outer pants and the inner ones and still keep everything smooth. And look in here." He lifted up one shoe and took out a pocket flash and shot a beam inside. "The sock's caught on a little snag in one of the metal eyelets. That's kept it from collapsing, and you can still see the faint impress of toes in there. Try slipping your foot out of a laced-up shoe and see if you can get that result."

I was getting dressed again and feeling like a damned fool.

"Got any other inspirations?" Abrahams grinned.

"The only inspiration I've got is as to where to go now."

"Some day," the Inspector grunted, "I'll learn where you go for your extra-bright ideas."

"As the old lady said to the elephant keeper," I muttered, "you wouldn't believe me if I told you."

The Montgomery Block (Monkey Block to natives) is an antic and reboantic warren of offices and studios on the fringe of Grant Avenue's Chinatown and Columbus Avenue's Italian-Mexican-French-Basque quarter. The studio I wanted was down a long corridor, beyond that all-American bend where the Italian newspaper *Corriere del Popolo* sits catty-corner from the office of Tinn Hugh Yu, Ph.D. and Notary Public.

Things were relatively quiet today in Dr. Verner's studio. Slavko Catenich was still hammering away at his block of marble, apparently on the theory that the natural form inherent in the stone would emerge if you hit it often enough. Irma Borigian was running over vocal exercises and occasionally checking herself by striking a note on the piano, which seemed to bring her more reassurance than it did me. Those two, plus a couple of lads industriously fencing whom I'd never seen before, were the only members of Verner's Varieties on hand today.

Irma ah-ah-ahed and pinked, the fencers clicked, Slavko crashed, and in the midst of the decibels the Old Man stood at his five-foot lectern-deck, resolutely proceeding in quill-pen longhand with the resounding periods of *The Anatomy of Nonscience*, that never-concluded compendium of curiosities which was half Robert Burton and half Charles Fort.

He gave me the medium look. Not the hasty "Just this sentence" or the forbidding "Dear boy, this page *must* be finished"; but the in-between "One more deathless paragraph" look. I grabbed a chair and tried to watch Irma's singing and listen to Slavko's sculpting.

There's no describing Dr. Verner. You can say his age is somewhere between seventy and a hundred. You can say he has a mane of hair like an albino lion and a little goatee like a Kentucky Colonel who never heard of cigars. ("When a man's hair is white," I've heard him say, "tobacco and a beard are mutually exclusive vices.") You can mention the towering figure and the un-English mobility of the white old hands and the disconcerting twinkle of those impossibly blue eyes. And you'd still have about as satisfactory a description as when you say the Taj Mahal is a domed, square, white marble building.

The twinkle was in the eyes and the mobility was in the hands when he finally came to tower over me. They were both gone by the time I'd finished the story of the Stambaugh apartment and the empty man. He stood for a moment frowning, the eyes luster-less, the hands limp at his sides. Then, still standing like that, he relaxed the frown and opened his mouth in a resonant bellow.

"You sticks!" he roared. (Irma stopped and looked hurt.) "You stones!" (The fencers stopped and looked expectant.) "You worse than worst of those that lawless and uncertain thoughts" (Slavko stopped and looked resigned.) "imagine howling," Dr. Verner concluded in a columbine coo, having shifted in mid-quotation from one Shakespearean play to another so deftly that I was still looking for the joint.

Verner's Varieties waited for the next number on the bill. In majestic silence Dr. Verner stalked to his record player. Stambaugh's had been a fancy enough custom-made job, but nothing like this.

If you think things are confusing now, with records revolving at 78, 45, and 33⅓ rpm, you should see the records of the early part of the century. There were cylinders, of course (Verner had a separate machine for them). Disc records, instead of our present standard sizes, ranged anywhere from 7 to 14 inches in diameter, with curious fractional stops in between. Even the center holes came in assorted sizes. Many discs were lateral-cut, like modern ones; but quite a few were hill-and-dale, with the needle riding up and down instead of sideways—which actually gave better reproduction but somehow never became overwhelmingly popular. The grooving varied too, so that even if two companies both used hill-and-dale cutting you couldn't play the records of one on a machine for the other. And just to make things trickier, some records started from the inside instead of the outer edge. It was Free Enterprise gone hogwild.

Dr. Verner had explained all this while demonstrating to me how his player could cope with any disc record ever manufactured. And I had heard him play everything on it from smuggled dubbings of Crosby blow-ups to a recording by the original *Florodora* Sextet— which was, he was always careful to point out, a double sextet or, as he preferred, a duodecimet.

"You are," he announced ponderously, "about to hear the greatest dramatic soprano of this century. Rosa Ponselle and Elisabeth Rethberg were passable. There was something to be said for Lillian Nordica and Lena Geyer. But listen!" And he slid the needle into the first groove.

"Dr. Verner—" I started to ask for footnotes; I should have known better.

"Dear boy . . . !" he murmured protestingly, over the preliminary surface noise of the aged pressing, and gave me one of those twinkles of bluest blue which implied that surely only a moron could fail to follow the logic of the procedure.

I sat back and listened. Irma listened too, but the eyes of the others were soon longingly intent on foils and chisel. I listened casually at first, then began to sit forward.

I have heard, in person or on records, all of the venerable names which Dr. Verner mentioned—to say nothing of Tebaldi, Russ, Ritter-Ciampi, Souez and both Lehmanns. And reluctantly I began to admit that he was right; this was *the* dramatic soprano. The music was strange to me—a setting of the Latin text of the *Our Father*, surely eighteenth century and at a guess by Pergolesi; it had his irrelevant but reverent tunefulness in approaching a sacred text. Its grave sustained lilt was admirable for showing off a voice; and the voice, unwavering in its prolonged tones, incredible in its breath control, deserved all the showing off it could get. During one long phrase of runs, as taxing as anything in Mozart or Handel, I noticed Irma. She was holding her breath in sympathy with the singer, and the singer won. Irma had let out an admiring gasp before the soprano had, still on one breath, achieved the phrase.

And then, for reasons more operatic than liturgical, the music quickened. The sustained legato phrases gave way to cascades of light bright coloratura. Notes sparkled and dazzled and brightness fell from the air. It was impeccable, inapproachable—infinitely discouraging to a singer and almost shocking to the ordinary listener.

The record ended. Dr. Verner beamed around the room as if he'd done all that himself. Irma crossed to the piano, struck one key to verify the incredible note in alt upon which the singer had ended, picked up her music, and wordlessly left the room.

Slavko had seized his chisel and the fencers were picking up their foils as I approached our host. "But Dr. Verner," I led with my chin. "The Stambaugh case . . ."

"Dear boy," he sighed as he readied the old one-two, "you mean you don't realize that you have just heard the solution?"

"You will have a drop of Drambuie, of course?" Dr. Verner queried formally as we settled down in his more nearly quiet inner room.

"Of course," I said. Then as his mouth opened, " 'For without Drambuie,' " I quoted, " 'the world might never have known the simple solution to the problem of the mislaid labyrinth.' "

He spilled a drop. "I was about to mention that very fact. How . . . ? Or perhaps I have alluded to it before in this connection?"

"You have," I said.

"Forgive me." He twinkled disarmingly. "I grow old, dear boy."

Ritualistically we took our first sip of Drambuie. Then:

"I well remember," Dr. Verner began, "that it was in the autumn of the year 1901 . . .

. . . that the horror began. I was by then well established in my Kensington practice, which seemed to flourish as it never had under the ministrations of its previous possessor, and in a more than comfortable financial position. I was able at last to look about me, to contemplate and to investigate the manifold pleasures which a metropolis at once so cosmopolitan and so insular as London proffers to the unattached young man. San Francisco of the same period might perhaps compare in quality; indeed my own experiences here a few years later in the singular affair of the cable cabal were not unrewarding. But a man of your generation knows nothing of those pleasures now ten lustra faded. The humours of the Music Halls, the delights of a hot bird and a cold bottle shared with a dancer from Daly's, the simpler and less expensive delights of punting on the Thames (shared, I may add, with a simpler and less expensive companion)—these claimed what portion of my time I could salvage from my practice.

But above all I was devoted to music; and to be devoted to music meant, in the London of 1901, to be devoted to—but I have always carefully refrained from the employment of veritable and verifiable names in these narratives. Let me once more be discreet, and call her simply by that affectionate agnomen by which my cousin, to his sorrow, knew her: *Carina.*

I need not describe Carina as a musician; you have just heard her sing Pergolesi, you know how she combined nobility and grandeur with a technical agility which these degenerate days associate only with a certain type of light soprano. But I must seek to describe her as a woman, if woman she may be called.

When first I heard the tittle-tattle of London, I paid it small heed. To the man in the street (or even in the stalls) *actress* is still a euphemism for a harsher and shorter term, though my experience of actresses, extending as it has over three continents and more than my allotted three score and ten of years, tends to lead me, if anywhere, to an opposite conclusion.

The individual who stands out from the herd is the natural target of calumny. I shall never forget the disgraceful episode of the purloined litter, in which the veterinarian Dr. Stookes accused me of—but let us reserve that anomaly for another occasion. To return to Carina: I heard the gossip; I attributed it to as simple a source as I have indicated. But then the evidence began to attain proportions which the most latitudinarian could hardly disregard.

First young Ronny Furbish-Darnley blew out his brains. He had gambling debts, to be sure, and his family chose to lay the stress upon them; but his relations with Carina had been common knowledge. Then Major MacIvers hanged himself with his own cravat (the MacIvers tartan, of course). I need hardly add that a MacIvers had no gambling debts. Even that episode might have been hushed up had not a peer of so exalted a name that I dare not even paraphrase it perished in the flames of his ancestral castle. Even in the charred state in which they were recovered, the bodies of his wife and seven children clearly evinced the clumsy haste with which he had slit their throats.

It was as though . . . how shall I put it? . . . as though Carina were in some way a "carrier" of what we had then not yet learned to call The Death Wish. Men who knew her too well hungered no longer for life.

The press began to concern itself, as best it might with due regard for the laws of libel, with this situation. Leading articles hinted at possible governmental intervention to preserve the flower of England from this insidious foreigner. Little else was discussed in Hyde Park save the elimination of Carina.

Even the memorable mass suicides at Oxford had provided no sensation comparable to this. Carina's very existence seemed as much in danger as though Jack the Ripper had been found and turned over to the English people. We are firm believers in our English justice; but when that justice is powerless to act, the Englishman aroused is a phenomenon to fear.

If I may be pardoned a Hibernian lapse, the only thing that saved Carina's life was . . . her death.

It was a natural death—perhaps the first natural action of her life. She collapsed on the stage of Covent Garden during a performance of Mozart's *Così fan tutte*, just after having delivered the greatest performance of that fantastic aria, *Come scoglio*, that a living ear has heard.

There were investigations of the death. Even my cousin, with an understandable personal interest, took a hand. (He was the only one of Carina's close admirers to survive her infection; I have often wondered whether this fact resulted from an incredible strength or an equally incredible inadequacy within him.) But there was no possible doubt that the death was a natural one.

It was after the death that the Carina legend began to grow. It was then that young men about town who had seen the great

Carina but once began to mention the unmentionable reasons which had caused them to refrain from seeing her again. It was then that her dresser, a crone whose rationality was as uncertain as her still persistent terror was unquestionable, began to speak of unspeakable practices, to hint at black magic as among milady's avocations, to suggest that her utterance (which you have heard) of flights of notes, incredibly rapid yet distinct, owed its facility to her control and even suspension of the mortal limitations of time.

And then began . . . the horror. Perhaps you thought that by *the horror* I meant the sequence of Carina-carried suicides? No; even that lay still, if near the frontier, within the uttermost bounds of human comprehension.

The horror passed those bounds.

I need not ask you to envision it. You have beheld it. You have seen clothing sucked dry of its fleshly tenant, you have seen the haberdashers' habitation sink flabbily in upon itself, no longer sustained by tissue of bone and blood and nerves.

All London saw it that year. And London could not believe.

First it was that eminent musicologist, Sir Frederick Paynter, FRCM. Then there were two young aristocrats, then, oddly, a poor Jewish peddler in the East End.

I shall spare you the full and terrible details, alluding only in passing to the Bishop of Cloisterham. I had read the press accounts. I had filed the cuttings for their very impossibility (for even then I had had adumbrations of the concept which you now know as *The Anatomy of Nonscience*).

But the horror did not impinge upon me closely until it struck one of my own patients, a retired naval officer by the name of Clutsam. His family had sent for me at once, at the same time that they had dispatched a messenger to fetch my cousin.

As you know, my cousin enjoyed a certain fame as a private detective. He had been consulted in more than one previous instance of the horror; but I had read little of him in the press save a reiteration of his hope that the solution lay in his familiar dictum: "Discard the impossible; and whatever remains, no matter how improbable, must be true."

I had already formulated my now celebrated counter-dictum: "Discard the impossible; then if *nothing* remains, some part of the 'impossible' must be possible." It was thus that our dicta and ourselves faced each other across the worn and outdated naval uniform on the floor, complete from the gold braid on its shoulders to the wooden peg below the empty left trouser leg, cut off at the knee.

"I imagine, Horace," my cousin remarked, puffing at his blackened clay, "that you conceive this to be your sort of affair."

"It is obviously not yours," I stated. "There is something in these vanishings beyond—"

"—beyond the humdrum imagination of a professional detective? Horace, you are a man of singular accomplishments."

I smiled. My cousin, as my great-uncle Etienne used to remark of General Masséna, was famous for the accuracy of his information.

"I will confess," he added, "since my Boswell is not within earshot, that you have occasionally hit upon what satisfies you, at least, as the truth in some few cases in which I have failed. Do *you* see any element linking Captain Clutsam, Sir Frederick Paynter, Moishe Lipkowitz and the Bishop of Cloisterham?"

"I do not." It was always discreet to give my cousin the answer which he expected.

"And *I do!* And yet I am no nearer a solution than . . ." His pipe clenched in his teeth, he flung himself about the room, as though pure physical action would somehow ameliorate the lamentable state of his nerves. Finally he paused before me, looked sharply into my eyes and said, "Very well. I shall tell you. What is nonsense in the patterns shaped by the reasoning mind may well serve you as foundation for some new structure of unreason.

"I have traced every fact in the lives of these men. I know what they habitually ate for breakfast, how they spent their Sundays, and which of them preferred snuff to tobacco. There is only *one* factor which they all possess in common: Each of them recently purchased a record of the Pergolesi *Pater Noster* sung by . . . *Carina*. And those records have vanished as thoroughly as the naked men themselves."

I bestowed upon him an amicable smile. Family affection must temper the ungentlemanly emotion of triumph. Still smiling, I left him with the uniform and the leg while I betook myself to the nearest gramophone merchant.

The solution was by then obvious to me. I had observed that Captain Clutsam's gramophone was of the sapphire-needled type

designed to play those recordings known as hill-and-dale, the vertical recordings produced by Pathé and other companies as distinguished from the lateral recordings of Columbia and Gramo-
phone-and-Typewriter. And I had recalled that many hill-and-dale
recordings were at that time designed (as I believe some wireless
transcriptions are now) for an inside start, that is, so that the
needle began near the label and traveled outward to the rim of
the disc. An unthinking listener might easily begin to play an
inside-start record in the more normal manner. The result, in almost all instances, would be gibberish; but in this particular
case . . .

I purchased the Carina record with no difficulty. I hastened to
my Kensington home, where the room over the dispensary contained a gramophone convertible to either lateral or vertical recordings. I placed the record on the turntable. It was, to be sure,
labeled INSIDE START; but how easily one might overlook such
a notice! I overlooked it deliberately. I started the turntable and
lowered the needle . . .

The cadenzas of coloratura are strange things in reverse. As I
heard it, the record naturally began with the startling final note
which so disheartened Miss Borigian, then went on to those daz-
zling *fioriture* which so strengthen the dresser's charge of time-
magic. But in reverse, these seemed like the music of some undis-
covered planet, coherent to themselves, following a logic unknown
to us and shaping a beauty which only our ignorance prevents us
from worshiping.

And there were words to these flourishes; for almost unique
among sopranos, Carina possessed a diction of diabolical clarity.
And the words were at first simply *Nema . . . nema . . .
nema . . .*

It was while the voice was brilliantly repeating this reversed
Amen that I became *literally* beside myself.

I was standing, naked and chill in the London evening, beside
a meticulously composed agglomeration of clothing which parodied
the body of Dr. Horace Verner.

This fragment of clarity lasted only an instant. Then the voice
reached the significant words: *olam a son arebil des men . . .*

This was the Lord's Prayer which she was singing. It is common
knowledge that there is in all necromancy no charm more potent
than that prayer (and most especially in Latin) *said backwards*.

As the last act of her magical malefactions, Carina had left behind her this record, knowing that one of its purchasers would occasionally, by inadvertence, play it backwards, and that then the spell would take effect. It had taken effect now.

I was in space . . . a space of infinite darkness and moist warmth. The music had departed elsewhere. I was alone in this space and the space itself was alive and by its very moist warm dark life this space was draining from me all that which was my own life. And then there was with me a voice in that space, a voice that cried ever *Eem vull! Eem vull!* and for all the moaning gasping urgency in that voice I knew it for the voice of Carina.

I was a young man then. The Bishop's end must have been swift and merciful. But even I, young and strong, knew that this space desired the final sapping of my life, that my life should be drawn from my body even as my body had been drawn from its shell. So I prayed.

I was not a man given to prayer in those days. But I knew words which the Church has taught us are pleasing to God, and I prayed with all the fervour of my being for deliverance from this Nightmare Life-in-Death.

And I stood again naked beside my clothes. I looked at the turntable of the gramophone. The disc was not there. Still naked, I walked to the dispensary and mixed myself a sedative before I dared trust my fingers to button my garments. Then I dressed and went out again to the shop of the gramophone merchant. There I bought every copy in his stock of that devil's *Pater Noster* and smashed them all before his eyes.

Ill though I could afford it, even in my relative affluence, I spent the next few weeks in combing London for copies of that recording. One copy, and one only, I preserved, you heard it just now. I had hoped that no more existed . . .

". . . but obviously," Dr. Verner concluded, "your Mr. Stambaugh managed to acquire one, God rest his soul . . . and body."

I drained my second Drambuie and said, "I'm a great admirer of your cousin." Dr. Verner looked at me with polite blue inquiry. "You find what satisfied *you* as the truth."

"Occam's Razor, dear boy," Dr. Verner murmured, associatively stroking his smooth cheeks. "The solution accounts economically for every integral fact in the problem."

"But look," I said suddenly. "It doesn't! For once I've got you cold. There's one 'integral fact' completely omitted."

"Which is . . . ?" Dr. Verner cooed.

"You can't have been the first man that thought of praying in that . . . that space. Certainly the Bishop must have."

For a moment Dr. Horace Verner was silent. Then he fixed me with the Dear-boy-how-idiotic! twinkle. "But only I," he announced tranquilly, "had realized that in that . . . space all sound, like the Our Father itself, was reversed. The voice cried ever *Eem vull!* and what is that phonetically but *Love me!* backwards? Only *my* prayer was effective, because only I had the foresight to pray *in reverse phonetics.*"

I phoned Abrahams to say I had an idea and could I do some checking in the Stambaugh apartment?

"Good," he said. "I have an idea too. Meet you there in a half-hour."

There was no Abrahams in the corridor when I got there; but the police seal was broken and the door was ajar. I went on in and stopped dead.

For the first moment I thought it was still Stambaugh's clothes spread out there. But there was no mistaking Inspector Abrahams' neat gray plainclothes—with no Abrahams in them.

I think I said something about *the horror.* I draw pretty much of a blank between seeing that empty suit and looking up to the far doorway and seeing Inspector Abrahams.

He was wearing a dressing gown of Stambaugh's, which was far too short for him. I stared at his grotesque figure and at the android parody which dangled from his hand.

"Sorry, Lamb," he grinned. "Couldn't resist the theatrical effect. Go on. Take a good look at the empty man on the floor."

I looked. The clothes were put together with the exactly real, body-fitting, sucked-out effect which we had already decided was impossible.

"You see," Abrahams said, "I remembered the vacuum cleaner. And the Downtown Merchants' parade."

I was back at the studio early the next morning. There was nobody from Verner's Varieties there but Slavko, and it was so relatively quiet that Dr. Verner was just staring at the manuscript of

The Anatomy without adding a word.

"Look," I said. "In the first place, Stambaugh's record player isn't equipped for hill-and-dale records."

"They *can* be played even on an ordinary machine," Dr. Verner observed tranquilly. "The effect is curious—faint and with an odd echoing overlap, which might even enhance the power of the cantrip."

"And I looked in his card catalog," I went on, "and he didn't have a recording of the Pergolesi *Pater Noster* by anybody."

Dr. Verner widened his overblue eyes. "But of course the card would vanish with the record," he protested. "Magic makes allowances for modern developments."

"Wait a minute!" I exclaimed suddenly. "Hey, I'm brilliant! This is one Abrahams didn't think of. It's *me*, for once, that solves a case."

"Yes, dear boy?" said Dr. Verner gently.

"Look: You *can't* play an inside-start record backwards. It wouldn't work. Visualize the spiraling grooves. If you put the needle in the outside last groove, it'd just stay there ticking—same like it would if you put it in the inside last groove of a normal record. To play it backwards, you'd have to have some kind of gearshift that'd make the turntable spin backwards."

"But I have," said Dr. Verner blandly. "It enables one to make extraordinarily interesting experiments in sound. Doubtless Mr. Stambaugh had too. It would be simple enough to switch over by mistake; he was drinking . . . Tell me: the spinning turntable that you saw . . . was it revolving clockwise or counter-clockwise?"

I thought back, and I was damned if I knew. Clockwise, I took for granted; but if I had to swear . . . Instead I asked, "And I suppose Captain Clutsam and the Bishop of Cloisterham had alternate counterclockwise gearshifts?"

"Why, of course. Another reason why such a serious collector as Mr. Stambaugh would. You see, the discs of the Fonogrammia company, a small and obscure firm but one boasting a few superb artists under exclusive contract, were designed to be so played."

I stared at those pellucid azure eyes. I had no notion whether counterclockwise Fonogrammia records were the coveted objective of every collector or a legend that had this moment come into being.

"And besides," I insisted, "Abrahams has demonstrated how it was really done. The vacuum cleaner tipped him off. Stambaugh had bought a man-sized, man-shaped balloon, a little brother of those monster figures they use in parades. He inflated it and dressed it in his clothes. Then he deflated it, leaving the clothes in perfect arrangement with nothing in them but a shrunken chunk of rubber, which he could withdraw by unbuttoning the shirt. Abrahams found the only firm in San Francisco that manufactures such balloons. A clerk identified Stambaugh as a purchaser. So Abrahams bought a duplicate and pulled the same gag on me."

Dr. Verner frowned. "And the vacuum cleaner?"

"You use a vacuum cleaner in reverse for pumping up large balloons. And you use it normally for deflating them; if you just let the air out *whoosh!* they're apt to break."

"The clerk" (it came out *clark*, of course) "identified Stambaugh positively?"

I shifted under the piercing blueness. "Well, you know identifications from photographs . . ."

"Indeed I do." He took a deliberately timed pause. "And the record player? Why was its turntable still revolving?"

"Accident, I guess. Stambaugh must've bumped against the switch."

"Which projected from the cabinet so that one might well engage it by accident?"

I pictured the machine. I visualized the switch and the depth to which one would have to reach in. "Well, no," I granted. "Not exactly . . ."

Dr. Verner smiled down at me tolerantly. "And the motive for these elaborate maneuvers by Mr. Stambaugh?"

"Too many threatening male relatives on his tail. He deliberately staged this to look oh-so-mysterious so nobody'd spot the simple fact that he was just getting the hell out from under. Abrahams has an all-points alarm out; he'll be picked up any time within the next few days."

Dr. Verner sighed. His hands flickered through the air in a gesture of infinitely resigned patience. He moved to his record cabinet, took out a disc, placed it on the turntable, and adjusted certain switches.

"Come, Slavko!" he announced loudly. "Since Mr. Lamb prefers rubber balloons to truth, we are conferring a signal privilege upon him. We are retiring to the other room, leaving him here alone with the Carina record. His cocksure materialism will surely wish to verify the effect of playing it in reverse."

Slavko stopped pounding and said, "Huh?"

"Come, Slavko. But first say a polite good-bye to Mr. Lamb. You may not be seeing him again." Dr. Verner paused in the doorway and surveyed me with what seemed like genuine concern. "Dear boy," he murmured, "you won't forget that point about the reverse phonetics . . . ?"

He was gone and so (without more polite good-bye than a grunt) was Slavko. I was alone with Carina, with the opportunity to disprove Dr. Verner's fabulous narrative once and for all.

His story had made no pretense of explaining the presence of the vacuum cleaner.

And Inspector Abrahams' theory had not even attempted to account for the still-revolving turntable.

I switched on the turntable of the Verner machine. Carefully I lowered the tone-arm, let the oddly rounded needle settle into the first groove from the outer rim.

I heard that stunning final note in alt. So flawless was the Carina diction that I could hear, even in that range, the syllable to which it was sung: *nem*, the beginning of the reverse-Latin *Amen*.

Then I heard a distorted groan as the turntable abruptly slowed down from 78 to zero revolutions per minute. I looked at the switch; it was still on. I turned and saw Dr. Verner towering behind me, with a disconnected electric plug dangling from his hand.

"No," he said softly—and there was a dignity and power in that softness that I had never heard in his most impressive bellows. "No, Mr. Lamb. You have a wife and two sons. I have no right to trifle with their lives merely to gratify an old man's resentment of scepticism."

Quietly he lifted the tone-arm, removed the record, restored it to its envelope, and refiled it. His deft, un-English hands were not at their steadiest.

"When Inspector Abrahams succeeds in tracing down Mr. Stambaugh," he said firmly, "you shall hear this record in reverse. And not before then."

And it just so happens they haven't turned up Stambaugh yet.

End